GIDEON'S
CORPSE

By Douglas Preston and Lincoln Child

In answer to a frequently asked reader question:
The above titles are listed in descending order of publication, though almost all of them are stand-alone novels that need not be read in order. However, the pairs *Relic/Reliquary*, *Dance of Death/The Book of the Dead*, and *Fever Dream/Cold Vengeance* are ideally read in sequence.

GIDEON'S CORPSE

DOUGLAS PRESTON
&
LINCOLN CHILD

GRAND CENTRAL
PUBLISHING

NEW YORK   BOSTON

Grand Central Publishing
Hachette Book Group
237 Park Avenue
New York, NY 10017

www.HachetteBookGroup.com

Printed in the United States of America

RRD-C

First Edition: January 2012
10 9 8 7 6 5 4 3 2 1

Grand Central Publishing is a division of Hachette Book Group, Inc. The Grand Central Publishing name and logo is a trademark of Hachette Book Group, Inc.

The Hachette Speakers Bureau provides a wide range of authors for speaking events. To find out more, go to www.hachettespeakersbureau .com or call (866) 376-6591.

The publisher is not responsible for websites (or their content) that are not owned by the publisher.

Library of Congress Cataloging-in-Publication Data
Preston, Douglas J.
 Gideon's corpse / Douglas Preston and Lincoln Child. — 1st ed.
   p. cm.
ISBN 978-0-446-56437-3 (regular edition) — ISBN 978-1-4555-0417-6 (large print edition) 1. Nuclear terrorism—Fiction. I. Child, Lincoln. II. Title.
PS3566.R3982G47 2012
813'.54—dc23
                        2011028119

To Barbara Peters

Acknowledgments

The authors thank Patrick Allocco, Douglas Child, Douglas Webb, and Jon Couch for their invaluable assistance with certain details of this book.

GIDEON'S CORPSE

1

GIDEON CREW STOOD at the window of the conference room, looking out over the former Meatpacking District of Manhattan. His gaze followed the tarred roofs of the old buildings, now hip boutiques and trendy restaurants; moved past the new High Line park thick with people; past the rotting piers; and came to rest on the broad expanse of the Hudson River. In the hazy sun of early summer, the river for a change looked like real water, the surface a mass of blue moving upstream with the incoming tide.

The Hudson reminded him of other rivers he had known, and streams and creeks, and his thoughts lingered on one stream in particular, high in the Jemez Mountains. He thought about a deep pool in it and the large cutthroat trout he was sure lurked in its dappled depths.

He couldn't wait to get the hell out of there, out of New York City, away from that withered gnome named Glinn and his mysterious company, Effective Engineering Solutions.

"I'm going fishing," he said.

Glinn shifted in his wheelchair and sighed. Gideon turned. The man's crippled hand appeared from under the blanket that was shrouding his knees. It contained a brown-paper package. "Your payment."

Gideon hesitated. "You're paying me? After what I did?"

"The fact is, based on what you've told me, our payment structure has changed." Glinn opened the package, counted out several banded bricks of hundreds, and laid them on the table in the conference room. "Here is half of the hundred thousand."

Gideon snatched it up before Glinn could change his mind.

Then, to his surprise, Glinn handed him the other half. "And here's the rest. Not as payment for services rendered, however. More in the way of, shall we say, an advance."

Gideon stuffed the money into his jacket pockets. "An advance on what?"

"Before you leave town," Glinn said, "I thought you might like to drop in on an old friend of yours."

"Thanks, but I've got a date with a cutthroat trout in Chihua-hueños Creek."

"Ah, but I was so hoping you'd have time to see your friend."

"I don't have any friends. And if I did, I sure as hell wouldn't be interested in 'dropping in' on them right now. As you so kindly pointed out, I'm living on borrowed time."

"Reed Chalker is his name. I believe you worked with him?"

"We worked in the same Tech Area—that's not the same as working *with* him. I haven't seen the guy around Los Alamos in months."

"Well, you're about to see him now. The authorities are hoping you could have a little chat with him."

"The authorities? A chat? What the hell's this about?"

"At this moment, Chalker's got a hostage. Four of them, actually. A family in Queens. Held at gunpoint."

Gideon laughed. "Chalker? No way. The guy I knew was a typical Los Alamos geek, straight as an arrow, wouldn't hurt a fly."

"He's raving. Paranoid. Out of his mind. You're the only person within range who knows him. The police want you to calm him down, get him to release those hostages."

Gideon didn't reply.

"So I'm sorry to tell you, Dr. Crew, but that cutthroat trout is going to be enjoying life just a little bit longer. And now you really do need to go. That family can't wait."

Gideon felt a swell of outrage at the imposition. "Find someone else."

"No time. There are two children involved, along with their mother and father. It seems the father is Chalker's landlord, rented him a basement apartment in their row house. Frankly, we're very lucky you're here."

"I hardly knew Chalker. He stuck to me like a limpet—but only briefly, after his wife left him. Then he got religion and drifted away, much to my relief."

"Garza will take you over. You'll be liaising with Special Agent Stone Fordyce, FBI."

"Liaising? Why is the FBI involved?"

"It's standard operating procedure whenever someone with a high-level security clearance like Chalker gets into trouble, on the chance he might go, ah, out of school." Glinn fixed his lone good eye on Gideon. "This isn't some undercover operation like last time—just a straightforward assignment. If all goes well, you should be on your way back to New Mexico in a day or two."

Gideon said nothing. He had eleven months of life left—or at least that's what they had told him. But then again, the more he thought about it, the more he began to wonder, and he intended to take the first opportunity to get a second opinion. Glinn was a master manipulator, and Gideon didn't trust either him or his people.

"If he's as crazy as you say, he might just turn that gun on me."

"Two kids. Eight and ten. Boy and a girl. And their parents."

Gideon turned, expelled a long breath. "Jesus. I'm giving you one day—*just* one day. And I'm going to be pissed at you for a long, long time."

Glinn bestowed a cold smile on him.

2

THEY ARRIVED AT a scene of controlled chaos. The setting was a nondescript working-class street in the ironically named neighborhood of Sunnyside, Queens. The house was part of a long row of attached brick houses, facing an identical row across a street of cracked pavement. There were no trees on the block; the lawns were overgrown with weeds and brown from lack of rain. The air hummed with the roar of traffic on nearby Queens Boulevard, and a smell of car exhaust drifted in the air.

A cop showed them where to park, and they got out. The police had set up roadblocks and barricades at both ends of the street, and the place was packed with squad cars, their lightbars flashing. Garza showed ID and was waved through a barricade, which held back a seething crowd of rubberneckers, many drinking beer, a few even wearing funny hats and carrying on as if it were a block party.

New York City, thought Gideon with a shake of his head.

The police had cleared a large area in front of the house in which Chalker had taken hostages. Two SWAT teams had been deployed, one in a forward post behind an armored rescue vehicle, the other back behind a set of concrete barricades. Gideon could see snipers peeking above several rooftops. In the middle distance, he could hear the occasional blaring of a voice over a megaphone, apparently a hostage negotiator trying to talk Chalker down.

As Garza pushed toward the front, Gideon experienced a sudden flash of déjà vu, a spasm of nausea. This was the way his father had been killed, exactly like this: with the megaphones, the SWAT teams, the snipers and barricades—shot in cold blood, surrendering, with his hands up...Gideon fought to push the memory aside.

They passed through another set of barricades to an FBI command post. An agent detached himself from the group and came over.

"Special Agent Stone Fordyce," said Garza, introducing him. "Assistant commander of the FBI team on site. You'll be working with him."

Gideon eyed the man with instinctual hostility. The guy was straight out of a TV series, dressed in a blue suit, starched white shirt, and repp tie, ID hanging around his neck, tall, handsome, arrogant, self-assured, and ridiculously fit. His narrow blue eyes looked down at Gideon as if examining a lower form of life.

"So you're the *friend*?" asked Fordyce, his eyes lingering on Gideon, particularly on his clothes—black jeans, black Keds without laces, secondhand tuxedo shirt, thin scarf.

"I'm not the maiden aunt, if that's what you mean," Gideon replied.

"Here's the deal," the man went on, after a pause. "This friend of yours, Chalker, he's paranoid, delusional. Classic psychotic break. He's spouting a bunch of conspiracy ideas: that the government kidnapped him, used him for radiation experiments, and beamed rays into his head—the usual. He thinks his landlord and landlady are in on the conspiracy and he's taken them hostage, along with their two kids."

"What does he want?" Gideon asked.

"Incoherent. He's armed with what we think is a 1911-style Colt .45. He's fired it once or twice for show. Not sure if he actually knows how to use it. You got any knowledge of his prior experience with weapons?"

"I would've thought none," said Gideon.

"Tell me about him."

"Socially inept. Didn't have a lot of friends, got burdened with a world-class dysfunctional wife who put him through the wringer. Dissatisfied with his job, talked about wanting to become a writer. Finally ended up getting religion."

"Was he good at his job? Smart?"

"Competent but not brilliant. As for brains, he's way more intelligent than, say, the average FBI agent."

There was a silence as Fordyce took this in and did not react. "The brief says this guy designed nuclear weapons at Los Alamos. Right?"

"More or less."

"You think there's a chance he's got explosives rigged in there?"

"He may have worked with nuclear weapons, but a firecracker would've freaked him out. As for explosives—I sincerely doubt it."

Fordyce stared at him, went on. "He thinks everyone here is a government agent."

"He's probably right."

"We're hoping he'll trust someone out of his past. You."

Gideon could hear in the background more megaphoned words, then a distorted, screamed reply, too far away to make out. He turned toward the sound. "Is that *him*?" he asked in disbelief.

"Unfortunately."

"Why the megaphone?"

"He won't talk on a cell or landline, says we're using it to beam more rays into his head. So it's megaphone only. He shouts his replies out the door."

Gideon turned again in the direction of the sound. "I guess I'm ready whenever you are."

"Let me give you a crash course in hostage negotiation," said Fordyce. "The whole idea is to create a feeling of normalcy, lower the temperature, engage the hostage taker, prolong the negotiations. Stimulate his humanity. Okay? Our number one goal is to get him to release the kids. Try to dig out something he wants and trade the kids for it. You following me so far?" He seemed doubtful Gideon was capable of basic reasoning.

Gideon nodded, keeping his face neutral.

"You have no authority to grant anything. You can't make promises.

Get that? Everything has to be checked with the commander. Anything he asks for, be sympathetic, but say you've got to check with the commander. This is a crucial part of the process. It slows things down. And if he wants something and the answer's a no, you don't get blamed. The point is to wear him out, stop the momentum."

Gideon was surprised to find himself in general agreement with the approach.

A cop appeared with a bulletproof vest. "We're going to suit you up," said Fordyce. "In any case, there shouldn't be any risk—we're putting you behind bulletproof Plexiglas."

They helped him strip off his shirt and put on the vest, tucking the extensions into his upper pants, then fitted him out with an invisible earpiece and remote mike. As he dressed, he could hear more megaphoned conversation in the background, interspersed with hysterical, incoherent responses.

Fordyce consulted his watch, winced. "Any new developments?" he asked the cop.

"The guy's getting worse. The commander thinks we may need to move into the termination phase soon."

"Damn." Fordyce shook his head and turned back to Gideon. "Another thing: you'll be working from a script."

"A script?"

"Our psychologists have worked it up. We'll give you each question through the earpiece. You ask it, then wait a moment after he replies to get the response from us."

"So you really don't need me at all. Except as a front."

"You got it. You're a rented body."

"Then why the lecture on hostage communication?"

"So you'll understand what's going on and why. And if the conversation gets personal, you might have to ad lib a little. But don't go shooting your mouth off or making promises. Gain his sympathy, remind him of your friendship, reassure him everything's going to be fine, that his concerns will be taken seriously. Be calm. And for God's sake, don't argue with him about his delusions."

"Makes sense."

Fordyce gave him a long, appraising look, his hostility softening somewhat. "We've been doing this a long time." A beat. "You ready?"

Gideon nodded.

"Let's go."

3

Fordyce led Gideon through a final set of barricades to the front line of concrete barriers, armored vehicles, and Plexiglas shields. The armor under his shirt felt bulky and foreign. Now he could hear the megaphone clearly.

"*Reed,*" came the electronic voice, calm and avuncular, "*an old friend of yours is here and wants to talk to you. His name is Gideon Crew. Would you like to talk to him?*"

"Bullshit!" came the reply, in an almost incoherent scream. "*I don't want to talk to anybody!*"

The disembodied voice was coming from the front door, which was standing ajar. All the curtains had been pulled and there was no one to be seen, hostages or Chalker.

A gravelly voice sounded in his earpiece. "Dr. Crew, do you read me?"

"I read."

"I'm Jed Hammersmith, I'm in one of the vans, sorry we can't meet in person. I'll be guiding you. Listen to me carefully. First rule is, you mustn't respond to me when I speak to you through the earpiece. When you're out there, obviously you can't be seen to be communicating with anyone else. You're talking only to him. Understand?"

"Yes."

"You lie! All of you! End the charade!"

Gideon felt a chill. It almost didn't seem possible this was the Chalker he knew. And yet it was his voice, distorted by fear and madness.

"We would like to help you," the megaphone said. "Tell us what you want—"

"You know what I want! Stop the kidnapping! Stop the experiments!"

"I'm going to be feeding you questions," said Hammersmith's calm voice in Gideon's ear. "We've got to move fast now; things aren't going well."

"I can see that."

"I swear to God I'm going to blow his brains out unless you stop messing with me!"

There was an inarticulate scream from the house, a woman's pleading. And below that, Gideon could hear the high-pitched wailing of a child. It chilled him to the bone. His own childhood memories— his father standing in a stone doorway, Gideon himself running across a green lawn toward him—came back stronger than ever. He tried desperately to tune them out, but every blast of the megaphone just served to bring them back.

"You're in on it, you bitch!" Chalker screamed to someone at one side of him, *"you're not even his wife, you're just another agent. This is all bullshit, all of it. But I'm not playing along! I won't take this anymore!"*

The megaphone voice responded, preternaturally calm, as if talking to a child. *"Your friend Gideon Crew wants to talk to you. He's coming out now."*

Fordyce pushed a mike into his hand. "It's wireless, set up to loudspeakers on the van. Go."

He pointed toward a bulletproof Plexiglas shelter, narrow and enclosed on three sides and the top, leaving the back open. After a moment's hesitation, Gideon stepped from behind the ARV into the glass box. It reminded him of a shark cage.

He spoke into the mike. "Reed?"

A sudden silence.

"Reed? It's me, Gideon."

More silence. And then, *"Oh my God, Gideon, have they gotten to you, too?"*

Hammersmith's voice sounded in his earpiece, and Gideon repeated his words. "Nobody's gotten to me. I was in town, heard the news, came down here to help. I'm not with anybody."

"Liar!" Chalker shrieked back, high and quavering. *"They've gotten you, too! Has the pain started yet? Is it in your mind? In your guts? It will be! Oh yes, it will—!"* The voice suddenly stopped, replaced by a violent retching.

"Exploit the pause," came Hammersmith's voice. "You need to gain control of the conversation. Ask him, How can I help?"

"Reed," said Gideon. "How can I help?"

More retching—then silence.

"Let me help, please. How can I help you?"

"There's nothing you can do! Save your own ass, get away from them. These bastards will do anything—look what they did to me! I'm burning up! Oh Christ, my gut—!"

"Ask him to step out where you can see him," said Hammersmith in Gideon's ear.

Gideon paused, recalling the snipers. He felt himself go cold; he knew if any of the snipers had a clear shot, they'd take it. *Just like they did with my father . . .* He also reminded himself that Chalker had a family in there, at gunpoint. He could see some men on the roof of the row house. They were getting ready to lower something through the chimney, a device that looked like a video camera. He hoped to hell they knew what they were doing.

"Tell them to turn off the rays!"

"Tell him you really want to help him, but he needs to tell you how."

"Reed, I really want to help you. Just tell me how."

"Stop the experiments!" Suddenly Gideon saw movement in the doorway. *"They're killing me! Turn off the rays or I blow his head off!"*

"Tell him we will do all that he asks," came the disembodied voice of Hammersmith. "But he has to step out where you can talk to him face-to-face."

Gideon said nothing. Try as he might, he couldn't get the image of his father out of his head: his father, hands in the air, shot in the face...No, he decided, he wasn't going to ask that. At least, not yet.

"Gideon," said Hammersmith, after a long pause, "I know you can hear me—"

"Reed," Gideon said, cutting off Hammersmith, "I'm not with these people. I'm not with anyone. I'm here to help you."

"I don't believe you!"

"Don't believe me, then. But hear me out."

No response.

"You say your landlord and landlady are in on it?"

"Don't go off script," warned the voice of Hammersmith.

"They aren't my landlady and landlord," came Chalker's response, ramping up, hysterical. *"I never saw them before! The whole thing's a setup. I've never been here before in my life, they're government agents! I was kidnapped, held for experiments—"*

Gideon held up a hand. "Reed, hold on. You say they're in on it and it's a setup. What about the kids? Are they part of it?"

"It's all a setup! Aaaahhh, the heat! The heat!"

"Eight and ten years old?"

A long silence.

"Reed, answer my question. Are the kids acting? Are they conspirators, too?"

"Don't confuse me!"

More silence. He heard Hammersmith's voice. "Okay, this is good. Follow up."

"No confusion here, Reed. They're children. Innocent children."

More silence.

"Let them go. Send them out here to me. You'll still have two hostages."

The long silence stretched on, and then there was a sudden movement, a high-pitched scream, and one of the kids appeared in the doorway—the boy. He was a little kid with a mop of brown hair, wearing an I ♥ My Grandma T-shirt, and he came out into the light, keening in fear.

For a moment Gideon thought Chalker was releasing the kids. But when he saw the nickel-plated .45 shoved into the boy's neck, he realized he was wrong.

"You see this? I'm not kidding! Stop the rays or I kill the kid! I'm counting to ten! One, two—"

The mother was screaming hysterically in the background. "Don't, please don't!"

"Shut up, you lying bitch, they're not your kids!" Chalker turned and fired the gun once into the darkness of the house behind him. The woman's screaming stopped abruptly.

With one brusque movement, Gideon stepped out from behind the Plexiglas cubicle and walked into the open area before the house. There were shouts, cops yelling at him—*get back, get down, the man's armed*—but he kept walking until he was less than fifty yards from the front door.

"What the hell are you doing? Get back behind the barrier, he'll kill you!" Hammersmith shouted into his earpiece.

Gideon plucked the earpiece out, held it up. "Reed? You see this? You're right. They were telling me what to say." He tossed the earpiece on the asphalt. "But not anymore. From now on we talk straight."

"Three, four, five—"

"Wait, for God's sake, *please*." Gideon spoke loudly. "He's just a child. Listen to him screaming. You think he's faking that?"

"Shut up!" Chalker screamed at the boy, and, remarkably, the boy stopped. He stood, trembling and pale, his lips fluttering. *"My head!"* Chalker shrieked. *"My—"*

"Remember when those school groups came to see the lab?" Gideon said, struggling to keep his voice calm. "You loved those kids, loved showing them around. And they responded to you. Not to me. Not to the others. To you. Remember that, Reed?"

"I'm burning up!" Chalker screamed. *"They got the rays on again! I'll kill him, and the death will be on your head, not mine! You HEAR me? SEVEN, EIGHT—"*

"Let the poor boy go," Gideon said, taking another step forward. It deeply frightened him that Chalker couldn't even count straight. "Let him go. You can have me instead."

With a brusque motion, Chalker turned, aimed the weapon at Gideon. *"Get back, you're one of them!"*

Gideon held his arms out toward Chalker almost beseechingly. "You think I'm in on the conspiracy? Take your best shot. But please, *please*, let the kid go."

"You asked for it!" And Chalker fired.

4

AND MISSED.

Gideon dropped to the tarmac, his heart suddenly pounding so hard it seemed to knock itself against his rib cage. He squeezed his eyes tight shut, waiting for another explosion, a searing pain, and oblivion.

But a second shot did not come. He heard a confusing welter of noise, voices shouting over one another, the rasp of the megaphone. Slowly, slowly, he opened his eyes, looked toward the house. There was Chalker, barely visible in the doorway, holding the boy in front of him. He could tell from the way the man handled the weapon, his shaking hand, his stance and grip, that it was probably the first time in his life he had fired a handgun. And he was shooting from fifty yards.

"*It's a trick!*" Chalker shrieked. "*You're not even Gideon! You're a fake!*"

Gideon got up slowly, keeping his hands in sight. His heart refused to slow down. "Reed, let's just do the trade. Take me. Let the little boy go."

"*Tell them to turn off the rays!*"

Don't argue with his delusion, they had told him. It was good advice. But how the hell should he respond? "Reed, everything will be all right if you just release the boy. And the little girl."

"*Turn off the rays!*" Chalker crouched behind the boy, using him as cover. "*They're killing me! Turn off the rays or I blow his head off!*"

"We can work it out," Gideon called. "Everything's going to be fine. But you have to let the boy go." He took another step, and another. He had to get close enough for a final rush—if it became necessary. If he didn't rush Chalker, tackle him, the little boy would die and the snipers would take Chalker out—and Gideon didn't think he could bear seeing that happen.

Chalker screamed as if in agony. *"Stop the radiation!"* His whole body was shaking as he waved the gun around.

How do you respond to a lunatic? Desperately, Gideon tried recalling the advice Fordyce had given him. *Engage the hostage taker, stimulate his humanity.*

"Reed, look into the boy's face. You'll see how truly innocent he is—"

"My skin's on fire!" Chalker cried. *"I was counting! Where was I? Six, eight—"* He suddenly grimaced, his face contorted with pain. *"They're doing it again! The burning, burning!"* Once again he pushed the gun into the child's neck. Now the boy began to scream—a high, thin sound, otherworldly.

"Wait!" Gideon yelled. *"No, don't!"* He began walking more quickly toward Chalker with his hands up. Forty yards, thirty—a distance he could cover in a few seconds...

"Nine, TEN! TEN! Ahhhhhh!—"

Gideon saw the finger tighten on the trigger and he sprinted straight at him. At the same time, with an inarticulate roar, the male hostage suddenly appeared in the hallway and fell upon Chalker from behind.

Chalker wheeled backward, the gun firing harmlessly.

"Run!" Gideon screamed at the boy as he dashed toward the house.

But the boy did not run. Chalker struggled with the hostage, who was clinging to his back. They spun around together and Chalker slammed him into the wall of the entryway and wrenched free. The man rebounded with a fierce cry and swung at Chalker, but he was a flabby man in his fifties and Chalker deftly sidestepped the blow and punched him to the floor, knocking him senseless.

"Run!" Gideon yelled at the boy again as he jumped the curb.

As Chalker swung the gun around toward the father, the boy leapt onto the scientist's back, pounding him with his small fists.

"Dad! Get away!"

Gideon tore up the walkway toward the front steps.

"Don't shoot my dad!" the boy shrieked, flailing.

"Turn them off!" Chalker screamed, whirling around, distracted by the child, swinging the handgun back and forth as if seeking a target.

Gideon took a flying leap at Chalker, but the gun went off before he made contact. He slammed the scientist to the ground, seized his forearm, and broke it against the banister like a stick of firewood, the weapon tumbling from his grip. Chalker shrieked in agony. Behind him, the boy's heartbreaking cries shrilled out as he hunched over his father, who was lying prone on the floor, the side of his head gone.

Pinned, Chalker writhed underneath Gideon like a snake, roaring insanely, spittle flying...

...And then the SWAT team came bursting through the door and thrust Gideon violently aside; Gideon felt hot blood and body matter spray across one side of his face as a fusillade of shots cut off Chalker's ravings.

The sudden, awful silence that followed lasted only a moment. And then, from somewhere inside the house, a little girl began to cry. "Mommy's bleeding! Mommy's bleeding!"

Gideon rolled to his knees and puked.

5

THE CHARGE OF SWAT team responders, CSI coordinators, and emergency medical personnel rolled in like a wave, the area immediately filling with people. Gideon sat on the floor, absently wiping the blood from his face. He felt shattered. No one took any notice of him. The scene had abruptly changed from a tense standoff to controlled action: everyone had a role to play; everyone had a job to do. The two screaming children were whisked away; medical personnel knelt over the three people who had been shot; the SWAT teams did a rapid search of the house; the cops began stringing tape and securing the scene.

Gideon staggered up and leaned against the wall, hardly able to stand, still heaving. One of the medics approached him. "Where's the injury—?"

"Not my blood."

The medic examined him anyway, probing the area where Chalker's blood had splattered across his face. "Okay," he said. "But let me clean you up a bit."

Gideon tried to focus on what the medic was saying, almost drowning from the feeling of revulsion and guilt that overwhelmed him.

Again. Oh my God, it's happened again. The presence of the past, the horribly cinematic and vivid memory of his own father's death, was so strong that he felt a kind of mental paralysis, an inability to work his mind beyond the hysterical repetition of the word *again*.

"We're going to need this area vacated," said a cop, moving them toward the door. As they spoke, the CSI team laid down a tarp and began setting down their small sports bags on it, organizing their equipment.

The medic took Gideon's arm. "Let's go."

Gideon allowed himself to be led away. The CSI team unzipped their bags and began removing tools, flags, tape, test tubes, and evidence Baggies, snapping on latex gloves, putting on hairnets and plastic booties. All around him, there was a sense of winding down: the tenseness, the hysteria, was dissipating, replaced by a banal professionalism: what had been a drama of life and death was now just a series of checklists to be completed.

Fordyce appeared out of nowhere. "Don't go far," he said in a low voice, taking his arm. "You need to be debriefed."

Hearing this, Gideon looked at him, his mind gradually clearing. "You saw the whole thing—what's to debrief?" He just wanted to get the hell away, get back to New Mexico, put this horror show behind him.

Fordyce shrugged. "The way it is."

Gideon wondered if they'd blame him for the death of the hostage. Probably. And rightfully so. He'd fucked up. He felt sick all over again. If he'd only said something different, the right thing, or maybe left the earpiece in, maybe they would have seen it coming, given him something to say . . . He'd been too close to the situation, unable to separate it from the shooting of his own father. He should never have let Glinn talk him into it. He realized to his dismay that his eyes were threatening to mist over.

"Hey," said Fordyce. "Don't sweat it. You saved the two kids. And the wife's going to make it—just a flesh wound." Gideon felt the man's grip tighten on his arm. "We've got to go now, they're securing the scene."

Gideon drew in a deep, shuddering breath. "Okay."

As they began to move toward the door, there was a strange ripple in the atmosphere, as if a chill wind had just blown through the house. Through his peripheral vision, Gideon noticed one of the CSI women freeze in place. At the same time he heard a low clicking noise, strangely familiar, but in his fog of guilt and nausea he couldn't quite place it. He paused as the crime scene investigator stepped over to her bag and rooted around in it, pulling out a yellow box with a gauge and a handheld tube on a long coiled wire. Gideon recognized it immediately.

A Geiger counter.

The machine was clicking quietly but regularly, the needle jumping with each beat. The woman looked at her partner. The entire room had fallen silent. Gideon watched, his mouth going dry.

In the suddenly quiet house the faint clicks were oddly magnified. The woman rose and held the Geiger counter out, slowly panning the room with it. The machine hissed, the clicks abruptly spiking. She jumped at the noise. Then, steadying, she took a step forward, and—almost reluctantly—began rotating it toward Chalker's dead body.

As the tube came closer to the body, the clicks climbed quickly in volume and frequency, an infernal glissando that morphed from hiss, to roar, and then finally to a shriek as the instrument's needle pinned all the way into the red.

"Oh my God," murmured the woman, backing away as she stared at the gauge, her eyes widening in disbelief. Suddenly she dropped the unit, turned, and ran out of the house. The instrument crashed to the floor, the roar from its counter filling the air, rising and falling as the tube rolled back and forth.

And then the entire room was in panicked motion, scrambling back, pushing, shoving, trying to get out. The CSI team broke into a run, followed by the photographers, cops, and SWAT members; in a matter of moments everyone was fleeing willy-nilly, clawing and shoving their way out the door, all sense of procedure vanishing. Gideon and Fordyce were carried along on the human wave. A moment later Gideon found himself out on the street before the house.

Only then did it begin to sink in. Gideon turned to Fordyce. The agent's face was deathly pale.

"Chalker was hot," Gideon said. "Hotter than hell."

"It would seem so," the agent said.

Almost without thinking, Gideon touched the sticky blood drying on the side of his face. "And we've been exposed."

6

THERE HAD BEEN a dramatic change in the crowd of police officers and professionals assembled behind the barricades. The scene of focused activity, the purposeful coming and going of uniformed people, dissolved. The first sign was a wave of silence that seemed to ripple outward. Even Fordyce fell silent, and Gideon realized someone was talking to him through his earpiece.

Fordyce pressed his finger against the earpiece and went still paler as he listened. "No," he said, vehemently. "No way. I didn't get anywhere near the guy. You can't do this."

The crowd had become motionless as well. Even those who'd fled the house had paused, watching and listening, as if collectively stunned. And then, abruptly, the crowd moved again—a rebound motion away from the house. The retreat was not exactly a rout, but rather a controlled recoil.

Simultaneously the air filled with fresh sirens. Soon choppers appeared overhead. A group of white, unmarked panel trucks began to arrive outside the barricades, escorted by additional squad cars; their rear doors opened up and alien-garbed figures began pouring out, hazmat suits emblazoned with biohazard and radiation symbols. Some were carrying riot control gear: batons, tear gas guns, and stun guns. Then, to Gideon's consternation, they began setting up barriers in front of the moving crowd, blocking the retreat. They shouted for people to stop moving, to stay where they were. The effect was dramatic—as people saw they might be prevented from fleeing, panic really began to take hold.

"What the hell's going on?" Gideon asked.

"Mandatory screening," replied Fordyce.

More barriers went up. Gideon watched as a cop started arguing and tried to push past a barrier—only to be forced back by several men in white. Meanwhile, the new arrivals were directing everyone into an area being hastily set up, a kind of holding pen with chain link around it, where more figures in white were scanning people with handheld Geiger counters. Most were being released, but a few were being directed into the backs of the vans.

A loudspeaker kicked in: *"All personnel remain in place until directed otherwise. Obey instructions. Stay behind the barriers."*

"Who are those guys?" Gideon asked.

Fordyce looked both disgusted and frightened. "NEST."

"NEST?"

"Nuclear Emergency Support Team. They're from the DOE—they respond to nuclear or radiological terrorist attacks."

"You think terrorism might be involved?"

"That guy Chalker designed nuclear weapons."

"Even so, that's quite a stretch."

"Really?" Fordyce said, slowly turning his blue eyes toward Gideon. "Back there, you mentioned something about Chalker finding religion." He paused. "May I ask...which religion?"

"Um, Islam."

7

Anyone who set off the Geiger counters was shoved into the vans like cattle. The partying rubberneckers had fled, leaving their funny hats and beer cans strewn about. Teams of monkey-suited hazmat people were going door-to-door, moving people out of their homes, sometimes forcibly, creating a scene of both pathos and chaos, with weeping elderly shuffling along in walkers, hysterical mothers, and wailing kids. Loud-speakers droned on about staying calm and cooperating, reassuring everyone it was for their own protection. Not a word about radiation.

Gideon and the rest squeezed together on parallel benches. The doors slammed shut and the van started up. Fordyce, opposite him, re-mained grimly silent, but most of the other people stuffed in the van looked shit-scared. Among them was a man Fordyce identified as the psychologist Hammersmith, whose shirt was bloodied, and a member of the SWAT team who had shot Chalker at point-blank range and who was also now decorated with his blood. *Radioactive* blood.

"We're fucked," said the SWAT team guy, a big beefy fellow with hammy forearms and an incongruously high voice. "We're going to die. There's nothing they can do. Not with radiation."

Gideon said nothing. The ignorance of most people about radia-tion was appalling.

The man moaned. "God, my head's pounding. It's starting al-ready."

"Hey, shut up," said Fordyce.

"Fuck you, man," the man flared. "I didn't sign up for this shit."

Fordyce said nothing, his jaw tightening.

"You hear me?" The man's voice was rising. "I didn't *sign up* for this shit!"

Gideon looked at the SWAT team member and spoke in low, measured tones. "The blood on you is radioactive. You'd better strip. And you, too." He looked at Hammersmith. "Anyone with the hostage taker's blood on any article of clothing, take it off."

This set off a frantic activity in the van, the sense of panic rising, a ridiculous scene in which everyone was suddenly stripping and trying to get blood off their skin and hair. All except the SWAT guy. "What does it matter?" he said. "We're fucked. Rot, cancer, you name it. We're all dead now."

"Nobody's going to die," said Gideon. "Everything depends on just how hot Chalker was and what kind of radiation we're dealing with."

The SWAT guy raised his massive head and stared at him with red eyes. "What makes you such a radiation rocket scientist?"

"Because I happen to be a radiation rocket scientist."

"Good for you, punk. Then you know we're all dead and you're a fucking liar."

Gideon decided to ignore him.

"Lying peckerwood."

Peckerwood? Exasperated, Gideon looked up at him again. Could he be crazy from radiation poisoning, too? But no, this was simple, mindless panic.

"I'm talking to you, punk. Don't lie."

Gideon combed his hair out of his face with his fingers and looked back down at the floor. He was tired: tired of this jackass, tired of everything, tired of life itself. He didn't have the energy to reason with an irrational person.

The SWAT team member rose abruptly from his seat and seized Gideon's shirt, lifting him out of his seat. "I asked you a question. Don't look away."

Gideon looked at him: at the engorged face, the veins bulging in his neck, the sweat popping on his brow, the trembling lips. The man looked so utterly and completely stupid, he couldn't help himself: he laughed.

"You think it's funny?" The SWAT guy made a fist, getting ready to strike.

Fordyce's punch to the man's gut came as fast as a striking rattler; he gave an *oof!* and fell to his knees. A second later Fordyce had him in a hammerlock. The agent bent over and spoke into his ear, in a low voice, something Gideon did not catch. Then he released the man, who collapsed on his face, groaned, and—after gasping for air—managed to rise back up to his knees.

"Sit down and be quiet," said Fordyce.

The man quietly sat down. After a moment he began to cry.

Gideon adjusted his shirt. "Thanks for saving me the trouble."

Fordyce said nothing.

"Well, so now we know," Gideon went on after a moment.

"Know what?"

"That Chalker wasn't crazy. He was suffering from radiation poisoning—almost certainly gamma rays. A massive dose of gamma radiation scrambles the mind."

Hammersmith raised his head. "How do you know?"

"Anyone who works up at Los Alamos with radionuclides has to learn about the criticality accidents that happened there in the early days. Cecil Kelley, Harry Daghlian, Louis Slotin, the Demon Core."

"The Demon Core?" Fordyce asked.

"A plutonium bomb core that was mishandled twice. It went critical each time, killing the scientists handling it and irradiating a bunch of others. It was finally used in the ABLE shot in '46. One thing they learned from the Demon Core was that a high dose of gamma radiation makes you go crazy. The symptoms are just what you saw with Chalker—mental confusion, raving, headache, vomiting, and an unbearable pain in the gut."

"That puts a whole new spin on things," said Hammersmith.

"The real question," said Gideon, "is the form that craziness took.

Why would he claim they were beaming rays into his head? Experimenting on him?"

"I'm afraid that's a classic symptom of schizophrenia," said Hammersmith.

"Yes, but he didn't *have* schizophrenia. And why would he say his landlord and landlady were government agents?"

Fordyce raised his head and looked at Gideon. "You don't think that poor fuck of a landlord *was* a government agent—do you?"

"No. But I wonder why he kept talking about experiments, why he denied having lived in the apartment. It doesn't make sense."

Fordyce shook his head. "I'm afraid it's starting to make sense to me. A lot of sense."

"How so?" Gideon asked.

"Put it together yourself. The guy works at Los Alamos. Has a top-secret security clearance. Designs nuclear bombs. Converts to Islam. Disappears for two months. Next thing, he shows up irradiated in New York City."

"So?"

"So the son of a bitch joined a jihad! With his help, they got their hands on a nuclear core. They mishandled it just like that Demon Core you mentioned, and Chalker got his ass irradiated."

"Chalker wasn't a radical," Gideon said. "He was quiet. He kept his religion to himself."

Fordyce laughed bitterly. "It's *always* the quiet ones."

There was a silence in the entire van. Everyone was listening intently now. Gideon felt a growing sense of horror: what Fordyce said had the ring of truth. The more he thought about it, the more he realized the man was probably right. Chalker had the personality for it; he was exactly the kind of insecure, confused person who would find his calling in jihad. And there was no other way to explain the intense dose of gamma rays he must have been exposed to, to make him so very hot.

"We'd better face it," said Fordyce as the van slowed. "The ultimate nightmare has come true. Islamic terrorists have got themselves a nuke."

8

THE VAN DOORS opened into an underground, garage-like space, where they were herded through a tunnel of plastic. To Gideon, who knew their radiation exposure was probably secondary and fairly minor, it seemed like overkill, more designed to follow some bureaucratic protocol than anything else.

They were shunted into a high-tech waiting area, all chrome and porcelain and stainless steel, with monitors and computer displays winking softly from all angles. Everything was new and had obviously never been used before. They were separated by sex, stripped, given three sets of showers, examined thoroughly, asked to undergo blood work, given shots, provided with clean clothes, tested again, and then finally allowed to emerge into a second waiting area.

It was an amazing subterranean facility, brand new and state of the art, clearly built after 9/11 to handle a radiological terrorist attack in the city. Gideon recognized various kinds of radiation testing and decontamination equipment, far more advanced than even what they had at Los Alamos. As extraordinary as the place was, he was not surprised: New York City would certainly need a major decontamination center like this.

A scientist entered the waiting room, smiling and wearing a normal white lab coat. He was the first person they'd had contact with who was not in a radiation or hazmat suit. He was accompanied by a small, gloomy man in a dark suit whose size belied an air of command. Gideon recognized him immediately: Myron Dart, who had been deputy director of Los Alamos when Gideon first arrived at the lab. Dart had been appointed from Los Alamos to government service of some kind. Gideon hadn't known him well, but Dart had always seemed competent and fair. Gideon wondered how he'd handle this emergency.

The cheerful scientist spoke first. "I'm Dr. Berk and you're all now clean," he said, beaming at them as if they had passed a final exam. "We're going to have individual counseling, and then you'll be free to resume your lives."

"How bad was the exposure?" Hammersmith asked.

"Very minor. The counselor will discuss with each person his or her actual exposure readings. The hostage taker's radiation exposure occurred elsewhere, not on site, and radiation exposure isn't like the flu. You can't catch it from someone else."

Now Dart stepped forward. He was older than Gideon remembered, his face long and narrow, shoulders sloped. His dress was impeccable as usual: gray suit with an understated pinstripe, beautifully cut, the lavender silk tie giving him an incongruously fashionable look. He carried with him a quiet air of self-assurance. "My name is Dr. Myron Dart, and I'm commander of the Nuclear Emergency Support Team. There's one very important thing I need to impress on all of you." Dart placed his hands behind his back while his gray eyes perused the group, slowly and deliberately, as if he were about to speak to each person individually. "So far, the news that this was a radiological incident hasn't leaked out. You can imagine the panic if it were to do so. Each and every one of you must keep absolutely quiet about what happened today. There are only two words you need to know: *no* and *comment*. That goes for everyone who is going to ask you what happened, from reporters to family. And they *will* ask."

He paused. "You will all be signing nondisclosure papers before your release. I'm afraid you won't be released until you sign these papers. There are criminal and civil penalties for violating the terms of the nondisclosure, spelled out in the documents. I'm sorry, but this is the way it has to be, and I'm sure you'll understand."

Not a word was said. Dart himself had spoken mildly, but something about the very quietness of his voice told Gideon the guy wasn't kidding.

"I apologize," said Dart, "for the inconvenience and the scare. Fortunately, it appears the exposure for all of you was slight to none. I will now turn you over to the very competent hands of Dr. Berk. Good day."

And he left.

The doctor consulted his clipboard. "Let's see. We're going to proceed alphabetically." Now he was like a camp counselor. "Sergeant Adair and Officer Corley, please come with me?"

Gideon glanced around at the assembled group. The SWAT team member who had freaked out in the van was no longer with them, and he thought he could hear, faintly, somewhere in the bowels of that vast facility, the man screaming and threatening.

Suddenly the door opened and Myron Dart reentered, accompanied by Manuel Garza. Dart looked seriously put out. "Gideon Crew?" His eyes fastened on Gideon, and he fancied he saw recognition in those eyes.

Gideon rose.

Garza came over. "Let's go."

"But—"

"No discussion."

Garza walked rapidly to the door, Gideon hurrying to keep up. As they passed Dart, the man looked at him with a cool smile. "You have interesting friends, Dr. Crew."

9

DURING WHAT PROMISED to be a long crosstown ride to Little West 12th Street, in gridlock traffic, Garza said nothing, his eyes straight ahead, concentrating on driving. The nighttime streets of New York were their usual blaze of light, action, noise, and bustle. Gideon could feel the man's dislike of him radiating from his face and body language. Gideon didn't care. The silence let him prepare for what he was sure was going to be an unpleasant confrontation. He had a pretty good idea of what Glinn would want now.

When Gideon was twelve, he had witnessed his father gunned down by FBI snipers. His father had been a civilian cryptologist working for INSCOM, the United States Army Intelligence and Security Command, and had been involved with the group that developed codes. The Soviets broke one of those codes only four months after it was introduced, and twenty-six operatives and double agents had been rolled up in a single night, all tortured and killed. It was one of the worst intelligence disasters of the Cold War. They had said it was his father's fault. His father had always suffered from depression, and under the pressure of the accusations and investigations he broke down, took a hostage, and was shot and killed in the doorway of Arlington Hall Station—after he had surrendered.

Gideon had witnessed the entire thing.

In the years following, Gideon's life had gone off the rails. His mother began drinking. A succession of men came and went from the house. They moved from town to town, following one broken relationship or school expulsion after another. As his father's money had dwindled, they lived in houses, then apartments, trailers, motel rooms, and boardinghouses. His strongest memory of his mother during those years was of her sitting at the kitchen table, glass of Chardonnay in her hand, cigarette smoke curling about her raddled face with its thousand-yard stare, Chopin's Nocturnes playing in the background.

Gideon was an outsider and he developed a loner's interests: math, music, art, and reading. One of their moves—he was seventeen at the time—had brought them to Laramie, Wyoming. One day, he'd gone into the local historical society and spent the day, killing time instead of going to school. Nobody would find him—who'd think of looking there? Occupying an old Victorian house, the historical society was a dusty warren of rooms with dark corners, packed with memorabilia and Western bric-a-brac—six-shooters that killed famous outlaws nobody had ever heard of; Indian artifacts; pioneer curios; rusty spurs; bowie knives; and a miscellany of paintings and drawings.

He found refuge in a room in the back where he could read. After a while his attention was attracted by a small woodblock print, one of many badly hung prints wedged uncomfortably along a wall. It was by an artist he had never heard of, Gustave Baumann, and it was called *Three Pines*. A simple composition, with three small, straggly trees, growing on a barren ridge. But somehow, the more he stared at the print, the more it drew him in; the more remarkable, even miraculous, it became. The artist had managed to imbue those three pines with a sense of dignity, of worth, of essential *treeness*.

The back room at the historical society became his refuge. They never figured out where he was. He could even strum his guitar and the deaf old lady who dozed at the admissions desk never noticed. He didn't know how or why, but over time Gideon fell in love with those snaggle-toothed trees.

And then his mother lost her job and they were going to have to move again. Gideon hated to say good-bye to the print. He couldn't imagine never seeing it again.

And so he stole it.

It turned out to be one of the most thrilling things he'd ever done. And it had been so easy. A few casual questions revealed that the historical society had virtually no security, and its set of dusty accession catalogs was never checked. So one bitterly cold winter's day he walked in with a small screwdriver in his back pocket, removed the print from the wall, and put it under his coat. Then, before leaving, he wiped down the wall the print had been hung on to get rid of the dust mark, shifted two other prints to cover up the screw holes and obscure the gap. The entire process took five minutes, and when he was done nobody would even know a print was missing. It was, truly, a perfect crime. And Gideon told himself it was justified—nobody loved the print, nobody saw the print, nobody even looked at it, and the historical society was letting it rot in a dark corner. He felt virtuous, like a father adopting an unloved, orphaned child.

But what a delicious thrill it had been. A physical sensation. For the first time in years he felt alive, his heart pounding, his senses razor-keen. Colors seemed brighter; the world looked different—at least for a while.

He hung the print above the bed in his new room in Stockport, Ohio, and his mother never noticed it, never remarked on it.

He was sure the print was almost worthless. A few months later, browsing through various auction catalogs, he discovered it had a value of six to seven thousand dollars. At the time his mother was in desperate need of rent, and he considered selling it. But he couldn't imagine parting with it.

But by that time he needed another thrill. Another fix.

So he began to haunt the nearby Muskingum Historical Site, where they had a small collection of etchings, engravings, and watercolors. He picked out one of his favorites, a lithograph by John Steuart Curry called *The Plainsman*, and stole it.

Piece of cake.

It came from an edition of two hundred fifty, and so was untraceable and thus easy to sell on the legitimate market. The World Wide Web was just coming into being, which made it all so much easier and anonymous. He got eight hundred dollars for the print—and his career as a small-time historical society and art museum thief was launched. His mother never had to worry about rent again. Gideon made up vague stories about odd jobs and helping after school, and she was too addled and desperate to question where the money was really coming from.

He stole for money. He stole because he loved certain specific pictures. But most of all, he stole for the thrill. It created a high like nothing else, a feeling of self-worth, of floating above the hidebound, mindless, and blinkered masses.

He knew these were not worthy feelings, but the world was a messed-up place, so why not step outside the rules? He hurt nobody. He was like Robin Hood, lifting unappreciated works of art and putting them in the hands of people who truly loved them. He went on to college, soon dropped out, moved to California, and ultimately devoted himself full-time to visiting small museums, libraries, and historical societies, selling what he had to and keeping the rest.

And then he got the call. His mother was dying in a DC hospital. He went to her side. And on her deathbed she told him the story: of how his father hadn't been responsible for the cryptological security breakdown, after all. Just the opposite: he had pointed out the flaws and been ignored. And then, when it went bad, they'd made him the fall guy, framed by the general in charge of the project—the same general who ordered that he be shot in the act of surrendering.

His father had been scapegoated. And then murdered.

When he learned this, Gideon's life was transformed. For the first time he had a real goal, a worthwhile goal. He cleaned up his act, went back to college, got a doctorate in physics, and went to work at Los Alamos. But all the time, in the background, like the drone note of a bagpipe, he'd carried on a search: a search for the evidence he needed to clear his father's name and wreak vengeance on the general who had murdered him.

It had taken years, but in the end he'd found what he'd needed—and he had taken his revenge. The general was now dead, his own father vindicated.

Yet it was no good: revenge didn't bring people back to life, or re- trieve ruined and wasted years. Still, he had his life ahead of him, and was determined to make the most of it.

Then, shortly afterward—little more than a month back—the supreme catastrophe had occurred. Gideon had been told he had a condition known by the picturesque name of a vein of Galen aneurys- mal malformation. It was an abnormal tangle of arteries and veins deep in the brain. It was inoperable, there was no treatment, and it would kill him within a year.

Or at least, that's what he'd been told. By Eli Glinn—the man who had given him his first assignment as an operative.

He allegedly had one year to live. And now, as Garża and he crawled through New York gridlock toward the Effective Engineering Solutions headquarters, Gideon had no doubt that Glinn, once again, wanted to take a chunk of that year away from him: convince him to take on another operation for EES. He wasn't sure how Glinn would do it, but he was pretty sure it was connected to what had just hap- pened with Chalker.

As the car turned onto Little West 12th Street, Gideon steeled him- self for the confrontation. He would be cool, but firm. He would keep his dignity. He would not engage. And if all that failed, he'd simply tell Glinn to go fuck himself and walk out.

10

IT WAS MIDNIGHT as they entered EES headquarters. The hushed confines seemed to swallow Gideon in cool white spaces. Even at the late hour, technicians moved about among the strange models, layouts, and tables covered with shrouded and mysterious equipment. He followed Garza to the elevator, which delivered them at a glacial pace to the top floor. A moment later he was standing in the same Zen-like conference room, Glinn seated in his wheelchair at the head of the vast bubinga wood table. The window he had stood by earlier that day now had its blinds drawn.

Gideon felt exhausted, gutted and cleaned like a fish. He was surprised and a little irritated to find Glinn uncharacteristically animated.

"Coffee?" Glinn asked. His good eye was fairly sparkling.

"Yes." Gideon collapsed into a chair.

Garza left with a frown, and returned with a mug. Gideon dumped in cream and sugar and drank it down like a glass of water.

"I have good news and bad news," said Glinn.

Gideon waited.

"The good news is that your exposure to radiation was exceedingly minor. According to the tables, it will increase your chances of dying from cancer by less than one percent over the next twenty years."

Gideon had to laugh at the irony of this. His voice echoed in the empty room. No one else joined in.

"The bad news is that we suddenly face a national emergency of the highest order. Reed Chalker was irradiated in what seems to have been a criticality event involving a mass of fissile material. He was affected by a combination of alpha particles and gamma rays from a source that appears to be highly enriched, bomb-grade U-235. The dose was in the range of eighty grays, or eight thousand rads. A massive, *massive* dose."

Gideon sat up. That was astonishing.

"Yes. The amount of fissile material capable of causing such an event would be at least ten kilograms. Which just happens to be more than enough uranium for a substantial nuclear weapon."

Gideon took this in. It was worse than he had imagined.

Glinn paused, then went on. "It seems clear that Chalker was involved in preparing a terrorist attack with a nuclear device. During these preparations, something went wrong and the uranium went critical. Chalker was irradiated. It also appears likely to our experts that the remaining terrorists spirited off the bomb, leaving Chalker to die. But he didn't die right away—radiation poisoning doesn't work like that. He went insane and in his confusion took hostages. And here we are."

"Have you found *where* he was preparing the bomb?"

"That's the highest priority now. It can't be too far from his apartment in Sunnyside, because it seems he returned there on foot. We're flying radiation monitors over the city and any moment we'll have a hit, since a criticality event like this would leave a minor plume of radiation—with a characteristic signature."

Glinn almost rubbed his hands together. "We're in on the ground floor, Gideon. You were there. You knew Chalker—"

"No," said Gideon. Now it was time to get up. He rose.

"Hear me out. You're the man for this job, no doubt about it. This isn't undercover. You'll go in as yourself—"

"I said no."

"You'll partner with Fordyce. It is an unavoidable requirement of the assignment, imposed by the National Nuclear Security Administration. But you'll be given a broad investigative mandate."

"Absolutely not."

"You only need to pretend to work with Fordyce. In reality you'll be a lone operator, beholden to no one, working outside the normal rules of law enforcement."

"I already did what you wanted," said Gideon. "In case you didn't notice, I fucked it up and three people were shot. And now I'm going home."

"You didn't make a mistake and you can't go home. We've got days, maybe hours. Gideon—*millions of lives are at stake.* Here's the address you need to go to first." He shoved a piece of paper at Gideon. "Now get going, Fordyce is expecting you."

"Fuck you. I really mean that. *Fuck you.*"

"You've got to hurry. There's no time." Glinn paused. "Don't you think you should do something more worthwhile with the months you have left than just go fishing?"

"I've been thinking about that. All that talk of my dying, of my terminal disease. You're the biggest bullshit artist I've ever met—for all I know, this could just be another patented Eli Glinn lie. How do I know those X-rays were mine, anyway? The name was cut out."

Glinn shook his head. "In your heart you know I'm telling the truth."

Gideon flushed with anger. "Look. What could I possibly do to help? They've got the NYPD, FBI, this NEST group, ATF, CIA, and I'm sure any number of black agencies in on this. I'm telling you, I'm going home."

"That is *precisely* the problem." Glinn raised his voice, angry himself. His crippled claw smacked the tabletop. "The response is over the top. It's so unwieldy that our psychoengineering calculations show they'll never stop the attack. It'll be investigative gridlock."

"Psychoengineering calculations," Gideon repeated sarcastically. "What a crock." He finally started for the door. Garza blocked his path with a faint curl of contempt on his lips.

"Get out of my way."

There was a brief standoff, then Glinn said, "Manuel, let him go."

Garza stepped aside with insolent slowness.

"When you go out on the street," said Glinn, "do me one favor: look at the faces of the people around you and think about how their lives are going to change. Forever."

Gideon didn't even wait to hear the rest. He rushed out the door, crushed his finger against the elevator button, and took it down to the first floor, cursing its slowness. When the doors opened he ran across the vast workroom, through the sets of doors, and down the hall; the front door opened electronically as he approached.

Once outside, he jogged down the street to a boutique hotel, where a line of cabs were standing. Screw his luggage. He would go to the airport, get back to New Mexico, hole up in his cabin until this whole thing was over. He had done enough damage. He grasped the handle of the cab and opened the door, hesitating a moment as he looked at the crowds of trendy people going in and out of the hotel. He recalled Glinn's advice. He found the people he saw repulsive. He didn't care how their lives might change. Let them all die. He might well be living with death; why not them, too?

That was his answer to Glinn.

Suddenly he felt himself shoved aside and a drunk man in a tuxedo barged past him, stealing his cab. The man slammed the door, leaned out the window with a grin of triumph, exhaling martini fumes. "Sorry, pal, he who hesitates...Have a nice trip back to Des Moines."

With a raucous laugh from its passenger, the cab pulled away and Gideon stood there, shocked.

How their lives are going to change. Glinn's words echoed again in his mind. Was this world, those people, that man, worth saving? Somehow, the very loutishness of the man hit home in a way no random kindness from a stranger would have. The man would wake up the next morning and no doubt regale his friends on the trading floor about the out-of-town dickhead who didn't know how to commandeer a New York City cab. Good. Fuck him. More proof they were not worth saving. Gideon would retreat to his cabin in the Jemez Mountains and let these assholes fend for themselves...

But as this thought ran through his mind, he faltered. Who was he to judge? The world was made up of all kinds of people. If he fled to his cabin and New York was taken out by a nuke, where would that leave him? Was it his responsibility? No. But by running away, he would have still put himself lower than that tuxedoed scumbag by orders of magnitude.

Whether he had eleven months or fifty years, it would be a long and lonely space of time in which he would never, ever forgive himself.

For a long, furious moment he hesitated. And then, boiling with rage and frustration, he turned and retraced his steps down Little West 12th Street to the anonymous door of Effective Engineering Solutions, Inc. It opened as he approached, as if Glinn were expecting him.

11

CHALKER'S BODY LAY on a porcelain gurney encased in a large glass cube, like an offering to some high-tech god. The corpse had been autopsied and was splayed open, a riot of red among gray steel, glass, and chrome, various organs arrayed around it—the heart, liver, stomach, and other body parts Gideon did not recognize and didn't want to recognize. There was something uniquely unsettling about seeing the guts of someone you'd known personally—it wasn't just another image on the evening news.

Chalker's personal effects were arranged on a table next to the body: his clothes, wallet, keys, belt, credit cards, papers, change, ticket stubs, Kleenex, and various other items—all tagged. All, evidently, radioactive.

At a console, medical personnel and technicians were operating a set of eight robotic arms inside the glass cube, each one of which terminated in a different set of grisly-looking dissecting instruments—bone chisels, shears, mallets, forceps, knives, skullbreakers, spreaders, and other tools of cadaveritude. Despite the highly dissected condition of the body, the work was still progressing.

"Lucky thing," said Fordyce, removing his notebook. "We didn't miss the autopsy completely."

"Funny, I was thinking just the opposite," said Gideon.

Fordyce glanced at him and rolled his eyes.

Gideon heard a whirring sound. One of the robotic arms, which terminated in a circular saw, began to move, the blade spinning up to a high-pitched whine. As the technicians murmured into headsets, the blade lowered toward Chalker's skull. "Torquemada would have loved this stuff," Gideon said.

"Looks like we're just in time for the removal of the brain," Fordyce said, licking his finger and turning the pages of his notebook to find a blank one.

The whine became muffled as the saw sank into Chalker's forehead. A dark liquid began running into the drain along the edge of the gurney. Gideon turned away, pretending to examine some papers in his briefcase. At least, he thought, there was no smell.

"Agent Fordyce? Dr. Crew?"

Gideon glanced over to see a technician with big glasses, a ponytail, and a clipboard, standing beside them expectantly.

"Dr. Dart will see you in his office now."

With a feeling of relief, Gideon followed the technician toward a cubicle at the far end of the high-tech area. Fordyce went along, grumbling about being taken away from the autopsy. They entered a spartan space no more than nine by twelve feet. Dart himself was sitting behind a small desk covered with heavy, squared stacks of folders. He rose and offered his hand, first to Fordyce, then to Gideon.

"Please sit down."

They took seats in folding chairs set up in front of the desk. Dart spent a moment organizing some already-organized papers. He had a face that did little to conceal the bones of the skull underneath; his eyes, full of vitality, were so deeply set that they gleamed out of two pools of darkness. At Los Alamos he had been a bit of a legend, a rather humorless geek physicist with a doctorate from CalTech who was unexpectedly a decorated soldier—a most unusual combination— having won two Silver Stars and a Purple Heart in action in Desert Storm.

Dart finished organizing the papers and looked up. "This is a pretty unusual portfolio they've given you two."

Fordyce nodded.

"As commander of NEST," Dart went on, "I've already thoroughly briefed the FBI. But I see they want you to have a little extra."

Gideon said nothing. He had no intention of taking the lead. That's what Fordyce was there for: to run interference, take the heat, and, if necessary, present his ass for kicking. Gideon intended to lie low.

"We're an independent team," said Fordyce. "We appreciate you giving us this private briefing, sir." His voice was mild, nonconfrontational. Here was a man who knew how the game was played.

Dart's eyes swiveled to Gideon. "And I've been told you've been hired by a private contractor whose identity is classified."

Gideon nodded.

"I thought I recognized you. We worked together at Los Alamos. How did you happen to get from there to here?"

"It's a long story. I'm on an extended vacation from the lab."

"You were on the Stockpile Stewardship Team, as I recollect. Same as Chalker." This little fact hung in the air. It was hard for Gideon to gauge how much Dart knew or what he thought about it.

"You were in on the incident," Dart continued.

"They brought me in to try to talk him down...but it didn't work out." Gideon felt his face flush.

Dart seemed to sense the awkwardness. He waved his hand. "I'm sorry about that. It must have been tough. They tell me you saved the two kids."

Gideon didn't answer. He felt the flush deepen.

"All right, moving on." Dart opened a file and shuffled more papers. Fordyce had his notebook out and ready. Gideon chose to take no notes; he had discovered in graduate school that note taking interfered with his ability to assemble the big picture in his mind.

Dart spoke rapidly while looking at the papers in front of him. "The autopsy and analysis of the personal effects of Chalker are not finished, but we have preliminary results."

Fordyce began scribbling.

"Nuclear spectroscopy from swipes of Chalker's hands and neutron activation tests showed conclusively that there were traces of highly enriched uranium 235 on his palms and fingers. He'd handled it in the past twenty-four hours. Chalker's clothes were contaminated with absorbed and adsorbed radioactive isotopes, including cerium 144, barium 140, iodine 131, and cesium 137. These are the classic fission products of a U-235 criticality event. The iodine 131 has a half-life of eight days, and we found a high level of it, so we know the accident took place no more than twenty-four hours ago."

Dart glanced at Fordyce. "If some of this is confusing to you, Agent Fordyce, Dr. Crew will explain it later."

He examined other sheets of paper. "The contents of his pockets have been inventoried. There was an admission ticket stub in his pocket, dated Friday last week, to the Smithsonian Air and Space Museum."

Fordyce scribbled faster.

"Slow down before you burn out a tendon," Gideon said, nudging Fordyce.

"There was a train ticket receipt, one way, Washington Union Station to New York Grand Central, dated yesterday afternoon. There was a piece of paper with a website address written on it and several phone numbers. The phone numbers are being analyzed."

Fordyce glanced up. "The website address?"

"I'm afraid I'm not authorized to release that information."

There was a silence. "Excuse me," said Fordyce, "but I thought we were authorized to receive all information."

Dart looked at him with his brightly gleaming eyes. "In an investigation like this," he said, "there has to be a certain level of compartmentalization. Each investigator is given what he needs to know, and not more. We all have to work within parameters." His glance shifted to Gideon. "For example, I've been denied information about the private contractor you're working for." He smiled, then went on in his dry voice. "An analysis of Chalker's vomitus indicated his last meal took place at around midnight. It was crab soup, bread, ham, lettuce, tomatoes, Russian dressing, and french fries."

"Whew," Gideon said. "No wonder he's radioactive."

Another shuffle. "We recovered two credit cards, a driver's license, a Los Alamos ID card, and various other items from his wallet. Those are being analyzed now."

"What about the autopsy?" Fordyce asked.

"The preliminary results indicate damage to his thyroid gland, consistent with exposure to iodine 131. This—" He glanced at Fordyce—"is a major fission product of U-235 and indicates Chalker was exposed for some time to a low level of radioactivity before the criticality incident."

"Do you have a sense of how long?" Gideon asked.

"Cell necrosis indicates more than eleven days." Shuffle. "There were also classic indications of a massive exposure to ionizing radiation in the criticality incident, with exposure on the order of eight thousand rads. The skin and the internal organs all showed evidence of acute radiation syndrome, beta as well as gamma burns. The exposure was from the front, with the greatest exposure on the hands. The traces of highly enriched uranium on his hands suggest he was actually handling the material when it went critical."

"Without gloves?" Gideon asked.

Dart looked at him. "Yes. And that's something we're wondering about, too, why he didn't wear protective gear. Unless of course he . . . did not expect to live much longer." A short silence followed this statement, and then Dart shut the file. "That's all we have so far."

Gideon said, "If that's true, we don't have a lot of time."

"Why's that?"

"It seems to me he was assembling the bomb."

"How do you know?" asked Fordyce, turning to him.

"The simplest nuke—the one terrorists would build—is a gun-type bomb. Two pieces of U-235 are fired together in a tube to achieve critical mass. With a bomb like that, you keep those two halves shielded and you don't bring the pieces anywhere near each other until it's time to actually assemble the bomb. Because those two pieces, if they get too close without proper shielding, will exchange neutrons, go critical, and let loose with a burst of gamma radiation exactly like what hit Chalker."

"So you're saying Chalker was assembling the weapon and botched it?" asked Fordyce.

"That's exactly what I'm saying."

"So was the weapon ruined?"

"Not at all," said Gideon. "It might be a little hot, but nothing a suicide bomber would need to worry about. The fact that the uranium went critical would have caused physical changes in the core that will, unfortunately, *enhance* the yield. It'll make the bomb more powerful."

"Son of a bitch," muttered Fordyce.

"Very good, Dr. Crew," said Dart. "Our own internal evaluation team has come to much the same conclusions."

Fordyce asked, "What about his laptop computer? I heard they recovered one from his apartment."

"The contents are encrypted. We haven't been able to extract any information yet."

"Then you should let me look at it. I recently finished a six-month tenure in the FBI's Cryptology Unit."

"Thank you, Agent Fordyce, but we've got a crack team on it and I personally feel your talents would be better used in other areas."

There was a brief silence before Fordyce spoke again. "Any indication of the target?"

Dart looked at him steadily. "Not yet."

Fordyce took a deep breath. "We need access to Chalker's apartment."

"Naturally you'll have access. But NEST is first in the queue." Dart consulted a calendar. "It's going to be a couple of weeks, I'm afraid. We've got a long line of government agencies ahead of you."

Gideon waited for Fordyce to react, but to his disappointment the agent didn't respond. They rose to leave.

"May I have a private word with you, Special Agent Fordyce?" Dart said.

Gideon looked at Dart in surprise.

"I'm sorry, Dr. Crew, this is between us."

Fordyce watched as Crew left. He wasn't sure what Dart's game was—he seemed like a straight shooter, but then everyone, even the best, had a game. Fordyce's strategy had always been to hide his own game while figuring out the game of everyone around him. It had gotten him through FBI minefields for years.

After the door shut, Dart folded his hands and stared at Fordyce. "I'd like this to remain between us. I'm a little concerned, because, frankly, I find this assignment of yours to be rather odd."

Fordyce nodded.

"I knew Dr. Crew briefly at Los Alamos. He's more than bright. I have a high opinion of his abilities. But up on the Hill he had a reputation as a freelancer, someone who felt the rules were for others, not him. The qualities that make him a brilliant and creative scientist may not translate well into a criminal investigation like this. I'm asking you to keep an eye on him and make sure he doesn't go off... half-cocked. That's all."

Fordyce kept his facial expression strictly neutral. It was true Gideon had a reckless, wiseass air about him that Fordyce didn't like. He understood why Dart thought he had an attitude—because he did. But Crew was his partner, and although he wasn't sure he trusted or even liked him, partnership loyalty trumped that. "Very well, Dr. Dart."

Dart rose, extended his hand. "Thank you and best of luck."

Fordyce rose and shook the hand.

12

GIDEON CREW STARED at the mess in disbelief. Even at two in the morning, there were now so many emergency and government vehicles, barriers, command and control stations, and staging areas around Chalker's apartment that they had been forced to park several blocks away. As they pushed their way closer to the row house where the hostage taking had occurred, the area became a zoo of law enforcement, vast and chaotic, with individuals from scores of government agencies moving about, layers of checkpoints, red tape, and peremptory challenges. Thank God, Gideon thought, for Fordyce, his shield, and his ferocious scowl, which enabled them to cut an efficient swath through it all.

The barriers were also keeping back a seething crowd of television crews, reporters, and photographers, all mingling with rubberneckers and people evicted from their homes, some of whom were protesting, waving homemade signs and shouting. Amazingly, so far the government had been able to keep a lid on the explosive news that radiation was involved and that they might be dealing with a loose nuke in the hands of terrorists.

Gideon did not expect that lid to stay on much longer. Too many people already knew. And when it came off, God only knew what would happen.

As they worked their way to the front of the alphabet soup of responders, they came to the central command and control center: three mobile vans in a U-shaped formation, festooned with satellite dishes. A set of stanchions had been set up, like an airport security apparatus, managing a crush of law enforcement personnel moving in and out. Beyond, the street had been cleared and, in the brilliant glow of artificial lights, Fordyce could see several people in radiation suits moving about on the front lawn and inside the building.

"Welcome to New Clusterfuck City," Gideon said.

Fordyce walked toward someone in an FBI uniform. "Special Agent Fordyce." He extended his hand.

"Special Agent Packard, Behavioral Science Unit."

"We need to get into the apartment."

Packard gave a cynical snort. "If you want in, you got to get in line. The six guys in the apartment right now have been there for three hours already, and there must be a hundred more waiting. The 9/11 response was a lot more organized than this." The man shook his head. "What unit are you with?"

"I'm liaising with a private security contractor."

"Jesus, a private contractor? You might as well take a vacation in Hawaii and come back in two weeks."

"So who are these guys that get to go first?" Fordyce asked.

"NEST, naturally."

Gideon touched Fordyce's shoulder and nodded at one of the figures in radiation suits. "Wonder who his haberdasher is?" he murmured.

Fordyce seemed to get the hint. He paused a moment, considering. Then he turned back to Agent Packard. "Where do you get the suits?"

Packard nodded toward another van. "Over there."

Fordyce grasped his hand. "Thanks, brother."

As they moved away, Gideon said, "So you're ready for a little guerrilla action? I mean, those jihadists have a nuke. Two weeks is going to be way too late."

Fordyce said nothing, simply wending his way through the crowd toward the van. Gideon followed. It was hard to know what the FBI agent was thinking from looking at his stony face.

A changing tent had been set up behind the van, with racks of suits and respirators. Radmeters were fitted to the sleeves of each suit. Fordyce ducked under the canvas barrier and, with Crew in tow, walked up to the racks and began pawing through them.

Immediately a man in a NEST uniform came over. "What's going on?" he asked.

Fordyce gave him a blue-eyed stare, plucked his shield from the chain around his neck, and almost pushed it into the man's face. "We need access. Now."

"Look," the man said shrilly, "how many times do I have to tell you people, FBI will get its turn?"

Fordyce stared at him. "No FBI have been in there yet? At all?"

"That's right. NEST has a lot of work to do first."

"Dart's group?"

"That's right. National security protocol in the event of a nuclear emergency says that NEST is the lead agency."

A long silence. Fordyce had again seemed to shut down. Gideon realized it would be up to him to do whatever it was they had to do to get in; Fordyce was too rule-bound and had too much to lose. Gideon, on the other hand, had nothing at all to lose.

"Thank goodness for that," said Gideon, taking a suit from the rack and stepping into it. "No wonder Dart was so eager to get us seconded to NEST."

He found Fordyce's sapphire stare on him, and he smiled back pleasantly. "Hurry up. You know Dart, he'll be pissed if we don't have our report in by dawn."

The man relaxed. "Sorry. Didn't mean to challenge you, I didn't realize you're assigned to NEST."

"No problem," said Gideon, eyeing Fordyce and wondering if the special agent was going to get with the program. "Come on, Stone, we don't have all day."

Still, the agent hesitated—and then, to Gideon's relief, began donning his own suit.

"Wait. I've got to see your authorization papers. And I'm supposed to help you select your gear."

Fordyce zipped his suit up the front and bestowed a friendly smile on the man. "Paperwork is on its way. And thanks, but we already know our gear."

"I've got to at least see your temp ID."

"You're going to make me take this off to show you an ID?"

"Well, gotta see ID."

Fordyce smiled, put a hand on the fellow's shoulder. "What's your name, son?"

"Ramirez."

"Hand me those respirators, Ramirez."

Ramirez handed him the respirators. Fordyce handed one to Gideon.

Gideon took it. "Dart authorized us personally. If you have any questions, call him."

Ramirez was still looking at Fordyce. "Well, Dart doesn't like to be disturbed—"

Fordyce fitted the respirator to his face, which effectively cut off his ability to communicate with Ramirez. Gideon followed suit. He saw that the respirator was fitted with a small radio transmitter. He flicked it on, set it to a private channel, indicated for Fordyce to do the same.

"You read, Fordyce?"

"Loud and clear," Fordyce's voice crackled back.

"Let's get going before, ah, it's too late."

They began to move past Ramirez.

"Wait," said Ramirez apologetically. "I really got to see that ID."

Gideon lifted his respirator. "We'll show it to you when we unsuit. Or you can check with Dart—but be sure to catch him at the right moment. He's kind of irritable right now."

"You're not kidding," said Ramirez, shaking his head.

"So you can imagine how pissed he'll be if his two handpicked guys get delayed."

Gideon eased the respirator back over his head before Ramirez could reply. They hopped the last barrier and strode toward the row house.

"Nice work if you can get it," said Gideon into the intercom, with a chuckle. "And by the way, that suit doesn't do a *thing* for you."

"You think it's funny?" said Fordyce, suddenly angry. "I've been dealing with that crap all of my career and there's nothing funny about it. And by the way, I'm going to say this was all your idea."

They gave the basement apartment, where Chalker had spent the last two months of his life, a swift walk-through. It was small and stark, consisting of a tiny room in the front, a pullman kitchen and bathroom, and a back room with a single window. The apartment was scrupulously clean and smelled faintly of Pine-Sol and bleach. Six NEST personnel moved about slowly, scanning with various instruments, picking up fibers and dust, taking photographs. Nothing had been touched.

The front room was empty, save for a rug by the door with a row of flip-flops, and a second, small but sumptuous Persian rug in the middle.

Gideon paused, staring the rug. It was askew, out of line with the lines of the room.

"Prayer rug," came Fordyce's tinny voice over the intercom. "Pointing in the direction of Mecca."

"Right. Of course."

The only other item in the room was a Qur'an, open, resting on an elaborately carved book stand. Fordyce examined it and saw it was a bilingual edition, English and Arabic, and well worn. Many of the pages had been marked with strings.

It would be interesting to see which verses had attracted Chalker's special attention. Gideon glanced at the page it was open to and his attention was immediately arrested by one verse, which had been marked:

Has there reached you the report of the Overwhelming Event?
Some faces, that day, will be humbled, working hard and exhausted.
They will burn in an intensive Fire.
They will be given drink from a boiling spring.

He looked up at Fordyce, who was also gazing at the book. He nodded slowly.

Fordyce pointed at the kitchen, then moved into it for a closer examination. It was as clean and bare as the rest of the apartment, everything in its place.

"Are we allowed to open the refrigerator?" Gideon asked Fordyce over the radio.

"Don't ask. Just do it."

Gideon opened the door. Inside was a carton of milk, a package of dates, leftover pizza in a carton, cheese, some Chinese food cartons, and other miscellaneous items. The freezer contained frozen lamb cubes, Ben & Jerry's ice cream, and a bag of raw almonds. As he shut the door, Gideon noticed a calendar affixed to the side of the refrigerator with a magnet, a photograph of the Taj Mahal filling its upper half. In the calendar grid below, a number of appointments had been scribbled in Chalker's hand. Gideon scanned them with interest while Fordyce came up behind.

Gideon grasped the calendar page and turned it back a month, then another. It was crabbed with cryptic appointments. "Jesus," he murmured into the intercom, dropping the calendar back to the current month. "You see that?"

"See what?" asked Fordyce, staring at the empty calendar. "It's blank."

"That's just it. The appointments just stop. There're no appointments after the twenty-first of this month."

"Which means?"

"We're looking at the appointment calendar of a suicide bomber. *And all his appointments end ten days from now.*"

13

THEY EMERGED INTO the street, the sodium lights bright after the dim apartment. Gideon blinked, tried to adjust his eyes.

"Ten days," said Fordyce, shaking his head. "Do you think they'll still try to maintain that schedule after all this?"

Gideon said, "I think it's quite possible they might *accelerate* it."

"Jesus Christ." A chopper passed over, flying low, trailing a net of radiation detectors, and Gideon could hear and see the lights of others hovering in the sky over various parts of the city.

"They're looking for the terrorists' lab," said Fordyce. "How far do you think Chalker could have gone, irradiated like that?"

"Not far. Quarter mile, at most."

They had almost reached the barriers. Gideon pulled off his respirator and said, "Let's keep the suits."

Fordyce looked at him steadily. "I'm beginning to think you like stirring the pot."

"We've got ten days. So, yeah, let's stir the pot. Vigorously."

"So what do we need the suits for?"

"To get our asses into the terrorists' lab. Which we are going to go looking for—right now. The warehouses of Long Island City are right across Queens Boulevard—that's an obvious place to start. I'm telling you, after getting irradiated, Chalker couldn't have gone far from the scene of the accident. He was barely mobile."

Fordyce at least didn't say no. They reached the car, pulled off the suits, and tossed them in the back. Gideon kept the communications device, tucking it into his pocket and retaining the earbud, so that he could listen in on the chatter. Fordyce fired up the vehicle. As they moved beyond the barriers and eased through the rubberneckers—incredible they were still out at three AM—a change began to take place in the crowd. There was a movement, a wave of fear, even panic. People started moving away, slowly at first, and then faster. There were shouts and a few screams, and they began to run.

"What the hell's going on?" Fordyce said.

Gideon rolled down the window. "Hey, you, what's happening? Hey!"

A scruffy teenager on a skateboard careened past them, and others streamed by. A man came huffing up, face red, and seized the rear car door handle, yanking open the door.

"What's going on?" Gideon shouted.

"Let me in!" he cried. "They've got a bomb!"

Gideon reached back, shoved him out. "Find another car."

"They're going to nuke the city!" the man cried, coming forward again. "Let me in!"

"Who?"

"The terrorists! It's all over the news!" He lunged again at the car as Gideon slammed the door, Fordyce shooting the locks.

The man pounded on the windows with sweaty fists. "We've got to get out of the city! I've got money. Help me! Please!"

"You're going to be fine!" Gideon shouted through the glass. "Go home and watch *Dexter*."

Fordyce punched the accelerator and the car lurched out into the street; he quickly crossed the boulevard and gunned his way into a quiet industrial side street, away from the panicking crowds. It was incredible: lights were going on in all the apartment buildings surrounding them.

"Looks like the news finally broke," Fordyce said. "The shit's really going to hit the fan now."

"It was only a matter of time," said Gideon. His earpiece was starting to ramp up, voices swamping the public frequencies. The response teams were evidently becoming taxed by panicking people and emergency calls.

They were moving slowly along Jackson Avenue, amid a wasteland of old warehouses and industrial sites stretching off in every direction.

"Needle in a haystack," said Fordyce. "We'll never find it on our own."

"Yeah, and once *they* find it, we'll never get in, especially after that stunt we pulled back there." Gideon thought for a moment. "We've got to find a lead that no one else has thought of."

"A lead no one else has thought of? Good luck." And Fordyce turned the wheel and headed the car back toward Queens Boulevard.

"Okay, I've got it!" said Gideon, suddenly excited. "Here's what we're going to do."

"What?"

"We're going to New Mexico. We're going to look into Chalker's past life. The answer to what happened to him lies out west. Face it—we're not going to accomplish shit here."

Fordyce gazed at him steadily. "The action's here, not there."

"That's exactly why we can't stay here, wrestling with all these bureaucrats. Out there, at least we'll have a fighting chance to make a difference." Gideon paused. "Got a better idea?"

Unexpectedly, Fordyce grinned. "La Guardia's only ten minutes away."

"What? You like the idea?"

"Absolutely. And we'd better leave now, because I guarantee you that in a few hours every seat on every plane out of New York City is going to be booked for the foreseeable future."

A low-flying helicopter churned overhead, trailing detectors. A moment later a voice cut through the babble on Gideon's earpiece.

"I got a hit! I'm getting a plume!"

It was drowned out in static and other voices.

"...Pearson Street, near the self-storage..."

"They got a hit," Gideon told Fordyce. "A radioactive plume over Pearson Street."

"Pearson Street? Jesus, we just passed it."

"We'll be the first on the scene. About time we got a break."

Fordyce pulled the sedan into a four-wheel powerslide. A moment later they were screeching around the corner of Pearson. Several helicopters were hovering already, seeking the precise source, and sirens could be heard in the distance.

Pearson Street dead-ended at the railroad yards. The last buildings on the street were a massive, blank self-storage building, opposite a vacant lot strewn with trash, and some ancient warehouses. At the very end of the road stood a long, decrepit railroad storage shed.

"There," Gideon said, pointing. "That shed in the railroad yard."

Fordyce looked at him dubiously. "How do you know—?"

"See the broken lock? Let's go."

Fordyce drove up on the curb, screeching to a stop. They yanked on their suits, Fordyce grabbed two flashlights from the glove compartment, and they ran toward the shed. It was surrounded by a chain-link fence, but there were plenty of holes and tears in the fence and they quickly squeezed through. The sliding doors were chained, but the lock hung from only one link, its hasp cut.

Gideon shoved open the door. Fordyce switched on his flashlight, then handed the other to Gideon. Their twin beams revealed a disused space full of decaying piles of angle iron, ties, rails, rusted equipment, and piles of salt and crushed rock.

Gideon looked around frantically but could see nothing of interest. It was just one big, useless space.

"Damn," said Fordyce. "Must have been one of those warehouses we passed."

Gideon held up his hand, scanned the floor. There had been people walking here recently, a lot of scuff marks in the dust and grime. They led toward a far wall, where he could make out the huge double doors of a freight elevator. He sprinted over.

"There's a level below this one," he said, staring at the elevator panel. He punched the buttons, but they were dead.

Gideon cast around with his flashlight and quickly located the emergency stairs. He pushed through the door into the pitch dark of a stairwell. The sirens had now converged up above and he could hear muffled radios, slamming doors, loud voices.

Using their flashlights as guides, they made their way quickly down the stairs. The vast room at the bottom was largely empty, save for grids, hoists, and moving racks mounted from the ceiling. But there was an acrid stench of burned paper and plastic in the air, and as Gideon moved into the center of the room he made out, at the far end, a tight warren of spaces with shadowy, abandoned equipment. Fordyce had seen it, too, and they both walked over.

"What kind of a setup is this?" Fordyce asked, looking around.

Gideon had recognized it immediately, and it chilled him. "I've seen similar setups in historic photos at the Los Alamos bomb museum," he said. "Old photos of the Manhattan Project. It's a crude set of rails, poles, pulleys and ropes used to move radioactive material around without getting too close to it. Very low-tech but relatively effective, if you're in martyr mode and don't care about exposing yourself to elevated radiation."

As he walked past the alcoves, peering into each, he could see more remote-handling apparatuses: crude slides and structures, pieces of shielding and lead boxes, along with discarded HE wires and detonators—and what he recognized, with another chill, was a broken high-speed transistor switch.

"Jesus," said Gideon, his heart sinking. "I see everything here they'd need to build a bomb—including the high-speed transistors, maybe the most difficult thing to get besides the core itself."

"What the hell's that?" Fordyce pointed to another alcove, where Gideon could see a cage with bars and some food trash.

"Dog crate? Big one, by the size of it. Probably a rottweiler or a Doberman—to keep away the curious."

Fordyce moved slowly, methodically, examining everything.

"There's a fair amount of residual radiation here," said Gideon, looking at the radmeter built into his suit. He pointed. "Over there, at that apparatus, is probably where Chalker fucked up and the mass went critical. It's hotter than hell."

"Gideon? Take a look at this." Fordyce was kneeling before a pile of ashes, staring at something. As Gideon walked over, he could hear a babble of voices on the intercom, shouts and footsteps echoing from above. The NEST crew had entered the building.

He knelt beside Fordyce, trying not to stir the air and thus disturb the delicate pile. Masses of documents, computer CDs, DVDs, and other papers and equipment had been swept up into a large heap and all burned together, creating a gluey, acrid mess that still stank of gasoline. Fordyce's gloved hand was pointing to one large, broken piece of ash at the top. As Gideon bent closer, his flashlight shone off its crumpled surface and he could just make out what it had been: a map of Washington, DC, with what appeared to be extensive notations in Arabic script. Several landmarks had been circled, including the White House and the Pentagon.

"I think we just found the target," said Fordyce grimly.

There was a pounding of feet on the stairs. A phalanx of white-suited figures appeared at the far end of the room.

"Who the hell are you?" came a voice over the intercom.

"NEST," said Fordyce crisply, standing up. "We're the advance team—turning it over to you."

In the reflected beam of his flashlight, Gideon caught Fordyce's eye through the visor. "Yeah. Time to go."

14

THEY HAD SPENT hours at the FBI field office in Albuquerque, filling out endless paperwork for a pool vehicle and expense account. Now they were finally on the road, driving to Santa Fe, the great arc of the Sandia Mountains rising on their right, the Rio Grande to their left.

Even here, they met a steady stream of overloaded cars heading the opposite direction. "What are they running from?" Fordyce asked.

"Everyone around here knows that if nuclear war breaks out, Los Alamos is a primary target."

"Yeah, but who's talking about nuclear war?"

"If the terrorist nuke goes off in DC, God only knows what might happen next. All bets are off. And what if we find evidence the terrorists got the nuke from a place like Pakistan or North Korea? You think we wouldn't retaliate? I can think of plenty of scenarios where we might see a sweet little mushroom cloud rising over that hill. Which, by the way, is only twenty miles from Santa Fe—and upwind of it."

Fordyce shook his head. "You're getting way ahead of yourself, Gideon."

"These people don't think so."

"Jesus," said Fordyce. "We must've spent four hours with those damn people. And only nine days until N-Day." He used the insider term for the presumed day of the nuke detonation.

They drove for a moment in silence.

"I hate that bureaucratic shit," Fordyce finally said. "I've got to clear my head." He fumbled in his briefcase, pulled out an iPod, stuck it into the car dock, and dialed in a song.

"Lawrence Welk, here we come," muttered Gideon.

Instead, "Epistrophy" came blasting out of the speakers.

"Whoa," said Gideon, amazed. "An FBI agent who listens to Monk? You've got to be kidding me."

"What did you think I listened to—motivational lectures? You a Monk fan?"

"Greatest jazz pianist of all time."

"What about Art Tatum?"

"Too many notes, not enough music, if you know what I mean."

Fordyce had a heavy foot. As the speedometer crept up to a hundred miles an hour, the agent took the portable flasher out of the glove compartment and slapped it onto the roof, turning on the grille flashers as he did so. The rush of air and humming of the tires sounded an ostinato to Monk's crashing chords and rippling arpeggios.

They listened to the music in silence for a while, then Fordyce spoke. "You knew Chalker. Tell me about him. What made the guy tick?"

Gideon felt a swell of irritation at the implication that somehow he and Chalker were buddies. "I don't know what made the guy 'tick.'"

"What did you two do up at Los Alamos, anyway?"

Gideon sat back, trying to relax. The car approached a line of slower vehicles and a semi; Fordyce swung out into the fast lane at the last moment, the wind buffeting them as they blew past.

"Well," said Gideon, "like I said, we both worked in the Stockpile Stewardship program."

"What exactly is that?"

"It's classified. Nukes get old like everything else. The problem is, we can't test-fire a nuke these days because of the moratorium. So our job is to make for damn sure they're in working order."

"Nice. So what did Chalker do, in particular?"

"He used the lab's supercomputer to model nuclear explosions, identify how the radioactive decay of various nuke components would affect yield."

"Also classified work?"

"Extremely."

Fordyce rubbed his chin. "Where'd he grow up?"

"California, I think. He didn't talk about his past much."

"What about him as a person? Job, marriage?"

"He started at Los Alamos about six years ago. Had a doctorate from Chicago. Recently married, brought his young wife with him. She became a problem. She was sort of an ex-hippie, New Age type, from the South, hated Los Alamos."

"Meaning?"

"She didn't hide the fact that she was against nuclear weapons—she didn't approve of her husband's work. She was a drinker. I remember one office party where she got drunk and started shouting about the military-industrial complex and calling people murderers and throwing things. She totaled their car and racked up a couple of DUIs before they took away her license. I heard that Chalker did everything he could to keep the marriage going, but eventually she left, went to Taos with some other guy. Joined a New Age commune."

"What sort of commune?"

"Radical, anti-government, I heard. Self-sufficient, off the grid, grow their own tomatoes and pot. Left wing, but the weird kind. You know, the ones who carry guns and read Ayn Rand."

"Is there such a thing?"

"Out west—out *here*—there is. There were rumors she'd taken his credit cards, emptied their bank account, and was running through the money to support the commune. About two or three years ago Chalker lost his house, declared bankruptcy. That was a real problem with his work, because of the high-level security clearance. You're supposed to keep your financial affairs in order. He started getting warnings, and his clearance was downgraded. They moved him into another position with less responsibility."

"How'd he take it?"

"Badly. He was kind of a lost soul. Not a strong sense of self, a dependent personality type, going through the motions of life without knowing what he really wanted. He started to cling to me, in a way.

Wanted to be my friend. I tried to keep him at a distance, but it was difficult. We had lunch together a couple of times, and on occasion he joined me after work for a drink with co-workers."

Fordyce was now at one twenty. The car rocked back and forth, the sound of the engine and the rush of air almost drowning out the music. "Hobbies? Interests?"

"He talked a lot about wanting to be a writer. Nothing else that I can think of."

"Ever write anything?"

"Not that I know of."

"His religious views? I mean, prior to his conversion."

"I never knew of any."

"How did he convert?"

"He told me about it once. He rented a powerboat and went out on Abiquiu Lake, north of Los Alamos. I sort of got the impression he was depressed and considering suicide. Anyway, he somehow fell out or jumped out of the boat and found himself drifting away, his heavy clothes dragging him down. He went under a few times. But then, just as he was about to go under for the last time, he says he felt strong arms pulling him out. And he heard a voice in his head. *In the name of Allah, the Beneficent, the Merciful*, I think those were the words."

"I believe that's the first line of the Qur'an."

"He managed to climb back into the boat, which he said had suddenly drifted back toward him as if blown by an unseen wind. It was, in his view, a miracle. As he was driving home, he passed the Al-Dahab Mosque, which is a few miles from Abiquiu Lake. It was a Friday and services were being held. He stopped on a whim, got out, and went into the mosque, where he was welcomed very warmly by the Muslims. He experienced a powerful conversion right on the spot."

"That's quite a story."

Gideon nodded. "He gave away his stuff and started living a very ascetic life. He would pray five times a day. But he did it quietly, he was never in your face about it."

"Gave away what stuff?"

"Fancy clothes, books, liquor, stereo equipment, CDs and DVDs."

"Did he evince any other changes?"

"The conversion seemed to do him a world of good. He became a much more adjusted person. Better at work, more focused, no longer depressed. It was a relief to me—he stopped clinging. He really seemed to have found some sort of meaning in his life."

"Did he ever try to convert you, proselytize?"

"Never."

"Any problems with his security clearance after he became a Muslim?"

"No. Your religion isn't supposed to have anything to do with your security clearance. He continued on as before. He'd already lost his top clearance, anyway."

"Any signs of radicalism?"

"The guy was apolitical, as far as I could tell. No talk of oppression, no tirades against the wars in Iraq and Afghanistan. He shied away from controversy."

"That's typical. Don't draw attention to your views."

Gideon shrugged. "If you say so."

"What about the disappearance?"

"Very sudden. He just vanished. Nobody knew where he'd gone."

"Any changes just before that point?"

"None that I could see."

"He really fits the pattern," murmured Fordyce, shaking his head. "It's almost textbook."

They came over the rise of La Bajada and Santa Fe lay spread out before them, nestled at the base of the Sangre de Cristo Mountains.

"So that's it?" said Fordyce, squinting. "I thought it would be bigger."

"It's too big already," said Gideon. "So what's the next step?"

"A triple espresso. Piping hot."

Gideon shuddered. He was an inveterate coffee drinker himself, but Fordyce was something else. "You keep guzzling that stuff, you're going to need a catheter and urine bag."

"Nah, I'll just piss on your leg," Fordyce replied.

15

THAT EVENING FOUND them in the Collected Works bookstore on
Galisteo Street, their third coffee shop, following Fordyce's incessant
complaints about the quality of coffee in the city. It had been a long
afternoon, and Gideon had lost track of how many espressos Fordyce
had run through his renal system.

Fordyce drained yet another cup in a single swallow. "Okay, now
that's a coffee. But I gotta tell you, I'm sick of this shit," he said, smacking the cup down in irritation. "New Mexico's no better than New
York. All we do is stand in line with fifty investigators in front of us
picking their noses. We're twenty-four hours into the investigation and
we haven't done shit. Did you get a good look at that mosque?"

"It couldn't have been more overrun if bin Laden appeared there,
raised from the dead with his seventy-two virgins."

Their first stop had been a detour past Chalker's mosque, for
which they were still awaiting official access. The large golden dome
had been a quarter mile deep in official vehicles, countless lightbars
flashing. Their request to gain access, like all their requests, had disappeared into a bureaucratic black hole.

After the chaos of New York City, Gideon was disturbed to find
Santa Fe also in an uproar. While there wasn't quite the naked panic
here that was gripping New York City, there was a strong sense of impending doom lying over a city in turmoil.

New York, Gideon had to admit, had been on another scale. They had barely escaped La Guardia early that morning. The airport was packed with panicked people, most of whom had arrived even without tickets, trying to get out, anywhere would do. It was a scene of hideous chaos. Fordyce had only managed to get them seats on a plane by ramming his FBI credentials down everyone's throats and, on top of that, finagling sky marshal duty on the flight to Albuquerque.

Gideon sipped his coffee as Fordyce groused. The "liaising" in Albuquerque hadn't helped at all. In addition to being frozen out of the mosque, they were unable to access Chalker's house, his office up at Los Alamos, his colleagues, or any other person or place of interest. Investigative gridlock had taken hold even out here, with NEST and its cronies given first crack at everything, all the other government agencies jockeying into position in the queue behind. Even the regular FBI was making little headway against the bureaucratic headwind—only those agents detailed to NEST. On top of that, their little escapade back in Queens—getting into Chalker's apartment—had evidently come to Dart's attention. Fordyce had gotten a frosty message from the man's office.

As Fordyce got up to visit the men's room, the red-haired waitress came back around and offered Gideon a refill. "Does he want one?" she asked.

"Nah, better not, he's wired enough. You can lay one on me, though." He gave her his most winning smile and pushed his cup forward.

She refilled his cup with a smile of her own.

"More cream?"

"Only if you recommend cream."

"Well, I like cream in my coffee."

"Then I do, too. And sugar. Lots of it."

Her smile deepened. "How much do you want?"

"Don't stop until I say so."

Fordyce came back to the table. He looked from Gideon to the waitress and back again. And then, as he seated himself, he asked Gideon: "Those antibiotic shots doing anything for your chancres?"

The waitress hurried off. Gideon turned on him. "What the hell?"

"We're working. You can chat up waitresses on your own time."

Gideon sighed. "You're cramping my style."

"Style?" Fordyce snorted. "And another thing: You need to lose the black jeans and sneakers. You look like a damn over-the-hill punk rocker. It's unprofessional and it's part of our problem."

"You forget, we didn't bring luggage."

"Well, tomorrow I hope you'll dress properly. If you don't mind me saying."

"I do mind, in fact," Gideon said. "Better than looking like Mr. Quantico."

"What's wrong with Mr. Quantico?"

"You think looking like a hard-ass FBI agent is going to open doors, get people to relax, talk to you? I don't think so."

Fordyce shook his head and began tapping a pencil against his empty cup. After a few minutes, he said, "There's *got* to be a line of investigation nobody's thought of yet." His BlackBerry chimed—it had been chiming constantly—and he pulled it out, thumbed up the message, read it, swore, put it back. "Bastards are still 'reviewing the paperwork.'"

The gesture gave Gideon a thought. "What about Chalker's phone records?"

Fordyce shook his head. "We won't get within a thousand miles of them. No doubt they've been impounded and sealed."

"Yeah, but I've got an idea about that. Chalker was kind of scatterbrained, and he often misplaced his cell phone or forgot to charge it. He was always borrowing phones."

Now Fordyce looked up, faintly interested. "From who?"

"Various people. But mostly from this woman who worked in the cubicle next to his."

"Her name?"

"Melanie Kim."

Fordyce frowned. "Kim? I recall that name." He snapped opened his briefcase, took out a file, and flipped through it. "She's already on the witness list—which means we have to get official permission to talk to her."

"We don't need to talk to her. We just need to get her phone records."

Fordyce shook his head. "Talk about scraping the bottom of the barrel. So how are we going to tell her calls from his?"

Gideon frowned, thinking back. It was a good question. Fordyce went back to tapping his cup.

"About six months ago," Gideon said slowly, "Chalker dropped his iPhone. Busted it. For a week he kept borrowing her phone to make his calls."

Fordyce seemed to brighten. "You got a time frame on this?"

Gideon racked his brains. "Wintertime."

"That's a help."

Gideon cursed his poor memory. "Wait. I remember Melanie got all pissed off because she was trying to plan a New Year's Eve party and he kept borrowing her phone and not returning it for hours on end. So it was before New Year's."

"And it must have been before Christmas, then. You wouldn't have been at work between Christmas and New Year's."

Gideon nodded. "Right... And Christmas vacation began December twenty-second last year."

"So we're talking the week or so before that?"

"Exactly."

"I guess we'd better start the paperwork," said Fordyce wearily.

Gideon stared at him. "Screw the paperwork." He took out his own iPhone, began dialing.

"Waste of time," said Fordyce. "By law a telecom provider can't release cell phone records, even to the customer, except by mail to the customer's address of record. On top of that, we'd need a subpoena."

Gideon finished dialing. He punched through the menu selections and finally ended up with an operator.

"Hello, dear?" he asked, putting on an old lady's quavering voice. "This is Melanie Kim. My phone was stolen."

"Oh no," said Fordyce, plugging his ears. "I'm not hearing this. No way."

The operator asked for the last four digits of her Social Security number and her mother's maiden name. "Let's see..." warbled Gideon. "I can't seem to find it...I'll have to call you back with that information, dear." Gideon hung up.

"That was lame," said Fordyce, removing his fingers with a snort.

Gideon ignored him and called Melanie Kim herself, whose number he had on his own cell. She answered.

"Hey, it's Gideon."

"Oh my God, Gideon," said Kim, "you won't believe it, but the FBI have been here questioning me all day—"

"Tell me about it," Gideon said, gently interrupting her, keeping his voice at a whisper. "They've been giving me the third degree, too, and you know what? All the questions are about *you*."

"Me?" There was instant panic in her voice.

"They seem to think you and Chalker were...well, you know, an item."

"Chalker? That asshole? You've *got* to be kidding."

"Listen, Melanie, I got the distinct impression they're going to steamroll you. I felt like I had to warn you. They're out for blood."

"No way. I had nothing to do with him. I hated the guy!"

"They were even asking me questions about your mother."

"My *mother*? She died five years ago!"

"They hinted around that she was a communist while a student at Harvard."

"Harvard? My mother didn't come here from Korea until she was thirty!"

"Your mother was Korean?"

"Of course she was Korean!"

"Well, they kept pressing me and I finally told them I thought she was Irish, you know, mixed marriage and all...I don't know where I got that impression. Sorry."

"Irish? *Irish*? Gideon, you moron!"

"What was her maiden name? So I can straighten this out."

"Kwon! Jae-hwa Kwon! You'd *better* straighten it out!"

"I'll fix it, I promise. One other thing..."

"Oh please, no."

"They asked a lot of questions about your Social Security number. They said it wasn't a valid number, hinted that you might have committed identity fraud, you know, like to get a green card or something."

"Green card? I'm a damn citizen! I can't believe these idiots. What a horror show—"

He'd really gotten her going now, pushing all her hot buttons. Gideon felt a pang of guilt. Again, he gently interrupted her. "They were especially focused on the last four digits of your Social. Thought they were weird."

"Weird? What do you mean?"

"That they would just happen to be one two three four. Sounds, you know, made up."

"One two three four? It's seven six zero six!"

Gideon cupped the phone and whispered hoarsely, "Oh no, gotta go, they're calling my name again. I'll do what I can to defuse this. Listen, whatever you do, don't let on that I warned you."

"Wait—!"

He shut the phone, leaned back in the chair, exhaling. He could hardly believe what he had just done. And the next step was going to be even worse.

Fordyce stared at him, an unreadable expression on his face.

Gideon called the phone company back. In his little-old-lady voice, cracking with confusion and upset, he gave the operator Kim's personal information and reported that her phone was stolen; he wanted the phone canceled, the cell number, data, and address book all switched over to her son's iPhone, who was getting a BlackBerry and wanted to move his account. Then Gideon gave her his own phone number, Social, and mother's maiden name. When the operator said the transfer would take up to twenty-four hours, Gideon began to cry and in a weepy voice told a confused tale of a baby, a deformed puppy, cancer, and a house fire.

A few minutes later, he hung up. "Expedited. We'll have the info in thirty minutes, max."

"You're one rotten SOB, you know that?" And Fordyce smiled approvingly.

16

I<small>N THE WEEK</small> before December twenty-second, Kim's call register listed seventy-one outgoing calls during work hours. They quickly discarded the calls that came from numbers in Kim's address book and focused on the rest. There were groups of them, implying Chalker had borrowed the phone to make bunches of calls at the same time.

When they listed all of these calls, there was a total of thirty-four.

They divvied up the work, Gideon calling while Fordyce used his computer to access an FBI reverse-lookup database and gather personal information on the numbers. In half an hour they had identified each number and compiled a list.

They both stared at the list in silence. It seemed innocuous enough, consisting of work associates, a doctor's office, dry cleaners, a Radio Shack, several to the imam of the mosque, and a scattering of other miscellaneous calls. Fordyce got up and ordered another triple espresso, returning with the empty cup, having already consumed it on the way back to the table.

"He called the Bjornsen Institute of Writing three times," said Gideon.

Fordyce grunted.

"Maybe he was writing something. Like I said, he had an interest in writing."

"Call them."

Gideon called. He spoke for a moment, hung up, gave Fordyce a smile. "He took a writing workshop."

"Yeah?" Fordyce was interested.

"It was called *Writing Your Life*."

Another long silence. Fordyce gave a low whistle. "So he was, what, writing his memoirs?"

"Seems so. And that was four months ago. Six weeks later, he dropped out, disappeared, and joined the jihad."

As this sank in, Fordyce's face lit up. "A memoir...That could be pure gold. Where's this institute?"

"Santa Cruz, California."

"Let me call them—"

"Wait," said Gideon. "Better if we just go. In person. You call them ahead of time, that'll open up a can of worms. If the official investigation gets wind of it, we'll be shut out."

"I'm supposed to clear all our movements through the field office," said Fordyce, almost to himself. "If we fly commercial, I'd have to get permission..." He thought for a moment. "But we don't *have* to fly commercial. We can rent a plane at the airfield."

"Yeah, and who's going to fly it?"

"Me. I've got a VFR license." And he began dialing a number.

"Who are you calling?" Gideon asked.

"Local airfield."

Gideon watched Fordyce talk animatedly into the phone. He wasn't too keen on flying, especially in a small private plane, but he sure didn't want Fordyce to know that.

Fordyce put down the phone. "The FBO at the airfield can rent us a plane—but not for a few days."

"That's too long. Let's drive there instead."

"And waste all that investigative time just sitting in a car? Anyway, I've got an appointment in the FBI Albuquerque field office tomorrow at two o'clock."

"So what do we do in the meantime?"

This was followed by silence. Then Gideon answered his own question. "You remember I told you Chalker gave away most of his stuff?"

"Yeah."

"He offered me some of his book collection. Novels. Thrillers. I wasn't interested, and so he mentioned something about giving them to the library of one of the Indian schools around here. San Ildefonso, I think."

"Where's that?"

"A pueblo on the way to Los Alamos. They're a small Indian tribe, known for their dances and black pottery. Chalker was a fan of the dances, at least until he converted."

"Did he donate his computer? Papers?"

"No, he just gave away the stuff he considered decadent—books, DVDs, music."

There was a silence.

"So maybe we should go over to San Ildefonso," said Gideon. "Check out those books."

Fordyce shook his head. "They're from his pre-conversion days. They won't tell us anything."

"You never know. There might be papers stuck into them, notes in the margins. You said we had to do something—so here's something to do. Besides—" and Gideon leaned forward—"it's the one place we can guarantee there won't be a line in front of us."

Fordyce stared out the window. "You've got a point."

17

Dr. Myron Dart sat in the conference room of the Department of Energy's Emergency Response Center, eight stories below the streets of Manhattan. A single black folder rested on the polished wood of the conference table. The clock on the wall behind him read two minutes to midnight. He knew he was exhausted and running on fumes, but there could be no letup. It was times like these he was grateful for his marine training, where they pushed you to the limit, then beyond, and then even beyond that.

The door to the room opened and the tall, wraith-like form of Miles Cunningham, his personal assistant, entered. He nodded at Dart, his ascetic features betraying no emotion. Every day Dart offered thanks for his almost supernaturally competent, monk-like assistant, who seemed to have transcended the vagaries of human emotion. Behind Cunningham trooped in the rest of the NEST top hierarchy. They took their seats around the table in perfect silence.

Dart glanced over his shoulder, saw the minute hand click over. Midnight exactly. He tried to cover up his pleasure at the exactitude. He had trained his staff well.

Now he opened the black folder that lay before him. "Thank you for attending this emergency meeting on such short notice," he began. "I'm going to brief you on the latest developments."

He looked over the top sheet. "First, some very good news: the cryptanalysts at the FBI broke the encryption on Chalker's computer. We also have in hand the forensic analysis of what Chalker was carrying in his pockets, and we've analyzed the contents of his apartment." He glanced around at his deputies. "The salient points are as follows. The computer is still being analyzed but so far we've found little beyond files of jihadist rantings, streaming-video AVIs of the preaching of various radical clerics, and religious tracts relating to common jihadist goals such as the usual 'smiting of the infidel' stuff. His browser history showed numerous visits to radical websites. Unfortunately, from what we've found so far the material is quite generic. We didn't find specific email exchanges with individuals, no direct links to individual terrorists, al-Qaeda, or other radical groups. In short, we haven't yet found information about the specific identity of his co-conspirators, specific details of the plot, or on how the nuke was actually acquired."

His gray eyes moved around the table again. "Does anyone have any thoughts on what we might infer from this?"

There was a moment of silence. Then somebody spoke up. "The computer was a backup machine?"

"My thoughts exactly. Anything else?"

"Could it have been planted? As bait, perhaps?"

"Another possibility."

A short discussion ensued and when it had reached its fruitful end Dart skillfully brought the conversation back around to the next point.

"I've instructed the teams to keep looking for another computer, or computers. However—" and here his tone developed an edge— "Chalker's machine did include extensive photographs and videos of five Washington landmarks: the Lincoln Memorial, the Capitol, the Pentagon, the Smithsonian Castle, and the White House. There was nothing on any New York landmark."

There was a low murmuring around the table. "Washington?" someone said.

"Correct."

"Could this be a plant? A diversion?"

"At first we thought that might be the case, and then we analyzed the contents of Chalker's apartment and the contents of his pockets. As you'll recall, we recovered in his pocket a scrawled web address. This address proved to be quite revealing. The website it referenced was encrypted, and it had been shut down and the information removed from the server—located in Yemen—but we were able to recover a mirror image of it via the CIA's classified web archiving department. They put their best people on it and finally broke the encryption. There we did learn some details of the bomb design, plus the same list of five targets in Washington, along with three others that seem to have been discarded at some point in the past: the Air and Space Museum, the Dirksen Senate Office Building, and the Cannon House Office Building. Beyond that, the site was woefully short on specifics. Remember, however, that among the contents of his pockets was an admission stub to the National Air and Space Museum."

A pause as Dart carefully turned a piece of paper over.

"His apartment contained additional religious tracts, DVDs, and documents, as well as a copy of the Qur'an in English, which certain passages marked involving fire, war, and Armageddon."

Another turn of paper.

"There was a calendar on Chalker's refrigerator. It was full of appointments he seems to have made. They were all cryptic, just shorthand letters. The key point is this: the appointments abruptly end on the twenty-first of this month. After that, the calendar is blank."

He paused, his eyes slowly moving around the table, making sure everyone understood the significance. "Analysis indicates that Chalker was exposed at the Long Island City location where the bomb appears to have been assembled. However, the evidence is clear that the bomb was successfully completed. Although the lab had been emptied and burned, the remains of a map of Washington was found, again with those same five sites circled."

He closed the folder and leaned forward, his face growing dark. "The conclusion we've reached is this: the target is Washington, DC, not New York. And the probable date of the attack is the twenty-first of this month. We have very little time."

An attendee raised a hand. Dart acknowledged him with a flicker of his eyes.

"Why assemble a bomb destined for DC in New York?"

"An excellent question. Our belief is that New York is much better suited for this sort of clandestine activity—a huge, sprawling, anonymous, multi-ethnic city where people mind their own business. It also has a large, sympathetic population of radical Islamists. DC, on the other hand, is a more tightly controlled environment, with higher security overall and a very small Islamic population. We believe that's the reason they chose to make the bomb in New York and transport it to DC."

Another silence.

"Accordingly, we will *immediately* be shifting our base of operations to DC. I want you all to get ready to move—now. The formal orders are in prep."

Dart stood up and began to pace behind his chair. "The computer contained no smoking guns, and the other evidence we have isn't specific enough. Despite their missteps, these terrorists have been careful. And yet we've obtained the two most vital pieces of information: where, and possibly when. By tomorrow morning, I expect each and every one of you to be in Washington, in the new operations center. Your folders contain the details and security protocols. We will of course be drawing in all available assets from the FBI, local law enforcement, and the armed forces."

He stopped pacing. "As we speak, the president and the vice president are moving to the Presidential Emergency Operations Center. In the coming twenty-four hours, Congress and the cabinet, as well as other critical government officials, will be shifted to the Congressional Bunker and certain undisclosed locations. The National Guard is being mobilized to handle the orderly evacuation of civilians."

Once again, his gaze riveted the group. "It is our firm hope that—knowing what we now know—we'll be able to thwart this attack. However, we must be extremely cautious in the way we handle the general public. You have all seen the panic that has gripped New York, the disorderly exodus, the gyrations in the financial markets. We have to expect that an even worse panic will grip Washington, especially when we start evacuating. The key to managing the panic is to manage the press. People need information. It'll be a disaster if they suspect us of holding back. We obviously can't hide the probable location of the attack. *But it is of the utmost importance that the possible date of the attack not become known.* That information is both uncertain and highly inflammatory. Any leak of that date will be tracked down and treated as nothing short of treason. Are we understood?"

Affirmations from around the table.

"Are there any questions?"

"Do we have any information on where the terrorists got the nuclear material?" someone asked.

"So far, we haven't identified any missing nuclear material from our own arsenal, although our records in some instances are incomplete or missing. We're looking into all the possibilities—including Pakistan, Russia, and North Korea."

When there were no more questions, Dart ended the meeting. "I expect you to hit the ground running in DC tomorrow morning. It's going to be a long night for all of us. We'll have another briefing at noon in the Twelfth Street Command Center. And now, good evening."

The conference room emptied as quickly as it had filled. As Dart picked up the black folder and rapped it smartly against the table, Cunningham, his assistant, approached. "Any orders, sir?"

"I want you to get in touch with that FBI agent, Fordyce. See if he and Crew have made any progress in Santa Fe. This whole investigation is a lumbering monster, but those two are just nimble enough to come up with something fresh. I want to keep an eye on them."

18

San Ildefonso Pueblo lay alongside the Rio Grande in a long grove of cottonwood trees. It was situated at the base of the Jemez Mountains, at the point where the road to Los Alamos began the climb into the foothills. Gideon had been to many Indian dances at San Ildefonso, particularly the famous Buffalo Deer Dance—it was a popular pastime among people who worked at the lab. But today the pueblo was almost deserted as they drove through it, past the dirt plaza and old adobe buildings.

As they approached, an overloaded pickup truck lumbered past, coating their car with dust.

Even the Indians are leaving, he thought.

In the plaza, they saw a group of Indian men, wrapped in Mexican blankets, sitting on wooden stools along one side, in the shade of an adobe wall. At least they didn't look panicked, drinking their morning coffee before a row of wooden drums.

"Wait," said Fordyce. "I want to talk to them." He slowed the car and stopped under an old cottonwood tree.

"What for?"

"Ask directions, maybe."

"But I know where the school is—"

Fordyce threw the car into park and was already getting out. Gideon followed, irritated.

"Hi, there," Fordyce greeted them.

The men watched them approach with stolid faces. It was evident to Gideon they were involved in some sort of drum practice, perhaps getting ready for a dance, and did not welcome the interruption.

"Any dances today?" Fordyce asked.

A silence, and then one said: "Dances have been canceled."

"Don't forget to put that in your notebook," Gideon muttered.

Fordyce removed his FBI shield. "Stone Fordyce. FBI. Sorry to interrupt you."

This was met by dead silence. Gideon wondered what the hell Fordyce was up to.

He put away the badge and gave them a disarmingly friendly smile. "Maybe you read about what's going on in New York City?"

"Who hasn't?" came the laconic reply.

"We're investigators on the case."

This got a reaction. "No shit," one of the men said. "What's going on? You got a lead on the terrorists?"

Fordyce held up his hands. "Sorry, guys, I can't tell you anything. But I was hoping you might help me with a few questions."

"You bet," said one man, evidently the leader. He was short and solid, with a square, serious face, a bandanna tied tightly around his head. They had all risen.

"This fellow who died of radiation exposure in New York, Reed Chalker, gave his book collection to San Ildefonso. Did you know that?"

The look of astonishment on their faces indicated they did not.

"I understand he was a fan of the dances."

"We get a lot of people coming down from Los Alamos to see the dances," said the leader. "A lot of our people work up there, too."

"Is that right? Your people work up there?"

"Los Alamos is the pueblo's biggest employer."

"Interesting. Anybody know Chalker?"

Shrugs all around. "It's possible. We could ask around."

Fordyce produced his cards and handed them out to everyone. "That's a great idea. Ask around. You learn of anyone here who knew

Chalker, even slightly, get in touch. Okay? There must have been a reason why he gave his book collection to the school, and I'd sure like to know that reason. You all could really help the investigation. I mean it. Now we're heading over to the school—is it this way?"

"Just go straight, take a left, you'll see it. There may not be anyone around. School's canceled. A lot of our people are leaving."

"I understand." Fordyce shook hands warmly all around and left the men in a group, talking animatedly.

"That was good," said Gideon, impressed despite himself.

Fordyce grinned. "It's like fishing."

"Don't tell me you're a fisherman, too."

"Love it—when I get the chance."

"Fly?"

"Bait."

Gideon scoffed. "That's not fishing. And here for a minute I thought we had something else in common."

He caught a glimpse of the Rio Grande through the trees, the sunlight glinting off the river as it ran over a bed of stones, and he had a momentary flashback to a trout stream far away and many years ago, fishing with his father during the good time, his father explaining that success in fishing, as in life, depended mostly on how long you kept your fly on the water. "Luck," he used to say, "is where preparation meets opportunity. The fly is the opportunity, the preparation is the cast. And the fish? That's the luck."

He quickly pushed that particular memory aside, as he habitually did whenever thoughts of his father arose. It was disturbing to find even here, at this remote Indian pueblo, that people were leaving. Then again, they were in the very shadow of Los Alamos.

The school lay beside the ancient cottonwood groves along the river, flanked by dusty baseball diamonds and tennis courts. It was a weekday morning but the school, as the men had indicated, was mostly empty. An eerie silence hung over the campus.

They checked in with the office and, after filling out a visitors' book, were escorted to the small school library, a room looking out over the soccer field.

The school librarian was still there, arranging books, a stout lady with long black braids and thick glasses. She got interested when Fordyce showed his ID and they mentioned Chalker's book collection. Again, Gideon was surprised at how eager she was to help.

"Oh yes." She shuddered. "I knew him. I did. And I can't *believe* he became a terrorist. I just can't believe it. Do they really have a bomb?" Her eyes widened.

"I'm not allowed to discuss the details," said Fordyce kindly. "I'm sorry."

"And to think he gave us his book collection. I have to tell you, everyone here is very worried. Did you know they let school out early for the summer? That's why we're so deserted around here. I'm leaving myself, tomorrow."

"Do you remember Chalker?" Fordyce interrupted patiently.

"Oh yes. It was about two years ago." She was almost out of breath at the recollection. "He called and asked if we needed books, and I said we'd love to have them. He brought them in that afternoon. There were two, maybe three hundred. He was actually a nice fellow, very nice! I just can't *believe* it . . ."

"Did he say why he was giving them away?" Fordyce asked.

"I don't recollect. I'm sorry."

"But why to the pueblo? Why not to the Los Alamos public library or some other place? Did he have a friend here?"

"He really didn't say."

"Where are the books now?"

She gestured. "They're all mixed up. We shelved them with the others."

Gideon looked about. There were several thousand books in the library. This was going to be more of a chore than he'd anticipated.

"Do you remember any titles in particular?" Fordyce asked, jotting notes.

She shrugged. "They were all hardbacks, mostly mystery novels and thrillers. Quite a few signed first editions—he'd been a collector, apparently. But that didn't matter to us—to us, a book is meant to be read. We just shelved them where they belonged."

While Fordyce talked, Gideon drifted away and began to peruse the fiction section, pulling down books at random and flipping through them. He didn't want to admit it to Fordyce, but he feared his idea might turn out to be a waste of time. Unless by sheer chance he came across one of Chalker's books with a significant piece of paper stuck into it, or some telling note in the margins. But that seemed unlikely—and book collectors did not normally annotate their books, especially autographed editions.

He drifted along the aisle of fiction, starting with Z and going on down the shelves in reverse alphabetical order, plucking out a book here and there, Vincent Zandri, Stuart Woods, James Rollins...He riffled through books at random, looking for notes or papers, or—he smiled to himself—rough sketches of atomic weapons perhaps, but finding nothing. In the background, he could hear Fordyce questioning the librarian with a gentle but persistent thoroughness. Gideon couldn't help but be struck by the man's competence. Fordyce was a strange combination of methodical, by-the-book determination and impatience with rules and red tape.

Anne Rice, Tom Piccirilli...He pawed through book after book with a rising irritation.

And then he paused. Here was a signed book, a copy of a David Morrell novel, *The Shimmer*, with the author's signature under a scribbled *Best wishes*.

Nothing telling there. He flipped through the pages but there was nothing else. He shoved it back. A little farther on, he encountered another signed book, this one by Tess Gerritsen, titled *The Bone Garden*. Another generic dedication: *To Reed, Best Regards*. And another, *Killing Floor*, signed by Lee Child, *To Reed, My Best*. Chalker had good taste, at least.

Fordyce droned on in the background, extracting every last drop of information from the librarian.

Gideon worked his way down to the B's. *The Abbey in the Oakwood* by Simon Blaine was personalized: *To Reed, with affectionate regards*. And it was signed *Simon*.

He paused before putting it back on the shelf. Did Simon Blaine sign all his books just *Simon*? There was another Blaine novel next to it, *The Sea of Ice. To Reed, with my best, Simon B.*

Fordyce appeared at his side. "Dead end," he murmured.

"Maybe not." Gideon showed the two books to Fordyce.

Fordyce took them, flipped through them. "I don't get it."

"*With affectionate regards*? And signed by first name only? Sounds like Blaine knew him."

"I doubt it."

Gideon thought for a moment, then turned to the librarian. "I'd like to ask you a question."

"Yes?" She hurried over, glad to have a chance to talk again.

"You seem to have a lot of books by Simon Blaine."

"We have all of his books. And come to think of it, most of them came from Mr. Chalker."

"Ah," said Fordyce. "You didn't tell me that."

She gave an embarrassed smile. "I just now thought of it."

"Did Chalker know Blaine?"

"I don't know," she said. "Perhaps. After all, Blaine lives in Santa Fe."

Bingo, thought Gideon. He cast a triumphant eye on Fordyce. "There you have it. They *did* know each other."

Fordyce frowned. "A man like Blaine, a bestselling author— National Book Award winner, it says here—isn't likely to have had much of a friendship with a geek from Los Alamos."

"I resemble that remark," said Gideon, in his best Groucho Marx imitation.

Fordyce rolled his eyes. "Did you see the date on that book? It was published two years before Chalker converted. And the fact that he gave away Blaine's books along with the others does not exactly indicate a deep friendship. Frankly, I don't see a lead here." He paused. "In fact, I'm starting to wonder whether or not this whole trip west has done nothing but cost us crucial time."

Gideon pretended not to hear this last remark. "It's worth visiting Blaine. Just in case."

Fordyce shook his head. "Waste of time."

"You never know."

Fordyce laid a hand on his shoulder. "That's true—in this business sometimes the craziest idea pans out. I don't mean to dismiss it out of hand. But you'll have to do this one alone—you're forgetting I've got a meeting in Albuquerque later today."

"Oh yeah. Do I need to be there?"

"Better if you're not. I plan to kick ass. I want access to the house, to the mosque, to the lab, to his colleagues—I want to make sure we're a real part of this investigation. *That's* how we're going to make a difference."

Gideon grinned. "You go, girl."

19

Simon Blaine lived in a large house about half a mile from the plaza, along the Old Santa Fe Trail. With the car gone with Fordyce to Albuquerque, Gideon walked from the plaza to the house. The weather was glorious, a warm, high-altitude summer's day, not too hot, the sky a royal blue, just a few thunderheads forming over the distant Sandia Mountains. He wondered if Blaine would still be around. The damn town was now half empty.

Eight days to N-Day. The clock was ticking. Still, he was glad to be in Santa Fe instead of New York, which was a total mess. Most of the Financial District, Wall Street, the World Trade Center site, and the area of Midtown around the Empire State Building had been abandoned—followed inevitably by looting, fires, and National Guard deployments. In the past day a political furor had erupted, with hysterical political attacks on the president. Certain divisive media figures and radio personalities had leapt into the fray, exploiting the situation to their own gain, whipping up public sentiment. America was not handling the crisis well at all.

He shook off these thoughts as he arrived at Blaine's address. The house was hidden behind an eight-foot adobe wall that ran alongside the road. The only things visible beyond the wall were the tops of aspen trees growing in profusion, rustling in a steady wind. The gate itself was solid wrought iron and weathered barnwood, and Gideon was unable to find even a crack to peer through. He eyed the intercom set into the adobe next to the gate, pressed the buzzer, and waited.

Nothing.

He pressed again. Nobody home? Only one way to tell.

He strolled along the wall until he came to the corner of the property. He was used to scaling walls and had little trouble leaping up, grasping the top, and pulling himself over the rough adobe. In a moment he had dropped down the other side, landing in a grove of aspen trees hidden from the house. Nearby, an artificial waterfall splashed over a pile of stones into a small pond. Beyond it, across a billiard-green lawn, lay a low, sprawling adobe house with many portals and verandas and at least a dozen chimneys.

Through the windows he saw a figure moving. Someone *was* home. He was irritated that they hadn't responded to his ring. Fingering the ID he'd finally been issued—and which, it had seemed, Fordyce gave him with a certain reluctance—he followed the wall back to the gate, pressed the button to open it, so it would appear he'd entered this way. As it swung open, he walked out into the driveway and strode up to the front door of the house. He rang the bell.

A long wait. He rang again and—finally—heard hollow footsteps in the entrance hall. The door swung open to reveal a skinny young woman in her mid-twenties, with a long swaying cascade of hair, wearing jeans, a tight white shirt, cowboy boots, and a fierce scowl. She had that quite unusual combination of dark brown eyes and golden hair.

"Who the hell are you?" she asked, hands on her hips, tossing her hair out of her face, "and how'd you get in?"

Gideon had already been considering what the best approach might be, and her defiant demeanor settled the question. With an easy smile, he reached with insolent slowness into his pocket, brought out the ID, and did a Fordyce, extending his hand deep into her personal space. "Gideon Crew, FBI liaison."

"Get that thing out of my face."

Continuing to smile, Gideon said, "You probably should take a look at it. Last chance you'll get."

With a cold, answering smile, she reached out but, instead of taking the ID, swatted his hand out of her face.

For a moment, Gideon stood surprised. Her face was defiant, her eyes flashing, the pulse of her heart in her slender neck—this was a tiger. As he pulled out his cell phone, he felt almost sorry about having to do this to such a woman. He dialed the police and spoke to a dispatcher he and Fordyce had previously chatted up—or rather "liaised with," to use Fordyce's jargon. "This is Gideon Crew. I need backup at Nine Ninety Old Santa Fe Trail. I'm on scene, and I've been assaulted by a resident on the premises."

"I didn't assault you, jerkoff!"

What a mouth. "Your action, knocking my hand away, meets the definition of assault." He gave the woman a grin. "The shit just hit the fan. And I don't even know your name yet."

She glared back with her fierce brown eyes and—after a long stare-down—finally wavered, her face loosening. She wasn't so tough after all. "You're really FBI?" Her glance raked his clothes—black jeans, lavender shirt, Keds. "You sure as hell don't look it."

"FBI *liaison*. Investigating the terrorist incident in New York. I'm here on a friendly little call to ask Mr. Simon Blaine some questions."

"He's not here."

"Then I'll wait."

Gideon could hear faint sirens. Damn, the police were quick around here. He saw her eyes dart toward the sound.

"You should've called," she said. "You had no right to trespass!"

"My right to enter the premises extends to the door. You've got about five seconds to decide whether you want to escalate this into something really ugly or cooperate one hundred percent. Like I said, this was a friendly visit and it doesn't have to turn into a felony charge."

"A felony charge?" The sirens got louder as the cars approached the gate. He could tell from the frightened look that she was crumbling fast. "All right. All right, I'll cooperate. But this is blackmail, pure and simple. I won't forget it."

The first squad car came through the open gate, followed by others. Gideon met the lead car in front of the house. He showed ID, leaned in. "Officers? Everything's under control—total cooperation now from the occupants of the house. Your quick response did the trick. Thank you so much."

The police were reluctant to leave—they were excited to be involved, even peripherally, in the investigation, and it wasn't often that they were called to a famous writer's house—but Gideon coolly persuaded them that it was a misunderstanding. After the cops left, he turned and smiled at the woman, gestured toward the door. "Shall we?"

She stepped into the house, then turned. "This is a no-shoe house. Take 'em off."

Gideon pulled off the Keds. Quite pointedly she, herself, did not remove her cowboy boots, on which Gideon could spy what looked like dried horseshit. She walked across the entrance hall's Persian rug into the living room. It was a spectacular space, with white leather sofas, a vast fireplace, and what Gideon recognized as prehistoric Mimbres pots in various display cases.

She sat down, still saying nothing.

Gideon took out a notebook and settled into a chair opposite her. He couldn't help but notice how pretty she was—downright beautiful, in fact. He was starting to feel bad about bullying her. Nevertheless, he tried to maintain a stern, unforgiving demeanor. "Your name, please?"

"Alida Blaine." She answered in a flat monotone. "Should I be calling the family lawyer?"

"You promised to cooperate," he said sternly. There was a long silence and then he softened. "Look, Alida, I just want to ask some simple questions."

She smirked. "Are Keds the new FBI uniform?"

"It's a temporary assignment."

"Temporary? So what do you do normally? Play in a rock band?"

Maybe Fordyce had been right about his dress. "I'm a physicist."

Her eyebrows shot up. Gideon didn't like how she kept turning the conversation on him as a subject, and he quickly followed with a question. "Can you tell me what your relationship is to Simon Blaine?"

"Daughter."

"Age?"

"Twenty-seven."

"Where's your father now?"

"At the movie set."

"Movie set?"

"They're making a film of one of his books, shooting it at the Circle Y Movie Ranch south of town."

"When will he be home?"

She looked at her watch. "Any time now. So what's this about?"

Gideon made an effort to relax, smile. Guilt was starting to creep over him. He just wasn't cut out to be a cop. "We're trying to find out more about Reed Chalker, the man involved in the terrorist plot."

"Oh, so *that's* it. Wow. But what in the world does that have to do with us?" He sensed her anger starting to morph into curiosity. She crossed her arms, slid open a drawer in a side table, removed a pack of cigarettes. She lit one, exhaled.

Gideon thought of bumming, decided that would not be a cool move. She really was beautiful, and he was having trouble maintaining the cool demeanor. He forced himself back to the business at hand. "We think your father knew Reed Chalker."

"I doubt it. I keep my father's schedule. I'd never heard that man's name until I read it in the newspaper."

"Chalker had a complete collection of your father's books. All signed."

"So?"

"It was the way they were signed. *To Reed, with affectionate regards. Simon.* The wording suggested they might know each other."

At this, Alida leaned back and laughed harshly, exhaling smoke. "Oh man, are you guys barking up the wrong tree! He signs all his books like that. Thousands of them. Tens of thousands."

"With his first name?"

"It saves time. It's also why he only uses the first names of the people he's signing for. When you've got five hundred people in line, each with several books in hand, you can't be signing your full name. This guy Chalker, he worked up at Los Alamos, right? That's what the papers are saying."

"That's right."

"So it wouldn't have been a big deal for him to get to my father's signings."

Gideon felt a creeping sense of failure. Fordyce had been right: this was a dead end, and he was making a royal fool of himself.

"Do you have evidence of that?" he asked as gamely as he could.

"Go ask down at the bookstore. He does a local signing there every year, they'll confirm it. He signs all his books *Simon* or *Simon B.* and writes either *With Affection* or *Warmest Regards*. To every Tom, Dick, and Harry in line. It has nothing to do with friendship."

"I see."

"Is this the kind of half-assed investigation you people are running?" she said, all hostility gone now, leaving amusement and scorn in their place. "And you're up against terrorists with a nuke? That scares the shit out of me."

"We have to follow up every lead," said Gideon. He took out Chalker's picture. "If you could just look at this and see if you recognize it?"

She looked at it, squinted, then looked more closely. Her whole face changed. "What do you know. I do recognize him. He used to come to all my father's book signings in town. Kind of a groupie, buttonholed him, tried to engage him in conversation with a hundred people in line behind him. My father humored him because that's his job, really, and he would never be rude to a reader." She handed the picture back. "But I can tell you my father was *not* this man's friend."

"Is there anything else you can tell me about him?"

She shook her head. "No."

"What did they talk about?"

"I really don't recall. Probably the usual stuff. Why don't you ask my father?"

As if on cue, the door slammed and a man walked into the room. For a famous author, Simon Blaine was disarmingly small, with a head of white curls and a smiling, pixie-like face, as smooth and unlined as a boy's, with a button nose, ruddy cheeks, and friendly, dancing eyes. A large smile broke out when he saw his daughter. He went over, gave her a hug as she rose—she was several inches taller than him—and then turned to Gideon as he rose in turn, extending his hand. "Simon Blaine," he said, as if Gideon wouldn't know who he was. He wore an ill-fitting suit a size too large for his slender frame, and it flapped as he shook Gideon's hand with enthusiasm. "Who is your new friend, MD?" His voice, incongruously, was deep and compelling—although it held traces of a Liverpudlian accent, making the man sound ever so faintly like a baritone Ringo Starr.

"I'm Gideon Crew." He glanced from father to daughter and back again. "MD? She's a doctor?"

"No, no, that's my nickname for her. Miracle Daughter." And Blaine looked at Alida with evident affection.

"Crew's not a friend of mine," said Alida hastily, stubbing out the cigarette. "He's an investigator for the FBI. Looking into the nuclear terrorist business in New York."

Blaine's eyes widened in surprise. They were a deep hazel-brown, flecked with bits of gold: a most unusual color. "Well, well, now. How interesting!" He took Gideon's ID, examined it, returned it. "How can I be of help?"

"I have a few questions, if you don't mind."

"Not at all. Please, sit down."

They all sat down. Alida spoke first. "Daddy, the nuclear terrorist who died in New York, Reed Chalker, collected your books. He came to all your book signings. You remember him?" She shook another cigarette out of the pack, tapped it on the table, lit up.

Blaine frowned. "Can't say I do."

Gideon handed him the picture and Blaine examined it. He looked almost like a leprechaun, his lower lip protruding in concentration, his white curls sticking out in tufts from either side of his head.

"You remember, he was the guy who used to bring a whole bagful of books, came to every signing, always at the front of the line."

The lower lip suddenly retracted and the bushy eyebrows went up. "Yes, yes, I do! Good Lord, that was Reed Chalker, the terrorist from

Los Alamos?" He handed the photo back. "To think he was a reader of mine!" He did not seem displeased.

"What did you talk about with Chalker?" Gideon asked.

"It's hard to say. I do a book signing every year at Collected Works in Santa Fe, and we often get four, five hundred people. They go by in a sort of blur, really. Mostly they talk about how much they love the books, who their favorite characters are—and sometimes they want me to read a manuscript or they ask questions about how to break into writing."

"And they often talk about what a shame it was that Daddy didn't win that Nobel," said Alida forcefully. "Which I happen to agree with."

"Oh, bosh," said Blaine, making a dismissive gesture. "National Book Award, Man Booker—I've gotten more awards than I deserve."

"Did he ever ask you to read anything of his? He was an aspiring writer."

"I've got a question for you," said Alida, staring at Gideon. "You're a physicist working for the FBI?"

"Yes, but that's irrelevant—"

"Do you also work at Los Alamos?"

Gideon was floored at her insight. Not that it mattered; it was no secret. "One of the reasons I was asked to join the investigation," he said in measured tones, "is that I worked in the same department with him at Los Alamos."

"I knew it." She sat back, crossing her arms and smiling triumphantly.

Gideon turned back to Blaine, once again trying to get the conversation off himself. "Do you recall if he ever showed you anything he'd written?"

Blaine thought for a moment, then shook his head. "No, he didn't. And anyway, I have a firm policy against reading other people's work. Really, all I remember of him is an eager, fawning sort of young man. But I haven't seen him in some time. I don't believe he came to any of my recent signings—did he, MD?"

"I don't think so."

"Did he ever mention his conversion to Islam?" Gideon asked.

Blaine looked surprised. "Never. And I *would* have remembered something like that. No, he must have talked about the usual things. The only thing I really remember about him was that he was persistent and, as I recall, he always held up the line."

"Daddy is too kind," Alida said. "He'll let people talk to him for hours." With the arrival of her father, her foul mood seemed to have melted away.

Blaine laughed. "That's why I bring Alida. She's the heavy, she keeps the line moving, she gets the spellings of everyone's names for me. I spell as badly as Shakespeare. Honestly, I don't know what I'd do without her."

"Did you ever see Chalker outside a signing?"

"Never. And he's certainly not the kind of person I'd have to the house." Gideon felt a strong wave of British snobbery wash over him with this last statement, revealing still another side to Mr. Simon Blaine. And yet he couldn't blame the man for the sentiment—he himself had assiduously avoided having Chalker to his apartment. He was one of those clinging people you didn't want to let into your life.

"He never talked about writing with you? I understand he might have been writing a memoir. If we could get our hands on that, it would be important for the investigation."

"A memoir?" Blaine asked, surprised. "How do you know?"

"He attended a writers' workshop in Santa Cruz called *Writing Your Life*."

"*Writing Your Life*," repeated Blaine, shaking his head. "No, he never mentioned any memoir."

Gideon sat back, wondering what else to ask. He could think of nothing. He took out his cards, gave one to Blaine and then, after a faint hesitation, another to Alida. "If you think of anything else, please give me a call. My partner Special Agent Fordyce and I will be flying to Santa Cruz the day after tomorrow, but you can always reach me on my cell."

Blaine took the card and slipped it into his shirt pocket without glancing at it. "I'll see you out."

At the door, Gideon thought of one final question. "What was it about your books that Chalker liked so much? Any particular characters, perhaps, or plots?"

Blaine screwed up his face. "I wish I could remember...Except that, it seems to me, he once said he thought the most vivid character I'd ever created was that of the abbot in *Wanderer Above the Sea of Fog*. Which puzzled me, because I consider the abbot to be the most evil character I've ever created." He paused. "Maybe to a man like that, the two were synonymous."

20

FORDYCE ENTERED THE hotel bar, strode across the carpet, and took a seat next to Gideon. "What's your toxin?" he asked.

"Margarita. Patrón Silver, Cointreau, salt," said Gideon.

"I'll have the same," Fordyce told the bartender. He turned back to Gideon with an expansive grin. "I said I was going to kick ass—and I did."

"Tell me about it."

Fordyce pulled a file out of his briefcase and slapped it on the table. "It's all right here. We've not only got clearance to interview the imam of the mosque—Chalker's mentor—but also a warrant allowing us to enter the Paiute Creek Ranch with a subpoena for Connie Rust, Chalker's ex-wife, compelling her cooperation."

"How'd you do it?"

"I called Dart's office directly, spoke to his assistant, a guy named Cunningham. He said he'd clear the brush for us and he did. And get this: Chalker's wife hasn't been interviewed yet. She's a virgin."

"Why not?"

"Typical bureaucratic snafu. The original Title Eighteen Notice of Intent was defective, they had to redo it, get it re-signed by a pissed-off judge."

"How'd you get them to agree?"

"I called in a chit. A big one. And to tell you the truth, nobody thinks the wife is worth the trouble. They divorced long before his conversion, they haven't been on speaking terms, and apparently she's a sad case." He put away his papers. "We'll hit the ranch at dawn. Then we're scheduled for tea with the imam at two o'clock."

"Tea with the imam. Sounds like a BBC comedy series."

Fordyce's drink arrived and he punched it down with scarcely less gusto than a triple espresso. "So. What do you know about this Paiute Creek Ranch?"

"Not all that much," said Gideon. "It has a dicey reputation. Some say it's a cult sort of like the Branch Davidian compound, armed patrols and locked gates. A guru named Willis Lockhart runs the show."

"They've got a clean record," said Fordyce. "I checked. No allegations of child abuse, no bigamy, no weapons violations, taxes paid up."

"That's encouraging," said Gideon. "So what's your plan?"

"Go in easy, don't spook them, show the warrant nice and polite, pick up the wife, leave. We have to bring her for interrogation to the Santa Fe command center, but we'll have a chance to hear what she has to say on the way there."

"And if the ranch people don't cooperate?"

"Call for backup."

Gideon frowned. "That ranch is deep in the mountains. Backup would take an hour or more."

"In that case, we leave nice, come back mean. With a SWAT team in tow."

"Hello, Waco."

Fordyce sat back in irritation. "I've been at this for years, believe me, I know how to do this."

"Yeah, but I have another idea..."

Fordyce held up his hands in a mock-dramatic gesture. "Please. I've had enough of your 'ideas.'"

"The problem is getting in there. Warrant or no warrant, they probably aren't going to let us in. And even if they do, how are we going to find the wife? You think they'll just fetch her for us? That ranch covers thousands of acres, and we'll have to have their cooperation—"

Fordyce swiped one hand across his neatly clipped head. "All right, all *right*. So what's your bright idea?"

"We go in undercover. As...well..." Gideon thought for a moment. What kind of person would they let into the ranch?

Fordyce snorted. "Jehovah's Witnesses?"

Gideon took a sip of his margarita. "No. We'll go in with a business proposition."

"Oh yeah?"

"New Mexico just passed a medical marijuana law." He went on to explain his nascent idea to Fordyce. The FBI agent was silent a long time, staring into his ice cubes, and then raised his head.

"You know, it's not a bad plan."

Gideon smirked. "I'm going to enjoy watching you muss up your perfect hair and finally lose that junior executive FBI outfit."

"I'll let you do the talking. You already look like a stoner."

21

THEY HIT THE Salvation Army store early the next morning, the moment it opened. Gideon flipped through the racks, scooping up outfits and handing them to Fordyce, who carried them with ill-concealed grace. Then they swung by a theatrical supply company before returning to Fordyce's hotel room with their haul. Gideon spread the clothes out on the bed while Fordyce watched with a frown.

"Is this really necessary?" he asked.

"Stand over there." Gideon spread out a shirt, laid the pants underneath, frowned, switched the shirt for another, then another, then socks, squinting at each combination.

"Jesus," Fordyce complained, "we're not going on Broadway here."

"The difference is that if our little play is a flop, you'll get a bullet instead of a rotten tomato. Trouble is, you look like you were born a Fed."

He mixed and matched the outfits again, adding shoes and socks, a baseball cap and a wig, finally assembling something to his liking. "Try these on," he said.

"Son of a bitch." Fordyce shed his suit and donned the outfit. He hesitated with the hair. It had been a woman's wig, with real hair, that Gideon had given a bad haircut to.

"Go ahead," said Gideon. "Don't be shy."

Fordyce put on the wig, adjusted it.

"Now the cap. Put it on backward."

The cap went on. But that didn't look right: Fordyce was too old. "Turn it right way around."

Finally Fordyce stood in front of him, in full costume. Gideon circled him appraisingly. "Too bad you shaved this morning."

"We've got to go."

"Not yet. I need to see you walk around."

As Fordyce took a turn around the hotel room, Gideon groaned. "You've got to put your heart in it, for God's sake."

"I don't know what more I can do. I already look like a jerk."

"It's not just about the look. It's about the mental attitude. You've got to act the part. No, not just act it—*be* it."

"So who am I supposed to be?"

"A cocky, wiseass, arrogant, cunning, self-satisfied, don't-give-a-shit, morally bankrupt prick. Think about that while you walk around the room."

"So how does a morally bankrupt prick walk?"

"I don't know, you've got to *feel* it. Put in some attitude. Throw in a little pimp roll. Give us a curl of the lip. Tilt your chin."

Fordyce, with an irritated sigh, did a second turn.

"Aw, shit," said Gideon. "Can you lose the poker up the ass?"

Fordyce turned to him. "We're wasting time. If we don't get there soon, we won't have time for the imam."

With another muttered curse, Gideon followed Fordyce down toward the waiting Suburban. He wondered just how good a radar these people would have. To him, Fordyce still walked and talked just like a Fed.

Maybe they wouldn't notice. But if they did, he'd better have a plan B.

22

THE PAIUTE CREEK Ranch lay north of Santa Fe in an isolated part of the Jemez Mountain range. Gideon and Fordyce bumped and ground their way up a washed-out mining road and into a series of ponderosa-covered hills and valleys just below a peak. The road ended at a brand-new chain-link fence with a set of locked gates.

As they got out of the Suburban, Gideon glanced over at Fordyce.

"You go first, I want to watch you walk again. Remember what I said."

"Stop staring at my ass." Fordyce started toward the gate, and it just about drove Gideon crazy to see how stubbornly the whiff of law enforcement clung to the agent. But he had to admit, the clothes were good—it was the way he carried himself that was a problem. If he kept his mouth shut, then maybe, just maybe, no one would notice.

"Remember," Gideon muttered, "I'm doing the talking."

"You mean, the bullshitting. Which you're an expert at."

Gideon peered through the fence. A hundred yards down the dirt track stood a small log cabin, and through the ponderosa pines he could glimpse more cabins, a barn, and the gables of a large ranch house. In the distance, some green fields were laid up alongside Paiute Creek.

Gideon shook the fence. "Yo!"

Nothing. Had all of them left, too?

"Hey! Anybody home?"

A man stepped out of the nearby cabin and came walking over. He had a long tangle of black hair and a long, squared-off beard in the mountain man style. As he approached, he casually unsheathed a machete stuck into his belt.

Gideon could feel Fordyce tensing up next to him.

"Relax," he murmured. "It's better than a .45."

The man stopped ten feet from the fence, holding the machete dramatically across his chest. "This is private property."

"Yeah, I know," said Gideon. "Look, we're friends. Let us in."

"Who you here to see?"

"Willis Lockhart," Gideon said, proffering the name of the commune's leader.

"Is he expecting you?"

"No, but we've got a business proposition for him that he'll want to hear—I guarantee it. I'm sure he would be pissed if we were turned away without him getting a chance to hear it. *Good* and pissed."

The man considered this a moment. "What kind of proposition?"

"Sorry, man, that's for Lockhart's ears only. It's about money. M-O-N-E-Y."

"Commander Will is a busy man."

Commander Will. "Well, are you going to let us in or not? 'Cause we're busy, too."

A hesitation. "You armed?"

Gideon held out his arms. "No. Feel free to check." And they had, in fact, left their sidearms in the car. Fordyce had his ID, the warrants, and the subpoena rubber-banded to his shin, under his pants.

"Him?"

"No."

The man sheathed his machete. "All right. But the commander isn't going to like it if you guys aren't who you say you are."

He unlocked the gate and they filed through. The man gave them a cursory pat-down. Gideon noted that he locked the gate behind

them, which was too bad. Still, getting in had taken a lot less jawbon-
ing than he'd anticipated.

They passed a corral where some commune members were working cattle, branding and cutting—ordinary-looking cowboy types.
Around a bend, the big ranch house came into closer view, three
stories tall, with new-looking gabled wings and a huge wraparound
porch. Beyond, in a large field, he could see a serious array of solar
panels surrounded by chain link and razor wire, several monster satellite dishes, and a small microwave tower.

"What do you think they need all that shit for?" Fordyce murmured.

"In case the Playboy Channel on regular cable goes down,"
Gideon said jokingly, but he, too, stared hard at the array.

As they approached the main house, they entered a beautifully restored historic mining town, complete with log cabins, corrals, and a
hitching post with a couple of saddled horses tied up. The authenticity
was spoiled by a parking lot behind the ranch house, in which stood
a small fleet of identical Jeeps, earthmoving equipment, and several
large trucks.

They mounted the wooden porch of the main house; the man
knocked on the door, then entered. They followed him in. Gideon
was surprised to find that the downstairs parlor had been fixed up as
a modern-looking conference room, with a rosewood table, corpo-
rate chairs, whiteboards, and even a plasma screen. The whiteboard
had some partial differential equations scribbled on it that Gideon did
not recognize, but he knew enough to realize were very sophisticated.
Beyond the parlor, he got a glimpse of a classroom in session, where
a group of kids listened to a teacher in a gingham dress. The whole
place had a weird, steampunk feel to it.

"Upstairs," said their escort.

As they mounted the stairs, Gideon caught a bit of what the
teacher was saying—something about how government biologists had
developed the HIV virus for genocidal purposes.

He caught Fordyce's eye.

Gaining the landing, Machete Man led them down a long corridor.

Several of the doors were open; in one, a barely dressed, curvaceous woman lolled on a bed of purple satin sheets. She glanced out at them indifferently.

"Do you suppose she's, ah, the *vice* commander?" Gideon asked as they stopped before a closed door. "The perks of power."

"Stow it," Fordyce growled as Machete Man knocked on the door. A voice called them in.

The room was done up in high Victorian whorehouse style, with red velvet wallpaper, opulent Victorian sofas and chairs, Persian rugs, brass lamps with green glass shades. Sitting behind a desk was a man in his fifties, extremely fit, with long hair, the same squared-off beard—it seemed to be a popular look—and Rasputin-like eyes. He was dressed in a blue shawl-lapel coat, brocaded vest, old-style ascot, and gold chain: the very image of a gambling-house dandy.

Totally hokey.

Gideon felt himself relaxing. Equations or no equations, these people were lightweights. This was no Manson Family. No Waco compound. His elaborate subterfuge was starting to look unnecessary.

"What do they want?" the man asked sharply, looking at Machete Man.

"They say they have a business proposition for you, Commander."

Lockhart's keen eyes turned to them, scanned Gideon, then scanned Fordyce. They remained on Fordyce for a moment—a little too long. Gideon's heart sank.

"Who are you?" he asked Fordyce, his voice tinged with suspicion.

"He's a Fed," said Gideon, with sudden inspiration.

Fordyce whipped his head around and Lockhart rose in his chair. Gideon gave an easy laugh. "Or, rather, an ex-Fed."

Lockhart remained standing, staring.

"ATF, retired," said Gideon. "You know these jokers can retire at forty-five? Now my pal's in another line of business—not unrelated to his previous work."

A long silence. "And what line of business might that be?"

"Medical marijuana."

The commander's bushy eyebrows rose. After a moment he eased himself back down in his seat.

Gideon went on. "The name's Gideon Crew. My partner and I are looking for a secure place to site a growing operation—something in the mountains, well protected, on good irrigated land far from prying eyes and marijuana thieves. With a source of reliable labor." He allowed himself a little smile. "It's a bit more profitable than the alfalfa you're growing, it's legal, and of course there are certain, ah, in-kind *perks.*"

Another long silence as Lockhart stared at Gideon. "Well now, what if we already had our own little 'medical' marijuana plantation up here? Why would we need you?"

"Because what you're doing is illegal and you can't sell it. I've got the permits and I've got a dispensary in Santa Fe all ready to go, first one in town. The volume will be *enormous.* And I repeat: it's all legal."

Now Fordyce interjected, bestowing a grin on Lockhart. "My days at ATF left me with excellent contacts in the business."

"I see. And what made you think of us?"

"My old friend Connie Rust," said Gideon.

"And how do you know Connie?"

"Well, see, I was her former purveyor of cannabis, before she joined up with you folks."

"And where did you get your supply?"

"Where else?" Gideon gestured at Fordyce.

Lockhart glanced back at the agent. "This was during your time at ATF?"

"I never said I was Mister Perfect."

Lockhart seemed to ponder this and apparently found it plausible. He picked up a walkie-talkie lying on his desk. "Bring Connie up here. Right away."

He laid it back down. They waited in silence. Gideon's heart began to pound. So far, so good.

A few minutes passed. Then a knock came at the door and a woman stepped in.

"Here's an old friend of yours, Connie," said Lockhart.

She turned to them, a wreck of a woman, her skin raddled by drink and weed, her lips loose and wet, her bleached-blond hair with two inches of brown roots. Another long gingham dress covered her emaciated form.

"Who?" she asked, her watery blue eyes scanning them both uncomprehendingly.

Lockhart gestured at Gideon. "Him."

"I've never seen—"

But Fordyce wasn't waiting to hear more. He reached down, whipped out his badge and papers from his leg, while Gideon stepped over to Rust and took a firm grasp of her arm.

"Stone Fordyce," the agent rapped out as he pulled off the wig. "FBI. We've got a warrant and subpoena to compel the testimony of Connie Rust, and we are hereby taking her into custody." He tossed the papers onto Lockhart's desk. "We're leaving. Any effort to impede us will be felony obstruction of justice."

As Lockhart stared at them, thunderstruck, they turned and barged out through the door, Gideon hauling along the bewildered and unresisting woman.

"What the *fuck*?" Gideon heard the shout from behind them. "Don't let them go!" As they ran down the stairs he could hear Lockhart yelling into his walkie-talkie.

In a moment they were out the door and jogging down the dirt street. That was when Rust began to shriek: a high-pitched scream that was almost animalistic in its bewilderment and terror. But she did not struggle; she was passive to the point of being limp.

"Keep it going, keep it going," said Fordyce. "We're almost there."

As they came around the bend, passing the large barn, they realized they were not almost there. The commune members who'd been working cattle were pouring into the dirt road, blocking it—many of them with long cattle prods in their hands. Gideon counted seven.

"Federal agents acting on a warrant!" boomed Fordyce. "Do not interfere! Make way!"

They did not make way. Instead they began to advance at a menacing walk, cattle prods held in front of them.

"Oh no," said Gideon, slowing.

"Keep going. It may be a bluff."

Gideon continued hustling Rust along, Fordyce leading the way.

"FBI, engaged in official business!" Fordyce roared as they trotted forward, his shield extended.

The sheer force of his determination slowed the cowboys, caused them to hesitate. But then Rust's high-pitched keening sound seemed to stiffen their resolve.

The opposing groups were now almost on top of each other. "Stand down," shouted Fordyce, "or you will be arrested and charged with felony obstruction!"

But instead of standing down, the cowboys renewed their advance. The leading man jabbed at the agent with his cattle prod. Fordyce twisted away, but the second prod got him in the side. There was a crackle of electricity and he went down with a roar.

Gideon let Rust go—she collapsed to the ground in a sobbing heap—and seized a shovel leaning against the barn. He lunged forward with the shovel, smacking the prod out of the second man's hand. It spun off into the dirt and Gideon swept the shovel back into the man's side. The man fell to the ground, clutching his midriff. Gideon dropped the shovel and scooped up the cattle prod, turning to face the others, who immediately surged forward with a collective shout, wielding their prods like swords.

23

SWORDS. THANKS TO a cute girl with swashbuckling proclivities, Gideon had briefly dabbled with fencing in high school. He'd quit when she quit, before he'd gotten any good at it. In hindsight, that seemed like a mistake.

The men circled him warily, Gideon backing up toward the side of the barn. He could see Fordyce, still on the ground, struggling to rise. One of the men gave him a swinging kick in the side, flipping him over.

That pissed Gideon off. He lunged at the closest man, making contact while pressing the prod's fingertip switch. Howling in pain, the man went down and Gideon swung at the next, parrying his thrust and knocking aside the man's prod before feinting at a third opponent. Behind his back he heard shouting: Fordyce was now back on his feet, staggering, roaring, and swinging away like a drunken maniac.

The third man jabbed again at Gideon, hitting his prod with a flash of sparks. Gideon hopped back, then lunged, but he was off-balance, the opponent advancing, thrusting and jabbing with the prod, Gideon parrying, electricity crackling. The second man came at him from the side just as Gideon scored a hit, his opponent going down with a zap and scream, writhing in the dirt. Gideon spun and knocked aside the other man's thrust. Out of the corner of his eye he saw Fordyce unleashing a roundhouse into another opponent, breaking his jaw with an audible crack, then leaping onto another like a wild animal, the man struggling to bring his long prod around to jab Fordyce with its fork.

More men converged on Gideon, backing him up against the side of the barn as he fended off their thrusts and swings. But there were too many for him to handle alone. One of them came in fast, slashing at him, while another jabbed him in the side; he felt a sudden white-hot blast of pain and cried out; legs buckling, he crumpled against the barn wall as the men closed in.

Suddenly Fordyce appeared behind them, now swinging the shovel like a baseball bat, smacking one attacker broadside in the head and causing the others to spin around to defend themselves. He parried their jabs with the shovel, the prods clanging and spraying sparks with every contact.

But there were too many: they were badly outnumbered, now both of them backed up against the barn doors. Gideon rose to his knees; Fordyce grabbed his arm and heaved him to his feet. "Inside the barn," he said.

A final swing of the shovel and a maniacal scream cleared their way to the open barn door, and they ran inside. After the brilliant light of the outdoors, Gideon was temporarily blinded by the sudden darkness.

"We need weapons," said Fordyce hoarsely as they retreated into the back, stumbling, feeling their way behind rows of equipment and stacks of alfalfa. Half a dozen cowboys poured in the door, fanning out, their shouts and voices echoing in the enclosed space.

"Well, lookee here." Gideon seized a chain saw leaning up against a post, grabbed the starter, and gave it a yank.

It fired up with an ugly rumble. He lifted the saw by the front handle, goosed it. Its roar filled the space.

The cowboys froze.

"Follow me." Gideon ran straight toward the massed cowboys, swinging the chain saw in front of him, pressing the throttle control all the way down. The saw's engine rose to an earsplitting scream.

The cowboys backed up and broke into a fearful retreat as Gideon reemerged into the sunlight.

"Let's get the hell out of here!" he yelled at Fordyce.

And then he heard another roar. Around the side of the barn came their old escort from the log cabin—but now instead of a machete he, too, was wielding a chain saw.

There was no option: Gideon turned and met the man's charge face-on, chain saws roaring. In a moment their saws came together with a mighty crash and a burst of sparks, the inertial force causing a kickback so violent that it knocked Gideon sideways, almost throwing him to the ground. The man, with the advantage of momentum, advanced with a swing of his shrieking blade, the chain a flashing blur along its edge; Gideon blocked it again with his own blade, and they clashed with another immense kick and shower of sparks. Again Gideon was driven back and the man advanced—he was clearly an expert with the chain saw.

Gideon was no such expert. If he was to have any chance to survive—any chance at all—it would be by using his lame experience as a high school fencer.

I'll try a coupé lancé, Gideon thought with something close to desperation. He thrust the tip of his blade at the man's chest, which his opponent all too easily parried with a sideswipe, the blades making contact for the third time with another terrific grating noise and cascade of sparks.

Gideon was thrown back against the side of the barn, and the man—smiling now—came sweeping in, his blade glancing off the wood of the barn as Gideon ducked, lost his balance, and fell. Fordyce tried to move in but the man forced the agent back with a lunge of his saw. And now the man was on top of him, his beard vibrating as he plunged the blade down toward Gideon, who held his own chain saw up as protection; he parried the whirling blade with his own and it twisted away, the vicious kick forcing the man backward. Seizing the opportunity, Gideon sprang to his feet, and—as the man turned back toward him, roaring—he suddenly leapt forward in a flunge, thrusting his chain saw ahead, then twisting it to one side. It tore through the sleeve of the man's workshirt and left a bloody stripe across his upper arm.

"A hit, a very palpable hit!" Gideon cried.

The flesh wound just served to make the bearded man even angrier. He rushed forward, swinging the chain saw above his head as if it were a mace, then bringing it crashing down on Gideon's own saw. There was a moment of grinding, sparks flying, and then with a mighty wrenching sound the saw was jerked from Gideon's hands. This was followed immediately by a sharp *crack!* as the chain of the man's saw snapped. It was an old saw, without a chain catcher, and the chain whipped around like a lash, laying open the man's face from mouth to ear. Blood sprayed everywhere, coating Gideon, as the man fell back with a scream, dropping the saw and clutching at his face.

"Behind you!" Fordyce roared.

Gideon scrambled up, seizing his own chain saw by its kickback protector, and swung around just in time to meet a group of cowboys rushing him with cattle prods; his saw blistered an arc through them, cutting the prods off at the hilts and scattering the men in terror.

And then Gideon heard the sound of shots.

"Gotta go!" Fordyce yelled, hauling Connie Rust to her feet and throwing her over his shoulder. They ran toward the fence. Gideon sank the chain saw blade into the links and chewed open a ragged hole, which they tumbled through, bullets kicking up dirt around them.

A moment later they'd reached the Suburban; Gideon tossed aside the chain saw and leapt into the driver's seat while Fordyce threw Rust into the backseat, climbing in on top of her and keeping her down.

Tunk tunk! A pair of rounds turned the windshield into an opaque web of cracks.

Gideon punched a hole through the sagging glass with his fist, ripped out the dangling pieces, then threw the Suburban into gear and fishtailed out, leaving behind a huge cloud of dust.

As the sound of the shots became more distant, Gideon heard Fordyce groan from the backseat.

"You all right?" he asked.

"I'm just thinking of the paperwork."

24

GIDEON FINALLY RELAXED as they left the maze of dirt roads behind and exited onto Highway 4 near Jemez Springs. They had not, to his relief, been chased or followed from the Paiute Creek Ranch. He slowed the Suburban as they eased through town, the streets thronging with tourists down from Santa Fe.

During the wild drive out of the mountains, Connie Rust—in the backseat with Fordyce—had fallen quiet. Now she began to whimper, over and over again. "What's going to happen to me?"

"Nothing bad," said Fordyce, his voice calm, reassuring. "We're here to help you. I'm sure you've heard about what your ex-husband was involved in."

This brought another bout of sobbing.

"We just want to ask you some questions, that's all." Gideon listened as Fordyce explained—with infinite patience, as if speaking to a child—that they had a subpoena, which required her to answer all their questions truthfully, but that she had nothing to worry about, that she was not a suspect, that she would not be locked up, and that in fact she was a very important person whose help they were depending on. He continued on in a deep-voiced murmur, gently overriding Rust's self-pitying outbursts, until she appeared to calm down.

A final sniffle. "What do you want to know?"

"My colleague," said Fordyce, "Gideon Crew, used to work with your ex-husband up in Los Alamos. He'll be asking the questions."

Gideon heard this with surprise.

"Meanwhile," Fordyce went on, "we're going to switch drivers so he can talk to you undistracted." He turned to Gideon. "Right, partner?"

Gideon pulled over.

Outside the car, Fordyce took him aside. "You knew Chalker," he murmured. "You know what to ask."

"But you're the interrogation expert," Gideon protested in a whisper.

"She's ready to talk now."

Gideon got into the backseat next to her. She was still sniffling, dabbing at her nose with a Kleenex but otherwise calm. She even looked a little pleased at the attention. Gideon felt at a loss. Interrogations were not his thing.

Fordyce started up the car and pulled back out onto the road, driving slowly.

"Um," said Gideon, wondering where the hell to start. "Like Agent Fordyce said, I was a colleague of your ex-husband's up on the Hill."

She nodded dumbly.

"We were friends. I think you and I met once." He thought it better not to remind her it was at the Christmas party where she got drunk.

She looked at him again, and he was shocked at the depth of disorientation in those eyes. "Sorry, I just don't remember you."

What to ask? He racked his brains. "During your marriage, did Reed ever show an interest in Islam?"

She shook her head.

"What about his work? Did he ever express any negative views about what he was doing up at the lab, with bombs and such?"

"He was gung ho about his work. Proud of it. Disgusting." She blew her nose. Talking about Chalker seemed to clear her mind—somewhat.

"Why disgusting?"

"He was a tool of the military-industrial complex and never realized it."

"Did he ever express any views against the United States? Express sympathy for any terrorist organizations?"

"No. He was a flag waver from way back. You should've seen him after 9/11. 'Nuke the bastards.' Little did he know Bush and Cheney organized the whole thing."

Gideon did not venture a comment on this opinion. "Didn't it then seem strange to you that he converted to Islam?"

"Not at all. When we were married, he used to drag me to the Zen center for meditations, to these pseudo-Indian Native American Church meetings, EST, Scientology, the Moonies—you name it, he tried it."

"So he was sort of a spiritual seeker."

"That's a nice way of putting it. He was a pain in the ass."

"Why did you divorce?"

She sniffled. "Just what I said: he was a pain in the ass."

"Did you remain in contact with him after your divorce?"

"He tried to. I was sick and tired of him. When I joined the ranch, he finally left me alone. Willis read him the riot act."

"Riot act?"

"Yes. Willis told him he would beat the crap out of him if he contacted me again. So he didn't. He was a coward."

Fordyce suddenly spoke from the front seat. "Do you and Willis have a relationship?"

"We did. Then he dedicated himself to celibacy."

Yeah, right, thought Gideon, recalling the young woman he had glimpsed lolling in a bed next to Willis's office.

"So what's the idea behind the ranch, the purpose of it?" asked Fordyce.

"We've seceded from this bogus country. We're off the grid, self-sufficient. We grow all our own food, we take care of each other. We're the harbingers of a new age."

"And why is this necessary?"

"You people are prisoners of your government. You have no idea. Your politicians are suffering from the disease of power. It's totally corrupt and yet you don't see it."

"What do you mean by 'the disease of power'?" Fordyce asked.

"All power structures, by their very nature, eventually get taken over by psychopaths. Almost all governments in the world have been taken over by gifted psychopaths who have a great command of human psychology and use normal people to their advantage. This race of pathological deviants can't feel compassion, they have no conscience. They have an insatiable need for power—and they rule the world."

It was a recited speech and it had a shopworn air, although it was not without interest, at least to Gideon. He had occasionally felt that way himself.

"So what do you plan to do about it?" Fordyce asked.

"We'll sweep it all away and start afresh."

"How will you sweep it away?" asked Gideon.

She suddenly shut up, her lips tightening.

After a moment, Fordyce asked: "So what do you do at the ranch?"

"I was originally part of the technical team, but now I work in the garden."

"Technical team?"

"That's right." She tilted her head up pathetically. "We're no Luddites. We embrace technology. The revolution will be delivered with technology."

"What kind of technology?"

"Internet, the web, mass communications. You saw our satellite dishes. We're highly connected."

"Will the revolution be violent?" asked Gideon pleasantly.

"The psychopaths will not leave voluntarily," she said grimly.

They were approaching the outskirts of Santa Fe, passing the prison, the grasslands giving way to suburban developments. "Any interest at the ranch in your ex-husband's work?" asked Fordyce. "I mean, he designed atomic weapons. Might be a good way to sweep away the psychopaths."

More silence. Then, "That's not the reason *I* was invited."

"Why were you invited?" said Fordyce.

"Because . . . Willis loved me."

This pathetic declaration was the last thing she would say. No matter how they asked or cajoled, she remained silent. They delivered the grim witness to the NEST central command complex in Santa Fe without her speaking another word.

"Let 'em have sloppy seconds," said Fordyce as they left, gunning the car and heading north. "We're off to see the imam."

25

THE AL-DAHAB MOSQUE stood at the end of a winding road, a sprawling adobe building with a golden dome framed against red bluffs. It formed a striking picture in red, gold, and blue, surrounded by a sea of government vehicles. The cars and vans filled the capacious parking lot, and more were rudely parked on the grounds to either side.

As they approached, Gideon heard shouting and turned to see a small but vociferous band of protesters off to one side, held behind police barricades, shouting and waving signs covered with sentiments like MUSLIMS GO HOME.

"Will you look at those morons?" said Gideon, shaking his head.

"It's called free speech," said Fordyce, pushing along.

A mobile command unit had been set up in the parking lot, a capacious trailer with a cluster of communications equipment on top. As Fordyce looked for a place to park the Suburban, Gideon asked: "Why set up here? Why not haul everyone downtown for questioning?"

Fordyce snorted. "Intimidation. Invade their space."

They went through several checkpoints and a metal detector, their credentials scrutinized, before being escorted into the mosque. It was spectacular: a long broad hallway led into the domed interior, beautifully tiled in blue, with complex, abstract patterns. They bypassed the domed central section and were led to a closed doorway in the back. A mass of NEST agents came and went, with guards milling about the door. There were few Muslims to be seen—everyone appeared to be a government agent.

Once again their creds were checked and then the door was opened. The small, spare room beyond had been turned into an interrogation room, not unpleasant, with a table in the middle, several chairs, microphones dangling from the ceiling, videocameras on tripods in the four corners.

"The imam will be in momentarily," said a man wearing a NEST cap.

They waited, standing up. The door opened again a few minutes later and a man entered. Much to Gideon's surprise he was a Westerner, and he wore a blue suit, tie, and white shirt. He had no beard, no turban, no robes. The only thing unusual about him was his stockinged feet. He was about sixty, a powerful, heavyset man with black hair.

He entered wearily and took a seat. "Please," he said. "Sit down. Make yourselves comfortable."

When he spoke, Gideon had a second surprise: the man had a strong New Jersey accent. Gideon glanced over to Fordyce, saw he was not sitting down, and decided to remain standing himself.

The door closed.

"Stone Fordyce, FBI," the agent said, flashing his badge.

"Gideon Crew, FBI liaison."

The imam seemed utterly uninterested—indeed, exhaustion appeared to overwhelm the faint traces of anger that remained in his face.

"Mr. Yusuf Ali?" Gideon asked.

"That's me," said the imam, crossing his arms and looking past them.

They had discussed ahead of time how to proceed. Gideon would go first and be the sympathetic questioner. Fordyce would interrupt at a certain point and be the heavy. The good-guy, bad-guy routine, as hackneyed as it was, had never been bettered.

"I was a friend of Reed's up at Los Alamos," said Gideon. "When he converted, he gave me some of his books. I couldn't believe it when I heard what he'd done in New York."

No reaction from the imam. He continued to stare past them.

"We're you surprised when you heard?"

Finally the imam looked at him. "Surprised? I was *floored*."

"You were his mentor. You were present when he recited the Shahada, the Testimony of Faith. Are you saying you didn't see any sign of his growing radicalism?"

A long silence. "That's got to be the fiftieth time I've been asked that question. Do I really have to answer it again?"

Fordyce broke in. "You got a problem with answering that particular question?"

Ali turned to look at Fordyce. "The fiftieth time, yes, I do. But I'll answer it anyway. I saw no sign, not any, of radicalism. On the contrary, Chalker seemed uninterested in political Islam. He was focused purely on his own relationship with God."

"That seems hard to believe," said Fordyce. "We've got copies of your sermons. In here we find comments critical of the US government, criticizing the war in Iraq, and other statements of a political nature. We've got other testimony regarding your anti-war, anti-government opinions."

Ali looked at Gideon. "Were you in favor of the war in Iraq? Are you in favor of all the government's policies?"

"Well—"

"We're asking the questions around here," interrupted Fordyce.

"The point I'm making," said the imam, "is that my views about the war are no different from many other loyal Americans. And I *am* a loyal American."

"What about Chalker?"

"Apparently, he wasn't. This may shock you, Agent Fordyce, but not everyone who's against the Iraq War wants to blow up New York City."

Fordyce shook his head.

Ali leaned forward. "Agent Fordyce, let me tell you something new. Something fresh. Something I haven't told the others. Would you like to hear it?"

"I would."

"I converted to Islam when I was thirty-five. Before that, I was Joseph Carini and I was a plumber. My grandfather came from Italy in 1930, a fifteen-year-old kid with a dollar in his pocket, dressed in rags. He came all the way from Sicily. He pulled himself up by his bootstraps in this country, got a job, worked hard, learned the language, bought a house in Queens, got married, and raised his kids in a nice, safe, working-class neighborhood. Which to him was like paradise, compared with the corruption, poverty, and social injustice of Sicily. He *loved* this country. My father and mother felt the same way. We managed to move out to the suburbs—North Arlington, New Jersey. They were so grateful for the opportunities given them by this country. So was I. What other country in the world would welcome a penniless fifteen-year-old kid who didn't speak English and give him the opportunities he had? And I've benefited from those same freedoms here, which allowed me to leave the Catholic Church—which I did for very personal reasons—convert to Islam, move out west, and eventually become imam of this beautiful mosque. Only in America would this be possible. Even after 9/11 we Muslims out here were treated with respect by our neighbors. We were as horrified as everyone else by that terrorist attack. We've been allowed to practice our religion unmolested, in peace, for many years."

Here he paused significantly. In the silence, the shouts and chants of the protestors faintly filtered in from outside. "At least, until now."

"Now, that's a fine, patriotic story," said Fordyce, an edge to his voice, but Gideon could see the little speech had taken some of the wind from his sails.

The rest of the interview limped along, going nowhere. The imam insisted there were no radicals in the mosque. They were mostly converts and virtually all were American citizens. The finances of the mosque and school were an open book; all the information had been turned over to the FBI. The charities they supported were all registered and, again, their books had been thrown open to the FBI. Yes, there was general opposition among the members to the wars in Iraq and Afghanistan, but then again, some of their congregation were actually serving in the Persian Gulf. Yes, they taught Arabic, but that was, after all, the language of the Qur'an, and didn't imply some sort of hidden allegiance to specific political attitudes or prejudices.

And then their time was up.

26

F ORDYCE WAS DARK and silent as they left, threading their way out among the throngs of law enforcement. Finally, as they approached the Suburban, he burst out, "The guy's good. Too good, if you ask me."

Gideon grunted his assent. "A real Horatio Alger, it seems. But if he's a liar, he's a damn good one." Gideon refrained from adding, *and I should know.* "It would be easy enough to check the story out."

"Oh, I'm sure it'll check out. A guy like that's careful."

"It might be worth finding out why he left the Catholic Church."

"And I'd give you ten-to-one odds he's hoping we'll do just that, given the way he emphasized that part of his story."

They neared the group of protestors corralled behind police barricades, their shrill, angry shouting like sandpaper in the quiet desert air. Out of the cacophony, individual voices rose and fell.

Suddenly Fordyce stopped, cocked his head. "You hear that?"

Gideon paused. Someone was shouting about a canyon and bomb building.

They walked over to the protestors. Seeing they were finally getting some attention, they redoubled their yelling and sign waving.

"All right, shut up a minute!" Fordyce boomed at them. He jabbed a finger. "You! What were you just saying?"

A young woman in full Western dress, boots, hat, and massive buckle, stepped forward. "They go sneaking up into Cobre Canyon just before sunset—"

"You've seen them yourself?"

"Sure I have."

"Seen them from where?"

"The rim. There's a trail I ride there, along the rim, and I've seen them below, walking up Cobre Canyon, carrying bomb-making materials. They're building a bomb in there."

"Bomb-making materials? Like what?"

"Well, backpacks full of stuff. Look, I'm not kidding, they're building a bomb."

"How many times have you seen them?"

"Well, just once, but once is all it takes to realize—"

"When?"

"About six months ago. And let me tell you people—"

"Thank you." Fordyce got her name and address and they headed back to the car. He slipped behind the wheel, still pissed. "What a waste of time."

"Maybe not, if that tip on Cobre Canyon pans out."

"Worth checking out, I suppose. But that woman was just repeating a rumor—she didn't see any of that herself. What really interested me were those two guys following us out of the mosque."

"We were followed?"

"You didn't see them?"

Gideon found himself blushing. "I wasn't looking."

Fordyce shook his head. "Don't know who they were, but I got a good long video of them."

"Video? When the hell did you shoot video?"

Fordyce grinned, lifted a pen from his pocket. "Ninety-nine bucks, Sharper Image. Beats filling out forms in triplicate and waiting weeks to get the official interrogation videotape from NEST." He started the engine, his face becoming serious. "We've pissed away three days. A week until N-Day, maybe less. And look at this mess. Just look at it. Scares the shit out of me."

He gestured scornfully back at the sea of law enforcement as he peeled out, leaving a cloud of dust lingering in the thin desert air.

27

Myron Dart stood inside the Doric fastness of the Lincoln Memorial, staring moodily at the expanse of marble beneath his feet. Although it was a hot early-summer day—the kind of muggy, torpid afternoon that Washington specialized in—it was still relatively cool inside the memorial. Dart was careful not to look up at the statue of Lincoln. Something about its awesome majesty, something in the president's wise and benevolent gaze, invariably choked him up. He couldn't afford emotion right now. Instead, he turned his attention to the text of the second inaugural address, engraved in stone: *With firmness in the right, as God gives us to see the right, let us strive on to finish the work we are in.*

Those were good words. Dart made a quiet vow to keep them in mind over the next couple of days. He was dog-tired and needed their inspiration. It wasn't just the pressure: it was the country itself. It seemed to be falling apart, the loud and discordant voices of demagogues, talking heads, and media personalities drowning out the rest. The immortal lines from Yeats's great poem came to mind: *The best lack all conviction, while the worst are full of passionate intensity.* This crisis had brought out the worst in his fellow Americans, from the looters and financial speculators to the religious nuts and political extremists—even to the cowardice of many average people, fleeing their homes willy-nilly. What in the world had happened to his beloved country?

He must not think of that now, must stay focused on the job at hand. He turned and left the memorial, pausing briefly on the top step. Ahead, the Mall stretched away to the distant Washington Monument, the monument's needle-like shadow striped across the greensward. The park was empty. The usual sunbathers and tourists were gone. Instead, a convoy of half-tracks rumbled down Constitution Avenue, and two dozen army Humvees were parked behind concrete barricades installed on the Ellipse. There was no civilian traffic to be seen anywhere. The leaves hung limp on the trees, and in the distance sirens droned on and on and on, rising and falling in a monotonous, post-apocalyptic lullaby.

Dart walked briskly down the steps to the approach road, where an unmarked NEST van was idling, flanked by several National Guard troops armed with M4 carbines. He stepped up to the double doors in the rear of the van and rapped on them with his knuckles. The doors opened and he climbed in.

The interior of the van was chilly and dark, illuminated only by the green and amber glow of instrumentation. Half a dozen NEST employees were seated, some monitoring a variety of terminals, others murmuring into headsets.

Miles Cunningham, his personal assistant, approached out of the gloom. "Report," said Dart.

"The Lincoln Memorial hidden cameras and motion sensors are installed and online," Cunningham said. "The laser grid should be operational within the hour. We'll have real-time surveillance capability for a quarter mile around the monument. A mouse, sir, won't be able to move without us observing it."

"And the Pentagon, the White House, and the other possible targets?"

"Similar nets are being put in place, all scheduled to be one hundred percent operational by midnight. Every security net will feed back through dedicated landlines to a centralized monitoring node at the command center. We have banks of trained observers ready to work in shifts, monitoring twenty-four seven."

Dart nodded his approval. "How many?"

"About five hundred, with another thousand NEST personnel in support—not counting, of course, the military, National Guard, FBI, and other liaison agency assets and personnel."

"What's the total of deployed personnel?"

"Sir, it's impossible to say in such a rapidly evolving situation. A hundred thousand or more, perhaps."

Way too many, thought Dart. The investigation had been, inevitably, a monstrosity from the very beginning. But he said nothing. Practically the entire complement of NEST was on the ground in Washington, pulled in from across the country, resources stretched to the breaking point. But then, it was the same with the army, the marines, the National Guard: the elite of the armed forces of an entire nation had descended on the city, at the same time that residents and government workers were leaving.

"The latest from the Device Working Group?" Dart asked.

Cunningham removed a file. "Here, sir."

"Summarize it for me?"

"They're still disagreeing on the size of the device and its potential yield. Size depends greatly on the technical sophistication of the fabricators."

"What's the latest estimate range?"

"They say it could be anything from a heavy suitcase bomb weighing fifty kilograms to something you'd have to carry around in the back of a van. Yield from twenty to fifty kilotons. A lot less if the bomb misfired, but even in that case there would be an enormous spread of radiation."

"Thank you. And the New Mexico branch of the investigation?"

"Nothing new, sir. Interrogations at the mosque have been inconclusive. They've got hundreds, thousands of leads, but so far they've turned up nothing of real note."

Dart shook his head. "The fire is here, not there. Even if we knew the name of every single terrorist in on the plot, it wouldn't help much. They've gone to ground. Our real problem now is interdiction and containment. Get Sonnenberg in New Mexico on the horn. Tell him that if he doesn't start getting results within twenty-four hours,

I'm going to start redeploying some of his assets back here to Washington, where they're really needed."

"Yes, sir." Cunningham began to speak again, then stopped.

"What is it?" Dart asked immediately.

"I had a report from the FBI liaison out there. Fordyce. He requested, and received, permission to subpoena Chalker's ex-wife. She's living in some kind of commune outside of Santa Fe. He also plans to interview other persons of interest."

"Did he mention who the other suspects were?"

"Not suspects, sir, just individuals they'll be contacting. And, no, there were no other names."

"Has he submitted a report on the ex-wife yet?"

"No. But subsequent interrogations of her by NEST personnel turned up nothing useful."

"Interesting. A commune? That's worth following up on, even if it is a little far-fetched." Dart glanced around. "As soon as the security nets are in place, I want the beta-testing to begin. Assemble the probe teams, start them running. Check for any holes or weak spots in the grids. Tell them to be creative—and I mean *creative*."

"Yes, sir."

Dart nodded. He grasped the handle of the rear door.

"Dr. Dart, sir?" Cunningham asked diffidently.

"What?"

Cunningham cleared his throat. "If you don't mind my saying so, sir, you should take a break. You've been going for over fifty hours straight, by my reckoning."

"We all have."

"No, sir. We've all taken breaks. You've been driving yourself without letup. May I suggest you go back to the command center, get a few hours of rest? I'll let you know if anything urgent comes up."

Dart hesitated, refrained from making another sharp retort. Instead, he made an effort to soften his tone. "I appreciate your concern, Mr. Cunningham, but I'll sleep when it's over." And with that, Dart opened the door and stepped out into the sunlight.

28

THE WEST SANTA FE Airfield dozed under a limpid sky. As Fordyce pulled into the parking lot, Gideon made out a single hangar, with a cinder-block building affixed to one end as if an afterthought.

"Where's the runway?" he asked, looking around.

Fordyce gestured vaguely past the hangar toward a large expanse of dirt.

"You mean, past that dirt area?"

"It *is* the dirt area."

Gideon was a poor flier on the best of occasions. In a comfy first-class seat in a roomy jet, with the overhead lighting low and his iPod fired up, noise-canceling headphones, and a cabin attendant to refresh his drink, he could get by, pretend he wasn't trapped in a flimsy metal tube blasting through the air miles above the ground. He glanced uneasily at the scattering of small planes parked on the dirt. There would be no pretending in one of those.

Fordyce grabbed a briefcase from the backseat, then got out of the car. "I'll go see the FBO about that rental I told you about. We were lucky to get the Cessna 64-TE."

"Lucky," Gideon said unhappily.

Fordyce strolled off.

Gideon sat in the car. He'd always managed to avoid small planes before. This was not good. He hoped he wouldn't panic, make an ass of himself in front of Fordyce. Too bad the man had a pilot's license. *Calm down, idiot*, he thought. *Fordyce can handle himself. There's nothing to worry about.*

Five minutes later, Fordyce emerged from the box-like building and waved at Gideon. With a hard swallow, Gideon got out of the car, arranged his face into a semblance of unconcern, and followed the agent past the hangar, past a row of parked planes, to a yellow-and-white craft with an engine on each wing. It looked like a tin bug.

"This is it?" Gideon asked.

Fordyce nodded.

"And you're sure you can fly it?"

"If I can't, you'll be the first to find out."

Gideon gave him the broadest grin he could manage. "You know what, Fordyce? You don't really want me along. Why don't I stay here in Santa Fe and follow up on some of the leads we've developed. That wife, for example—"

"Nothing doing. We're partners. And you're riding shotgun." Fordyce opened the pilot's door, climbed in, fiddled with a few of the controls, then got back out again. He started walking around the plane, peering at this, touching that.

"Don't tell me you're the mechanic, too."

"Preflight walkaround." Fordyce inspected the ailerons and tail elevator, then opened a little door and pulled out what looked like an oil dipstick.

"Wash the windows while you're at it, please," Gideon said.

Ignoring this, Fordyce ducked under one of the wings, at the same time pulling something from his pocket that looked like an oversize syringe with a soda straw inside it. He opened a small cap, pushed the device up into the wing. Bluish liquid drained into the syringe, which Fordyce then held up to the light. A little ball sat in the bottom of the straw-shaped section.

"Now what are you doing?" Gideon asked.

"Checking the fuel for water." Fordyce continued peering at the light blue liquid. Then he grunted, replaced the fuel.

"You're done, right?"

"Hardly. There's a tank in each wing, five fuel points per wing."

Gideon sat down despairingly on the grass.

When—eventually—Fordyce motioned for him to get into the passenger seat and put on his headset, Gideon felt vastly relieved. But then followed even more exhaustive checks: engine start checklist, taxi checklist, before-takeoff checklist. Fordyce rattled off everything with gusto, and Gideon feigned interest. It was a full half hour before the engines were on and they had moved into takeoff position. Sitting there, in the tiny compartment, Gideon felt a sense of claustrophobia begin to build.

"Jesus," he said. "We could have walked to Santa Cruz by now."

"Don't forget—this was your idea." Fordyce peered out at the windsock, determining the wind direction. Then, goosing the engines, he slowly turned the plane.

"What if—" Gideon began.

"Shut up for a minute," Fordyce interrupted, his voice thin and tinny over the plane's intercom. "We're doing a short-field takeoff and I have a lot to do if we're going to clear those." He pointed to a row of cottonwoods a thousand feet ahead.

Gideon shut up.

Fordyce spoke into his headset. "West Santa Fe traffic, Cessna one four niner six niner, taxiing onto active runway three four for takeoff."

He adjusted his headset, did a final check of his seat belt harness and door lock, then released the parking brake and throttled forward. "West Santa Fe traffic, Cessna one four niner six niner, taking off runway three four, northwest departure."

They flounced along the dirt, slowly gaining speed, Gideon holding on for dear life.

"We're rotating at Vr, one twenty-five KIAS," Fordyce informed him. "So far, so good."

Gideon gritted his teeth. *The bastard's enjoying this*, he thought.

Suddenly the shuddering and jouncing stopped and they were airborne. The prairie fell away below them and blue sky filled the windows. All at once the plane didn't seem so cramped. It was agile and light, more like an amusement park ride than a lumbering passenger jet. Gideon felt a small thrill of exhilaration despite himself.

"Climbout at Vx," Fordyce said. "One seven five knots."

"What's Vx?" Gideon asked.

"I'm talking to the flight recorder, not you. Stay shut up."

They climbed steadily, both engines working hard. When they reached four thousand feet, Fordyce took out the flaps and throttled back to cruising speed. The little plane started to level off.

"Okay," he said. "The captain has turned off the 'no talking' light."

Takeoff safely past, the engines dialed back to a drone, Gideon almost believed he could enjoy himself a little. "Are we going to be flying over anything interesting?"

The plane suddenly gave a lurch and a rattle, and Gideon gripped his armrests in terror. They were crashing. Another lurch, and another, and he could see the landscape sawing back and forth below them.

"Touch of turbulence at this altitude," said Fordyce easily. "Think I'll take her up another thousand." He glanced over at him. "You okay?"

"Fine," said Gideon, with a forced smile, trying to relax his steel fingers. "Just fine."

"To answer your question, we'll be flying over the Petrified Forest, Grand Canyon, Death Valley. We'll refuel at Bakersfield, just to be safe."

"Should've brought my box Brownie."

The plane leveled out at the higher altitude, which seemed to be free of turbulence, smooth as silk. Gideon felt a growing relief.

Fordyce pulled a set of aviation maps from his briefcase, placed them on his knees. He looked at Gideon. "Got any ideas about what we should look for on this little trip?"

"Chalker wanted to be a writer. The fact he went to this writer's conference *after* getting religion showed it was one of his few interests that persisted post-conversion. Maybe he wanted to write about the conversion itself: remember, the conference was about autobiographical writing. If he gave a copy of a manuscript to someone at the conference to critique—or if someone remembered what he read aloud at a seminar—that might be interesting."

"Interesting? It'd be dynamite. But if it exists there's probably a copy on his laptop, which means there are a thousand people in Washington reading it already."

"Probably. Maybe. But not all writers use computers for their work, and if there was incriminating stuff in there he could very well have erased it. Anyway, even if it's on his computer, do you think we'll ever see it?"

Fordyce grunted and nodded. "Good point."

Gideon settled back in his seat, distractedly glancing at the brown-and-green landscape drifting away beneath them. After a slow start, their investigation was finally picking up—the wife, the mosque, Blaine, and now this. He had a tingling feeling that somewhere, somehow, one of those leads would bring them to a pot of gold.

29

HE WAS ON a magic carpet, floating gently through white-cotton clouds on gossamer threads. Warm breezes, too low and soft to make any noise, caressed his face and teased his hair. The carpet was so smooth, its movements so soothing, it seemed he was not moving— and yet, far below, he could see the landscape passing beneath him. It was an exotic landscape of glittering domes and spires, wide lush jungles, purple fields sighing their vapors to the sky. Far above, the distant sun threw benevolent rays over the tranquil scene.

And then the carpet gave a sudden, violent lurch.

Blearily, Gideon opened his eyes. For a moment, still in thrall to the dream, he reached out as if to grasp and steady the fringes of the carpet. Instead, his fingers encountered metal, knobs, the smooth face of a glass dial.

"Don't touch that!" Fordyce barked.

Gideon sat up suddenly, only to be restrained by the seat harness. Immediately, he remembered where he was: in a small plane, heading for Santa Cruz. He smiled, remembering. "More turbulence?"

No answer. They were flying through some bad weather, it seemed—or was it? He suddenly realized that what he thought were clouds were actually gouts of thick black smoke billowing out of the left engine, obscuring the view outside.

"What's happened?" he cried.

Fordyce was so busy he didn't answer for ten seconds. "Lost left engine," he replied tersely.

"Is it on fire?" The last clinging remnants of sleep vanished, replaced by sheer panic.

"No flames." Fordyce slammed a lever down, worked some switches and dials. "Shutting off fuel to the engine. Leaving electrical system on—no sign it's electrical, can't afford to lose avionics and gyroscope."

Gideon tried to say something, found he had lost his voice.

"Don't worry," said Fordyce, "we still have one engine. It's just a question of stabilizing the plane with asymmetrical thrust." He worked the rudder, then glanced quickly over the controls. "Monkeys find pussy in the rain," he muttered slowly, then repeated it, like a mantra.

Gideon stared straight ahead, hardly able to breathe.

Fordyce paid no attention to him. "Primer locked," he said. "Transponder at emergency squawk." Then he pressed a button on his headset. "Mayday, mayday, this is Cessna one four niner six niner on emergency channel, one engine out, twenty-five miles west of Inyokern."

A moment later there came a crackling over Gideon's intercom. "Cessna one four niner six niner, this is Los Angeles Center, please restate your emergency and your position."

"One four niner six niner," Fordyce said, "one engine out, twenty-five miles west of Inyokern."

A brief pause. "One four niner six niner, Los Angeles Center, closest airport on your current heading is Bakersfield, runway sixteen and thirty-four. Airport thirty-five miles out at ten o'clock."

"One four niner six niner," said Fordyce, "heading ten o'clock for Bakersfield."

"Squawk seven seven hundred, and ident," came the voice from Los Angeles Center.

Fordyce pressed a button on the console.

"This is Los Angeles Center. Contact at thirty-four miles out from Bakersfield."

The thick smoke had diminished somewhat, and Gideon could see that the sky had clouded over. The land below was foggy and indistinguishable, just the occasional patch of green revealed amid tufts of gauzy gray.

He took a look at the altimeter: the needle was slowly sliding downward. "Are we descending?" he croaked.

"Law of gravity. Once we get to the single-engine service ceiling, we should be fine. We're only some thirty-odd miles from Bakersfield. Let me try the left ignition one more time." He flicked a switch, flicked it again. "Shit. Dead."

Gideon felt pain in the tips of his fingers and he realized he was gripping the seat with all his might. He slowly loosed his hold, willed himself to relax. *It's cool. Fordyce has it under control.* Fordyce was an able and experienced pilot. The man knew what to do. So why did he feel so panicked?

"Stabilizing at one thousand nine hundred AGL," Fordyce said. "We'll be on the Bakersfield runway in ten minutes. Now you'll have a story you can take home to—"

Suddenly there was a violent explosion to their right, a rattle that ran through the entire fuselage. Gideon jumped, instinctively shielding his face with his arm. "What the hell was that?"

Fordyce looked white. "Right engine detonating."

"*Detonating?*" Clouds of oily dark smoke were now pouring from the other engine. It made an ugly, half-coughing, half-grinding noise, then died, the propeller feathering to a stop.

Once again Gideon found himself without words. This was the end—that much was clear.

"We can still glide," Fordyce said. "I'll do a dead-stick landing."

Gideon licked his lips. "Dead-stick landing?" he repeated. "That doesn't sound good."

"It isn't. Help me pick out a place to land."

"Help you—?"

"Look out the window, for fuck's sake, and find me some flat open ground!"

A most peculiar sense of disbelief gripped Gideon. This had to be a movie, this couldn't be happening. Because if this was real life, he'd be too petrified to move. Instead, he found himself scanning the horizon for a landing site. The ground-level fog had cleared somewhat, and now he could see that a bare ridge lay ahead of them. Beyond the ridge, the land fell away into a narrow valley still thick with fog, surrounded by steep forested hills.

"Can't see the ground—fog. How much time do we have?"

"Moment." Fordyce was working the controls yet again, nosing the U-shaped control yoke forward and dialing in the trim tabs. Despite the extremity of the emergency, his voice sounded calm.

"Trimmed for eighty," he finally said. "That gives us a few miles. What about that damn landing site?"

"It's still socked in ahead." Gideon blinked, wiped sweat from his forehead. "How the hell can you lose both engines?"

Instead of answering, Fordyce set his lips in a grim line.

Gideon stared out through the cockpit glass until his eyes hurt. They were descending toward the ridge. Beyond, the cloud cover was slowly breaking up. And then he saw it: through a gap in the clouds a tiny but unmistakable ribbon of asphalt running up the valley.

"There's a road up there!" he said excitedly.

Fordyce took a quick look at his map. "Highway 178." He got on the radio again. "Mayday, mayday, this is Cessna one four niner two niner on channel 121.5. Second engine out, repeat, second engine out. Am attempting emergency landing on Highway 178 west-southwest of Miracle Hot Springs."

Silence over the headset.

"Why isn't anybody responding?" Gideon asked.

"Too low," Fordyce said.

They were down to fourteen hundred feet above ground level, and the ridge was coming up fast. In fact, it looked like they weren't going to clear it.

"Hold on," Fordyce said. "We should just shave past that."

Eerily silent, they glided over the barren ridgetop, wind whistling past the dead propellers, fragments of mist trailing away beneath. Gideon realized he'd been holding his breath and now he let it stream out of his lungs. "Sink me," he muttered.

"Two miles, I'd guess," Fordyce said. "One thousand one hundred AGL. Steady on glideslope."

"Landing gear?"

"Not yet. That would increase our drag—*oh, fucking hell!*"

They had cleared the ridge and were gliding into the valley beyond. And now the landscape came into view through the parting mists: another low ridge, covered with a towering grove of sequoias, tall and majestic, standing between them and the highway beyond.

"Fucking hell," Fordyce whispered again to himself.

Gideon had never heard Fordyce lose it and that scared him more than anything. He looked down at his own hands, flexed them, as if to experience physical movement just once more. He realized, with a little flare of surprise, that he wasn't afraid of dying—that maybe this was better than what was coming...in eleven months. Maybe.

Fordyce's face had gone dead white, and sweat had beaded heavily on his forehead. "Sequoia National Forest," he said huskily. "I'm going for that gap, there. Hold on."

The plane was heading toward the uneven ridge, obscured by massive trees with tiny pointed tops. Moving the control yoke again, Fordyce angled the plane toward an enfilade between several of the giant trees. At the last possible moment, he veered the plane sharply to the right.

Gideon felt the world tilt and the nose of the plane drop heavily. "Christ," he murmured. Whether it was an epithet, or a prayer, or both, he wasn't sure. A moment of sheer terror as the huge, reddish trunks flashed past them just feet away, turbulence buffeting the plane—and then the sky was abruptly clear. The ribbon of Highway 178 curved gently ahead, a few cars crawling along it.

"Five hundred feet AGL," Fordyce said.

"Can we make it?" Gideon's heart was pounding. Now that they'd passed the trees and a chance for survival existed, he felt a sudden urge to live.

"Don't know. We lost a lot of altitude in that maneuver. And I still have one final turn to make—have to land with traffic, not against, if we stand any chance of walking away from this."

They began a slow turn toward the highway. Gideon watched as Fordyce lowered the landing gear.

"More trees ahead," Gideon said.

"I see them."

Another wrenching movement and Gideon heard the sudden *thwap thwap!* of branches on the underside of the plane, and then they were turning to align with the road, a bare thirty feet above the surface.

A truck was lumbering just ahead of them, grinding up a rise, and they descended toward it, seemingly on a collision course. Gideon closed his eyes. There was a *rubumbump!* as one of the plane's wheels bounced off the top of the truck's cab. As the truck's horn blared, the plane was shoved into a tilt; Fordyce pulled it straight, then settled the craft down onto the road ahead, holding the nose up high as the truck behind them fought to slow down, air brakes razzing.

They hit the tarmac with a lurch, came up, then back down with another jarring *thump*—and then they were skidding along the ground, finally coming to a stop in the middle of the highway. Gideon turned and saw the truck screeching to a stop behind them, jackknifing, spewing and spitting rubber from shredding tires. It slid to a stop barely twenty feet from them. Ahead, in the opposite lane, a car approaching from the other direction also slammed on the brakes.

And then all was silent.

For a moment, Fordyce sat like a marble statue, as the metal ticked and hissed around him. Then he prized his fingers from the control yoke, flicked off the master switch, pulled off his headset, and undid his safety harness.

"After you," he said.

Gideon climbed out of the plane on rubbery, nerveless legs.

They sat down, robotically, on the shoulder of the highway. Gideon's heart was going so fast he could barely breathe.

The trucker and the driver of the oncoming car came running up. "Damn!" cried the trucker. "What happened? You guys all right?"

They were all right. Other cars began stopping, people getting out.

Gideon didn't even notice. "How often does an engine just die like that?" he asked Fordyce.

"Not often."

"What about both engines? In exactly the same way?"

"Never, Gideon. Never."

30

A DAY AND A half later, Gideon Crew parked the Suburban—its windshield replaced—in the field beside his log-and-adobe cabin, killed the engine, and got out. He glanced around, breathing deeply, taking in for a moment the vast sweep of early-evening scenery laid out before him: the Piedra Lumbre basin; the Jemez Mountains surrounding him, fringed with ponderosa pines. The air, the view, were like a tonic. It was the first time he'd been back to the cabin since the business on Hart Island, and it felt good. Up here, the dark feeling that was almost always with him seemed to abate. Up here, he could almost forget everything else: the frantic investigation, his medical diagnosis. And the other, deeper things, as well: his blighted childhood; the colossal, lonely mess he'd made of his life.

After a long moment, he scooped up the shopping bags from the passenger seat, pushed open the door to the cabin, and walked into the kitchen alcove. The smell of wood smoke, old leather, and Indian rugs enveloped him. With the country in an uproar, cities evacuating, and the voices of the crazies and conspiracy freaks filling the talk shows and radio, here at least was a place that remained the same. Whistling the melody to "Straight, No Chaser," he began removing items from the shopping bags and arranging them on the counter. He took a moment to circumambulate the cabin, opening shutters and raising windowpanes, checking the solar inverter, turning on the well pump. Then he returned to the kitchen, looked over the array of ingredients, still whistling, and began pulling out pots, knives, and other equipment from various drawers.

God, it felt good to be back.

An hour later, he was opening the oven, checking the progress of his braised artichokes *à la provençale*, when he heard a vehicle approach. Looking out the kitchen window, he saw Stone Fordyce behind the wheel of a shabby FBI Crown Vic. In response, he threw half a stick of butter into a chafing dish and began heating it on the stove.

Fordyce stepped inside, glanced around. "This is what I call rustic charm." He glanced over into the alcove. "What's that, computer stuff?"

"Yes."

"That's a hell of a lot of equipment to run off solar power."

"I've got some serious battery storage."

Fordyce moved into the living room, tossed his jacket on a chair. "That's some road up here. I almost scraped off my muffler."

"Discourages visitors." Gideon nodded toward the kitchen table. "Bottle of Brunello open—help yourself." He had wondered if the wine would be thrown away on the FBI agent, but decided to try anyway.

"God knows I need it." Fordyce poured himself a generous bumper, took a sip. "Something smells good."

"Good? This is going to be the best meal you've ever eaten."

"Is that a fact?"

"I'm sick of eating airport and hotel food. Usually I only eat one meal a day, prepared by myself."

The agent took another sip of wine, eased himself down on the leather sofa. "So—find out anything?"

They had returned to Santa Fe directly from the crash site instead of continuing to the writing center. It had seemed more important to figure out who'd sabotaged the plane—if in fact it had been sabotaged. To save time, they had divvied up this day's investigative duties.

"Sure did." The butter foam was subsiding in the chafing dish, and he carefully transferred the *rognons de veau*—rinsed and peeled of their fat—from the butcher's paper into the dish. "I looked into that Cobre Canyon allegation. Hiked up the canyon. You won't believe what I found."

Fordyce rocked forward. "What?" he asked eagerly.

"A pile of rocks, some seashells, a prayer rug, a ritual ablution bowl, and a small natural spring."

"Meaning?"

"It's a shrine. Members of the mosque go out there to pray. No evidence of bomb making or anything other than praying."

Fordyce grimaced.

"And I looked into why our friend the imam left the Catholic Church. Years ago, he was abused by a priest. All hushed up, there was some kind of payment involved. Nothing public. His family signed a nondisclosure agreement."

"That's what he wanted us to find out. But couldn't tell us."

"Exactly. And I was also able to get a make on those two guys you videotaped at the mosque. Get this: one of them has a commercial pilot's license, used to fly for Pan Am."

Fordyce put down his glass. "No *shit*. Well, that ties in with what I found about our accident today."

"Lay it on me."

"I saw the preliminary report of the NTSB investigators. This was put on a fast track. There's no doubt about it—the plane was sabotaged. Somebody—maybe your friend the pilot—added jet fuel to the avgas in our Cessna."

"What does that mean?"

"That Cessna runs on one hundred low-lead. It needs an octane rating of one hundred to function. Adding jet fuel lowered the octane. As a result, the mixture basically burned through both pistons, one after the other." Fordyce took another sip of wine. "A misfueled engine can start and stop normally—up until the moment it burns up. The thing is, avgas is light blue in color. Jet fuel is clear, sometimes straw-colored. When I did that inspection, the color *did* look a bit off—too light—but it was still blue, so I thought we were okay. This was very deliberate, done by someone who knew exactly what he was doing."

There was a brief silence as the implications of this sank in.

"So what time did you finish your investigations?" Fordyce asked.

"Twelve thirty. One, maybe."

"Then where the hell were you all afternoon? I tried your cell phone like half a dozen times. You turned it off."

The dark feeling welled up again, suddenly. He hadn't planned to tell Fordyce anything at all, but nevertheless heard himself saying: "I had to have some tests done."

"Tests? What kind of tests."

"The personal kind."

The *rognons* had stiffened in the butter and were turning slightly brown; Gideon carefully transferred them onto a plate he'd been warming on the stovetop. Fordyce stared at the plate, a frown coming over his features.

"What in hell are those—?"

"Kidneys. Just give me a minute or two to prepare the reduction." Gideon added shallots, bouillon, spices, and a generous pour of the red wine to the chafing dish.

"Not eating those," Fordyce said.

"They're not even lamb kidneys—only veal. And Frank, my butcher in town, had beef marrow on hand—that's why we're eating *à la Bordelaise* instead of *flambés*." Gideon corrected the seasoning of the reduction, then carefully cut the kidneys into crosswise slices—done perfectly, a lovely pink at the center—mixed them in the chafing dish with the sauce, folded in the beef marrow, and then arranged them on two plates along with the braised artichokes from the oven.

"Bring the wine," he said, carrying the plates into the living area beyond the kitchen.

Fordyce followed reluctantly. "I'm telling you, ain't eating it. I don't do offal."

Gideon put the plates down on a low table before the leather sofa.

Fordyce took a seat on the sofa, stared sourly at his plate.

"Try it."

The agent lifted his knife and fork, poised them, hesitated.

"Go ahead. Be a man. If you don't like it, I'll get you a bag of Doritos from the kitchen."

He gingerly cut off a tiny piece with his fork, and tasted it suspiciously.

Gideon took a bite himself. Perfect. He wondered how anyone could resist.

"Guess it won't kill me," Fordyce said, placing a larger piece in his mouth.

For several minutes, the men ate in silence. Then Fordyce spoke again. "It seems funny, somehow, to be sitting out here, in the woods, eating dinner and drinking wine—which is excellent, by the way—when just yesterday we walked away from a plane crash. I feel like I've been, somehow, *renewed*."

This reminded Gideon of his diagnosis. And how he had spent his afternoon.

"How about you. Feel reborn?"

"No," said Gideon.

Fordyce paused, looked at him. "Hey—you all right?"

Gideon took a big gulp of wine. He realized he was drinking too quickly. Did he really want the conversation to go in this direction?

"Look, you want to talk about it? I mean, that was one hell of a scare."

Gideon shook his head, put down his glass. He had an overwhelming urge to talk about it.

"That's not the problem," he finally said. "I'm over that."

"So what is it?"

"It's that... every morning, first thing—I remember."

"Remember what?"

For a moment, Gideon did not reply. He didn't know why he'd said that. But no, that wasn't true: he'd said it for the same reason he'd invited Fordyce up to the cabin. Whether it was their shared investigation, or their mutual admiration for Thelonious Monk, or simply surviving yesterday's crash—he'd begun to look upon Stone Fordyce as a friend. Maybe—save, more or less, old Tom O'Brien back in New York—his only friend.

"I've been told I have a terminal illness," he said. "Every morning, I have about a minute or two of peace—and then I remember. That's why I don't feel reborn, renewed, whatever."

Fordyce stopped eating and looked at him. "You're shitting me."

Gideon shook his head.

"What is it? Cancer?"

"Something known as an AVM: a tangle of arteries and veins in the brain. Statistically, they say I've got around a year to live, give or take."

"There's no cure?"

"It's inoperable. Someday it's just going to...pop."

Fordyce sat back. "Jesus."

"That's where I was this afternoon. Getting another medical opinion. You see, I have reasons to doubt the first diagnosis. So I had an MRI."

"When will you get the results?"

"Three days." He paused. "You're the first person I've told this to. Didn't mean to lay a burden on you—it's just that...Jesus, I guess I had to tell someone. Blame it on the wine."

For a brief moment, Fordyce just looked at him. Gideon recognized the look: the man was wondering if he was being bullshitted or not. And then deciding he was not.

"I'm really sorry," Fordyce said. "I don't know what to say. My God, that's just awful."

"No need to say anything. In fact, I'd prefer it if you never mentioned it again. Anyway, it might all be horseshit. That's what this afternoon's tests will tell me."

"You'll let me know when you find out?" Fordyce asked. "One way or another."

"I will." He laughed awkwardly. "Great way to ruin a dinner party." He grabbed the bottle, refilled both their glasses.

"I've changed my mind," said Fordyce, a bit too heartily, eating the last of his kidneys. "I like kidneys. At least cooked à la Gideon."

They continued eating, the talk moving along more superficial paths.

At last, Gideon got up and put a Ben Webster CD on the stereo. "What's our next move in the investigation?"

"Sweat that pilot from the mosque."

Gideon nodded. "I'd like to go out to the movie ranch, check out Simon Blaine again."

"The writer? Oh yeah, no doubt he's a real desperado. Then we should go back to those crazy fuckers out at the ranch and kick some more ass. All those satellite dishes and high-tech equipment make me nervous. Not to mention hearing old lady Chalker's talk of a violent apocalypse."

"I'm not too keen on getting zapped again with a cattle prod."

"We go in with a SWAT team and haul Willis in by one testicle, along with those scumbags who assaulted us."

"Didn't you guys learn anything from Waco?"

"Better than wasting time with the writer."

"He's got a cute daughter."

"Oh *now* I get it," said Fordyce, with a laugh, pouring himself the last of the wine. "Investigating with your glands, I see."

"I'll get us another," said Gideon.

A Miles Davis CD and a second bottle of wine later, Gideon and Fordyce lounged in the cabin's living room. The sun had set, the evening had gotten chilly, and Gideon had started a fire, which crackled on the hearth, casting a firelight throughout the room.

"Best offal I've ever eaten," said Fordyce, raising his glass.

Gideon drained his glass. Putting it back on the table with a sloppy motion, he realized he was more than half drunk. "I've been meaning to ask you something."

"Shoot."

"Back in the plane, you kept muttering something about monkeys and pussy."

Fordyce laughed. "It's an aviation mnemonic. *Monkeys find pussy in the rain*. It's the checklist of things you have to do when an engine goes out: Mixture on rich, Fuel on, Pump, Ignition left and right, and so forth."

Gideon shook his head. "And here I thought it was the wisdom of the ages."

31

Stone Fordyce woke up to the theme song of *The Man from U.N.C.L.E.* He fumbled off his cell phone alarm with a curse and forced himself to sit up. He knew the pounding in his head was due to the wine, and he suspected the havoc in his stomach was from the damn kidneys he had eaten the night before.

He glanced at the clock: five AM. He had a routine report scheduled for seven thirty AM New York time, five thirty New Mexico time. That gave him half an hour to get his brain in order.

Ten minutes before the call, in the middle of shaving, his cell phone rang. With another curse, he wiped his hands and answered it.

"Am I speaking to Special Agent Fordyce?" The cool voice of Dr. Myron Dart was on the other end of the line.

"I'm sorry, I thought our conference call was for seven thirty," said Fordyce, irritated, wiping the shaving cream off the unshaven side of his face.

"The conference call has been canceled. Are you absolutely alone?"

"Yes."

"I have some information for you that has just come to my attention. Information of a . . . very sensitive nature."

The Circle Y Movie Ranch was located north of Santa Fe, in the Piedra Lumbre basin, a ten-thousand-acre ranch bisected by Jasper Wash and surrounded by mesas and mountains receding to the horizon. It was a hot June day, the high desert air clear and deep. The Circle Y was the most famous of the many so-called movie ranches surrounding Santa Fe, a working cattle ranch that also hosted a number of Western-style movie sets used by Hollywood studios in the making of films and television shows.

As Gideon drove along the winding ranch road, the image of a Western town rose from the plains, with a steepled church at one end and a classic Boot Hill graveyard at the other. A dusty main street ran the length of it. Approached from behind, however, it began to look a little strange, until the buildings proved themselves to be mere façades, braced into position by slapdash two-by-four scaffolding. Just beyond the ersatz village ran Jasper Creek, an intermittent stream, now dry, winding along a narrow arroyo between shelves of rock, dotted here and there with ancient cottonwoods.

It was a picture-perfect scene, everything painted gold in the early-morning sun, under sapphire skies. While the air was still cool, he could feel it was going to be a scorcher.

Gideon parked in a dirt lot at one side of the town in an area roped off for vehicles. He strolled toward the set. The place was bustling, with camera booms, cherry pickers, and lights rising above the ferment of activity, punctuated with the blast of megaphoned commands and people running hither and yon.

Most of the town had been roped off with plastic tape, and as Gideon approached the barrier a man with a clipboard intercepted him. "May I help you, sir?" he asked, blocking Gideon's way.

"I'm here to see Simon Blaine."

"Is he expecting you?"

Gideon removed his ID. "I'm with the FBI." He gave the man an ingratiating smile and, unable to stop himself, winked. *I could get used to this*, he thought.

The man took the ID and scrutinized it for a long time before handing it back. "What's it about?"

"Can't go into that."

"Mr. Blaine is occupied right now. Can you wait?"

"We're not going to have a problem here, are we?"

"Uh, no, absolutely not. But...let me go see if he's free."

The man bustled off. Gideon took the opportunity to duck under the tape and stroll into "town." The long main street ran between a saloon, livery stables, a general store, what appeared to be a whorehouse, a blacksmith's forge, and a sheriff's office. A tumbleweed rolled past, and Gideon noted that it was a real tumbleweed that had been spray-painted a golden yellow, and that it was being pushed along by a wind-machine parked behind a false façade. More painted tumbleweeds were stacked in a wire basket next to the machine, being released by a worker, one by one, with shouted instructions to the wind-man as to exactly where the tumbleweeds were to go.

A group of riders in Western garb came clip-clopping down the street on paint horses. The lead rider was Alida, her blond hair streaming behind her in the phony wind like a golden flame. She was dressed in full Western regalia: white shirt, leather vest, six-guns strapped on, woolly chaps, hat, boots—the works. She glanced his way, recognized him, and reined her horse to one side. With a frown she dismounted and came over, leading her horse by the reins.

"What are you doing here?" she asked crossly.

"Just checking in. Looking for your father."

"Please don't tell me you're still chasing that stupid lead."

"I'm afraid so," he said pleasantly. "Nice horse. What's his name?"

She crossed her arms. "Sierra. My father is *really* busy."

"Can't we do this in a nice, friendly way?"

She recrossed her arms and gave an irritated sigh. "How long do you want with him?"

"Ten minutes."

The man with the clipboard came back, his face creased with anxiety. "I'm very sorry, he just pushed his way in—"

Alida turned to him with a radiant smile. "I'm taking care of it." She turned back to Gideon, the smile vanishing as quickly as it came. "They're about to shoot the final sequence of *Moonrise* and they've got a big pyro scene coming up. Can't you wait until after that?"

"Pyro scene?"

"They're going to blow up and burn the town. Or at least a good part of it. The pyrotechnics are almost ready to go." She added after a moment, "You might enjoy it."

It would give him a little more time to hang around and ask her questions. If he could think of some. "How long will it take?"

She glanced at her watch. "About an hour. Once the explosions and fire start, it goes fast. You can talk to my dad afterward."

He nodded. "Fair enough." He glanced over her appraisingly. "You look like a star."

"I'm a stunt double."

"For anyone in particular?"

"The female lead, Dolores Charmay. She's playing Cattle Kate."

"Cattle Kate?"

"The only woman in the history of the West hanged for cattle rustling." Alida flashed him a brief smile.

"Ah. Now, that suits you. How many bad guys do you kill?"

"Oh, maybe half a dozen. I also have to gallop around, holler, fire my six-guns, ride through a curtain of fire, cause a stampede, get shot, and fall off my horse—the usual stuff."

A man came by, uncoiling a wire, two others behind wheeling a tank of propane. Behind the church, Gideon saw what looked like a giant gasbag being gingerly maneuvered into position.

"What's that?" he asked

"That's all part of the pyrotechnics. That gasbag will create a fireball. It looks spectacular, but there's no actual explosion. See, in the movie the bad guys have secretly stockpiled the town with arms and munitions, so a lot of great stuff is going to go off."

"Sounds dangerous."

"Not if it's done right. They've got a special pyro crew setting it up. Everything's planned and timed down to the last iota. It's as safe as a walk in the park. You just don't want to be *in* the town when it burns up—that's all."

She was warming to her subject and, to his relief, it seemed she was forgetting her dislike of him.

"And those things?" he asked, by way of encouragement. He pointed to some cylinders that were being buried in the ground.

"Those are flash pots. They're filled with an explosive mixture that goes off just like a bomb, shooting upward. Those lines over there go to nozzles and racks that release jets and sheets of burning propane to simulate building fires. You're going to love it when all this goes off—if you like explosions, that is."

"I love explosions," he said. "All kinds. In fact, one of the things I do at Los Alamos is design high-explosive lenses for nuclear implosion devices."

Alida stared at him, what little friendliness there was leaving her face. "How awful. You design nuclear *bombs*?"

He hastily changed the subject. "I only mention it because what you've got here isn't so different. I imagine all these pyrotechnics are connected to a central computer controller, which will fire them off in the right sequence."

"That's right. Once the sequence starts, they'd better be rolling, because there aren't any retakes and there's no turning back. If they miss the shot, a couple of million dollars' worth of pyrotechnics are wasted, not to mention most of the set." She slipped a pack of cigarettes from her breast pocket, shook one out, lit up.

"Um, should you be smoking here?"

"Absolutely not." She exhaled a long stream of smoke in his direction.

"Let me have one."

With a wry smile she slid one from her packet, lit it for him, flipped it, and inserted it between his lips.

A short, bowlegged, cranky-looking man with a shaved head came walking down the street on stubby legs, bawling in a megaphone. She held her cigarette behind her back and Gideon followed suit.

"Isn't that—?"

"Claudio Lipari. The director. A real Nazi."

Gideon noticed movement out of the corner of his eye and turned. A dozen sedans were arriving, bringing in a rolling cloud of dust, but instead of stopping in the parking lot they drove over the plastic tapes and continued on toward the town, fanning out as they came.

Lipari saw them. He stopped and stared, frowning.

"What's going on?" Alida asked.

"Crown Vics," said Gideon. "It's law enforcement."

The cars parked at the edges of town, surrounding the place. Doors opened and four men got out of each car—all wearing bulky blue suits leaving little doubt there was body armor underneath.

The director began walking toward the closest car, his face furious, waving them off with his arms and shouting, to no effect. The men in the blue suits came forward, spreading out, flashing their badges, moving in a well-coordinated action.

"Classic," said Gideon. "They're about to make an arrest. A big one." *Are they after Blaine?*

"God, no," said Alida. "Not right now."

To his surprise, Gideon saw Fordyce get out of the lead car. The FBI agent seemed to be scanning the area. Gideon waved his hand; Fordyce saw him and began walking over. His face looked grim.

"Something's wrong," said Gideon.

"This is unbelievable. This can't be about my father."

Fordyce arrived, face red, brow furrowed.

"What going on?" Gideon asked.

"I need to talk to you in private. Come over here." Fordyce pointed to Alida. "You move away, please."

Gideon followed Fordyce away from Alida and the bustling main street. They walked over to a quiet area behind one of the false façades. Gideon could see wires everywhere and a scattering of flash pots. Fordyce had his weapon out.

"You're making an arrest?" said Gideon.

Fordyce nodded.

"Who?"

The gun came up. "You."

32

GIDEON STARED FIRST at the pistol, and then at Fordyce. He glanced around and saw that, indeed, the blue suits were all in position, weapons drawn, blocking his avenues of escape.

"Me?" Gideon asked, incredulously. "What have I done?"

"Just turn around and put your hands on your head."

Gideon did as he was told, the butt of the cigarette still burning in his mouth. Fordyce began patting him down, removing his wallet, penknife, and cell phone. "You're quite the artist, aren't you?" Fordyce said. "A master manipulator. You and your friend Chalker."

"What the hell are you talking about?"

"You did a fine job of pretending to dislike the guy—and here it turns out you're best buddies, in with him from the beginning."

"I told you, I couldn't stand the bastard—"

"Right. All that stuff on your computer—frigging jihadist love letters almost."

Gideon's mind was moving a mile a minute. The cluster-fuck had turned into a veritable orgy of incompetence. This was truly incredible.

"You really had me going," Fordyce said. His voice had the bitter tone of a man betrayed. "That trip up to your cabin. Dinner and male bonding. And that sob story about your terminal illness. What a crock. This whole trip west was nothing but an intentional wild goose chase—I should have seen that on day one."

Gideon felt a surge of furious anger. He hadn't asked for this assignment. It had been forced on him. Already, he'd wasted a precious week of his life. And now this: he was probably going to spend the rest of his all-too-short life dealing with this bullshit—maybe even from the inside of a cell.

Screw 'em. What do I have to lose?

Fordyce finished patting him down. He grabbed one of Gideon's upraised arms by the wrist, jerked it behind him, slapped on the handcuffs. He reached up to grab the other wrist.

"Wait. The cigarette." Gideon plucked the smoldering butt from his lips—and tossed it into the flash pot adjacent to Fordyce.

It went off like a cannon, with a concussive boom that slammed both of them to the ground, followed by a huge outpouring of theatrical smoke.

Staggering to his feet, ears ringing, Gideon saw that his shirttail was on fire. The smoke engulfed them, swirling about in crazy billows. There was a sudden volley of shouts and cries.

He ran. Bursting out of the smoke bank, he saw Alida, back on her paint horse, staring at him. The blue suits were all beginning to converge—and their weapons were trained on him.

Another loud explosion took place, followed by a carronade of booms.

There was only one chance—one slim chance. He sprinted forward and leapt onto the back of Alida's horse.

"Ride!" he yelled, jamming his heels into the horse's flanks.

"What the *hell*—?" She reined in the horse.

But Gideon was on fire, and the horse, already spooked by the noise, wasn't going to wait. With a snort of terror he bolted, galloping down the street toward the church.

For just a second, Gideon got a glimpse of Simon Blaine, framed in the doorway of the sheriff's office, still as stone, looking at them with an indescribable expression on his face. Then Gideon began ripping off his burning shirt, popping all the buttons, searing his skin in the process while Alida screamed *"Get off my fucking horse!"* as she tried to get the panicked animal under control. Behind, he could hear another thunderous roar, followed by flash-booms, interspersed with shouting, the blue suits running this way and that, some racing for their cars, others pursuing him on foot. Now the entire town was starting to go up. People were fleeing in all directions, willy-nilly.

Alida swung back her fist and tried to bat him away, striking him in the chest, nearly dislodging him.

"Alida, wait—" he began.

"Get off my horse!"

A pair of Crown Vics were now coming after them, tearing down the disintegrating main street of the set, scattering cowboys and cameramen and spooking more horses. No way were they going to outrun those cars.

They galloped around the corner of the church, almost colliding with the huge pyro gasbag. Gideon saw the opportunity and took it—and jettisoned his burning shirt on top of the bag.

"Hang on!" he cried, gripping the edges of the saddle.

Almost instantly there was a tremendous *whoosh* and a wave of heat swept over them, a gigantic fireball engulfing the church. The edges of fire licked about them briefly as they raced on, singeing his hair with a crackle. The horse accelerated in a blind panic. The explosion triggered the rest of the F/X explosives, and World War III erupted behind them: terrific roars, bangs, blasts, flash-booms, soaring rockets. A glance backward from the galloping horse produced the tremendous sight of the entire town erupting in flames, balls of fire rising into the morning sky, buildings blasted into toothpicks, fireworks and rockets streaming up, people and horses knocked to the ground, the earth shaking.

Alida pulled one of her six-guns and began swinging it at him like a club, whacking him in the side of the head and bringing stars to his eyes. She prepared to swing again but Gideon grabbed her wrist and gave it a hard twist, sending the gun flying. And then, before she could stop him, he slapped the dangling, open end of the handcuff onto her wrist, shackling them together.

"You bastard!" she screamed, tugging at him.

"I fall, you fall. And we're both dead." He yanked the other six-gun out of her holster, disarming her, and shoved it into his belt.

"Bastard!" But the message had sunk in. She stopped trying to throw him off.

"Take us down the wash," he said.

"No way. I'm turning the horse around! I'm delivering you to the cops!"

"Please," he pleaded. "I've got to get away. I didn't do anything."

"Does it look like I give a shit? I'm taking you back, and I hope they lock up your ass and throw away the key!"

And then the FBI came to his rescue. He heard a volley of gunshots and a bullet whined past, others kicking up dust on either side. The damn idiots were shooting at them. They were going to kill them both rather than let him get away.

"What the hell?" Alida screamed.

"Keep going!" he cried. "They're shooting at us! Can't you see—?"

More shots.

"Holy shit, they really are," she said.

As if by magic, she had the horse under control. The animal was now running smoothly, purposefully. She pointed his head toward the edge of the rimrock above the creek. More bullets whizzed past. The horse ran for the edge, gathering speed to leap into the arroyo.

She glanced back. "Hang on, motherfucker."

33

GIDEON DESPERATELY GRIPPED the cantle of the saddle as the horse leapt off the rimrock and plunged down a steep, soft embankment, bounding down the slope in little more than a controlled fall. When the horse hit the bottom he staggered and skidded in the sand, throwing both riders forward, the three of them almost going down. But under Alida's expert handling, the animal recovered and she brought him to a halt, covered with sweat and trembling.

"We've got to keep going," Gideon said.

Ignoring him, Alida patted Sierra's neck, leaning over murmuring soothing words into his ear. In the background, Gideon could hear approaching cars, roaring and bouncing along the prairie above and beyond the edge of the canyon, out of sight.

She straightened up. "I'm surrendering you."

"They're going to shoot both of us."

"Not when they see me with a white flag." She grabbed her shirt and with one violent motion ripped it off, the snaps popping.

"Oh my," said Gideon.

"Fuck you." She held up the shirt, waving it as a white flag. Gideon made a grab for it but she stood up in the stirrups, holding it beyond his reach.

Gideon looked over his shoulder. He could hear the cars approaching the edge of the canyon, the big V8s roaring. There were shouts, slamming doors, and a head appeared above the rimrock about three hundred yards from them.

"We surrender!" Alida cried, waving the shirt. "Don't shoot!"

A shot rang out, kicking up sand in front of them.

"What the *hell?*" She waved the shirt frantically. "Are you blind? We give up!"

"They don't get it," Gideon said. "We'd better get out of here."

The horse began prancing as bullets kicked up sand around them. Thank God, Gideon thought, they were shooting with handguns. "Go, damn it!"

"Shit," Alida muttered, giving the horse her heels. Sierra took off. More heads began appearing along the south rim. They galloped along the dry bed of the wash, running the gauntlet as shots continued to ring out from above.

"Hang on." She dodged and weaved the horse as they thundered along, making a more difficult target. Shots whined by and Gideon hunched his back, expecting at any moment to feel a bullet hit home.

And yet—almost miraculously—within minutes they had outrun the shooters and were still in one piece. Alida slowed the horse to a canter, put her shirt back on, and they continued up the dry bed of the wash as it narrowed into a ravine between two steep hills, which—Gideon noted—would block any advance by FBI agents in cars.

She dropped down into a trot.

"We need to keep up the pace," Gideon said.

"I'm not killing my horse for you."

"They're shooting to kill, you realize."

"Of *course* I realize it! What in hell did you do?"

"They seem to think I'm one of the terrorists, the ones with the nuke."

"And are you?"

"Are you nuts? This investigation has been a balls-up from the beginning."

"They seem pretty damn convinced."

"You yourself said they were stupid."

"I said *you* were stupid."

"You never said I was stupid."

"Yeah, but I was thinking it. And you keep proving it."

The wash got steeper as it mounted the foothills of the Jemez Mountains, its bed strewn with black boulders. The horse picked his way among the rough terrain with care.

"Look, I'm no terrorist," Gideon said.

"I'm *so* reassured."

They rode in silence for half an hour as the wash climbed into the mountains, the terrain getting ever rougher, the piñon and juniper trees giving way to towering ponderosa pines. As the wash divided into tributaries, they took one after another, until they were in a maze of small ravines surrounded by slopes of heavy timber.

"Okay, here's what we're going to do," Alida said. "You're going to release me. I'll head back and you go on."

"I can't. We're cuffed together—remember?"

"You can break the chain. Pound it off with a rock."

After a moment, Gideon said, "Right now I can't let you go. I need your help."

"You mean, you need a hostage."

"I have to prove my innocence."

"I can't *wait* for that moment to turn you in."

They rode on in angry silence. The sun was now almost straight overhead.

"We need to find water," Alida said in a surly tone. "For my horse."

Past noon, they topped out on a high forested ridge that overlooked the valley behind them.

"Hold on," Gideon said. "I want to see what's happening below."

She halted the horse and Gideon turned around. Through the thick screen of trees he could see down into the grassy plains below. A huge cloud of smoke still billowed from the ruins of the movie set, with fire trucks parked all around, white jets of water arcing into the remains. His eye followed the course of Jasper Wash and there, at the beginning of the steep hills, he could make out rows of parked cars, people gathering, and what looked like a mass of searchers moving up the wash and fanning out. He could hear the faint baying of hounds.

Horses were being unloaded from a large stock trailer and riders were mounting up, forming a posse of sorts.

"That's some manhunt gearing up," said Alida. "And listen to that—choppers."

Sure enough, Gideon could hear a throbbing sound as three black specks resolved themselves in the distant blue sky.

"Wow, you are in some deep shit," she said.

"Alida, I don't know how to make you believe me, but I'm completely and totally innocent. This is a grotesque mistake."

She stared at him, then shook her head. "Those people down there don't think so."

They headed down from the ridge, made their way across another ravine, and then climbed steeply through stands of Douglas fir, enormous boulders and fallen timber impeding their progress. They found themselves traversing the hillsides, back and forth, trying to get around rocks and downed timber.

"We've got to lose the horse," said Gideon.

"No way."

"He's leaving too clear a track, and those dogs will be following the horse's scent trail. If we turn him loose, he'll divert them from us. And besides, the country's getting too rough for a horse."

"Forget it."

"If we let Sierra go, he'll get water sooner. There's no water in this part of the Jemez. Especially in June."

Alida was silent.

"He's exhausted. He's supporting two riders. He can't go on like this. Look at him."

Again she did not respond. The horse really was exhausted, soaking wet and all lathered up around his saddle skirts and breast collar.

"If they catch up to us, they just might shoot first, ask questions later. You saw what happened back there: those guys are so eager to kill me, they don't care about a little collateral damage."

They were working their way up a small tributary wash that ended in an enormous ridged mountainside, rising at steep angles all around them. There was no way to go but straight up.

Alida stopped the horse. "Get off," she said curtly.

They dismounted awkwardly, shackled together. She untied the saddlebags and tossed them to Gideon. "You carry these." She removed Sierra's bridle and reins, tied them securely to the saddle horn, and slapped the horse on the butt.

"Go," she said. "Get out of here. Go find yourself a drink."

The horse, puzzled, stared at her, ears pricked.

"You heard me. Git!" She slapped the horse again and he trotted off, stopping once again to look back in puzzlement. She picked up a stick, waved it. "Hyah! *Git!*"

The horse turned and ambled away down the canyon.

She spat and turned to Gideon. "Now I *really* hate you."

34

Aᴛᴛᴇʀ ᴀ ʟᴏɴɢ, arduous climb up the mountainside, in the late afternoon they topped the last ridge and found themselves looking across a wilderness of mountains and valleys, unbroken by roads or any sign of human life. They stopped to rest. From time to time Gideon had heard the throbbing of choppers, some passing fairly close overhead. But the forest was so dense that he'd been able to hide the two of them under thick vegetation before there was any chance they'd be spotted.

It was a vast area called the Bearhead: the remotest part of the Jemez Mountains. Gideon had fished the lower reaches of the Bearhead but had never been deep into it before. The sun was now setting, throwing the mountains into deep purple.

"A person could go in there and vanish forever," Alida said, squinting into the hazy distance.

"Right," said Gideon. He dropped the saddlebags and cleared his throat. "Excuse me, I'm afraid I have to pee."

She stared at him, her eyebrows arching in disdainful amusement. "Go ahead."

"Maybe you should turn around."

"Why? I didn't ask you to cuff us together. Go on, let's see what you've got."

"This is ridiculous." He unzipped his fly and peed, turning away from her as best he could.

"My, your face is red."

They descended a series of steep slopes, keeping to the cover of a gully, and found themselves in a heavy oak brush, forming an understory below towering firs and spruces. They pushed ahead, barely able to see where they were going, up and down precipitous slopes. It was hard travel, but they were well hidden.

"So what's the plan, Abdul?" Alida asked at last.

"That's not funny."

"As I see it, you're running from the combined law enforcement of the entire US of A, the sun is setting, you've got no shirt, we're in the middle of nowhere with no food and no water. And you don't have a plan. Wow."

"There are supposed to be some old mines in the Bearhead. We'll go to ground."

"Okay, we spend the night in a mine. And then?"

"I'm thinking, I'm thinking." *What would my old buddy Sergeant Dajkovic do in a situation like this?* he wondered to himself. Probably drop and do a hundred push-ups.

They hiked into the Bearhead, following elk trails that appeared and disappeared, until they came to the edge of a tiny meadow beside a dry creekbed. Beyond, partway up the hillside, stood the dark openings of several mines, with old shaft houses and tailing piles.

"Here's where we spend the night," Gideon said.

"I'm thirsty as hell."

Gideon shrugged.

He gathered handfuls of dry grass from the meadow and tied them into a tight bundle. They climbed up to the closest tunnel. At the mouth, he borrowed her lighter, lit the bundle, and then they moved cautiously into the passage, the firelight flickering over the massively timbered walls and ceiling. It was an old hard-rock tunnel that went straight into the hillside. He hoped to find signs of water, but it was as dry in the mine as it was in the creekbed outside.

The bottom of the mine was a bed of soft sand. Alida sat down and fished a cigarette out of her pocket, used the burning grass bundle to light it. She inhaled deeply, blew out a long stream of smoke. "What a day. Thanks to you."

"Um, may I—?"

"Unbelievable. You kidnap me, hold me hostage, get me shot at—and now you're bumming cigarettes."

"I never said I was perfect."

She held out a cigarette. "Give me the saddlebags."

He handed them to her and she unbuckled them, fished around, and took out two granola bars. She tossed him one, opened the other. Gideon took a bite, the crumbs clogging his dry mouth.

"Tomorrow, the first thing we do is find water," he said, gagging and putting the rest of the bar into his pocket.

They sat in silence for a while, in the dark, smoking.

"This is depressing," said Alida. "We need a fire."

They rose and went outside, filling their cuffed arms as best they could with dry pieces of oak. The sun had set and the air was now cool, stars sprinkling the sky. Gideon could hear, from time to time, the distant sound of choppers, but as the night deepened they faded away and all grew silent. He lit a small fire, the dry wood producing barely any smoke.

Alida yanked Gideon's cuff-chafed wrist. "Lie down. I'm going to sleep."

He lay down with her next to him, on their backs. For ten minutes, nobody spoke. Then Alida said: "Shit. I'm too upset to sleep. One moment I'm shooting a film, the next I'm shackled to a terrorist who's got the whole damn country after him."

"You don't really think I'm a terrorist. I hope."

A long silence. "I have to say, you don't look the type."

"You're damn right I'm not the type. There's been a ludicrous mistake."

"How do you know it's a mistake?" she asked.

Gideon paused. Fordyce's words came back to him. *You did a fine job of pretending to dislike the guy—and here it turns out you're best buddies, in with him from the beginning.* And then the craziest accusation of them all: *All that stuff on your computer—frigging jihadist love letters almost.*

"Jihadist love letters," he said out loud.

"What?"

"That's what the FBI agent who tried to arrest me said. That I had, quote, jihadist love letters, unquote, on my computer."

Another long silence.

"You know," Gideon went on, "you asked a very good question. Of course it wasn't a mistake. I've been *framed*."

"Oh yeah?" came the reply, in a voice laced with skepticism.

"First they tried to kill us by sabotaging our plane a few days ago. When that didn't work, they framed me."

"Why would anybody do that?"

"Because our investigation touched the person or group behind this." He thought a moment. "No, not touched—we must've scored a direct hit. Scared the shit out of someone. Sabotaging the plane, framing me—those are risky, desperate measures."

He paused, thinking.

"The question is, which computer of mine did they salt? I know it can't be my personal computer at the cabin—the entire hard disk is encrypted with an RSA 2048-bit key. Unbreakable. So they must have salted my computer up on the Hill."

"But isn't that a classified system?"

"That's just it. It's jacked into a highly classified, isolated network. But because of the security, the contents of every computer are accessible in their entirety to the network security officers and certain other officials. The network automatically logs everything and everyone on the system and records every keystroke, everything they do. So if someone monkeyed with my computer up at the lab, it would have to be an insider—*and it would be recorded.*"

In the dying glow of the fire, he could see Alida's eyes on him. "So what are you going to do about it?"

"Talk to Bill Novak. The network security officer. He's the guy with access to all the files."

"So you're going to have a nice chat. And he's just going to tell a wanted terrorist everything he needs to know."

"With that six-gun of yours pressed to his head, he will."

She laughed harshly. "You moron, it's a stage gun, loaded with blanks. Otherwise, I would've blown you right out of the saddle back there."

He slid it out of his belt, examined it, frowned. It was indeed loaded with blanks. "I'll think of something." He paused. "Anyway, we're going to Los Alamos."

"But that's across the Bearhead wilderness, twenty miles away!"

"You wanted a plan—you got it. And Los Alamos is the last place they'll think of looking for me."

35

Stone Fordyce paused, swiping the sweat from his brow, and checked his GPS. They were approaching an altitude of nine thousand feet, the ponderosa pines giving way to fir trees, the forest getting heavier. The powerful halogen beams of his men's flashlights swept through the trunks, casting stark shadows, and the pair of bloodhounds bayed their frustration at the pause. He held up his hand to listen, and all movement behind him ceased, the men falling silent. The dog handler hushed the dogs.

He knelt, examining the trail. It was getting fresher, the crumbled edges of dirt sharper and more defined. All day and through the evening they had steadily been gaining on the trail, and now they were very close: the dogs were frantic and straining at their leashes. Slowly he stood, keeping his hand up for silence and listening intently. Above the sighing of the wind in the trees he thought he could hear something else—the repeated sound of measured footfalls. The horse was moving laterally on the steep slope above them.

It was almost over.

"They're up there," he murmured. "Five-meter separation. Flank them on the right. Move!"

They exploded into action, the dogs baying loudly, the men fanning out and surging up the hill, weapons drawn. They were exhausted, but the closeness of their quarry gave them fresh energy.

Fordyce drew his own .45 and started up. Once again he felt a surge of self-blame. He should have seen it days ago. Gideon was a con artist par excellence—and he'd taken Fordyce for the ride of a lifetime. But all that was over now. Once they got Gideon, they'd make him talk and the plot would be blown open.

Make him talk. Screw the Geneva Convention—there was a live nuke out there. They would do what it takes.

Gasping but still pushing, they topped out on the ridge, Fordyce in the lead. The trail went right, and Fordyce jogged along it, keeping low and using the cover of the trees to good effect. The others surged behind.

He saw the glint of something ahead in the light, heard a flurry of movement, a shape moving in the trees. He threw himself behind a trunk, crouching, waiting—and a horse came into view, stamping and eyeing them nervously. The woman's paint horse.

Riderless.

The men fanned out, surrounding the nervous animal, which pranced about, flaring its nostrils and backing up.

Fordyce realized what had happened. A fury seized him for the moment before he got his breathing back under control. He rose, holstered his pistol.

"Lower the lights," he said evenly. "You're spooking it."

He approached the horse, hand out, and the horse came closer, nickering. He took the halter. The horse was missing its saddlebags, and the bridle had been tied to the saddlehorn. This was a horse that had been deliberately turned loose.

Once again, he had difficulty breathing and had to make an effort to hide his rage. It wouldn't do to show weakness in front of the men. As the men and dogs came up, he turned to them. "We've been following the wrong trail."

This was followed by a stunned silence.

"At some point back there, probably way back, they turned the horse loose and continued on foot. We've been following the horse. We'll have to backtrack and find where they turned off."

He looked around. His team consisted of NEST officers, some in bad physical shape, soaked with sweat. There were FBI agents detailed to NEST, the dog handler, and some local law enforcement that somehow managed to tag along. The group was too big.

"You—" He pointed to the least-fit local lawman—"and you, and you, take the horse back down. It's evidence, so keep chain of custody and turn it over to the forensic team."

He looked around. "We're going to have to move a *lot* faster. There are too many of us." He ruthlessly cut out some more deadwood, sending them back with the horse, waving away murmurs of protest.

Kneeling, he spread out the USGS topo maps, then took out the sat phone and dialed Dart. God, how he hated to make the call. As it rang, he looked around at the group he'd just dismissed, still standing around like cows. "What the hell are you waiting for? Get going!"

"Status." Dart's thin voice spoke, no preliminaries.

"We don't have him yet. They decoyed us away with the horse. We're going to have to backtrack."

A sharp exhale of displeasure. "So our choppers are in the wrong area?"

"Yes." Fordyce glanced at the map he'd spread out. "They should be redeployed deeper in the mountains. My guess would be an area called the Bearhead."

He heard a rustle of paper. Dart was looking at the same maps.

"We'll shift our aerial teams over there." A pause, then Dart asked: "What's his plan?"

"I'd guess he's just running. Simple as that."

"We need him. And there's something else. I've gotten reports of your people firing indiscriminately at them. This is totally unacceptable. We need them alive, damn it. We need to question them."

"Yes, sir. But they may be—probably are—armed. They're terrorists. The FBI rules of engagement are crystal clear that deadly force may be used in the case of preservation of life under the doctrine of self-defense."

"First of all, there's no proof that *she's* a terrorist. She may be...temporarily under his influence. And as for the rules of engagement, you deliver me two dead bodies and I will be very, very unhappy. Is that understood?"

"Yes, sir," said Fordyce, swallowing.

"Agent Fordyce, the only reason you're where you are right now is because I don't have anyone else on scene. Just you and twelve other special agents who were unable to make a simple collar. And who can't find him despite overwhelming advantages in manpower and equipment. So I ask you: are you going to get him or not?"

Fordyce stared hotly into the darkness of the mountains. "We're going to get him, sir."

36

A PALE LIGHT APPEARED in the mouth of the cave. Gideon raised his head. His mouth felt like damp chalk, his lips dry and cracking, and his bare back ached from sunburn. Propping himself on his elbow, he looked at Alida, still sleeping, her blond hair spread across the sand. As he gazed at her, she opened her eyes.

"We'd better get going," he said.

"No." Her voice was husky from disuse.

Gideon stared at her.

"Not until you take off these cuffs."

"I told you, I don't have a key."

"Then lay the links on a rock and pound them off. If we're going to find water, we've got to split up."

"I can't risk you running off."

"Where am I going to run to? Anyway, in case you hadn't noticed, I believe you. Look at you. You're no terrorist."

He glanced back at her. "What changed your mind?"

"If you were a terrorist," she went on, "you would have tried to use that fake six-gun on me as soon as I'd served my purpose. No— you're just some schmuck who was in the wrong place at the wrong time. So can we *please* take these damn cuffs off?"

Gideon grunted. He certainly wanted to trust her. "I'll need a piece of stiff wire and a knife."

She plucked a small knife and a thin key ring from a pant pocket, the latter of which he quickly straightened out. Then, using the key ring as a pick and the tip of the penknife as a tension wrench, he sprang the simple lock in a matter of thirty seconds or so.

"You lied to me. You could've picked that lock anytime."

"I had to trust you first." He looked around, picked up two empty beer cans—no doubt left by hunters—and stuffed them into his pockets. The cans would come in handy when and if they found water.

"Anything more of value in those saddlebags?" he asked.

"Why?"

"Because I'm not carrying them any farther."

She dug out a lighter and a few candy bars and slipped them into her pockets. Then they exited the mine and started walking south, staying to the wooded ravines and valleys as much as possible, moving apart but keeping each other in sight. They looked for water but found no sign. It was June, before the summer rains: the driest time in New Mexico.

The dry washes eventually came together into a deep ravine with sheer granite walls. As they climbed down it, Gideon heard the sound of an approaching chopper; moments later a fast-moving Black Hawk passed less than two hundred feet above them, doors open, M143 guns mounted left and right. It swept away and vanished beyond the walls of the ravine.

"Jesus, did you see those guns?" Alida said. "You think they'd shoot us?"

"They've already tried."

At noon, they finally found water: a small puddle at the bottom of a pour-off. They threw themselves down and lapped up the muddy fluid. Then they lay back in the shade of the overhang. As the water settled their thirst, a raging hunger took hold.

After a few minutes, Gideon roused himself and gobbled down the rest of the granola bar. "What about those candy bars?"

She pulled out two Snickers bars, which had melted in the heat. He tore the wrapper off one end of his and pressed the bar into his mouth, like toothpaste, swallowing as fast as he could.

"More?" he asked, his mouth still half full.

"That's all." Her own face was smeared with chocolate and mud.

"You look like a two-year-old the morning after Halloween."

"Yeah, and you look like her snot-nosed baby brother."

They filled the old beer cans with water and continued on, exiting the far end of the ravine and climbing another ridge.

As the day wore on, the chopper traffic increased, along with occasional fixed-wing aircraft flying in patterns. He had no doubt their pursuers were using infrared and Doppler radar, but the intense heat of the day—and the heavy tree cover—kept them safe. By late afternoon they were approaching the southern end of the Bearhead, an area that Gideon started to recognize.

At sunset, they finally reached the end of the mountains. They crept up to the top of the last ridge and—falling to their bellies and peering through the cover of a thicket of brush oaks—looked down on the town of Los Alamos, home of J. Robert Oppenheimer, the Manhattan Project, and the atomic bomb.

Despite its remarkable past—at one time its very existence had been top secret—Los Alamos looked like any other government town, ugly and generic, with fast-food joints, prefab apartment complexes, and nondescript office buildings. What made it different was its spectacular setting: the town and labs spread out on a series of isolated mesas projecting from the flanks of the Jemez Mountains. At over seven thousand feet, it was one of the highest-altitude cities in the United States. Originally chosen for its inaccessibility and remoteness, it was surrounded by sheer thousand-foot cliffs on one side and cut off by lofty mountains on the other. Gideon could just see, beyond the town, the immense crack in the earth known as White Rock Canyon, at the bottom of which, flowing unseen, the Rio Grande roared through a series of rapids and cataracts.

To the south of town Gideon could make out the major Tech Areas, heavily fenced areas dotted with huge, warehouse-like buildings. The look of the place caused him to shiver. Was it really the sanest idea to break in there? But he could see no alternative. Someone had framed him. He had to find out who.

He rolled on his side and took a long drink from the dirty beer can. He handed it to Alida. "As I hoped, the air search seems to be sticking mostly to the north."

"So what now? Cut the fence?"

He shook his head. "That's no normal fence. It's loaded with infrared sensors, motion sensors, pressures, alarm circuits—and there are video cameras hidden along its length. Even if we did get through, there are other, invisible rings of security I know nothing about."

"Cute. So we find a gap, go around?"

"There are no gaps. The security in the Tech Areas is pretty much fail-safe."

"Seems you're shit out of luck, Osama."

"We don't have to evade security. We'll go right in through the front gate."

"Yeah, right, with you at the top of the FBI's most wanted list."

He smiled. "I don't think I am. At least not yet. They have every reason to keep their pursuit of me secret. They think I belong to a terrorist cell—why broadcast to the cell that I've been identified, that I'm on the loose?"

Alida frowned. "I still think it's insanely risky."

"There's only one way to find out." And he rose to his feet.

37

THERE WERE NO floor buttons in the elevator, just a key, and an armed marine to operate it. Dart entered the elevator; the marine, who knew him well, still carefully checked his ID—knowing Dart would reprimand him if he didn't—then grasped the key and gave it a single turn.

The elevator descended for what seemed forever. As it did, Dr. Myron Dart took a moment to collect his thoughts and take stock.

As N-Day approached, entire sections of Washington had been evacuated and secured by large numbers of troops. Every square inch had been searched and re-searched with dogs, radiation monitors, and by hand. Meanwhile, the country held its collective breath, speculating endlessly on just where in Washington Ground Zero might be.

Many across the country were fearful that the massive response in DC would force the terrorists to pick another target. As a result, other large American cities, from LA to Chicago to Atlanta, were in a panic, with residents fleeing, tall buildings emptying out. There had been riots in Chicago, and citizens had pretty much evacuated themselves from anywhere near Millennium Park and the Sears Tower. New York City was a mess, with entire swaths of the city abandoned. The stock market had lost fifty percent of its value and Wall Street had shifted most of its trading operations to New Jersey. A long list of American landmarks had become shunned, with nearby residents fleeing—from the Golden Gate Bridge to the Liberty Bell. Even the

Gateway Arch in St. Louis was generating panic. It had become a theater of the absurd.

Along with the speculation and panic came the inevitable recriminations over the stalled investigation. NEST had come under a tidal wave of criticism, second-guessing, and public furor. They said it was incompetent, chaotic, disorganized, choking in bureaucracy.

Much of the criticism, Dart had to admit, was valid. The investigation had taken on a life of its own, a Frankenstein, a *lusus naturae* not subject to central control. He was not surprised. *It was, indeed, inevitable.*

The marine glanced at him. "Excuse me, sir?"

Dart suddenly realized he had murmured out loud. God, he was tired. He shook his head. "Nothing."

The elevator doors whisked open onto a passageway carpeted in blue and gold. A wall clock announced eleven PM, but this deep underground, under these circumstances, time of day had become essentially meaningless. As Dart stepped out, two more marines appeared, flanking him and leading him down the corridor. They passed a room full of people sitting at a monstrous wall of computer screens, all talking simultaneously into headsets; another room that contained a podium with the presidential seal, television cameras, and a bluescreen. There were conference rooms, a small cafeteria, temporary military barracks. Finally, they reached a closed door with a desk placed before it. A man behind the desk smiled as they drew near.

"Dr. Dart?" he asked.

Dart nodded.

"Go right in. He's expecting you." The man reached into a drawer and pressed something; there was a buzz and the door behind him sprang ajar.

Dart stepped through the door. The president of the United States sat behind a vast, unadorned desk. Two miniature American flags stood at opposite ends of it. Between them was a row of phones in various bright colors, like something you might see in a playroom. On a side wall were half a dozen monitors, each tuned to a different station, their audio output muted. The president's chief of staff stood silently to one side, hands folded in front. Dart exchanged nods with the chief, who was famously taciturn, and then turned his attention to the man behind the desk.

Beneath the renowned thatch of jet-black hair and the bushy eyebrows, the president's eyes looked sunken, almost bruised. "Dr. Dart," he said.

"Good evening, Mr. President," Dart replied.

The president swept one hand toward a pair of sofas that faced his desk. "Please sit down. I'll take your report now."

The door to the room was quietly shut from the outside. Dart took a seat, cleared his throat. He had brought no folder, no set of notes. Everything was burned into his mind.

"We have only three more days until the anticipated attack," he began. "Washington is as secure as is humanly possible. All resources, agencies, and personnel have been mobilized in this effort. Army checkpoints have been set up on all roads leading in or out of the city. The writ of habeas corpus has, as you know, been temporarily suspended, allowing us to take into custody anyone for almost any reason. A holding and processing facility for detained persons has been erected, on the Potomac just up from the Pentagon."

"And the evacuation of the civilian population?" the president asked.

"Complete. Those who wouldn't go have been taken into custody. We've had to keep the regional hospitals open, with skeleton staffs, for those patients who simply cannot be moved. But those are few."

"And the status of the investigation?"

Dart hesitated a moment before replying. This was going to be rough. "Nothing new of importance since my last briefing. Very little progress has been made on identifying the group or where the nuclear device is located. We have not been able to narrow down the actual target—that is, beyond the several already noted."

"What about the possible threat to other cities? Of the terrorists shifting their target?"

"Again, we have no useful information on other targets, sir."

The president erupted to his feet, started pacing. "By God, this is unacceptable. What about this terrorist still on the loose? Crew?"

"Unfortunately, Crew continues to evade our men. He escaped into the mountains and my men now have him trapped in a vast wilderness area where at least he can do no harm, where there's no cell coverage, no roads, no way for him to make contact with the outside world."

"Yes, but we need him! He could name names, he could name targets! Damn it, man, you people have to find him!"

"We're deploying massive assets into the search. We'll find him, Mr. President."

The president's slender figure swept from one side of the room to the next, turning briskly as he paced. "Tell me about the nuke itself. What more do we know?"

"The Device Working Group continues to disagree about how to interpret the patterns of radiation, the isotope ratios, the fission products they've detected. There are anomalies, it seems."

"Explain."

"The terrorists had access to the highest level of engineering expertise—Crew and Chalker were two of Los Alamos's most knowledgeable experts on nuclear weapons design. The question is how good their *fabrication* of the supposed weapon was. The actual machining of the bomb parts, the assembly, the electronics, is a very, very exacting business. Neither Chalker nor Crew had that kind of engineering expertise. Some in the Device Working Group feel the bomb they made might be so big, it could only be carried around in a car or a van."

"And you? What do *you* think?"

"I personally believe it's a suitcase bomb. I believe we have to assume they had engineering expertise beyond Chalker and Crew."

The president shook his head. "What more can you tell me about it?"

"The two sections of the charge have been well separated and shielded since the accident, as we can't find any trace of radiation anywhere. Washington is a sprawling city, spread out over a large area. We're dealing with the proverbial needle in a haystack. The very best assets from local, state, federal, and military resources have been tapped, and we've drawn heavily from all the many military bases near Washington. The city, quite literally, is crawling with troops, forming a massive dragnet."

"I see," the president said. He thought for a moment. "And what about the idea that all your effort might just cause the terrorists to divert the weapon to a less hardened target? The whole country's in a state of panic—and rightfully so."

"Our people have discussed that question at length," Dart replied. "It's true that there are many other targets that might prove attractive. But the fact is, all the indications we have are that the terrorists are fixated on Washington. Our experts on the psychology of jihadism tell us the symbolic value of the attack is far more important than numbers of people killed. And that means an attack on America's capital. I continue to believe myself, quite strongly, that Washington remains their target. Of course, we're assuming nothing, and assets in every major American city have been activated. But I think it would be a serious, *serious* mistake to draw additional assets from Washington to counter some purely hypothetical risk in another city."

The president nodded again, more slowly. "Understood. However, I want your people to identify a specific list of iconic targets in other cities and form a plan of protection for each one. Look, the American people have already voted on a list of targets with their feet—so get to work. Show them we mean to protect everything. Not just DC."

"Yes, Mr. President."

"You think with all this, they'll change the date?" the president asked.

"Anything's possible. In our favor is the fact that the terrorists don't know we've figured out the date. We've managed to keep that secret from the press and the public."

"And it had better stay secret," the president said. "Now, is there anything else I should know at the present time?"

"I can't think of anything, sir." He glanced at the chief of staff, who remained in the background, imperturbable.

The president stopped pacing and fixed Dart with a tired look. "I'm well aware of the torrent of criticism falling on you and the investigation. They're beating the hell out of me, too. And in many ways the investigation *is* massive and unwieldy and duplicative. But you and I both know this is the way it has to be; this is the way Washington works, and we can't change horses in the middle of a race. So carry on. And Dr. Dart, before our next briefing—in fact, as soon as possible— I'd like to hear that you've captured Gideon Crew. It seems to me this individual is the key to breaking the investigation."

"Yes, Mr. President."

By way of dismissal, the president offered Dart a smile—a tense, exhausted smile with neither warmth nor humor in it.

38

THE WILDERNESS ENDED and Los Alamos began as if someone had drawn a line, the trees suddenly giving way to a typical suburban neighborhood with ranch houses, postage-stamp lawns, play sets and kiddie pools, blacktopped driveways sporting station wagons and mini vans.

From the cover of the fringe of trees, Gideon stared across a dark lawn at one mini van in particular, an old 2000-model Astro. It was eleven o'clock at night, but the house was still dark. Nobody was home. In fact, as he looked around, he noted that almost all the houses were dark; an air of desertion, even desuetude, hung over the place.

"This is making me nervous," said Alida.

"There's nobody here. Looks like they've all left."

He walked boldly across the lawn, Alida following a few steps behind. They gained the side of the house and he turned back to her. "Wait here a moment."

There was no sign of a burglar alarm, and it was the work of two minutes—and long experience—to slip inside and assure himself the house was empty. Finding the master bedroom, he helped himself to a crisp new shirt that almost fit. He combed his hair in the bathroom, then grabbed some fruit and some sodas from the kitchen and went back to where Alida was waiting.

"I hope you're not too nervous to eat," he said, handing her an apple and a Coke. She bit ravenously into the apple.

Rising from a crouch, Gideon walked to the breezeway and got into the car. The keys were not in the ignition or the center console. He got out, opened the hood.

"What are you doing?" Alida mumbled through the apple.

"Hot-wiring it."

"Jesus. Is this another one of your little 'skills'?"

He closed the hood, got back in the driver's seat, started dismantling the steering column with a screwdriver he'd found in the glove compartment. A few moments later everything was ready, and with a cough the car started up.

"This is crazy. They're going to shoot us on sight."

"Get down on the floor and cover yourself with that blanket."

Alida got into the backseat and lowered herself out of sight. Without another word, Gideon backed out of the driveway and drove down the street. He soon found himself on Oppenheimer Drive, heading past Trinity, on his way to the Tech Area main gate. The town was deserted, but even this late in the evening, with a nuclear threat hanging over the country, work proceeded at Los Alamos. As they approached the gate, Gideon made out the brilliant sodium lights, the two armed guards in their pillboxes, the cement barriers, the always-friendly security officer.

There was a car ahead of them being checked through. Gideon slowed, stopped, waited. He hoped the guard wouldn't look at him too closely—his shirt was clean, of course, but his pants were a muddy mess. His heart was pounding like mad in his chest. He told himself that there was no reason for the FBI to publicize his name; no reason to notify Los Alamos security, considering that was the last place he'd go; and every reason to keep his identity secret while they hunted him down.

Then again, what if Alida was right? What if they had put out an APB on him? As soon as he reached the gate they'd nail him. This was crazy. He had a car—he should just turn around and get the hell out of there. He began to panic and threw the car into reverse, getting ready to stomp on the accelerator.

The car ahead went through.

Too late. He eased the car back into drive and pulled up, plucked his Los Alamos ID from around his neck and handed it to the guard…

The guard nodded to him nonchalantly, clearly recognizing him, took it, and went inside. That wasn't what normally happened. Had the man recognized the car as not belonging to him?

Once again Gideon shifted the car into reverse, his foot hovering over the gas pedal. There was no car in line behind him. If he blasted back out, he might reach the turnoff to the back road to Bandelier before they organized a chase. Then he'd ditch the car at the Indian ruins of Tsankawi and cross the San Ildefonso Indian Reservation on foot.

God, it was taking forever. He should go now, before the alarms went off.

And then the security guard appeared with a smile and the card. "Thanks, Dr. Crew. Here's your card. Working late, I see."

Gideon managed a smile. "The grind never stops."

"Ain't it the truth." And the man waved him through.

Gideon parked in the rear of the lot for Tech Area 33, where he worked. It was an enormous, warehouse-like building of white stucco and Pro-Panel. The building housed the offices and labs of part of the Stockpile Stewardship Team, along with access to the underground test chambers and a small linear accelerator for probing aging bomb fuel and other fissile materials.

In the dark of the car, Gideon checked the phony six-gun. It was a replica of an old Colt Model 1877 double-action revolver, nickel-plated, and fully loaded with blanks. Blanks or not, he hoped he wouldn't have to use it.

He shoved it into his waistband and covered it with his shirt. "We're here."

Alida threw off the blanket and rose. "Is that it? No more security?"

"There are other rings of security but not, at least, to visit an office." He checked his face in the mirror—not exactly clean, and not exactly shaven. He was known around his department as a slapdash dresser, so he hoped his present disheveled state would not be noted. Most of the physicists, it had to be said, were infamously sloppy; it was sort of a badge of honor.

He got out of the car. They walked through the parking lot and around toward the front of the building.

"Is this Bill Novak you told me about, the network security guy, going to be in?" Alida asked. "It's after eleven."

"Probably not. But there's always someone in the security office. Tonight it'll probably be Warren Chu. At least I hope so. He's not likely to give us much trouble."

They entered the building. An L-shaped hall ran through the front section; the labs were in the back and below ground. Gideon walked slowly, working on his breathing, trying to stay calm. He turned the corner and came to a closed door, knocked.

"Yeah?" came a muffled voice from inside. The door opened. Chu stood there, a round, smooth fellow with glasses and a cheerful expression. "Hey, Gideon. Where you been?"

"Vacation." He turned. "This is Alida—she's new. I'm showing her around."

The round face turned to Alida and the smile broadened. "Welcome to Mars, Earthling."

Gideon let his own expression turn serious. "Can I come in?"

"Sure. Is there a problem?"

"Yeah. A big one."

Chu's face fell as Gideon stepped aside. They walked into his tiny, windowless office. Chu swept the only extra chair clear, eyeing Gideon's muddy pants but not commenting on them. Alida sat down, Gideon stood. He smelled coffee and spied a box of Krispy Kreme donuts. He was suddenly starving.

"You mind?" He sidled up to the box, tipping it open.

"Be my guest."

Gideon took a glazed cruller and a New York cheesecake. He caught Alida's glance and took another two for her. He stuffed the cruller into his face.

"So what's up?" Chu looked annoyed at seeing four of his donuts vanish so quickly.

Gideon swallowed with effort, wiped the crumbs from his mouth. "It seems somebody used my computer while I was on vacation.

Hacked into it. I don't know how they bypassed my password, but they did. I want to know who."

Chu's face paled and he lowered his voice. "Jesus, Gideon, you know you've got to report that through proper channels. You can't come here. I'm just the tech guy."

Gideon lowered his voice. "Warren, I came to you because whoever did this seems to have it in for you."

"Me?" Chu's eyebrows shot up in astonishment.

"Yeah, you. Look—I know you didn't do it. But whoever did it plastered your picture on my screen, giving me the finger. And a cute little poem: *Warren Chu says Fuck you too.*"

"Are you serious? Oh my God, I can't believe it. Why would someone do that to me? I'll kill him, I swear I will." Chu was already turning to his monitor. "When did this happen?"

Gideon considered the time line. He had to have been framed at some point between the plane crash and his attempted arrest. "Between, um, four days ago and very early yesterday morning."

"Wow," Warren said, staring at his screen. "Your account's been frozen. And they never told me!"

"That's because they *suspect* you."

Chu practically pulled at his long hair. "I can't believe it. Who would do this?"

"Is there any way to get into my account and take a look around? Maybe we could figure out who did it, you know, before it gets out and security comes down on you like a ton of bricks."

"Hell, yes. I have the clearance to override this. If they haven't taken *that* away."

Gideon's heart quickened. "Really?"

"Sure." Chu's fingers were beating a furious tattoo on the keyboard. "How'd the hacker get your password?"

"I was hoping you'd tell me."

"You write it down somewhere?"

"Never."

"You ever log on in front of anyone?"

"No."

"Then it would have to be someone with high-security clearance."

Gideon watched intently as a series of numbers scrolled by on the screen, faster and faster. Chu was the very picture of nerdy outrage.

"Gonna find the mother," said Chu, clicking away. "Gonna find the mother... There—I've broken into your account!"

A final, triumphant rap of the keyboard and Gideon stared at the screen. It showed his post-login home page. Where would the incriminating "jihadist love letters" be?

"Let's check my email," he said.

Chu continued typing, and Gideon's secure email account popped up. Again Chu was forced to override the locked-up account.

Looking at the mass of emails, Gideon had an idea. "Are there any to or from Chalker?"

"Reed Chalker?" Chu seemed uneasy, but typed in the request. A list popped up, dating back to the months before Chalker disappeared. Gideon was stunned by the number of messages; he couldn't remember ever having corresponded with Chalker.

"Looks like you guys had a lot to talk about," said Chu. "How's this supposed to help us find the hacker?"

"Those emails were planted," said Gideon. "Planted by the hacker."

"Yeah?" Chu sounded doubtful. "That would have been quite a job."

"I never emailed Chalker. Well, hardly ever." Gideon reached past Chu, bent over the keyboard, highlighted a year-old email innocuously titled "vacation," and hit the ENTER key.

Salaam Reed,

To answer your question: you remember what I said about the world being divided into Dar al-Islam and Dar al-Harb—the House of Islam and the House of War. There is no middle ground, no halfway place. You, Reed, have now personally entered the House of Islam. Now the real struggle begins—with the House of War you left behind.

Gideon stared in disbelief. He'd never written that. It didn't just make him look like a co-conspirator with Chalker; it made him look like his *recruiter*. He quickly opened the next.

> My friend Reed, Salaam:
> Jihad is not just an internal struggle, but it's also external. There can be no peace for you as a good Muslim, no cessation of struggle, until all the world becomes Dar al-Islam.

He began paging forward through the emails. This was clearly a complex, highly sophisticated and exhaustive fraud. No wonder Fordyce had been taken in. He noticed a more recent email, opened it.

> The time is now. Do not hesitate. If someone receives the message of Islam and dies rejecting it, they are forever destined to Hellfire. Anyone who truly believes in the message, their previous sins are forgiven and they will spend eternity in Paradise. If you have belief, act on it. Do not worry what anyone else thinks. Your eternal life is at stake.

It continued in a similar vein, persuading Chalker to convert. Gideon read on with mounting outrage. Not only had he been framed, but he had been framed in a most sophisticated fashion—*by someone on the inside*.

39

W ARREN CHU GAZED at the emailed messages with growing horror and disbelief. These were not planted. How could they be? Nobody but a chief security administrator could do that.

He slowly turned and looked at Gideon, staring at him, as if seeing him for the first time. A thought went through his mind: you just never could see inside another person. He never would have guessed.

"I can't believe you wrote this," he burst out, almost without thinking.

"Damn it, Warren, I didn't," Gideon told him forcefully. "Those emails were planted!"

Chu was taken aback by his vehemence. Again, he wondered how such a thing could be done. It seemed highly unlikely. Not only that, but that business about himself being targeted as well? It was starting to smell phony.

He cleared his throat, tried to sound normal. "Right. Okay. Let me work on this for a while. See if I can figure out who did this, and how."

"You're a real pal, Warren." Gideon crammed the rest of the cheesecake donut into his mouth.

A beat. "Gideon, um, would you mind? I can't work with someone staring over my shoulder."

"Right. Sorry."

Gideon retreated to the other side of the office, at the same time—Chu noted with irritation—helping himself to yet another donut. The guy acted as if he hadn't eaten in days.

Chu opened another email, then another. This was scary stuff. The secure network ran as a Type II Virtual Machine environment: was it possible somebody had leveraged the VM monitor, maybe gained root access or swapped out the guest OS, then planted a keylogger or compromised the secure login feature somehow? It was theoretically possible—but it would take more skill than Chu himself had.

The more he thought about the robustness of the VM architecture, the isolated address spaces, and the virtual memory abstraction, the more difficult the hack seemed. And he had always thought Gideon just a little too independent...sketchy, even. But that meant—if these emails hadn't been planted—that Gideon was a terrorist, a traitor to his country, a potential mass murderer...Chu, overwhelmed by the thought, felt his bowels loosening.

What in God's name should he do?

Suddenly he realized that the woman who had come in with Gideon, the new employee, had come up behind him. He jumped as she laid a hand on his shoulder and squeezed, hard enough to send a message. He glanced up, looked around. Gideon was at the door now, looking out, left and right, down the halls, keeping a lookout. For the first time, Chu noticed a handgun stuffed into the waistband of his pants.

She leaned over him and whispered. "If you've got an alarm, activate it. Now."

"What?" Chu didn't quite understand.

"Gideon's with them. The terrorists."

Chu swallowed. Confirmation.

"Just do it and keep cool."

Chu felt unreality take hold. His heart surged in his chest and he felt the sweat glands on his face prickle. First Chalker, now Gideon. Unbelievable. But there were the emails, staring him right in the face—practically a smoking gun.

Casually, he reached beneath the desk, found the button, pressed it. He'd never done this before and wasn't sure what would happen.

A low siren went off. In the hallway, red lights began to flash.

"What the *hell?*" Gideon spun away from the doorway.

"Sorry, pal," said the woman, turning toward Gideon and crossing her arms in front of her. "You're busted."

40

GIDEON STARED AT her in disbelief. Surely he must have misheard or misunderstood something. "Alida, what are you doing?"

She turned to him, poised and collected. "I've been waiting for my opportunity. I told you I couldn't wait to turn you in. Remember?"

For the moment he was too shocked to feel any anger.

"You almost had me believing you back there," she said. "But when I saw those emails—"

"They were *planted!*"

"Yeah. And all those FBI agents, all those choppers, everyone shooting at you—I suppose that's all just a mistake, too. It's just too much to believe, Gideon. I'm not that gullible."

Gideon heard footsteps pounding down the corridor. He quickly drew the six-gun, fired it once into the air. Then he grabbed Chu's arm, turned his arm behind his back, and put the gun to his head. "Out," he barked. "Into the hall."

With a gasp of fear Chu scrambled to obey.

"The gun's a fake!" Alida cried, chasing after them.

"Trust me, it's real!" Gideon said. "Don't make me kill him!"

Gideon pushed Chu ahead of him, at a jog. The high-security checkpoint to the inner labs was just down the hall. They rounded the corner and came to the checkpoint, with two metal detectors and several guards—all of whom had their own weapons drawn.

"He's a dead man if you stop me!" Gideon shouted, shoving Chu through the metal detector, which went off with a shrill alarm.

"It's a stage gun, you idiots!" Alida yelled.

"You want me to prove it's real? If you follow, I shoot!" He continued on, thrusting Chu down the hall to the emergency stairs. He slammed open the door with his shoulder and dragged Chu down the stairs with him. The only person to follow was Alida.

"Bitch!" Gideon said as Alida threw herself on his back and tried to grab his gun. He knocked her aside but she came back at him again, punching him, again trying to rip the gun out of his hand.

"Stop it!" yelled Chu.

Gideon twisted away, pushing Chu through the doors at the bottom of the stairs and into the particle accelerator control room. Two operators stood there, at the large semicircle of monitors and instrumentation, staring in shock.

Gideon again heard the pounding of feet in the corridor outside.

"On the floor! Everyone!" He fired the gun into the ceiling.

The operators dove to the floor. Funny, Gideon thought grimly, how the makers of some of the world's most fearful weapons were in reality a bunch of rabbits.

Seconds later half a dozen security officers burst in, weapons drawn. They were not Los Alamos security—they were all wearing NEST uniforms.

"Drop the gun!" one shouted as they all leveled their weapons at him.

Gideon pulled Chu around as a shield, the gun pressed to the man's head. Chu issued an inarticulate croak.

"He's got a fake gun, damn it!" Alida cried.

The lead security officer swiveled around, leveling his gun at Alida. "You!" he yelled. "On the floor! Now!"

"Me? What the—"

With a jerk of his head, the officer signaled to two others, who immediately tackled her, slamming her to the ground. They began searching her roughly.

"Son of a *bitch*!" she screamed, writhing on the ground.

"Quiet!" One of the men struck her in the face.

Gideon couldn't believe it. They really thought she was a terrorist, too.

The NEST leader turned his gun back at Gideon. "Drop your weapon and release your hostage—or we open fire."

Gideon realized that, Chu or no, they weren't kidding: they would shoot right through Chu to nail him, if necessary.

"All right," he said.

It was over. He lowered the gun from Chu's head and held it out, letting it drop to the floor. Chu scrambled up and away, behind the guards. Slowly, Gideon raised his hands.

The two guards jerked Alida back up, their search completed. Blood poured from her nose, spotting her white shirt.

"Cuff her," the NEST leader said. "And you: Crew. Facedown on the ground. Slowly."

"Morons!" Alida yelled, trying to kick one of them. One of the guards struck her in the stomach, doubling her over.

"Leave her alone, she had nothing to do with it!" Gideon said.

"On the ground!" the man shouted at Gideon, leveling his gun.

Keeping his hands out, Gideon began to kneel—and that was when he saw an opportunity. As he went down, he steadied himself with a hand on the accelerator control console, laying it casually over a small switch covered with a red plastic cap—the emergency power cutoff switch. He rested one knee on the ground, then the other, while beneath his cupped hand he worked off the cover to the emergency switch, grasping it tightly.

"Hurry up and get down! Flat on the floor! *Flat!*" the NEST leader shouted impatiently, twitching the .45.

Gideon steadied himself. Then he said in a quiet voice: "If I pull this switch, we're all dead."

There was a sudden silence.

Gideon turned to the operators. "Tell them."

One of the operators glanced at Gideon, saw his fingers gripping the switch. The man turned white. "My God," he said. "That's the emergency power cutoff. We're at full power. If he pulls that...Jesus, don't do it!"

Nobody moved.

Thank you, my friend, Gideon thought. Aloud, he said: "Tell them what will happen if I do."

"It will shut off the power to the magnetic beam corridor. The beam will decollimate, and a whole lot of us will be blown to bits."

"You heard him," said Gideon calmly. "Shoot me, I fall, the switch gets pulled."

The security officers seemed paralyzed. Six pistols remained pointed at him.

"I'm a desperate man," Gideon said, his voice low. "And I have nothing to lose. I'm going to count to three. One—"

The head officer glanced left and right. He was sweating like hell, clearly certain that Gideon would do it.

"Two...I'm deadly serious here."

The leader laid his gun down, and the others quickly followed.

"Good decision. Now release her."

They released Alida. She fell to her knees, then got up again, breathing hard. She wiped the blood from her nose.

"For the record," said Gideon, "both of us are innocent. This is a frame job. And I'm going to find out who did it. So I'm sorry, gentlemen, but I'm going to have to leave you. Alida? Whether you like it or not, you'd better stick with me. Please collect their guns from the floor and hand them to me."

There was a long, smoldering hesitation. Their eyes met. Gideon could still see doubt, hesitation, and anger.

"Alida," he said, "I don't know how else to convince you except to appeal to your intuition. Please, *please* believe me."

After a moment's hesitation, Alida went around and collected the pistols from the floor and brought them over to Gideon. He ejected the magazines from all but one and stuck the magazines in his pocket. Then he unloaded the weapons of their chambered rounds, put these in his pocket, and dropped the empty firearms to the ground. He jammed the gun with the blanks into his belt. All the while he kept one hand on the cutoff switch. Finally, with the one loaded pistol in his hand, he took his hand away from the switch and, covering the men, went over to the door into the hallway, shut it, and turned the bolt.

Just in time—he could hear the thunder of feet in the hall outside.

A moment later he heard them at the door, trying to get in. There were shouts, pounding. Another alarm began to sound, this one louder.

"Everyone on the floor—except you." Gideon pointed the gun at the hysterical operator.

The man raised his hands. "Please. I'll do whatever you want."

"I know you will. Unlock the door to the accelerator tunnel."

The man scurried to the back of the room, hastening to obey. Using a magnetic key, he unlocked a small door in the rear wall and opened it. A faint green glow emerged. Beyond the door, a curved, tube-like tunnel stretched ahead, going almost to the vanishing point. To the right was a catwalk. To the left was a complex cylindrical device, stretching on into infinity, covered with wires and tubing, like the stage of some monstrous rocket. A deep humming sound issued from it. It was a small, straight-line accelerator, some two thousand feet long, but Gideon knew the accelerator tunnel connected to much older tunnels, dating back to the Manhattan Project. Where those tunnels went he had no idea—they were blocked off behind locked doors.

And yet they remained his only chance.

Gideon motioned Alida through the door. Then he took the magnetic key from the operator, relieved the second operator of his key, and followed Alida into the tunnel.

The door shut and locked behind them.

Gideon turned to Alida. "I need to know: are you with me or not? Because if you're not one hundred percent convinced of my innocence, this is as far as you're going. I can't risk another Judas moment like that."

The silence was interrupted by a flurry of pounding on the door, shouts, and the sound of a third alarm.

She stared back at him. "My answer to you is, we'd better start running like hell."

41

THEY SPRINTED DOWN the metal catwalk paralleling the live particle beam. "You know where we're going?" Alida cried, her feet pounding along behind him.

"Just follow me."

Shouts, suddenly loud, echoed down the tunnel behind them. *Damn*, Gideon thought. He'd hoped it would take them longer to get through the door.

"Stop or we shoot!" came the barked command.

They continued on. The accelerator was throbbing with high energy, and if the pipe got punctured by even a single round... "They're bluffing," Gideon said, "they won't shoot."

Thwang! The shot ricocheted off the ceiling above their heads, followed quickly by others: *Thwang! Thwang!*

"Sure, they won't shoot," Alida muttered, ducking as she ran.

Gideon could hear feet pounding on the catwalk behind them.

Thwang! Another round glanced off the wall, spraying them with chips.

Gideon stopped, spun around, fired back at them with the stage gun. Their pursuers hit the deck.

They ran on another twenty yards until Gideon found what he was looking for: an ancient metal door set into the cement wall. It was padlocked with an old brass lock.

"Shit!" muttered Alida.

Gideon turned and fired again with the fake gun, sending the guards sprawling to the ground a second time. Then he took out the real .45, pressed the barrel against the lock, and fired. The lock exploded. Gideon threw his weight against the metal door. It groaned but didn't open.

Alida tensed. "On three."

They slammed into the door simultaneously, forcing it open with a loud crack, just as more shots clanged off the door. They fell inside, slammed the metal door shut—and suddenly faced pitch blackness.

Alida flicked on her lighter, dimly illuminating a crude, branching tunnel. He grabbed her hand and took one of the tunnels at random, pulling her along at a run. The lighter went out with the movement.

He heard voices, a fresh groan of rusted steel. The metal door was being opened.

Still gripping Alida's hand, Gideon jogged ahead in the darkness, blind. They must have gone a few hundred yards when his feet tangled up with something on the ground and they fell together. He lay there in the dark, breathing hard, fumbling around until he found her hand again. He could hear voices behind them, echoing down the tunnel, distorted. They were not far. Did they have flashlights?

A lancing beam of yellow answered his question—but the sweep of the beam overhead briefly illuminated another branching tunnel in the nearby wall. As soon as the light passed, Gideon pulled Alida to her feet, and they ducked into the alcove.

Alida briefly flicked on her lighter. It went about twenty feet to a dead end—but at the far end of the cul-de-sac, an old rusted ladder climbed the stone wall. Gideon groped his way forward until he found the ladder, and they began to ascend. The voices behind them were getting louder; excited, aggressive.

Up they climbed, in the darkness. Below, Gideon saw a light flash into the alcove, but they had already climbed high enough to be invisible. They kept going, moving as silently as possible, until they reached the top of the ladder. Another flick of Alida's lighter revealed a horizontal tunnel, crowded with ancient, rusting equipment, apparently left over from the original Manhattan Project.

Gideon climbed out and helped Alida up, wondering how much of the stuff was still hot.

"Which way?" Alida whispered.

"No idea." Gideon started down the dark tunnel, moving in what he hoped was an easterly direction, toward White Rock Canyon. There were scraping sounds and voices in the shaft behind them: someone else was now climbing the ladder.

He stumbled over something on the ground. "Let me have the lighter."

She palmed it to him. He flicked it on and saw rail tracks laid onto the floor of the tunnel. An old handcar, or pump trolley, sat on a nearby siding.

A volley of shots sent them diving to the ground. Flashlight beams lanced up and around them.

"Get on the handcar," Gideon whispered. "Quickly."

In a second Alida had leapt onto the cart. Gideon gave it a shove, running it onto the main track and up to speed, then jumped on himself. The pump handle moved up and down with a creaking of metal, rusty and covered with dust but still in working order. Gideon worked the handle to keep it going as more rounds ricocheted through the cavern. The car went squealing along the metal track, gaining speed as it entered a downhill grade.

"Oh, shit," said Alida.

Gideon stopped pumping—but it made no difference. Faster and faster went the pump, its twin handles flying up and down on their own. The shots and cries began to recede.

"This was a really bad idea," said Alida, crouching and gripping the wooden sides of the handcar.

The car was now barreling downhill, in utter blackness, heading for only God knew where.

42

THEY CAREENED ALONG the track, unable to see anything. A stale cave-wind whistled past Gideon's head as he crouched in terror, groping for a better handhold, bracing for the inevitable crash.

"A brake!" yelled Alida. "This thing's got to have a brake!"

"Why didn't I think of that?"

He flicked on the lighter, and—in the brief spark before it went out—made out an old iron foot pedal on the side of the car, between the sets of wheels. Desperately, he jammed down on it with his foot. There was an earsplitting screech, an explosion of sparks burst around and behind them, and they were thrown forward as the cart decelerated, vibrating wildly, threatening to jump the tracks. He quickly eased up and applied the brake more evenly, slowly increasing the pressure. The cart wailed and groaned and finally came to a shuddering halt.

"Nice work, Casey Jones."

Gingerly Gideon got off, then flicked the lighter. The tunnel stretched on ahead, making what looked like the beginning of a long curve. Not far ahead, however, a large pile of rocks lay across the tracks, apparently having fallen from the ceiling. The tunnel was blocked across its entire width.

"Jesus," muttered Alida. "You stopped us just in time."

Gideon could still make out, far away, the distorted, echoing voices of the NEST team. They had only gained a few minutes.

"Come on," he said, taking her hand.

He jogged forward to the rock pile and they began to climb it, Gideon flicking on the lighter every few seconds in order to orient themselves. He could hear the sound of distant running.

"I don't need hand-holding," said Alida, trying to shake free of his hand.

"I do."

At last they reached the top of the pile and clambered down the other side. They made their way on down the tunnel as quickly as they could, climbing over two additional cave-ins, until at last they reached one that blocked the tunnel completely.

"Damn," said Alida, staring up at the rock pile. "Did we pass any side tunnels back there?"

"None," said Gideon, staring at the pile of loose rocks. He held the lighter up. The ceiling was rotten, but there was no opening or way through. It was a dead end.

"We'd better figure out something quick."

"Like I said, we didn't pass any side tunnels. But we *did* pass some blasting supplies."

"No. Oh no."

"You stay here."

Gideon picked his way back. The voices were getting louder, and he thought he could see the faint flicker of light in the dusty air. Their pursuers were coming on fast.

He reached the supplies—stacks of blasting mats, boxes of wadding, old drill bits, cord. There was a cache of wooden boxes in a far corner, and he ripped the rotten lid off one: blasting caps. He tried to lift the box but it collapsed, the caps spilling all over. Everything was rotten.

Now flashlight beams were flicking about, piercing the rising columns of dust. "Hey! Over there!" came a shout, followed by a shot.

Gideon extinguished the lighter, dropping into a crouch. If a bullet hit these blasting caps...

Another shot, the light beams playing about, looking for him. They were too close; there was no time to jury-rig a bomb. Only one thing to do. Crouching, he ran back down the dark tunnel for a few hundred feet, then turned and knelt. Aiming the live handgun with one hand, he flicked the lighter with the other. It cast just enough illumination for him to take aim at the heap of blasting caps. Beyond, a crowd of flashlight beams danced in the murk.

"There!" came a voice.

A volley of shots rang out as he squeezed off his own shot. There was a violent explosion, then a roar that punched him backward, knocking the wind from him, followed by a shuddering crash as the ceiling collapsed.

43

Shaking his head to bring himself back to his senses, Gideon scrambled to his knees in the blackness and crawled back the way he had come. The ground continued to shake with secondary collapses, rocks and pebbles falling all around him. He finally managed to get to his feet and, with a few more flicks of the lighter, make it back to the spot where Alida was waiting. She was crouching, coated with dust, and furious.

"What the hell did you do?"

"They were too close. I had to shoot at the blasting caps, blow the tunnel up."

"Christ almighty. And that huge noise afterward? Was that a cave-in?"

"Right. The ceiling collapsed, blocking the tunnel. Now we're safe—at least for the moment."

"Safe? Are you *nuts*? Now we're trapped!"

They began retracing their steps toward the fresh cave-in, looking for side tunnels or shafts they may have missed. There was nothing. Gideon was exhausted: his ears rang, his head pounded, and his mouth was full of muddy paste. They were both coated with dust and could hardly breathe in the choking air. Arriving at the cave-in, Gideon inspected it with the flame of the lighter. It was a massive heap of rocks, wall-to-wall, impassable. Gideon peered up at the irregular hole in the ceiling from which the rocks had fallen.

He snapped the lighter off and they were once again plunged into darkness. He could hear muffled voices from the far side.

"What now?" Alida asked.

They sat in silence for a while. Gideon finally removed the lighter, flicked it on, held it out.

"What are you doing?"

"Looking for movement of air. You know, like they do in novels."

But the flame burned utterly straight. The dust was so thick he could barely see. He flicked it off again. "It's possible," he said, "this cave-in opened a hole in the ceiling up there. I'm going up to check."

"Be careful. It's unstable."

Gideon climbed the pile of rock. Each footfall sent more rocks and pebbles sliding down, including some larger ones that detached from the ceiling and crashed onto the pile. The rocks led all the way up to the concave hole in the ceiling. He scrambled to the top, sliding back a little with each step, the dust choking him, invisible rocks raining down all around—and suddenly, at the very top, he found air that was fresh and clear. He looked up and saw a star.

They crawled out into the dark and lay in a patch of sweet-smelling grass at the bottom of a ravine, coughing and spitting. A small stream ran down the ravine, and after a moment Gideon got up, crawled to the stream on his hands and knees, washed his face, and rinsed his mouth. Alida did the same. They appeared to be below the Los Alamos plateau, in the warren of heavily forested tributary canyons cutting down to the Rio Grande. Gideon lay back on the ground, breathing hard and looking up at the stars. It was incredible they had escaped.

Almost immediately he could hear the throbbing sound of a chopper.

Damn. "We've got to keep moving," he said.

Alida stretched herself out on the grass, her filthy blond hair in tangles around her face, her once-white shirt the color of a dirty mouse, even the bloodstains obscured by dust. "Just give me a moment to catch my breath," she said.

44

WARREN CHU SAT at his desk, sweating profusely and wishing the whole thing would be over. The FBI agent paced in the small office like a caged lion, occasionally asking a question before settling back into yet another long, excruciating silence. The rest of the Feds and security agents had disappeared into the tunnels; at first he'd heard a fusillade of shots, then the noises had grown increasingly muffled and distant before ultimately fading to silence. But this agent, the one named Fordyce, had stayed behind. Chu shifted, trying to unstick his sweating buttocks from the faux-leather chair. The A/C in this billion-dollar facility was, as usual, barely adequate. Chu was aware his comportment during the hostage situation had not exactly been heroic, and that added to his uneasy feeling. He consoled himself with the thought that he was still alive.

Fordyce wheeled around yet again. "So Crew said that? Exactly that? That somebody hacked into his computer while he was on vacation?"

"I don't remember *exactly* what he said. Someone had it in for him, he said."

Pace, turn. "And he claimed the emails had been planted?"

"That's right."

The FBI agent slowed. "Is there any way they *could* have been planted?"

"Absolutely no way. This is a physically isolated network. It isn't connected to the outside world."

"Why not?"

Chu was taken aback by the question. "Some of the most sensitive information in the country is in this system."

"I see. So there's no way those emails could have been planted by someone on the outside."

"No way."

"Could someone on the *inside* plant them? Like, for example, could *you* have planted them?"

A silence. "Well," said Chu, "it wouldn't be impossible."

Fordyce stopped pacing, stared at him. "How would one go about it?"

Chu shrugged. "I'm one of the security administrators. In a highly classified network like this, somebody's got to have full access. To make sure everything's kosher, see. It would have taken a high level of technical skill—which I have. Of course, I didn't do it," he added hastily.

"You and who else could have done this—theoretically?"

"Me, two other security officers at my level, and our supervisor."

"Who's your supervisor?"

"Bill Novak." Chu swallowed. "But look, all four of us have gone through stringent background checks and security reviews. And they're watching us all the time. They've got access to everything in our personal lives: our bank accounts, travel, credit card statements, phone bills, you name it. As a practical matter, we've got no privacy. So for one of us to be involved in a terrorist plot—it's just inconceivable."

"Right." Fordyce resumed pacing. "Did you know Crew well?"

"Pretty well."

"You're surprised?"

"Totally. But then, I knew Chalker, too, and I was floored when I heard about him. You never can tell. Both of them were a little off-kilter as human beings, if you know what I mean."

Fordyce nodded and repeated, as if to himself, "You never can tell."

There was a noise in the hallway, then the door burst open and a few of the security officers came back in, coated in dust, sweat beading their temples, bringing with them a smell of earth and mold.

"What's going on?" Fordyce asked.

"They escaped, sir," said the one Chu assumed was the team leader. "Into the side canyons leading down to the river."

"I want the choppers deployed over the canyons," Fordyce said. "Especially those with infrared capability. I want men deployed along the river, with teams going up every single one of those side canyons. And get me up in a bird, pronto."

"Yes, sir."

Fordyce turned back to Chu. "You stay here. I may have more questions for you." And he was gone.

45

As Gideon and Alida bulled their way through the brush down the narrow canyon, the air above filled with choppers, the *thwap* of their rotors echoing up and down the stone walls, along with the drone of small planes and, perhaps, unmanned aerial vehicles. Spotlights flashed downward through the dusty air, columns of light roaming over the canyon walls. But the narrow canyons were choked with brush, with many overhanging rocks and alcoves, and so far they had found ample places to hide as the aircraft passed overhead.

Their progress was slow, interrupted frequently by the need to press themselves against the rock walls or cram under brush as spotlights passed them by. It was a warm night. Even though it was well after midnight, the rocks still held some heat of the intense sun, but the temperature was dropping fast. Gideon knew that, as the environment cooled, their presence would begin to show up better in the infrared sensing devices their pursuers had surely deployed.

Slowly they worked their way down toward the river.

A chopper suddenly passed very close overhead, its backwash whipping the bushes and raising furious clouds of dust. As the spotlight swept toward them, Gideon pushed Alida flat against the canyon wall. The blinding light passed over, then wobbled and came back, the chopper banking hard. The light fixed on them.

"Oh, shit," he muttered.

No point in hiding now. Gideon pulled Alida along and they scrambled down the canyon while the chopper went into a hover, the light following them. They climbed over fallen rocks, slid down pourovers. The canyon was dry, and it was hard to tell how far ahead the river lay.

More choppers appeared, taking positions in the sky. *"Cease moving,"* a voice boomed over the rotor noise. *"Raise your hands."*

Gideon slid over a boulder, helped Alida down. Ahead, the canyon plunged even more steeply.

"Halt! Or we fire!"

Gideon recognized Fordyce's voice. He was furiously angry: this was personal.

They came to the edge of another pour-over. This time, the drop was some ten feet to a muddy pool.

"Your final warning!"

They jumped just as a burst of automatic weapons fire sounded, hurtled downward, and landed heavily in water-covered mud. They struggled up out of the pool and staggered into a thicket of salt cedars, gunfire ripping and shredding the branches around them and smacking into the rock walls on either side. The searchlights temporarily lost them, roving widely through the heavy vegetation.

They came to a final pour-over, with nothing but blackness below. The searchlights hit them again.

"Jump!" Gideon cried.

"But I can't see a damn—"

"It's either that or get shot. *Jump!*"

They jumped—a sickening, terrifying plunge into blackness—and then landed in icy whitewater. Gideon felt himself tumbling head over heels in the torrent, racing and thundering along. They had reached the rapids of the Rio Grande, boiling through White Rock Canyon.

"Alida!" he cried, thrashing around. He got a glimpse of a white face to his left. "Alida!" He tried to swim, the strong current sweeping them both downstream among roaring cataracts and huge standing waves.

"Gideon!" he heard her cry. He reached out, contacted her body, then grasped her hand. There was nothing to do but ride it out.

The choppers had spread out, the spotlights sweeping wildly across the river; apparently they had misjudged, because they were focusing on a stretch of the river upstream of them. The canyon was narrow and deep here, and rules of separation seemed to be limiting the number of helicopters, as only three now were taking part in the search.

They continued to be swept helplessly along in the frigid waters at terrifying speed, clinging to each other as best they could. Gideon could barely keep his face above the churning, roiling river. As his eyes grew accustomed to the dark again, he could see farther—a terrifying descent of whitewater, huge haystacks, and standing waves. They flew over one haystack, tumbled and fought to right themselves, almost losing grip on each other. Gideon thrashed to the surface, took a huge breath, then was forced under again by the powerful current. Now they were both completely underwater, caught like leaves in the immense turbulence. He struck violently against an underwater boulder and Alida's grasp was jarred loose.

He fought his way back to the surface, coughing and gasping. He tried to call out, breathed in water, and began choking instead. He fought to stay on the surface, to orient himself in the current. The current was slowing just slightly, but still moving at a terrible pace. He managed to get his head up and gulped air, trying to get his breath back.

"Alida!"

No answer. He peered around but saw nothing besides whitewater and dark canyon walls. The three choppers were now quite a way upstream, but there were two others coming in below them, lights playing over the roiling surface of the river. As the first approached, Gideon held his breath and went under, keeping his eyes open. The big blue glow passed by; he rose, took another breath, and submerged until the second glow was behind him.

He came back up. *"Alida!"*

Still no answer. And now he could see and hear, up ahead, more whitewater. As it approached and the roar grew to fill the air, drowning out the choppers, he realized it was worse—far worse—than what they had passed through.

And there was no sign, none whatsoever, of Alida.

46

Stone Fordyce peered down through the open door of the chopper, manipulating the control stick of the "night sun," the chopper's powerful spotlight. As the pool of light played over the boiling surface of the river, he felt an unexpected catharsis, a certain sense of mingled relief and sadness—there didn't seem to be any way a person could survive those horrible rapids. It was over.

"What's beyond this whitewater?" Fordyce asked the pilot through his headset.

"More whitewater."

"And then?"

"The river eventually comes out into Cochiti Lake," said the pilot, "about five miles downstream."

"So there's five miles of this whitewater?"

"Off and on. There's one really bad stretch just downstream."

"Follow the river to Cochiti Lake, then, but take it slow."

The pilot wended his way down the river while Fordyce searched the surface with the spotlight. They passed what was obviously the violent whitewater: a bottleneck stretch between vertical walls with a rock in the middle the size of an apartment building, the water boiling up against it and sweeping around in two vicious currents, creating massive downstream whirlpools and eddies. Beyond that the river leveled out, flowing between sandbars and talus slopes. With no floating reference point, it was hard to judge how fast the water was moving. He wondered if the bodies would rise or sink, or perhaps get caught up on underwater rocks.

"What's the water temperature?" he asked the pilot.

"Let me ask." A moment later the pilot said, "About fifty-five degrees."

That'll kill them even if the rapids don't, thought Fordyce.

Still he searched, more out of a sense of professional thoroughness than anything else. The river finally broadened, the water growing sluggish. He could see a small cluster of lights downstream.

"What's that?" he asked.

The pilot banked slowly as the river made a turn. "The town of Cochiti Lake."

Now the top of the lake came into view. It was a long, narrow lake, evidently formed from damming up the river.

"I don't think there's anything more we can do along here," said Fordyce. "The others can continue their search for the bodies. Take me back to Los Alamos."

"Yes, sir."

The chopper banked again and rose, gaining altitude and accelerating as it headed northward. Fordyce felt in his gut that Gideon and the woman must be dead. No one could have survived those rapids.

He wondered if it was even necessary to interview Chu or the other security officers. The idea that someone had planted those emails to frame Crew was ridiculous and well-nigh impossible. It would have to have been an inside job, involving at least one top security officer—and to what end? Why even frame him?

But still he felt uneasy. Leaving a bunch of incriminating emails on a classified work computer was not the most intelligent move a terrorist could make. It was, in fact, stupid. And Crew had been anything but stupid.

47

Gideon Crew crawled up onto the sandbar, numb with cold, bruised and bleeding and aching from the ride through the rapids and his long struggle to reach the shore.

He sat up and clasped his hands around his knees, coughing and shivering and fighting to regain his breath. He'd lost both the stage gun and the real gun somewhere in the rapids. Upstream, he could hear the faint roar of rapids, and he made out the dull line of whitewater where the canyon opened up. He was sitting on a low sandbar that curved for hundreds of yards along an inside bend of the river. Before him the river ran sluggishly, the moon dimpling its moving surface.

Both upstream and downstream he could see the lights of helicopters, see the downward play of spotlights in the darkness. He had to get out of the open and under cover.

He managed to rise unsteadily to his feet. Where was Alida? Had she survived? This was too terrible—this was never part of the plan. He'd sucked an innocent woman into his problem, just as he had with Orchid, back in New York. And now, thanks to him, Alida might be dead.

"Alida!" he practically screamed.

His eye roamed the sweep of sand, shining in the moonlight. Then he saw a dark shape lying partway out of the water, one hand held crookedly over its head, frozen in place.

"Oh no!" he cried, stumbling forward. But as he approached he saw it was twisted, misshapen—a driftwood log.

He sank down on it, gasping for breath, immeasurably relieved.

The closest chopper was working its way down the river toward him—and he abruptly realized he was leaving telltale footprints in the sand. With a muffled curse, he picked up a branch and worked his way back, erasing his prints with it. The effort warmed him a little. He crossed the sandbar, still sweeping, waded across a side channel, reached the far side, and dove into a thicket of salt cedars just as the chopper roared overhead, its blinding searchlight moving back and forth.

Even after it had passed by he lay in the darkness, thinking. He couldn't leave this stretch of river until he found Alida. This was where the fast water slowed into a broad, sluggish flow, and this was where—if she were still alive—she would probably reach shore.

Another chopper roared overhead, shaking the bushes he was hiding in, and he covered his face from the flying sand.

He crawled out and peered up and down the river again, but could see nothing. There was a cutbank on the far side: if she was anywhere, she'd have to be on this side of the river. He began creeping through the heavy brush, trying to stay silent.

Suddenly he heard crackling behind him, and a heavy hand clapped onto his shoulder. With a shout he turned.

"Quiet!" came the whispered reply.

"Alida! Oh my God, I thought—"

"*Shhhh!*" She seized his hand and dragged him deeper into the bushes as another chopper swept toward them. They lay low as the backwash rattled the scrub.

"We've got to get away from the river," she whispered, pulling him to his feet and scooting through the brush up a dry creek. Gideon was disconcerted to find her in better shape than he was. He gasped for breath as they climbed a boulder-strewn wash, which grew progressively narrower and steeper.

"There," she said, pointing.

He looked up. In the dim moonlight he could see the jagged remains of an old basaltic flow, and at the base of it the dark opening of a cave.

They struggled up a scree slope, Alida pulling him along when he faltered, and in a few minutes they were inside. It wasn't a true cave—more like a broad overhang—but it shielded them from above and below. And it had a smooth floor of hard-packed sand.

She stretched out. "God, does that feel good," she said. There was a brief silence before she continued. "A really crazy thing happened back there. I saw this log lying on the shore, could've sworn it was your dead body. It really . . . well, really shocked me."

Gideon groaned. "I saw it, too, and thought it was you."

Alida gave a low laugh, which gradually trailed off into silence. In the darkness, she reached out and took his hand and gave it a squeeze. "I want to tell you something, Gideon. When I saw that log, the first thing that came into my mind was that, now, I wouldn't ever get the chance to say it. So here goes. I believe you. I know you're not a terrorist. I want to help you find out who did it—and why."

Gideon was momentarily speechless. He tried to come back with a wiseass response, but could think of nothing. After all that had happened—after being framed, attacked by his partner, shot at, chased across the mountains, pursued through the tunnels, run into the river, and almost drowned—he felt a surge of emotion at this sudden expression of trust. "What changed your mind?" he managed.

"I know you now," she went on. "You're sincere. You've got a kind heart. There's just no way you could be a terrorist."

She squeezed his hand again; and at that, with all the stress, the disbelief, the exhaustion, the inner loneliness, hearing a sympathetic word did something to Gideon. He began to choke up. Entirely against his will, he felt tears springing into his eyes and leaking down his face—and then he found himself sobbing like a baby.

48

AFTER A WHILE he managed to get himself under control. He wiped his eyes with his damp sleeve, then raised his head. He felt his face growing scarlet with shame.

"Well, well," Alida said. "A man who can cry." She smiled at him in the darkness, but it was a gentle smile, with no trace of irony.

"How embarrassing," he muttered. He couldn't remember the last time he had cried. He hadn't even cried on his mother's deathbed. It might have been on that terrible day in 1988, on the blazing green grass outside Arlington Hall Station, when he'd realized that his father wasn't still alive, after all, but had been shot dead by a sniper.

"I don't know what got into me," he said. He felt mortified to have broken down in front of Alida, of all people. But at the same time, a part of him felt relief. She seemed to sense his embarrassment and did not pursue the subject. For a long time they lay side by side, in silence.

Gideon propped himself up on an elbow. "I've been thinking. When Fordyce and I arrived in New Mexico, we interviewed just *three* people. We must've scored a direct hit and never realized it. One of those people was so frightened by that interview that he tried to kill us. First he sabotaged our plane, and when that didn't work, he did a frame job on me."

"Who are they?"

"The imam of the local mosque. A cult leader named Willis Lockhart. And then...of course, your father."

Alida snorted. "My father is no terrorist."

"Granted, it seems unlikely, but I can't rule out anyone. Sorry." A pause. "Why does he call you 'Miracle Daughter,' anyway?"

"My mother died giving birth to me. Since then, we've only had each other. And he's always looked on me as some kind of miracle." She smiled again despite herself. "So tell me about the other two."

"Lockhart runs a doomsday cult at a place called the Paiute Creek Ranch, in the southern Jemez Mountains. Chalker's wife had an affair with him and joined the cult, and it could very well be that Chalker was drawn into it, too. They're looking forward to apocalypse. They're no slouches when it comes to technology. They've got incredibly sophisticated communications and computing facilities, all run on solar power."

"And?"

"And, well, maybe—just maybe—they're trying to hasten along the apocalypse. You know, give it a little nudge by detonating a bomb."

"Are they Muslim?"

"Not at all. But it occurred to me that the cult might be planning to set off a nuke and see it *blamed* on the Muslims. Great way to start World War Three. It's the Charles Manson strategy."

"The Manson strategy?"

"Manson and his followers tried to start a race war by murdering a bunch of people and making it look like it was done by black radicals."

She nodded slowly.

There was a long silence before Gideon spoke again. "You know, the more I think about it, the more I feel in my bones that Lockhart and his cult are behind this. The imam and the members of his mosque seem like nice, rational people. But I get really bad vibes from Lockhart."

"So what's your plan?"

"I'm going to confront Lockhart." Gideon inhaled deeply. "It means crossing the mountains again to get to the Paiute Creek Ranch. We're going to head parallel to the river until we reach—"

"I've got a better plan," Alida interrupted.

He fell silent.

She held up a finger. "First, we take these wet clothes off, build a fire, and dry them out. Because it's cold and getting colder."

"Fair enough."

"Second, we sleep."

Another beat.

"Third, we need help. And I know just the person: my father."

"You're forgetting he's on my short list of suspects."

"Knock it off, for God's sake. He can hide us up at the ranch he has out of town. We'll use that as a base while we figure out who framed you."

"And your father is going to help a suspected nuclear terrorist?"

"My father is going to help *me*. And trust me, if I tell him you're innocent, he'll believe me. And he's a good man, with a strong sense of justice, of right and wrong. If he believes you're innocent—and he will—he'll move heaven and earth to help you."

Gideon was too weary to argue. He let the matter drop.

Working together, they built a small fire in the back of the shelter, concealed from the outside. The thin stream of smoke rose and trickled along the roof, exiting through a narrow crack. Alida blew on the fire until it was blazing merrily, then rigged up a couple of sticks to use as drying racks.

She held out a hand. "Let me have your shirt and pants," she demanded.

Gideon hesitated a moment, then reluctantly stripped. She pulled off her own shirt, bra, pants, and panties, and hung everything together on the line. Gideon was simply too wiped out to go through the motions of averting his eyes. It was, in fact, pleasant to watch the firelight play off her skin as she moved. Her long blond hair fell in wild tangles down her bare back, swaying with the movement of her body.

She turned to him and, somewhat reluctantly, he glanced away.

"Don't worry about it," she said, with a laugh. "I used to go skinny-dipping with the boys in the stock tank at our ranch all the time."

"Okay." He looked back and found her eyes also lingering on him.

She quickly adjusted the wet clothes, added a few more sticks to the fire, then sat down.

"Tell me everything," she said. "About yourself, I mean."

Slowly, haltingly, Gideon began to talk. Normally, he spoke of his past to no one. But whether it was the exhaustion, the stress, or simply having an interested and sympathetic human being nearby, he started to tell her about his life: how he became an art thief; how easy it had been to rip off most historical societies and rinky-dink museums; how he was able to do it most of the time without the victims even knowing they had been robbed. "A lot of those places don't take care of their art," he told her. "They don't display it or light it well, and nobody sees it. They may have an inventory list, but they never check it against their collections, so years might go by before they realize they've been robbed. If ever. It's the perfect crime, if you don't set your sights too high, and there are literally thousands of places out there just begging to be victimized."

Alida pulled a stray strand of damp hair away from her forehead with a finger. "Wow. Are you still doing it?"

"I quit years ago."

"Don't you ever feel guilty?"

Gideon couldn't quite put out of his mind the fact that he was talking to a nude woman. He tried to put it in perspective—after all, the fellows in *Le déjeuner sur l'herbe* didn't seem to have thought much about it. The clothes on the racks were starting to steam and would be dry soon, anyway. "Sometimes. Once in particular. I got arrogant and went to a fund-raising cocktail party at a historical society I had ripped off. I thought it would be funny. I met the curator in charge of the collection and he was all shaken up, upset. Not only did he notice the little watercolor was gone, but it turns out that was his particular favorite in the whole place. It was all he could talk about, he felt so bad. He really took it personally."

"Did you give it back?"

"I'd already sold it. But I gave serious thought to stealing it back for him."

Alida laughed. "You're terrible!" She took his hand in hers, gave it a little caress. "How'd you lose the end of your finger?"

"That's a story I never tell anyone."

"Come on. You can tell me."

"No. Really. I'm taking that secret to the grave."

Saying this, Gideon suddenly remembered that the grave, for him, might be a lot closer than for most people. It was a fact he recalled every single day, almost every single hour—but this time, sitting in the cave, the remembrance came on him like a blow to the gut.

"What is it?" Alida asked, sensing it immediately.

Without hesitating, he knew he was going to tell her. "There's a good chance that I'm not long for this world myself." He tried to laugh, his attempt to make light of it falling flat.

She stared at him, her brow furrowed. "What do you mean?"

He shrugged. "I allegedly have something called a vein of Galen aneurysmal malformation."

"A *what*?"

Gideon stared into the fire. "It's a tangle of arteries and veins in the brain, a big knot of blood vessels in which the arteries connect directly to the veins without going through a network of capillaries. As a result, the high arterial pressure dilates the vein of Galen, blowing it up like a balloon. At a certain point it bursts—and you're dead."

"No."

"You're born with it, but after the age of twenty it can start to grow."

"What can they do about it?"

"Nothing. It's inoperable. There are no symptoms and no treatment. And it'll kill me in about a year, more or less. I'll die suddenly, without warning, boom, sayonara."

He fell into silence, still staring into the fire.

"This is one of your jokes, right? Tell me you're joking."

Gideon remained silent.

"Oh my God," Alida whispered at last. "There's really nothing that can be done?"

After a moment, Gideon responded. "The thing is, I was told all this by a man back in New York. The one who hired me for this job. He's...a manipulator. There's a chance he might be making it all up. To find out one way or another, I got an MRI in Santa Fe a few days ago, but of course I haven't had a chance to get the results."

"So it's just hanging over your head, a potential death sentence."

"More or less."

"How awful."

Instead of answering, Gideon tossed a twig onto the fire.

"And you've been carrying this around with you, not sharing it with anyone?"

"I've told one or two others. Not in this much detail."

She was still holding his hand. "I can't imagine what that would be like. Wondering if your days are numbered. Or whether it's just some cruel joke." She raised her other hand, stroked his fingers, caressed the hair of his wrist. "How awful it must be."

"Yes." He looked up at her. "But you know what? At this particular moment, I feel pretty good. More than good, in fact."

She returned the look. Without a word, she took his hand and placed it on her naked breast. He traced its contours, feeling her warm skin, her nipple growing erect. Then she placed her own hand on his chest and slowly pushed him back, onto the sand. As he lay there, she knelt next to him and caressed his chest, his flat stomach. Then she swung over and straddled him, lowering herself and leaning close to kiss him, her breasts softly caressing his chest. And then she began easing him into her: gently at first, then with the pressure of swiftly increasing passion.

"Oh my God," he gasped. "What...are we doing?"

"We may have a lot less time than I thought," she answered huskily.

49

GIDEON AWOKE SUDDENLY. The sun was shining brightly into the mouth of the cave. Alida was gone. Something had woken him up.

And then he heard voices outside.

He sat up, immediately wide awake. He could hear the murmur of a man's voice and the crunch of footfalls coming up the scree slope to the overhang. Had Alida betrayed him again—after everything? It wasn't possible...or was it? Pulling on his pants, he grasped a heavy branch lying next to the dead fire and rose silently, tense, ready to fight.

The crunching drew closer and a silhouette appeared in the mouth of the cave: the outline of a man. Gideon could see nothing else in the glare. He readied himself for a lunge.

"Gideon?" came the man's voice—a voice he recognized. "Easy now, it's just us, Alida and Simon Blaine."

"Gideon?" It was Alida's voice. "It's okay."

Panic ebbing, he lowered the branch.

Blaine entered cautiously. "I'm here to help," he said in his Liverpudlian accent. "Is that all right with you?"

Alida followed her father into the cave.

Gideon tossed the branch aside and sat back. "What time is it?"

"About noon."

"How did you get here?" he asked.

It was Alida who answered. "I hiked toward Cochiti Lake, talked some guy in a trailer into using his phone. Called my dad."

Blaine stood in front of him, smiling and leprechaunish, in pressed jeans, a workshirt, and a silly looking leather cowboy vest, his white beard trimmed, his blue eyes piercing. Alida stood beside him.

Gideon rubbed his face. He had slept for so long, it was hard to collect his thoughts. Vivid memories of the previous night came flooding back.

"Dad's going to help us," she said. "Just like I promised."

"That's right," Blaine added. "My daughter tells me you've been framed and that you're no terrorist—and her word's certainly good enough for me."

"Thank you," said Gideon, feeling enormous relief. "Sorry I trashed your movie set."

"That's what insurance is for. Besides, we got a few takes anyway. Now, here's the plan. I've got my Jeep parked on a dirt road about four miles from here. The canyon and river are swarming with FBI and police and God knows who else. But it's rough, big country, and if we stick to the small side canyons we'll avoid them. They're mostly down by the lake, looking for your bodies."

Gideon looked carefully at Blaine. Concern and anxiety were written all over his face.

"I'm going to bring you both up to the ranch. It's isolated. They're all convinced you're a terrorist, Gideon, and they think my daughter's in on it. With the crazy atmosphere of terror and fear out there—the whole country is gripped with it—I'm not sure you'd survive being apprehended. You would not believe the panic out there, the *irrational* panic, and it's only getting worse. So we've got to work fast. We've got to figure out for ourselves who framed you, and why. That's the only way we can save you—and my daughter."

"I'm pretty sure it's that cult up at the Paiute Creek Ranch—"

"Maybe. Alida says you might suspect me, as well." Blaine looked at him with a peculiar expression.

Gideon blushed. "It doesn't seem likely. But someone Fordyce and I talked to was so alarmed that they tried to kill us...and framed me."

Blaine nodded. "You need to trust me. And I need to trust you. That's fundamental."

Gideon looked at the man. He didn't really know what to say.

Blaine smiled suddenly, gripped his shoulder. "You're a skeptic at heart. Fine. Let my actions speak for themselves, then. But let's get going."

It was a big Jeep Unlimited and they lay in the back, under blankets, while Blaine kept to remote forest roads and abandoned Jeep trails as he worked his way along the foothills of the mountains to his ranch. The roundabout route took several hours, and they finally reached the ranch in midafternoon. Blaine drove into the barn and Gideon and Alida got out. They stood in the fragrant, hay-scented dimness, talking.

"I'll need to use a phone," said Gideon. "I have to call my handlers."

"Handlers?" Blaine asked.

Gideon didn't respond. Instead, he followed Blaine and his daughter out of the barn, past Blaine's isolated writing studio, and down to the ranch house: a rustic, two-story, batten-board building dating from the nineteenth century, with a spacious front porch and a row of dormer windows.

Blaine directed Gideon to a table in the front hall that contained only two items: a telephone, and a framed photo of Blaine himself, signed *For my Miracle Daughter, with all my love.* Gideon picked up the phone and called Eli Glinn's number, the one he was instructed never to call except in the most extreme emergency.

Manuel Garza answered. Gideon cleared his throat, tried to compose his voice. "It's Crew. I need to speak to Glinn."

"This line is only to be used in an emergency."

Gideon let a moment pass, and then he managed to say, quite calmly, "You don't think this is an emergency?"

"You've gotten yourself into trouble, but I'm not sure I'd call it an emergency."

Again Gideon let a beat pass. "Just get him for me, will you, please?"

"Moment."

He was put on hold. A long minute passed. And then Garza came back on. "Sorry. Spoke to Mr. Glinn. He's busy, can't interface with you right now."

Gideon took a breath. "You actually spoke to him?"

"Exactly what I said. He was very specific that you're on your own now."

"That's a load of shit! You guys hired me for this job—and now you're just hanging me out to dry? You know I'm not a goddamn terrorist!"

"There's nothing he can do." Gideon noted a certain suppressed satisfaction in the man's voice.

"Pass this message on to him for me, then. I'm done. I quit. And when I get out of this mess, I'm coming looking for him. You know that nice scar he's got on one side of his face? I'm going to accessorize the other side. And that's just for starters. You tell him that."

"I will."

Gideon hung up. *Garza enjoyed that, the fuck.*

"Problem?" He found Alida looking at him, an expression of concern on her face.

Gideon swallowed, tried to shrug it off. "No bigger than any of my other problems." He turned to Blaine. "I'd like to borrow your Jeep, if I may. There's a fellow I need to visit up at the Paiute Creek Ranch."

Blaine spread his hands. "Be my guest. Just don't let the authorities catch you. Can I help you with anything else?"

Gideon paused. "Do you have any firearms?"

A broad smile. "I have rather a nice little collection. Care to take a look?"

50

THE SUN HAD SET, the crescent moon was down, and a very dark midnight approached. Gideon drove Blaine's Jeep off the Paiute Creek forest service road and into a thicket of gambel oaks. He backed it slowly into a clump of bushes, branches scratching against the paint, until the vehicle was well hidden from the road.

He got out. He had borrowed some of Blaine's clothes—a bit loose and a bit short, but serviceable—and was dressed entirely in black, his face darkened with charcoal, a wicked Colt Python .357 Magnum revolver with a four-inch barrel—in his opinion, the scariest-looking pistol made—in one hand and an old-fashioned strop razor in his pocket. He wasn't going to kill anyone—at least, he wasn't planning to—but appearance would be everything.

First he had some work to do. He removed a shovel and a pick from the back of the Jeep and selected a soft, loamy portion of the forest floor as a place to dig. He broke up the ground with the pick, then shoveled out the loose dirt, keeping the edges of the hole crisp and sharp with the blade. It was soft ground and in less than an hour he had created a shallow grave, a stark rectangle, about seven feet long, two feet wide, and three feet deep.

He packed the shovel back in the Jeep, rinsed his hands from a canteen, then took a sap, some zip ties, and a few other items from the seat and stuffed them all into his pockets. Leaving the grave site, he made his way through the dark ponderosa forest. The Paiute Creek Ranch lay at roughly eight thousand feet of altitude and, despite being summer, the night air was cool to the point of chilliness. He paused frequently to listen to the night sounds of the forest: the distant yipping of a pack of coyotes, the low bassoon of a great horned owl.

In half a mile he came to the chain-link fence surrounding the ranch settlement. Through the trees he could see the yellow glow of windows. Stopping at the fence, he listened intently, but no sound came from the compound. It was as he hoped: they were apparently on "ranch time," to bed at sunset, up before dawn.

A careful inspection indicated that there were no sophisticated alarms or sensors along the fence. Taking out a pair of fencing pliers, Gideon began to snip the chain links, creating a large flap that he pulled back and wired open. He crawled through and made his way carefully through the darkness to the rear of the main ranch house. All was quiet. A few dim yellow lights glowed in the lower windows, but—because the outfit was run on solar power and batteries—there were no bright spotlights or area lights.

He was convinced there would be some sort of night patrol: these people were paranoid and they would have posted guards. Moving with enormous care through the darkness, he drew up to the building and peered in the window. There, in a rocking chair, sat the cowboy with the squared-off beard, quietly alert, reading a book. An M16 was propped up against the sofa next to him.

Gideon was convinced Willis occupied rooms on the top floor. It was clearly the most comfortable accommodation at the ranch. One room had been his office, and he recalled seeing through an open door to a sumptuous bedroom with whorehouse-velvet walls and a canopy bed. That would be Willis's bedroom.

So he had to do something about the man downstairs.

He watched the man for a while. The man didn't look sleepy, he wasn't drinking, and—what unnerved Gideon most of all—he was reading James Joyce's *Ulysses*. This man was no dumb hick cowboy. The outfit was all show. This was a sophisticated and intelligent person who would not be easily fooled.

Gideon had anticipated running into some problem or other, and he realized he'd done so already. At all costs, he had to prevent the man from raising an alarm. He couldn't just go in and bash the man over the head. That would make too much noise and had a high probability of ending in a ruckus or fight. Besides, Ulysses had an assault rifle. He began to formulate a plan. It was high-risk, but he couldn't think of a better way.

Plucking a piece of paper from his pocket, Gideon scrawled a short note. He took a deep breath, then tapped on the window. The man looked up, saw Gideon's black face peering in, and rose abruptly from his chair, grabbing the rifle.

Quickly, Gideon put his finger to his lips and gestured for the man to come outside. But instead the man started for the stairs. Gideon rapped again, this time louder, and shook his head, again putting his finger over his mouth. Then he held up the note he had written.

> DON'T WAKE WILLIS!!
> MUST TALK TO YOU
> IMPORTANT!!

The man hesitated. He could not identify Gideon through the blackface and, Gideon hoped, would assume that Gideon might be a ranch insider. Who else would knock on the window like that?

Gideon gestured again, nodding and waving the man outside.

Shouldering the gun, the man headed for the door.

Gideon backed away from the house, into the edge of the trees, as the man came around the corner, looking this way and that. Gideon flashed his light, and the man approached.

"Who are you?" he whispered.

"Shhhh," Gideon whispered. "You wake Willis, we're in big trouble. This is important—*real* important."

The man frowned in suspicion. "What's this all about?" he asked, unshouldering the rifle. "Who are you and why the hell have you blacked your face?"

Gideon backed up a little, then shut off the light and moved rapidly and silently in a lateral direction.

The man stopped at the edge of the trees. "Lane, is that you?" He was looking around, still pointing the gun at where Gideon was no longer standing. "What do you want? Come out."

Gideon darted out and whacked the man across the side of the head with the cosh. With a moan, he sagged heavily to the ground. Fortunately, the rifle did not fire.

Seizing the man under the arms, Gideon dragged him deeper into the forest, tied him to a tree, blindfolded and gagged him, and then—with a certain hesitation—whacked him a second time.

Picking up the M16, he returned to the house, snuck inside, and carefully propped it back against the sofa. He quickly wrote a second note, just in case anyone came by, and left it on the rocking chair:

BACK IN A MOMENT
DON'T WAKE WILLIS!!

That might not fool anyone for long, but it would at least delay things. It had always amazed Gideon how most people chose to obey as a default reaction, even if the command was illogical or stupid. It was a reaction he had relied on many times, to good effect.

He snuck up the stairs. Now he faced the second problem: what to do if Willis had a woman in his room? He didn't believe for a moment the man was celibate.

He crept softly through Willis's dark, empty office. The door to the bedroom was locked. Gideon knelt, took out his tools, and—with infinite care and excruciating slowness—unlocked the door.

The room had a night-light—cute—and Gideon saw, to his enormous relief, that Willis was alone.

He walked silently over to the bed, a piece of gaffing tape already unrolled and ready to go. He leaned over Willis, who was sleeping on his back—and then in one smooth motion laid a knee hard across his chest, pinning him, while simultaneously pressing the blade of the straight razor against the man's neck.

"Cut your throat if you move or make a sound," he whispered hoarsely into the man's ear.

He had previously dulled the blade, but Willis didn't know that. With the razor pressed to his neck, the struggle ended. Willis lay there, the whites of his eyes gleaming in the darkness. His eyes went even wider as he recognized Gideon through the blackface.

Keeping the razor to the throat, Gideon said: "Open your mouth. Wide."

The man opened his mouth. Gideon placed the muzzle of the Colt Python into it, then removed the razor. "You're going to do as I say, right? Blink yes."

After a moment, Willis blinked.

"Stand up nice and slow. Keep the barrel between your teeth."

He eased himself off Willis and the man stood up, exactly as told.

"Hands behind your back."

Willis put his hands behind his back and Gideon cuffed them together with the zip ties. He removed the barrel from the man's mouth, took the roll of gaffing tape, and sealed his mouth.

"Now you and I are going to take a walk. I'm going to keep the muzzle of this gun pressed against the back of your head and I *will* pull the trigger if anything happens. We will walk out of the door, down the stairs, and off the ranch. I repeat: if anyone disturbs us, I shoot you in the head. So it's up to you to make sure no one disturbs us. Nod if you agree."

Nod.

"Is there anyone else sleeping up here?"

Nod.

"Point to the room."

With cuffed hands, Willis indicated the room next door, where Gideon had previously seen the woman lolling on the bed.

"Okay. She wakes up, you die. Now walk down the stairs and out the side door."

Willis was perfectly obedient. He did everything exactly as instructed. Within a minute they were in the darkness of the trees. Gideon switched on an LED lamp and walked Willis out past the hole in the fence and through the half mile of woods to where he had dug the grave.

When they arrived, Willis saw the grave in the light of the lamp and immediately staggered with fear. Gideon had to physically hold the man up. He made a muffled moan through the tape.

Gideon reached around and ripped it from the man's mouth. Willis gasped, staggered again. He was beyond frightened.

"Go lie down in the grave."

"No. Oh my God. No—"

"*In the grave.*"

"Why? Why in the grave—?"

"Because I'm going to kill you and bury you. Get in there."

Willis fell to his knees, blubbering, the tears streaming down his face. "No, please. Don't do this. Don't do it, don't, don't..." His voice choked up. He was coming apart before Gideon's eyes.

Gideon shoved him back and he fell, slipping into the hole, scrambling quickly out again in terror. Gideon took a step forward with the gun.

"Open your mouth."

"No. Please please *please* please please, *no, no, no*—"

"Then I'll just shoot you and roll your body in."

"But why, *why?* I'll do anything, *anything*, just tell me what you want!" His voice dissolved into a choking wail, his frame racked with sobs, a dark stain spreading from his crotch. And then he puked, once, twice, heaving and choking.

"I'll do anything..." he managed to squeak out, heavy drool hanging from his mouth.

It was time.

"Tell me about the nuke," Gideon said.

A silence, accompanied by a blank stare.

"The nuke," said Gideon. "Tell me your plans for the nuke. The nuke you plan to detonate in DC. Tell me about that and I'll let you go."

"Nuke?" Willis looked at him with utterly uncomprehending eyes. "*What nuke?*"

"Don't play stupid. Tell me about it and you're a free man. Otherwise..." And Gideon gestured toward the grave with the gun.

"What... what are you talking about? Please, *I don't understand...*" Willis stared at the gun, wide-eyed, his pleas turning into incoherent babbling.

Gideon looked at him, an awful realization dawning: this man knew nothing. He might be the leader of a cult, an egocentric and paranoid man with delusions of grandeur, but he was patently innocent of nuclear terror. Gideon had made a terrible mistake.

"I'm sorry." Gideon reached down, grasped Willis, and pulled him up. "I'm sorry. My God, I'm so sorry."

He cut off the ties and holstered the gun. "Go."

Willis stared blankly.

"You heard me, get out of here! *Go!*"

Still the man wouldn't run. He just stared blankly, dazed, still paralyzed with fear. With a curse of self-disgust, Gideon turned, walked into the bushes, got in the Jeep, started it up, and drove away, skidding through the dirt, slewing around, and gunning the engine, wanting nothing more than to get away as quickly as possible.

51

By the time Stone Fordyce arrived back at Los Alamos from an inspection of the teams dragging the lake and combing the banks of the river, it was past midnight. Midnight: it marked the turn of another day. *One day to N-Day.*

He was dead tired but that thought woke him up fast. As he approached the Tech Area, he was directed to the new command and control center being set up in a disused warehouse just outside the security perimeter. It amazed him how fast things had moved in his absence.

As he flashed his badge at the entrance, the guard said: "Stone Fordyce? The boss wants to see you. In the back."

"The boss? Who's that?"

"Millard. The new guy."

The boss wants to see you. Fordyce didn't like the sound of that.

He brushed past the guard, walked by the acres of cheap desks, each with its own computer and phone, to a cubicle hastily erected in the back corner, occupying one of the few areas of the warehouse with a window. The door was open, revealing a small, lean man in a suit standing behind a desk, back turned, speaking into the phone.

Fordyce gave a polite tap on the open door. All his professional instincts told him that this was not going to be a good meeting.

The man turned, held up a finger, kept talking. Fordyce waited.

He didn't know Millard, hadn't even heard the man's name before, but that didn't surprise him in an investigation like this, with everyone jockeying for inches of turf. And someone had to take charge on a local level—things had become increasingly chaotic, with many people in charge and no clear lines of command.

He studied Millard while waiting for him to get off the phone. He was a good-looking man in a WASPy sort of way: high cheekbones, fine green eyes, mid-fifties, a distinguished shock of gray hair at the temples, athletic and lean. He had an easygoing face and a mild-mannered voice. Fordyce hoped it would extend to his personality. But he doubted it.

Millard remained on the phone for a few more minutes, hung up, then gave Fordyce a smile. "Can I help you?"

"Agent Fordyce. I was told you wished to see me."

"Ah, yes. Name's Millard. Please, sit down."

They shook hands. Fordyce sat in the only other chair in the cubicle.

"This is a unique investigation," Millard said, his voice pleasant, even melodious. "We've got something like twenty-two law enforcement and intelligence agencies directly involved, along with sub-agencies and black agencies. Things get confusing."

Fordyce nodded in a noncommittal way.

"I think you would be the first to admit that things have gone seriously off-track in the New Mexico branch of the investigation. But now Sonnenberg's been sent back east, and I've been appointed by Dart to take charge of all aspects of the investigation. No more confusion."

A pleasant smile.

Fordyce smiled back, waited.

Millard leaned forward, clasping his hands. "I'm not going to beat around the bush. Your involvement in this case has been less than successful. You failed to identify your former partner as a suspect until it was pointed out to you, you failed to arrest him at the movie set, failed to locate him in the mountains, failed to apprehend him when he entered Los Alamos, and then allowed him to escape down to the river.

Your people can't find his dead body—if in fact he did drown. You've been in law enforcement long enough to know that this is not an acceptable record, especially in a case like this, with a city at risk, the entire country in a panic, the president and Congress having a fit, and most of Washington shut down."

He paused, folding his hands. His voice had remained quiet and pleasant. Fordyce said nothing. There was, in fact, nothing to say. It was all true.

"I'm going to move you out of the field and into the office, here, where your new responsibilities will be R and A."

R&A. Research and analysis. That was the fancy term the FBI used for that most odious of jobs, given to new agents as a sort of rite of passage. *Research and analysis.* He thought back to his own early days in the Bureau, one of a hundred agents parked in a windowless basement room, loaded up with stacks of gray metal cabinets full of files to read, search, and summarize. An investigation like this generated literally tons of paper every day—wiretap transcripts, financial records, emails by the bushel, interrogations, and much more—all of which had to be digested and summarized, with the relevant facts plucked out of the mass of useless information like poppy seeds tweezered out of a soggy cake...

"But before you assume your new responsibilities, take the weekend off," Millard said, breaking Fordyce's chain of thought. "You've been killing yourself. Frankly, you look like hell."

Another friendly smile and then Millard rose, extended his hand. "Are we okay?"

Fordyce nodded, taking the hand.

"Thanks for being a sport," he said, giving Fordyce a friendly pat on the back as he exited the office.

Fordyce paused outside the door of the warehouse, gulping air as he walked toward his car. He felt slightly sick. His career was over. Millard was right: he had fucked up big time. Once again, he felt a swelling of black anger at Gideon Crew.

But along with the anger came a certain uneasiness. Again. It always came down to two things. The biggest was Gideon leaving incriminating emails on his work computer. The more Fordyce had seen Gideon in action, the more he'd realized the guy was as smart as hell. The computer wasn't the only evidence against him, apparently: they had found a Qur'an and prayer rug in his cabin, along with some DVDs of radical Islamic preachers. But those discoveries, too, gave him pause. They seemed lame. Because at the same time, the CIA hadn't been able to break into Gideon's RSA-encrypted, security-protected home computers, despite the most sophisticated hacking tools in the toolkit of the CIA. A guy that careful, and that good, would not leave jihadist DVDs lying around.

The second was that Gideon had sabotaged the plane, putting himself at risk. Sure, if he were a jihadist he'd be looking for martyrdom. But he remembered Gideon during that flight; the guy was genuinely terrified.

He paused. If Gideon had been dirty, Fordyce felt sure he would have sensed it, felt *something* was wrong. But he hadn't. The guy felt genuine.

Maybe he hadn't fucked up, after all. Maybe everyone else had. Maybe Gideon *had* been framed.

With a muttered curse, he resumed walking to his car. He had his gun, badge, and a few days to satisfy himself whether or not Gideon really was guilty.

52

Fᴏʀᴅʏᴄᴇ ᴄᴏɴꜱᴜʟᴛᴇᴅ ᴛʜᴇ GPS built into his pool vehicle. The house was in a cul-de-sac, with pine forest and mountains rising up behind. It was well after midnight but the lights were on, the blue flicker of a TV seen through the gauzy curtains. The Novaks were still up.

This was clearly one of the prime lots of the suburban neighborhood: the last house on a dead-end lane, bigger than the others. Not to mention the Mercedes in the driveway.

He drove in, blocking the Mercedes, then got out and rang the bell. A moment later a woman's voice asked who it was.

"FBI," said Fordyce. He unfolded his shield, showed it through the narrow side window.

The woman opened the door immediately, almost breathlessly. "Yes? What is it? Is everything all right?"

"Everything's fine," said Fordyce, stepping inside. "Sorry to be bothering you at such a late hour." She was a fine-looking woman, very fit, trim little waist and a shapely butt, great skin, wearing white slacks and a cashmere sweater with pearls. Funny outfit for midnight television.

"Who is it?" came an irritated voice from what appeared to be the living room.

"FBI," the woman called back.

The TV went off immediately and Bill Novak, the head of security in Crew's department, emerged.

"What is it?" he asked matter-of-factly.

Fordyce smiled. "I was just apologizing to your wife for the late hour. I have a few questions of a routine nature. It won't take long."

"No problem," said Novak. "Come in, please, sit down."

They went into the dining room. Mrs. Novak turned on the lights. "Can I get you anything? Coffee? Tea?"

"Nothing, thanks." They all sat down at the table and Fordyce looked around. Very tasteful. Expensive. Some old silver on the dining table, a few oil paintings that looked like the real thing, handmade Persian rugs. Nothing outrageous—just expensive.

Fordyce took out a notebook, flipped over the pages.

"Do you need my wife?" Novak asked.

"Oh yes," said Fordyce. "If you don't mind."

"Not at all."

They seemed eager to please, not nervous. Maybe they didn't have anything to be nervous about.

"What is your annual salary, Dr. Novak?" Fordyce asked as he looked up from his notebook.

A sudden silence. "Is this really necessary?" the security head asked.

"Well," said Fordyce. "This is strictly voluntary. You're under no obligation to answer my questions. Please feel free to call your attorney if you desire legal advice or wish him or her to be present." He smiled. "One way or another, however, we would like your answers to these questions."

After a pause, Novak said, "I think we can proceed. I make a hundred and ten thousand dollars a year."

"Any other source of income? Investments? Inheritance?"

"Not to speak of."

"Any overseas accounts?"

"No."

Fordyce glanced at the wife. "And you, Mrs. Novak?"

"I don't work. Our finances are mingled."

Fordyce made a note. "Let's start with the house. When did you buy it?"

"Two years ago," said Novak.

"How much did it cost, what was your down payment, and how much did you finance?"

Another long hesitation. "It was six hundred and twenty-five thousand, and we put down a hundred and financed the rest."

"Your monthly payments?"

"About thirty-five hundred dollars."

"Which comes to, what, about forty-two thousand per year." Fordyce made another note. "Do you have any children?"

"No."

"Now let's talk about your cars. How many?"

"Two," Novak said.

"The Mercedes and—?"

"A Range Rover."

"Their cost?"

"The Mercedes was fifty, the Range Rover about sixty-five."

"Did you finance them?"

A long silence. "No."

Fordyce went on. "When you bought your house, how much did you spend on new furnishings?"

"I'm not really sure," said Novak.

"For example, these rugs? Did you bring them from your previous residence or purchase them?"

Novak looked at him. "Just what are you driving at?"

Fordyce allowed him a warm, friendly smile. "These are nothing more than routine questions, Dr. Novak. This is how the FBI starts almost any interview—with financials. You'd be amazed how quickly one can smoke out someone living beyond their means with just a few simple questions. Which is alarm number one in our business." Another smile.

Fordyce could see signs of tension in Novak's face for the first time.

"So . . . the rugs?"

"We bought them for the new house," Novak said.

"How much?"

"I don't remember."

"And the other furnishings? The silver collection? The wide-screen TV?"

"Mostly bought when we purchased the house."

"Did you finance any of these purchases?"

"No."

Another notation. "You seem to have had a lot of cash on hand. Was there a legacy involved, lottery or gambling winnings, an investment coup? Or perhaps family help?"

"Nothing significant to speak of."

Fordyce would have to plug the figures into a spreadsheet, but already they were at the outer limits of what was readily explainable. A man making a hundred grand a year would be hard-pressed to buy the cars he had around the same time he was making a down payment on his house, and paying cash on top of everything else. Unless he'd made a real estate killing on his previous house.

"Your previous house—was it nearby?"

"It was over in White Rock."

"How much did you sell it for?"

"About three hundred."

"How much equity did you have in that house?"

"About fifty, sixty."

Only fifty or sixty. That answered that question. There *was* unexplained wealth.

Fordyce gave Novak another reassuring smile. He flipped the pages of his notebook. "Now, getting to these emails that were found in Crew's account."

Novak looked relieved to see the change in subject. "What about them?"

"I know you've answered a lot of questions already about this."

"Always ready to help."

"Good. Could those emails have been planted?"

The question hung in the air for a moment.

"No," said Novak at last. "Our security is foolproof. Crew's computer was part of a physically isolated network. There's no contact with the outside world, no Internet connection. It's impossible."

"No contact with the outside. How about by somebody *inside* the network. A co-worker, say?"

"Again, impossible. We work with highly classified material. Nobody has access to anyone else's files. There are layers and layers of security, passwords, encryption. Trust me, there's no way, none, that those emails could have been planted."

Fordyce made a notation. "And this is what you've been telling investigators?"

"Certainly."

Fordyce looked at the man. "But you have access, don't you?"

"Well, yes. As the security officer I have access to everyone's files. After all, we have to be able to track what everyone is doing—standard operating procedure."

"So what you just told me is false. There *is* a way those emails could have been planted. *You* could have done it." In asking this question, Fordyce shifted his entire tone of voice, pitching it low and accusatory, emphasizing the word *you* in an openly disbelieving manner.

The air froze. But Novak didn't blink. After a moment, he said, "Yes, I could have planted them. But I didn't. Why would I?"

"I'll ask the questions, if you don't mind." Again Fordyce employed his most skeptical tone of voice. "You just admitted you told a falsehood to me and all the other investigators." He glanced at his notebook. "You said, and I quote: 'There's no way, none, that those emails could have been planted.' That's false."

Novak kept a steady eye on him. "Look, I misspoke. I wasn't considering myself in that statement because I know I didn't do it. Don't try to entrap me here."

"Could anyone else in your department have planted those emails?"

Another hesitation. "The three other security officers in my department might have been able to do it, but it would have taken two of them in cooperation, since they don't have the highest level of clearance."

"And are there others above you who could have done it?"

"There are those who have the authorization, but they would have had to go through me. At least, I think they would have. There are levels of security even I don't know about. The higher-ups might have installed a back door. I really don't know."

Fordyce felt a little frustrated. So far, Novak hadn't actually said anything incriminating, hadn't shown any cracks. His misstatement wasn't out of the ordinary—he had seen far worse from innocent people under questioning.

But the house, the cars, the rugs...

"May I ask you, Agent Fordyce, what makes you think those emails were planted?"

Fordyce decided to tip his hand a little. He fixed him with a glaring eye. "You know Dr. Crew. Would you call him stupid?"

"No."

"Would you call leaving incriminating emails on your work account a smart thing to do? Without even erasing them?"

A silence. Then Novak cleared his throat. "But he *did* erase them."

This brought Fordyce up a bit short. "Yet you recovered them. How?"

"Through one of our many backup systems."

"Can anything really be erased from one of your computers?"

"No."

"Does everyone know that?"

Another hesitation. "I believe most do."

"So we're back to my original question. Was Dr. Gideon Crew a stupid man?"

Now he saw Novak's façade just begin to crack. He had finally succeeded in raising the man's ire. "Look, I find the entire thrust of your questioning to be offensive, all these questions about my personal finances, these insinuations about planted emails, this late-night surprise visit. I want to help the investigation, but I will not sit here and be victimized."

Fordyce, with his long experience in questioning suspects, knew when he had reached the probable end of what had been a very useful interview. No point in provoking Novak further. He slapped his note-book shut and rose, turning back on his warm, chummy voice.

"Fortunately, I'm done. Thank you kindly for your time. It was all routine, no need to be concerned."

"I am concerned," said Novak. "I don't think it's right, and I'm going to file a complaint."

"Naturally, you're welcome to do so."

As he retreated to his car, he hoped to hell Novak wouldn't complain about him, or would at least wait a few days. A complaint would be most inconvenient. Because he was now halfway convinced that Novak was dirty in some way. That didn't exonerate Crew, of course, and Novak hardly looked like a terrorist.

But still... Was it possible Gideon *had* been framed?

53

GIDEON HAD PULLED the Jeep off the dirt road ten miles from the Paiute Creek Ranch. He had to calm himself down, organize his thoughts. He felt awful about what he'd just done to Willis. He had terrified the man, brutalized him, humiliated him. The man was far from being the nicest person in the world, but no innocent person deserved that kind of treatment. And he was clearly innocent. Could someone else at the cult be behind it? Impossible, not without Willis knowing.

Gideon had made a hideous mistake.

On top of that, it was one o'clock in the morning, the day before N-Day. *One day.* And he had no more idea who was behind the plot than when he arrived in Santa Fe, eight days ago . . .

He grasped the wheel, realizing that he was hyperventilating worse than ever. He had to get a grip on himself, clear his head, and think this through.

He turned off the engine, threw the door open, and stumbled out of the vehicle. The night was cool, a slow sigh of air moving through the branches of the pines, the stars twinkling above. He steadied himself, tried to regulate his breathing, and started walking.

The Paiute Creek Ranch had nothing to do with the terrorist plot. That much was clear. So he was back to Joseph Carini and the Al-Dahab Mosque. They had of course been the obvious perpetrators all along, and now it was confirmed. He had been too clever by far. The obvious answer, the simplest answer, was almost always the true answer. It was one of the fundamental principles of scientific inquiry— and criminal investigations.

But *was* it so obvious? Why would the Muslims frame him as a fellow Muslim, when such a move would only increase suspicion, focus more attention on them? After all, the investigation had already come down on them like a ton of bricks. There were hundreds of investigators crawling all around the mosque, going through their most private documents, questioning their members, digging out all their secrets. He and Fordyce had been two investigators out of hundreds. They hadn't learned anything of value, anything out of the ordinary, at least that he could see. And yet, whoever had attempted to frame him had taken huge risks, breaking into a highly classified computer system. It was someone who believed he had learned something so incriminating, so dangerous, that extraordinary measures had to be taken—

Suddenly he stopped in his tracks. Frame *him*. There was something he had been overlooking, blindingly obvious only now, after it had occurred to him. These actions were being taken against him, and him alone. After all, they hadn't framed Fordyce, too. In fact, Fordyce was hot on his ass.

After the plane wreck, after learning about the sabotage, Gideon had always assumed whoever was doing this was trying to kill them both, to stop their line of inquiry. But the fact was, they were only trying to stop him.

What had he done—what had he investigated, who had he talked to—on his own, without Fordyce?

As quickly as he had posed the question, the answer came.

He stared up at the dark sky, at the hard uncompromising points of starlight. Could it be possible? It seemed so incredibly improbable. But he'd proved it wasn't Willis, and he felt certain it wasn't the Muslims. As he turned around and began heading back to the Jeep, he couldn't help but remember the oft-repeated Sherlock Holmes dictum: *When you have eliminated the impossible, whatever remains, however improbable, must be the truth.*

54

Sitting in his cubicle in the 12th Street Command Center, Dart slowly replaced the telephone in its cradle. He glanced out the tiny, makeshift window. A black rectangle of night stared back at him. Then he picked up the telephone again and dialed. His hands shook slightly with a combination of exhaustion and rage. It was four o'clock in the morning but that made no difference.

The phone was answered on the first ring. "Special Agent in Charge Millard."

"Millard? It's Dart."

"Dr. Dart." Millard's voice tightened audibly.

"What's the status of the hunt for Crew?"

"Well, sir, while we've got a full complement of personnel still combing the area, we're nevertheless growing increasingly confident he and his accomplice drowned in—"

Dart found anger overmastering his habitual control. "Of course you're confident he drowned. Naturally. It's what he wants you to think. Not only haven't you caught him, but you let him waltz through the security perimeter of Los Alamos, run amok, and then waltz right out again."

"Sir, that isn't exactly the way it happened, and at the time I wasn't—"

"Do you want to know what I equate that to, Agent Millard? I equate that to a wanted felon walking into police headquarters, helping himself to weapons and ammunition, flipping the police chief the bird, and then walking out again."

This time, there was silence on the other end of the line. Dart realized he was already beyond the edge of control, but he didn't care.

In the silence, Miles Cunningham, Dart's personal assistant, stepped into the cubicle, placed a cup of coffee on the desk—hot, black—and stepped back out again. Dart had instructed him to cease his appeals for rest, instead ordering the man to bring him a fresh cup of coffee, every hour on the hour.

Despite the scalding temperature of the coffee, Dart took a huge swig, swallowed, cleared his throat. "Understand, Agent Millard," he continued. "I'm not holding you fully responsible. As you started to imply, your command of the New Mexico operations is new. But I am holding you responsible for everything that happens, going forward."

"Yes, sir."

"N-Day is tomorrow. Every hour, every *minute*, the terrorist Gideon Crew continues to remain at large increases the threat to us all. I very much doubt he drowned in the Rio Grande. He's still in the mountains somewhere. I want those mountains searched. End to end."

"That search is ongoing, sir, and our people are doing their best. But the area in question covers more than ten thousand square miles of wilderness, and it's extremely rugged."

"Gideon Crew is on his own, without food or water. You've got hundreds of men and millions of dollars of high-tech equipment. I'm not interested in excuses, I'm interested in results."

"Yes, sir. We're going all out. In addition to the dogs and ground search teams, we've deployed a large arsenal of remote sensing and monitoring equipment. Choppers with infrared and pattern-recognition computer systems. Predator drones, equipped with the latest synthetic aperture foliage-penetrating radar. But at the risk of offending, I have to report they've found nothing, and the evidence really does suggest that Crew and the woman drowned in the river."

"Have you found the bodies, Agent Millard?"

"No, sir."

"Until you do, I don't want to hear another word about drownings."

"No, sir."

Dart took another gulp of coffee. "Now, there's another problem I want to talk to you about. Agent Fordyce. The man has demonstrated incompetence, an inability to follow orders, and a tendency to freelance. It's come to my attention that he questioned the top Los Alamos security officer on his own, with no authorization and no required partner. He didn't even record the interview. Do you know what that means?"

"I think so, sir."

"It means that whatever he learned is rendered useless in court and unreliable for investigative purposes. If Novak was involved in some way, this totally undermines our chances of prosecuting him."

"I've already taken Fordyce off active field duty and reassigned him to R and A."

"I want him relieved of duty. Off this investigation. It's clear to me the man is having some kind of breakdown."

"Yes, sir."

"I want you to do it in a way that doesn't get FBI internal affairs up in arms. We're having enough conflict with the FBI as it is. Put him on leave—paid, of course. Call it a vacation, no return date specified."

"Very well, sir."

"Find Crew. And the woman. And for God's sake—bring them to me *alive*." Dart hung up, took another gulp of coffee, and stared back into the darkened window.

55

GIDEON ARRIVED BACK at the ranch about two o'clock in the morning, having pounded the Jeep along bad forest service roads the entire way. He found Alida still up, sprawled on a big sofa in the rustic living room before a fire, her blond hair spread across the leather.

She jumped up when he walked in, came over and embraced him. "I was so worried about you. My God, you look destroyed."

Gideon felt destroyed.

She led him to the sofa. "Drink?"

He nodded.

She kissed him gently, then went to the wet bar and began to mix a pitcher of martinis. From the sofa, he watched her pour gin and vermouth into a large shaker, scoop in ice, and shake the mixture vigorously, wondering the whole time just how the hell he was going to manage this. She seemed so happy, so beautiful, she practically glowed.

"Did you find Willis?" she asked, squeezing the zest of a lemon into a pair of glasses. "Did you confront him?"

"He...he wasn't around," Gideon lied. An awful feeling, a horrible feeling, settled over him. He was going to have to act with Alida. He was going to have to misdirect, pretend, *lie*...A flickering recollection of their magical night in the cave only made it worse.

"Do you still think it's Willis?"

Gideon nodded. "Say, where's your father?"

"He drove back to our house in Santa Fe. He's got to get up early tomorrow—has to catch a plane." She brought over the martinis and he took his. Exactly the way he liked it: straight up, with a twist, little chips of ice swirling around. Gideon took a sip, felt the liquid burn his throat.

She eased herself down next to him, leaned against him, nuzzled his face. "I'm so glad you're back. You know, I've been thinking, Gideon. Thinking about us."

He took another sip. "Your father's going on a trip? Where?"

"Maryland, I think." Her lips brushed his neck and she murmured, "I'm having a hard time keeping my wits about me, with you here. That was some evening we had in the cave—I can't get it out of my head. Maybe this isn't a good time to talk, but, as I said, I've been thinking…"

"Right," said Gideon, taking refuge again in his drink. "What's he doing in Maryland?"

"Research, I think. For his next novel." Another nuzzle. "Are you okay?"

"Fine, I'm fine. Just tired. And I'm still dirty, with all that charcoal." He waved vaguely at his black-smeared face.

"I like it. Sexy."

"Do you know what the novel's about?"

"Something to do with viruses, I think."

"Does your father ever teach writers' workshops?"

"Sure. He enjoys that. Can we talk about something else right now?"

Gideon swallowed. "In a moment. There's a workshop in Santa Cruz I've heard about, called *Writing Your Life*."

"My father teaches at that one every year. He adores Santa Cruz."

Gideon had to cover his expression with a hefty slug of the drink. He was already feeling the effects of the alcohol.

"So he likes teaching?" he said.

"He loves it. After his disappointment over the Nobel, I think he finds it consoling."

"You mentioned the Nobel before. What happened, exactly?"

Alida sipped her own drink. "He was on the short list a few times, but didn't get it. And then he learned through the grapevine why they'd never give it to him—because his politics were wrong."

"Politics? How so?"

"He used to be a British citizen. And when he was a young man, he was in MI6—that's the British intelligence service. Sort of like the CIA."

"I know what it is." Gideon was stunned. "I had no idea."

"He never, ever talks about it, even to me. Anyway, I don't know about the Nobel for a fact myself. It's just what people say. The Nobel Committee refused Graham Greene for the same reason—he worked in British intelligence. Those damn Swedes just don't like the idea of a writer being involved in espionage and counter-intelligence. John le Carré won't get one, either!" She snorted.

"Was your father upset?"

"He doesn't admit it, but I know he was. I mean, he was only doing his patriotic duty to his country. It's humiliating." Her voice had climbed slightly. "Look at all the great writers passed over—James Joyce, Vladimir Nabokov, Evelyn Waugh, Philip Roth. The list goes on and on. And who do they give it to instead? Writers like Dario Fo and Eyvind Johnson!" She sat back with a *thump*.

Gideon was so taken aback by her sudden passion he had temporarily forgotten how guilty this whole act of dissembling made him feel. "Aren't you . . . well, worried about your father going to Maryland right now? I mean, that's close to DC."

"He's not going anywhere near the evacuation zone. Anyway, I'm sick of talking about my father. I really want to talk to you about us. Please."

She grasped his shoulder and looked into his face, her dark brown eyes glistening. With tears? Certainly with love. And Gideon couldn't stop feeling the same unbearable tug at his own heart. "I just . . ." he started, stumbled. "I'm just concerned about your father, given this terrorist situation. I'd like to know where he's going in Maryland."

She looked at him with a small flash of impatience. "I can't remember. Some army base. Fort Detrick, I think. Why is this so important?"

Gideon knew that Fort Detrick was hardly more than a stone's throw from Washington. Was Simon Blaine planning to mobilize his people there for the final push? Why an army base? It was surely no coincidence that Blaine was traveling back east to an army base, thirty hours before N-Day. His head reeled at the possibilities. "Your father must know a lot of people in the intelligence community."

"He does. When he was in MI6, I believe one of the things he did was act as a liaison with the CIA. At least, I once saw a citation they gave him. Classified. It was the one time he left his safe open."

"And he's flying out tomorrow morning?"

She laid a hand on his arm, the impatience breaking out again. "That would be *this* morning, since it's two AM already. Gideon, what's this interest in my father? I want to talk about us, *our* relationship, *our* future. I know it's sudden, I know guys don't like to be ambushed like this, but, damn it, I know you feel the same way I do. And you of all people know *we may not have a lot of time.*"

"I'm sorry, I didn't mean to avoid the subject." He tried to cover up his runaway interest by adopting a slightly accusatory tone. "It's just that I thought your father was going to help us. Now he's running away."

"He *has* helped us! He's not running away, either. Look, we're safe here, we can use this as a base to find out who framed you. All we have to do is track down that man Willis. It makes sense that he and his crazy cult are behind this. He'll be caught, the hunt will be over, and you and I will be cleared."

Gideon nodded, feeling awful all over again. "Yes. I'm sure that will happen." He gulped the rest of his drink.

She sat back. "Gideon, are you ready to talk? Or are you just trying to forestall it with all these questions about my father? I don't want to force myself on you."

He nodded dumbly, attempted a smile. He was already wishing for a second drink. "Sure."

"I hesitate to bring up a painful subject, but... Well, you know I'm direct. I say what I think, even if I put my foot in my mouth. I hope you know that about me by now."

"I do," he croaked.

She drew closer. "I know you may have a fatal condition. That doesn't frighten me off. I'm ready to make a commitment to you. That's what I've been thinking about. That's what I've wanted to tell you. I haven't felt this way about a guy...well, ever."

Gideon could hardly manage to look at her.

She took his hands in hers. "Life is short. Even if it's true, and you only have a year—well, let's make that year count. Together. You and me. Will you do that? We'll roll up a lifetime of love into one year."

56

Fordyce followed Millard through the sea of desks and cubicles that formed the new command and control center. A glorious dawn was breaking outside, but in the converted warehouse, the air was dead and close and the lighting fluorescent.

Millard was a true company man, thought Fordyce; always pleasant, never sarcastic, tone of voice mild—and yet, underneath it all, a raging asshole. What was the word the Germans used? *Schadenfreude.* Taking pleasure in the misfortune of others. That described Millard's attitude perfectly. The moment Millard had phoned asking for a meeting, Fordyce had been able to guess what it was about.

"How are you feeling, Agent Fordyce?" Millard asked, his voice laden with false empathy.

"Very good, sir," Fordyce replied.

Millard shook his head. "I don't know. You look tired to me. Very tired, in fact." He squinted at Fordyce as if he were an object behind museum glass. "That's what I wanted to talk to you about. You've been working yourself too hard."

"I don't think so. I'm really feeling fine."

Millard shook his head again. "No. No, you look exhausted. I appreciate your team spirit, but I simply can't allow you to go on working yourself like this." He paused, as if gathering himself for the kill. "You need to take a vacation."

"You already told me to take a few days off."

"This is not a—how should I say it?—a quick break. I want you to take some *serious* time off from the job, Agent Fordyce."

That was it—the line he'd been waiting to hear. "Time off? Why?"

"To recharge your batteries. Regain an objective outlook."

"How long are we talking about, exactly?"

Millard shrugged. "That's a little hard to say at present."

An indefinite leave of absence. That's what they called it. Fordyce realized that, once he was out the door, that would be it. If he was going to do something, he had to do it now—right now. They only had *one day*.

"Novak is dirty," he said.

This was such a non sequitur that Millard stopped short. "Novak?"

"Novak. Chief of security for Tech Area Thirty-three. He's dirty. Take him in, sweat him, do what it takes."

A long silence. "Perhaps you'd better explain."

"Novak's living a lifestyle way beyond his means. Luxury cars, a big house, Persian rugs, all on a hundred and ten thousand a year. His wife doesn't work, and there's no family money."

Millard looked at him sideways. "And why is this significant?"

"Because there's only one person who could've planted those emails in Crew's account, and it's Novak."

"And how do you know all this?"

Fordyce took a breath. He had to say it. "I interviewed him."

Millard stared at him. "I'm aware of that."

"How?"

"Novak complained. You barged into his house after midnight, no authorization, didn't follow any interview protocols—what did you expect?"

"I had no choice. We're out of time. The fact is, the guy lied to investigators, told them it was impossible to plant those emails. He forgot to mention *he's* the only one who could have done it."

Millard stared at him long and hard, his lips compressed. "Are you saying Novak framed Crew? For money?"

"All I'm saying is, the guy's dirty. Take him in now, sweat the bastard—"

Millard's lips became almost invisible. The man's skin seemed to tighten across his face, as if he were drying out. "You are out of line, mister. Your behavior is unacceptable, and these demands are improper and, frankly, outrageous."

Fordyce couldn't take it anymore. "Improper? Millard, N-Day is tomorrow. *Tomorrow!* And you want me to—"

A loud commotion erupted at the main door. A man was shouting, his shrill manic voice echoing in the warehouse space, rising above the hubbub of voices swirling around him. He had apparently just been brought in, and as his outrage rang out, Fordyce heard disjointed accusations of police brutality and government conspiracies. Clearly a nut case.

And then Fordyce heard Gideon's shouted name mingling with the incoherent mix.

"What the hell?" Millard flashed him another look. "Don't you go anywhere. I'll get back to you in a moment."

Fordyce followed Millard to the front, where the man was haranguing a large group of agents. He was shocked to see it was Willis Lockhart, the cult leader. He hadn't been brought in, it seemed—he had come in on his own. But what a change: he was wild, his face haggard, spittle on his lips. From the outraged, furious rant, Fordyce gathered that Gideon Crew had showed up at the ranch the previous night, kidnapped Willis at gunpoint, brought him to a grave he'd dug in the woods, brutalized him, tortured him, threatened to kill him, all the while demanding answers to questions about nukes and terrorism and God knows what else.

So Gideon was still alive.

Willis screeched about how it was all a plan, a plot, a conspiracy, before his rantings dissolved into incoherency.

At that moment, Fordyce was suddenly and utterly convinced: Gideon Crew was innocent. There was no other explanation—none—for why he would have gone to the Paiute Creek Ranch and done what he did to Willis. He had been framed. Those emails had been planted. And just as clearly, it meant that Novak was in on the terrorist plot. Even though he already half believed it, now the conclusion was inescapable.

"Hey! Hey, you!"

Lockhart's scream interrupted this epiphany. Fordyce looked up to see the cult leader staring at him, extending a shaking finger. "It's him! There he is! It's the other guy who came up to the ranch last week! They started a fight, trashed the place, left my people hurt! You son of a bitch!"

Fordyce glanced left and right. Everyone was staring at him, Millard included.

"Fordyce," Millard said in a strange voice, "is this another man you interviewed?"

"Interviewed?" Lockhart shouted. "You mean brutalized! He attacked half a dozen of my people with a chain saw! He's a maniac! Arrest him! Or are all of you part of it as well?"

Fordyce glanced at Millard, glanced at the exit. "The man's crazy," he said in a calm voice. "Look at him."

He saw on everyone's faces a certain relaxation, a certain relief that these accusations were as crazy as all the others. Everyone's face, that is, except Millard's.

Suddenly Lockhart lunged at Fordyce, and there was an eruption of chaos as a dozen agents rushed in to intervene.

"Let me at him!" Willis yelled, clawing at the air. "He's the devil! He and that man Gideon Crew!" He swung a powerful forearm, connecting with an agent, slammed into another. In the resulting confusion, the pushing and hollering and shoving, Fordyce managed to duck down, dart through the crowd, and slip out the door. He headed straight for his car, got in, started the engine, and took off.

57

As DAWN BROKE, Gideon stood by the leather sofa, his head pounding, pulling on his clothes while Alida lay nude on the bearskin rug before the fireplace, still asleep, her blond hair in a wild tangle, her smooth skin glowing against the coarse dark nap of the rug. Out the windows of the cabin, dark clouds smeared across half the sky, and a humid wind lashed the pines. A storm was brewing.

Confused memories of the night before knocked about in his head: too many drinks, more spectacular sex, and God only knew what unwise things said or promised. Gideon felt awful. What had he done? He was a complete asshole. To allow himself to be drawn into that, when he suspected her father of being a terrorist and all the while plotting how to stop him, bring him down...it was monstrous.

What should he do? Should he take Alida into his confidence? No, that wouldn't work—she would never, ever believe that her father, Simon Blaine, bestselling author, ex-spy, was the ringleader of—or at least involved in—a nuclear terrorism plot. Who would? He had to keep lying to her, and he had to do this alone. He had to go to Maryland, find Blaine, and stop him. And he couldn't get on a plane, couldn't do anything requiring an ID. His only way of getting back east was to drive—in Alida's Jeep.

It seemed impossible. Why would a man like Blaine be involved in a terrorist plot like this? But he was. Gideon was sure of it now. There was simply no other answer.

As he thought about his position, once again he felt overcome with self-loathing. Yet what choice did he have? This was about more than clearing his own name. Countless lives were at stake. Nobody would believe him; he was a wanted man; and so he was compelled to act alone. There was no escaping it.

As he pulled on his shirt, his eye once again fell on the curves of Alida's body, her face, her lucent hair... Was it possible he was actually in love with her?

Of course it was.

Enough, *enough*. But even as he was trying to pull his eyes away, she opened her own. And winced.

"Ouch," she said. "Hangover."

He tried to force a grin onto his face. "Yeah. Me too."

She sat up. "You look like hell. I hope I didn't break you." She gave a wicked smile.

He hid his face by bending down to tie his shoes.

"And where are you so all fired up to go this morning?"

He forced himself to look up. "Paiute Creek Ranch. I'm going to confront Willis."

"Good. It's him, I just know it. Let me come along."

"No, no. Could be dangerous. And your presence might detract from getting the truth out of him."

She hesitated. "I get it. But I'm worried. Be careful."

Gideon tried to arrange his face into a semblance of normality. "I'll need to borrow the Jeep."

"No problem. Just stick to the back mountain roads."

He nodded.

She stood up and before he could escape she put her arms around him, pressed her lips to his, and sidled her naked body up against him. A long, lingering kiss followed, the warmth of her body creeping through his clothing. Gideon surrendered to it. Finally, she released him.

"That was for luck," she said.

Gideon could only nod dumbly. She went to a drawer, plucked out the keys, tossed them to him.

He caught them. "Um, just in case—gas, whatever—do you have any money?"

"Sure." She picked her pants off the floor, rummaged in the pockets, extracted a wallet. "How much?"

"Whatever you can spare, I guess."

She pulled out a bunch of twenties, and without counting handed them over with a radiant smile.

He tried to move but felt as if frozen. He couldn't do this—not to her. And yet here he was, about to do it. Stealing her car, taking her money, lying to her, going after her own father. But, damn it, what choice did he have? His position was impossible. If he stayed here with Alida, countless people would die and he might still end up in jail. If he left...

"I may not be back for a while," he told her. "I have a few other things to do. Don't wait up for me tonight."

She looked at him with real concern. "All right. But stay away from people—any people. My father mentioned roadblocks on the main routes going in and out of the mountains, Los Alamos, and Santa Fe. Watch yourself."

"I will."

He stuffed the money in his pocket, dodged another kiss, and rushed to the Jeep. He jumped inside, started the engine, and peeled out, leaving a cloud of dust. He tried not to look back but couldn't help himself—and saw her standing in the doorway, still naked, one leg slightly cocked, her blond hair cascading down her shoulders, waving.

"Fuck, fuck, *fuck!*" He pounded on the steering wheel as he headed down the ranch road. Rounding a bend, he came to Blaine's writing hut, surrounded by trees and out of view of the main ranch. On impulse, he drove up to it and got out. Using the Jeep's tire iron, he smashed a window, climbed in, took Blaine's laptop computer, tossed it and a charger into the back, and then continued on.

58

GIDEON'S FIRST STOP was the Goodwill Industries Thrift Store out on Cerrillos Road. He parked the expensive, late-model Jeep far from the entrance and walked through a Walgreens, where he bought a disposable cell phone before going into the thrift store. Heading for the racks, he pulled off a hasty selection of sports jackets, shirts, pants, suits, and various pairs of shoes in his approximate size. He also found some sunglasses, a toupee, some cheesy man-jewelry, and a large suitcase.

Paying for it with some of Alida's cash, he drove down the block to a theatrical supply store and bought spirit gum, sealers, face paints, pencils and crayons, scabs, effects gels, nose and scar wax, a bald-cap, some hairpieces, a lace beard, a prosthetic paunch, and a few cheek pieces and inserts. He had no idea how he might use anything or even what he might need, so he bought everything.

Back to the Jeep, and then he drove farther south on Cerrillos to the edge of town, where he found an anonymous motel that looked like it might cater to the trade. With a quick-and-dirty makeup job, he transformed himself into a low-life pimp, which went well with the black Jeep Unlimited he was driving. The clerk didn't bat an eye when Gideon paid cash for an hourly rate, claimed to have lost his ID, and tipped the man a twenty, telling him to keep an eye out for a "classy young lady" who, of course, would never arrive.

Loading all the theatrical supplies into the suitcase, along with Blaine's computer, he went into his rented room, spread the clothes out on the bed, and began mixing and matching them into various disguises. It was a process he had undertaken many times before.

In his days as an art thief, he usually robbed small private museums and historical societies during daylight hours, when they were open but almost deserted. After the first few heists, he always went in disguise, and as the years went by he got better and better at it. A good disguise was far more than mere appearance; it was about assuming a new character, walking differently, talking in a new way, even thinking differently. It was the purest, most refined form of Method Acting.

But creating the actual new persona was never easy. It had to be subtle, believable, not over the top, and yet with a few telling details that the average person would remember and which would be key to misleading investigators. A totally forgettable character would be a waste of time, but on the other hand, a too eccentric character would be dangerous. The process took time, thought, and imagination.

As he sorted through the clothes, laying out one shirt, then another, mixing and matching them with various pants and shoes, a character began to take shape in his mind—a mid-forty-ish man, out of shape, recently divorced, kids gone, laid off from his job, looking to rediscover and renew himself with a car trip cross-country. A *Blue Highways* sort of odyssey. He'd be a writer—no, make that an *aspiring* writer. He'd be keeping notes of his journey, ready to share his observations about America with anyone he ran into. His wallet had been stolen first day out—no ID now but that was cool in a way, a kind of freedom, a welcome release from the enslaving bonds of society.

Now that he had it, he quickly assembled the outfit: loafers, black jeans, L.L. Bean oxford pin-striped shirt, Bill Blass sport jacket, baldcap with a fringe of hair on the longish side, skin with the slightly raddled look that marked the drinking man, Ray-Bans, a Pendleton "Indy" hat with a broad brim. A small but memorable diamond-shaped scar on his right cheek and a modest paunch completed the picture.

Going through the familiar process of creating a new persona, and a disguise to go with it, felt good. And—for at least a few minutes—he was able to forget Alida.

Now that he was done, he turned to the computer and fired it up. It was, just as he'd expected, password-protected, and his few feeble attempts to guess the password failed. Even if he broke the password, no doubt there would be other layers of security. Blaine's plan might be on that computer, but it might as well be on the moon for all the good it would do him, if he couldn't get through that password.

No time for that now. He shoved it in the suitcase with the other stuff, exited the motel room, tossed everything in the back of the Jeep, and took off. The vehicle had a GPS and when he plugged in the address for Fort Detrick, Maryland, it informed him the distance was eighteen hundred seventy-seven miles and would take thirty hours. By driving at five miles over the speed limit, stopping only for gas, he might shave it down to twenty-five, twenty-six hours. He didn't dare push it any faster—without a driver's license he couldn't risk a traffic stop.

He looked at his watch. It was already ten o'clock in the morning. Blaine had said his plane was leaving early: he'd already be in the air. Gideon had checked with the airlines, and there had been no direct flights to DC that morning—he would have to change planes, and with the loss of two hours due to time zone changes, Blaine would not be at Fort Detrick until that evening at the earliest. The event would almost certainly go down tomorrow, N-Day—the infamous day on the appointment calendar he had seen in Chalker's apartment.

He would be there by noon tomorrow. Whether that gave him time to intersect and confront Blaine he could only guess. Of course, it was entirely possible Blaine wasn't going to Fort Detrick at all. That could have been a ruse; the man might instead be heading straight to Washington. But Gideon would have to deal with that problem when he got east.

He had no idea what he was going to do when he got there. In fact, he didn't have the first notion of a plan, a strategy, a mode of attack. But at least—he thought as he started the engine—he had twenty-six unbroken hours to think one up.

59

Stone Fordyce eased his car down the hideous dirt road toward Blaine's ranch. He was filled with misgivings. Under any other circumstances, he would have said to hell with it. But these were not normal circumstances. Washington was, perhaps, one day away from being nuked. And the investigation was now totally screwed up, headed in the wrong direction. Millard and Dart had it wrong: Gideon had been most certainly framed. By a Los Alamos insider. And that insider—probably Novak—was somehow involved with the terrorist plot. It was the only conclusion he could draw.

Actually, he'd come to a second conclusion: Gideon hadn't run away. He was still in the neighborhood, trying to prove his innocence by searching for the guilty party. That was why he'd gone to Los Alamos, at huge risk to himself. And then he'd confronted Lockhart, again at high risk. Gideon was a clever fox, as sly as they came, but even he wouldn't go to such extreme measures unless he was truly innocent. Somewhere along the way, Gideon had managed to convince Alida Blaine that he was no terrorist—that was the only way to explain her ongoing involvement, her not contacting the authorities.

So where was Gideon? He couldn't have walked from Los Alamos to the Paiute Creek Ranch, back across the mountains, in such a short space of time. He had no horse. Therefore, he must have used a car.

But whose?

As soon as Fordyce asked the question he knew the answer. Gideon and Alida were being helped. Who would they turn to? It was so obvious he couldn't believe no one had thought of it. They were being helped by Alida's father—the writer, Simon Blaine.

From there, it had been a trivial matter to learn that Blaine had a ranch in the Jemez Mountains. And once it was obvious to him, Fordyce realized it would eventually be obvious to Millard, as well. The investigation might be off-base, but Millard wasn't stupid. Somebody, at some point, would think to raid Blaine's ranch.

He just hoped to hell it hadn't already happened.

But as he approached, he saw that everything looked quiet. The ranch buildings were scattered around a large central field, through which ran a burbling creek, with stands of timber hiding various outbuildings, barns, and corrals.

He pulled off the road well short of the ranch, got out his service piece, and exited the car. There were no vehicles, no signs of life. He moved into the trees and approached the main house quietly, stopping every few minutes to listen. Nothing.

Then, when he was about a hundred yards away, he heard the banging of a door and Alida Blaine came striding out, her long blond hair streaming behind her, walking across the yard.

Fordyce stepped out into the sunlight, gun and badge on display. "Miss Blaine? Federal officer. Don't move."

But she took one look and broke into a run, heading straight toward the thick forest at the far side of the meadow.

"Stop!" he cried. "FBI!"

She only ran faster. Fordyce took off after her, sprinting at high speed. He was a fast runner, in excellent shape, but she was really flying. He realized that if she got into those trees, she knew the country and might just get away.

"Stop!" He redoubled his speed, sprinting like a madman, and began to close the gap. They entered the trees but he was still gaining, and in a few hundred yards was close enough to launch himself at her and tackle her from behind.

They landed heavily on a bed of pine needles, but she rolled and fought like a mountain lion, screaming and punching, and it took all his ability, and a few high school wrestling moves, to subdue and pin her.

"Jesus Christ, what the hell's your problem?" he yelled. "You're damn lucky I didn't shoot you!"

"You don't have the balls," she spat back, her face red, furious, still struggling.

"Will you just calm down and listen?" He could feel blood trickling down his face where she had raked his cheek with her hand. God, she was a wild one. "Look, I know Gideon was framed."

The struggling stopped. She stared at him.

"That's right. I know it."

"Bullshit. You're the one that tried to arrest him." But she said this with a little less conviction.

"Whether bullshit or not, I've got a gun trained on you, so you're going to goddamn well listen to me. You got that?"

She was quiet.

"All right." And Fordyce briefly explained the arc of his reasoning. But in doing so he didn't mention Novak's name or go into any details—the last thing he needed was more freelancing on the part of Gideon. Or her.

"So you see," he said, "I know both of you are innocent. But no one will listen to me, the investigation is completely off-base—and it's up to us to pursue this line on our own."

"Let me up," she said. "I can't think with you lying on top of me."

He cautiously let her up. She stood, slapping away the pine needles and dust. "Let's go into the house," she said.

"Is Gideon inside?"

"No. He's not on the ranch."

He followed her into the house, into a large rustic living room with Navajo rugs on the walls, a bearskin on the floor, and an elk skull over the mantelpiece of a big stone fireplace.

"Want anything?" she asked. "Coffee?"

"Coffee. And a Band-Aid."

"Coming up."

The coffee tasted wonderful. He looked at her discreetly as she rummaged for a bandage. This was one hell of a woman. Like Gideon: formidable.

"What do you want?" she asked as she tossed him a Band-Aid box.

"I need to find Gideon. We took on this assignment together and I intend to complete it—with him, partners."

She thought about this, but only for a moment. "Fair enough. I'm in."

"No, you're not in. You have no idea how dangerous this is going to be. We're professionals—you're not. You'd be a serious hindrance and a danger to us both—not to mention yourself."

A long silence.

"Well," she finally said, "I guess I can accept that. You and Gideon can use the ranch as your base."

"Can't do that, either. This ranch is likely to be raided—not today, maybe, but soon. It's just a matter of time. You've got to get the hell out of here. And I've got to find Gideon. Now."

More silence. She was thinking it through, and he was pretty confident she'd understand what she had to do.

Finally, she nodded. "Okay. Gideon's taken the Jeep and he's headed up to the Paiute Creek Ranch to confront Willis. Because sure as hell, he and his weirdo cult are behind this."

Fordyce managed to cover up his surprise. Gideon had *already* confronted Willis—the day before.

"He went up to Paiute Creek... *this* morning?"

"Right. Left at dawn."

So Gideon was lying to her, too. What the hell was the man really up to? He was on the track of someone, Fordyce was sure of that—and he had some reason for not sharing the information with her.

"All right," he said. "Give me the plate number and a description of the vehicle, and I'll take it from there."

She gave him the info, while he wrote it down.

He rose. "Miss Blaine? May I offer you some advice?"

"Sure."

"You need to go to ground. Now. Because it's as I said: sooner rather than later, they're going to raid this ranch—and with the mentality of this investigation, you might not survive it. Understand? Until we find out who's really behind this, your life is not safe."

She nodded.

"All right," he said. "Thanks for your cooperation. I'm outta here."

60

GIDEON HAD REACHED Tucumcari, and he pulled into a Stuckey's to fill up on gas. It was about one in the afternoon and he'd been making excellent time. He felt a certain relief. He'd made a clean getaway and he was driving a vehicle unknown to law enforcement. He had twenty-three more hours of driving ahead of him, more or less. Alida's money might not be enough to get him all the way, but if he had to raid a cash register or two he'd deal with that when the time came.

After filling up, he went into the Stuckey's, in full disguise as Mr. Touchy-Feely-Middle-Aged-Divorced-Man-on-a-Road-Trip-of-Self-Discovery, and stocked up on beef jerky, Cheetos, Twinkies, and Ring Dings, along with a case of Coke and a box of NoDoz. He found a plastic hospital urinal and—after a momentary hesitation—added it to his basket. That would shave some time off his run. He brought everything to the counter, purchased it, and carried the bulging bag to his car. He got in and was about to start the engine when he felt something cold against the nape of his neck.

"Don't fucking move," came the low, hoarse voice.

Gideon froze. He glanced at the glove compartment, where he'd stashed the Python.

"I've already got your .357," came the voice.

Now Gideon recognized the voice as Fordyce's. Unbelievable. How had this happened? This was a disaster—the ultimate disaster.

"Listen to me well, Gideon. I know now you're innocent. I know you were framed. And I also know the security director, Novak, was in on it."

Gideon wasn't sure he'd heard correctly. He struggled with disbelief. Was this some kind of gambit? What was Fordyce up to?

"The investigation is seriously off-track. I need you. We need to partner together, just like before, and finish this assignment. Gideon, you're a foxy son of a bitch, and I don't know if I trust you any farther than I could throw you, but I swear to God we're the only ones who can prevent that nuke from going off."

This was becoming more convincing. "How did you find me?" he asked.

"I put out a routine 'Attempt to Locate' on the Jeep's plate, got a report you were headed east on I-40, drove like hell, and found you here." There was a pause. "Look, I know it's hard to wrap your head around. Like everyone else, I was fooled. I thought you were guilty. But now I know different. I don't know where you're headed, what lead you're following up, but I damn well know you're going to need help."

Gideon looked at him in the rearview mirror. "How'd you get the plate number?"

"I—I figured, since you were on the run with Alida Blaine, that you might be using one of her family cars."

Gideon said nothing. So the vehicle *wasn't* unknown to law enforcement, after all.

"Here's your Python." Fordyce handed it back to him. Gideon could see it was still loaded. "To show my good faith."

Gideon glanced into the rearview mirror again, looked into Fordyce's eyes, and saw sincerity. The man was telling the truth.

"Let's go. We're racing against the clock." Gideon started the Jeep.

"Wait. We can take my pool car. I've got a siren, the works."

"You're AWOL from the investigation—?"

"They put me on leave."

"This car's marginally safer. They might come looking for you first."

Fordyce paused. "Makes sense."

Gideon pulled out of the Stuckey's, back onto the interstate. "While we drive," he said, "I'm going to tell you what I've learned. And you tell me what you know. And then I've got a laptop in the back that needs to be broken into. You once said you worked in the FBI's decryption section. Think you can help?"

"I can try."

Gideon set the cruise control at seventy-nine. Then, with the car humming along the interstate, he began to tell Fordyce everything.

61

AFTER CROSSING THE Texas Panhandle, they stopped near the Oklahoma border so Fordyce could pick up a cigarette-lighter converter for the laptop's AC adapter. On the long trip across Texas, Gideon had explained to the agent how he'd deduced that Blaine was the one behind the terrorist plot, and in turn Fordyce told him how he'd figured out that Gideon was innocent and the security director, Novak, was involved.

"What I don't know," Fordyce said, "is whether Novak was part of the plot from the beginning, or if he was paid for just the frame job."

"From your description of his house, it seems like he's had more money than he should for some time now," Gideon replied. "My bet is that he's one of the original players." He paused. "No wonder Blaine was willing to help me, a fugitive on the lam. He probably wasn't too happy that Alida became involved, but he must have figured that if I stayed on the loose, I'd prove just another distraction for the authorities."

He paused again. "What I *can't* figure out is Blaine himself. Why the hell would he, of all people, want to set off a nuke in Washington? I just don't see the motivation. He's a patriot, an ex-spy."

"You'd be surprised how people can change. Or what their motivations might be."

"Alida told me Blaine was denied a Nobel Prize because of his past. Perhaps that embittered him."

"Perhaps. And perhaps we'll find the answer on this laptop." Fordyce plugged in the computer and pressed the POWER button.

From the driver's seat, Gideon looked over as the hard disk trundled, various start-up messages flashed by, then the login screen appeared.

Gideon muttered, "Like I said. Password-protected."

"O ye of little faith," Fordyce retorted.

"Can you crack it?"

"That remains to be seen. Look at the splash screen, it's running the NewBSD variant of UNIX—an odd choice for a novelist."

"Don't forget, he's ex-MI6. Who the hell knows what software they run?"

"True. But I doubt this is Blaine's working machine." He pointed at the laptop's screen. "Check out that version number: NewBSD 2.1.1. This OS is at least six years old."

"Is that bad?"

"It might be good—the security won't be as strong. Didn't you see any other computers in his office?"

"I didn't hang around casing the joint. I just grabbed the first one I saw."

Fordyce nodded. Then he pulled his BlackBerry from his pocket and began pressing buttons.

"Who are you calling?" Gideon asked.

"I'm accessing the mainframe at FBI Crypt. I'm going to need a few tools to do this job properly."

Gideon waited while Fordyce typed a laborious series of commands. Then, with a grunt of satisfaction, the agent attached a flash memory stick to the BlackBerry's USB port. "I can boot into half a dozen operating systems with this gizmo," he said, tapping the memory stick. "Thank God this laptop's got USB."

"What next?" Gideon asked.

"I'm going to run a dictionary attack on Blaine's login password."

"Right."

"If it isn't too long or obscure, and if the total exhaust time on the OS password monitor is within reason, maybe we'll catch a break."

Gideon glanced over dubiously. "Blaine's no dummy."

"True. But that doesn't mean he's technically savvy." Fordyce snugged the flash drive into one of the laptop's USB ports and re-booted the machine. "This little honey can try two hundred and fifty thousand passwords a second. Let's see just how paranoid Simon Blaine really is."

For the next ninety minutes, Gideon drove the Jeep at precisely seventy-nine miles per hour, passing Elk City, then Clinton, then Weatherford. The sun would soon be setting, and a starry sky would fill the night dome of the prairie. As they neared Oklahoma City, without progress, Gideon began to feel increasingly restless. Fordyce, too, was growing impatient, peering at the screen and muttering under his breath. Finally, with a curse, he yanked the flash drive from the laptop's slot and powered down the machine. "Okay," he growled. "Score one for Blaine."

"So we're screwed?" Gideon asked.

"Not yet we're not." When the laptop rebooted and the login prompt appeared, Fordyce rattled off a quick blast of keystrokes:

```
LOGIN: root
PASSWORD: ****
```

Immediately a storm of text scrolled up the screen.

"Bingo!" Fordyce said.

Gideon looked at him. "Did you get into his account?"

"No."

"Then what good is it?"

"I got into the system account. Just type *root* for both the login name and password and, presto, you're super-user. You'd be amazed at how many people either don't know enough or are too lazy to change the default system account passwords on these older UNIX systems."

"Can you get into his account or his files from there?"

Fordyce shook his head. "No, I can't. But maybe I don't need to."

"Why the hell not?"

"Because as super-user, I can access the standard UNIX password file." He plugged the flash drive back in, typed a long string of commands, then sat back in his seat, beaming. He pointed at the screen. "Check it out."

Gideon looked over.

```
BlaineS:Heqw3EZU5k4Nd:413:adgfirkgm~:/home/
subdir/BlaineS:/bin/bash
```

"That's his account name and password, the latter scrambled with DES."

"Data encryption standard? I thought that couldn't be cracked."

Fordyce smiled.

Gideon frowned. "Uh-oh. Let me guess. The government built a back door into the encryption standard."

"You didn't hear it from me."

For about ten minutes, Gideon drove while Fordyce typed, sometimes pausing to peer at the screen, now and then muttering under his breath. Finally, with a withering curse, he punched the back of the seat.

"No joy?" Gideon asked.

Fordyce shook his head. "I can't break the DES algorithm. Blaine's a lot more sophisticated than I thought. He or someone used a hardened DES variant. I'm totally stuck. I can't think of anything else to do."

The Jeep fell into silence.

"We can't just give up," Gideon said.

"You got any ideas?"

"We can try guessing the password."

Fordyce rolled his eyes. "My dictionary attack just tried over a billion passwords in twelve common languages, including words, combinations of words, names, and place-names, not to mention a compilation of the million most commonly used passwords. It's the best brute-force attack program in existence. And you think you can do better by *guessing?*" He shook his head.

"At least we know what *not* to guess at. Your dictionary attack is just a dumb program. We know a lot more about Simon Blaine than it does. Look, it's worth a shot. We've already got his account name, right?" Gideon thought for a moment. "Maybe he used the name of one of the characters in his books. Get on your BlackBerry, find his website, and grab the names of any characters you find."

Fordyce grunted approval and got to work.

A few minutes later, Fordyce had compiled a list of a dozen names. "Dirkson Auger," he said, looking at the first on the list. "Blaine really gets paid for making up names like that?"

"Try it."

Fordyce lifted the lid of the laptop. "I'll try Dirkson first."

Error.

"Auger."

Error.

"Try them together," Gideon suggested.

Error.

"Try the names again in turn, only backward this time."

Error.

"Son of a bitch," Fordyce muttered.

"Do the same with the rest."

Before Gideon had driven another fifteen miles, Fordyce threw up his hands. "It's hopeless," he said. "I've tried them all. Even if it *was* one of these names, if Blaine had any sense he'd have thrown in a few extra characters to add some noise, or changed letters to numbers, or something. There are just too many variants."

"The thing about passwords," Gideon said after a minute or two, "is that, unless you're using a password manager, you have to remember the damn thing."

"So?"

"So maybe it isn't a character in a book. Maybe it's the name of a real person. He wouldn't be likely to forget that. And the most obvious person would be Alida."

"Obvious, all right. Way too obvious." Fordyce typed in the name anyway, tried a bunch of variations. "Nope."

"Okay, so do what you suggested a minute ago. Change some of the letters to numbers or symbols."

"I'll change the *l* to a *1*." Fordyce tried this password. "Nada."

"Try something else. Change the *i* to a dollar sign."

More typing. "Strike three," said Fordyce.

Gideon licked his lips. "I remember reading that most decent passwords are composed of two parts, a root and an appendage. Right? So add something on the end."

"Like what?"

"I don't know. *Xyz*, maybe. Or *00*."

Still more typing. "This is getting old, fast," Fordyce told him.

"Wait a minute—I just thought of something. Blaine has a pet name for Alida. *Miracle Daughter*. He sometimes calls her MD. Try that after her name."

Fordyce typed. "No go. Not in front, in back, or in the middle."

Gideon sighed. Maybe Fordyce was right. "Just keep trying all the variables." He concentrated on the road ahead while Fordyce typed quietly beside him, trying one variant after another.

Suddenly the FBI agent gave a whoop of triumph. Gideon glanced over and saw a fresh welter of text scrolling up the screen.

"You got in?" he asked in disbelief.

"Damn right!"

"What was the password?"

"*A1$daMdee*. Kind of sentimental, don't you think?" And Fordyce settled in to browse the computer's files as the skyline of Oklahoma City came into view.

62

Twelve hours later they were crossing Tennessee. Fordyce slouched in the passenger seat, nose buried in the laptop. For twelve hours, he had been poring over it, browsing its many thousands of files, with no hits; nothing but book drafts, endless chapter revisions, correspondence, outlines, movie treatments, notes, and the like. The computer seemed completely and totally devoted to writing—and nothing else.

Gideon glanced over. "Any luck?" he asked for about the thirtieth time.

Fordyce shook his head.

"What about emails?"

"Nothing of interest. No exchanges with Chalker, Novak, or anyone else up at Los Alamos." It seemed more and more likely, Fordyce reflected, that there had been another computer in Blaine's office that Gideon had failed to grab. But he didn't say anything.

In the background, Gideon was listening to NPR, which—as usual—was spewing a mixture of news and speculation about the impending nuke attack on Washington. The investigation had managed to keep the presumed N-Day—today—a secret, but the massive movements of troops, the evacuations of Washington, and all the other preparations in major cities around the country were garnering frantic media attention. The country was in a state of intense and escalating anxiety. People knew that things were coming to a head.

Anxiety and outrage ruled the airwaves. A parade of self-appointed experts, pundits, talking heads, and politicians offered their conflicting views, one after the other, excoriating the stalled investigation and offering their own insights. Everyone had a theory. The terrorists had abandoned their plan. The terrorists had shifted their attack to another major American city. The terrorists were lying low, biding their time. The terrorists were all dead from radiation poisoning. The liberals were to blame. The conservatives were to blame. The terrorists were communists, right-wingers, left-wingers, fundamentalists, anarchists, bankers, you name it.

It went on and on. Fordyce couldn't help but listen with a kind of repulsed fascination, wanting to ask Gideon to turn it off yet unable to.

He glanced out at the road ahead of them. They were approaching the outer suburbs of Knoxville. He stretched again, looked back down at the laptop. It was incredible how many files a writer could generate. He was about three-quarters through them, and there was nothing to do but keep going.

As he opened the next file—something called "OPERATION CORPSE"—he was jolted by the sudden whoop of a siren and flashing lights in his rearview mirror. He glanced over at the speedometer and saw they were still going seventy-nine—in a zone where the speed limit had just dropped to sixty.

"Oh shit," he muttered.

"No driver's license," said Gideon. "I'm dead."

Fordyce laid aside the computer. The cop whooped his siren again. Gideon put on his blinker, slowed, eased over into the breakdown lane, and came to a stop.

"Play it by ear," said Fordyce, his mind working fast. "Tell him you had your wallet stolen, that your name is Simon Blaine."

The cop got out of his car, hitching up his pants. He was a state trooper, big and square, with a shaved head, knobby ears, mirrored shades, and a frown on his thick lips. He came up, tapped on the window. Gideon rolled it down.

The trooper leaned in. "License and registration?"

"Hello, Officer," Gideon said politely. He reached over into the glove compartment and rummaged around, pulling out the registration. He handed it to the cop. "Officer, my wallet was stolen at a rest stop back there in Arkansas. As soon as I get back to New Mexico I'll be getting a replacement license."

A silence while the trooper glanced over the registration. "Are you Simon Blaine?"

"Yes, sir."

Fordyce hoped to hell the guy wasn't a fiction reader.

"You say you have no license?"

"I have a license, Officer, but it was stolen." He had to engineer this one fast. He pitched his voice in a confidential tone. "My dad was a state trooper just like you, shot in the line of duty—"

"Please step out of the car, sir," said the trooper, impassive.

Gideon moved to comply, fumbling with the doorknob while he continued talking. "Routine traffic stop, two guys, turned out they'd just robbed a bank..." He continued fumbling. "Damn door..."

"Out. Now." The man brought his hand to rest on the butt of his sidearm, as a precaution.

Fordyce could see that this was already going the wrong way. He took out his shield and leaned over Gideon, showing it to the trooper. "Officer?" he said. "Special Agent Fordyce, FBI."

The trooper, startled, took the shield and examined it through the mirrored shades. He handed it back to Fordyce, making a show of being unimpressed. Then he turned to Gideon once again. "I asked you to step out of the car."

Fordyce was irritated. He opened his door and got out.

"You remain in the car, sir," said the trooper.

"Excuse me," said Fordyce, sharply. He walked around the front of the car and approached the trooper, staring at his shield. "Officer Mackie, is it? As I said, I'm a special agent from the DC field office." He did not offer his hand. "My associate here is an FBI technical liaison. We're traveling undercover. We're both assigned to NEST, working on the terrorist case. I've given you my name and shown you my badge number, and you're welcome to check out my affiliation. But I am sorry to say you are *not* going to see any ID from this gentleman and you'll just have to accept that. Do you understand?"

He paused. Mackie said nothing.

"I said, do you *understand* me, Officer Mackie?"

The trooper remained unmoved. "I will check out your affiliation, thank you. May I have your identification back, sir?"

This wasn't acceptable: the last thing Fordyce wanted was for Millard to learn he was two-thirds of the way across the country in Simon Blaine's Jeep. But...If the man needed the identification back, it meant he hadn't noted his name. Fordyce took another step toward the trooper and lowered his voice. "No more of this bullshit. We need to get to Washington, and we're in a big-time hurry. That's why we were speeding. Because we're traveling undercover, we can't slap a siren on the vehicle or travel with an escort. Call in my ID, check it out—no problem. You do that. But in case you haven't been listening to the news, there's a crisis going on, and my associate and I sure as hell can't wait around while you check us out." He paused, scanning the man's face to see if he was penetrating that stolid exterior.

The state trooper remained more or less impassive. A tough one. Well, so be it. He raised his voice to a shout.

"And I might just add, *Officer*, that if your activities blow our cover, you'll find yourself at the bottom of the Mariana Shit Trench. We're on a critical mission and you've already wasted too much of our time."

And now, finally, Fordyce saw the man's truculent, brick-like face flush with fear and anger. "I'm just doing my job, sir, you've no business talking to me like that."

Fordyce eased off abruptly, exhaled, laid a hand on the man's shoulder. "I know. I'm sorry. We're *all* just doing our jobs—in a tough situation. I'm sorry for speaking to you sharply, Troop. We're under a lot of stress here, as you might imagine. But we really do need to keep going. By all means, call in my name and badge number, check it out—but please don't hold us up."

The man straightened. "Yes, sir. I understand. I think we're done here. I'm going to radio your plate number ahead and let everyone know you'll be coming through on official law enforcement business, so you can exceed the speed limit at least as far as the state line."

Fordyce gave his shoulder a squeeze. "Appreciate it, Troop. Very much." He slipped back into the passenger seat and Gideon took off. After a moment, Fordyce said, "Father a state trooper shot in the line of duty? Fucking lame. Lucky I was around to pull your fat out of the fire."

"You had the badge, I didn't," Gideon said. Then he added, grudgingly: "Still, you did good."

"Damn right." Fordyce frowned. "Lot of good it's going to do us. We're, what, seven hours out of DC and we still don't have a clue what Blaine's up to. This laptop is as clean as the driven snow."

"There's got to be something in there. You can't plan a huge conspiracy like this and not have it leak into your work in some way."

"What if we're wrong? What if he's innocent, after all?"

Gideon fell silent. Then he shook his head. "For personal reasons, a huge part of me wishes he was. But he's behind this. He has to be. Nothing else makes sense."

With a weary sense of futility, Fordyce went back to OPERATION CORPSE. He knew what he'd find, the same thing he'd found in all the other endless files: the straightforward work of a dedicated and prolific writer.

OPERATION CORPSE was a ten-page outline for a novel, apparently one Blaine had never written—at least, not by that title. Fordyce rubbed his eyes, began skimming the synopsis, then stopped. As he stared at the screen, he felt his heart just about do a flip. He blinked once, twice. Then he went back to the beginning and began again, more slowly this time.

When he reached the end, he looked over at Gideon. "Oh my God," he said in a low voice. "You aren't going to believe this."

63

GIDEON TRIED TO focus on the road as Fordyce began to talk. "There's a book proposal here, just ten pages. It's titled OPERATION CORPSE."

Gideon eased off the accelerator, slowing down to eighty so he could devote more attention to Fordyce. "A book proposal?"

"Yeah. An outline for a thriller."

"About nuclear terrorists?"

"No. About smallpox."

"Smallpox? What does that have to do with anything?"

"Just listen." Fordyce paused, gathering his thoughts. "You need to understand some background first. The outline explains that, as a human disease, smallpox was completely wiped out in the wild back in 1977. All remaining viral cultures held in laboratories were destroyed...*except for two*. One is currently at the State Research Center of Virology and Biotechnology in Koltsovo, Russia. And the other is at USAMRIID, in—" Fordyce paused for effect—"Fort Detrick, Maryland."

Gideon felt himself go cold. "No *shit*."

"The outline tells the story of a gang that plans to steal the smallpox from Fort Detrick. They want to get their hands on it and threaten to release it—in order to blackmail the world. They want a hundred billion dollars and their own small country—an island in the Pacific.

They plan to keep the smallpox as protection, a guarantee of sorts, on their island and live out their lives in luxury and comfort."

"So far, I don't see the connection."

"The rub is *how* they're going to steal the smallpox: by creating a fake Islamic terrorist plot to detonate a nuke in DC."

Gideon glanced at the agent. "Sink me."

"And here's the kicker: they fake the terrorist plot with an irradiated corpse—left in an apartment in New York City, made to look like it was killed in a radiation accident involving a nuclear bomb core. And the apartment is salted with phony evidence linking the man to radical Islamists and a jihadist terror cell."

"Chalker," Gideon said.

"Exactly. Not to mention a calendar with the intended date, and a burned map of Washington with potential targets."

The wheels in Gideon's mind began to turn. "Fort Detrick is only forty miles from Washington."

Fordyce nodded. "Right."

"So the threat to DC will have drawn off most of the soldiers at Fort Detrick."

"Exactly," said Fordyce. "Not only will the nuclear threat empty Fort Detrick of soldiers, but it'll also strip away most of the security from USAMRIID, leaving the smallpox vulnerable."

"Unbelievable," said Gideon.

"In the outline, they have an inside contact who's given them the codes to get into the vault where the virus is. They walk in, punch in the codes, open the biosafe holding the smallpox, take out a few frozen cultures, and walk out. The smallpox cultures are stored in these cryogenically sealed disks that are so small they can be hidden in your pocket." Fordyce tapped the laptop. "It's all here—in a book outline Blaine wrote *six years ago*. And get this: it says here the idea for the book was based on an actual covert operation launched by the British during World War Two, called Operation Mincemeat. British intelligence floated a corpse off the coast of Spain. Supposedly, it was the body of a high-level Brit officer drowned in a plane crash. In the pockets of the corpse were secret documents indicating that the Allies were going to invade Italy through Greece and Sardinia. But the whole thing *was a plant*—a scheme to misdirect the Germans from England's true invasion plans. And it totally fooled the Germans, all the way up to Hitler himself."

There was a brief silence as Gideon processed this. "British intelligence," he murmured. "MI6. Just like Blaine."

"The only difference," Fordyce went on, "is that Chalker wasn't a corpse."

"Even alive, he was damn effective," said Gideon. "Even a massive dose of radiation takes time to kill. They must've kidnapped him, kept him locked up, and performed God only knows what kind of brainwashing on him."

"That dog crate in the lab we found," Fordyce said. "It probably wasn't for a dog, after all."

"So those crazy rantings of Chalker about being kidnapped, experimented on, weren't so crazy after all." Gideon paused. "They framed him for being a jihadist—just like they framed me."

Fordyce tapped at the keyboard. "Let me read you something. It says in this proposal that, since it's been forty years since smallpox was seen in the wild, most people alive today have no resistance to it. It would scythe right through the human race. Check this out."

Variola major, or smallpox, is considered by many epidemiologists to be the worst disease ever to afflict humankind. Depending on the strain, the mortality rate can run as high as one hundred percent. *Variola* is as infectious as the common cold and spreads like wildfire. Even those who survive are physically scarred for life and often blind as well.

Smallpox causes one of the most frightening and terrible deaths known. It commences with high fever, muscle pain, and vomiting. A rash develops, covering the body with hard, distended pustules, often forming on the tongue and palate. In its fulminating form, the pustules merge to form a single pustule-like covering to the victim's entire body. The blood leaks out of the vessels into the muscles and organs, and the eyes fill up with blood and turn bright red. The symptoms of the disease are often accompanied by acute mental distress in which neurological changes cause the victim to suffer an overwhelming feeling of suffocating terror, a dread of impending doom. All too often, that fear becomes reality.

The World Health Organization has stated that a single case of smallpox appearing anywhere in the world would be a "world-wide medical emergency of the highest order" and would require "a complete and total quarantine of the infected region combined with an emergency 'ring of vaccination' program as containment. It seems likely that significant military force would be required to implement an effective quarantine of infected areas."

When Fordyce finished reading there was silence in the car, the humming of the tires filling the space.

"So Blaine had an idea for a novel," said Gideon. "He worked out all the details, wrote the proposal. It was going to make a terrific thriller. And then he realized it was too good to waste on a book. He decided to do it—for real."

Fordyce nodded.

"I bet he went for it when he met Chalker and realized what a golden opportunity had just fallen into his lap. I mean, what better scapegoat for his irradiated corpse than a nuclear scientist at Los Alamos who'd converted to Islam?"

"Yes," said Fordyce. "And another thing: I'd bet we're dealing with a larger group here—not just Blaine. Novak's in on it, and there must be others. This isn't the kind of thing you can pull off solo."

"You're right. And I'll bet one of those others is—or was—an airplane mechanic."

"But here's what I don't get. Without a real nuke, how did they irradiate Chalker?"

Gideon considered this. "There are other ways. The most obvious would be with the radio-isotopes used in medical diagnoses."

"That stuff's easily available?"

"Not easily. But it is available to those with the right licenses. The thing is, medical isotopes *are* generally fission products of uranium or plutonium, the result of controlled criticality reactions. Of course, they'd have to calculate radioactive isotope ratios based on medical radioactivity, due to the fission yields driving these isotopic ratios."

"I have no idea what you're talking about."

"What I mean is, it could be done. You could fake a nuclear core accident by leaving traces of medical radio-isotopes in just the right ratios. Not only that, but medical radio-isotopes could have been used to irradiate Chalker, as well."

"What about the U-235 they found on Chalker's hands?" asked Fordyce.

"If you had an inside contact at Los Alamos—like Novak, say— that wouldn't be difficult. All you'd need is a few nanograms. Someone could obtain that amount by simply swiping the tip of a gloved finger on a piece of U-235. The glove would bring away many nanograms of material that could then be transferred to Chalker's hands with a mere handshake."

"So why didn't anyone consider the possibility this was faked?"

"It's so improbable," Gideon answered. "So...outré. Would you ever have guessed?"

Fordyce thought about this a moment. "Never."

"Blaine must have rented that Queens apartment, supposedly for Chalker. No wonder Chalker said it wasn't his place—chances were he'd never been there before. They probably kept him in that basement cage until he was suitably disoriented. Then they irradiated him, put a gun in his hand, and stuck him in Sunnyside with an innocent family. All for blackmail, for money."

"If you're talking smallpox, for a whole hell of a lot of money, no doubt."

Gideon shook his head. "Jesus, that's cold."

They flashed past a sign announcing they were entering Virginia. Gideon slowed further.

"N-Day is here," said Fordyce, glancing at his watch. "And we've got maybe five hours to figure out how we're going to stop this thing."

64

THEY DROVE THROUGH the Appalachian foothills of southwestern Virginia in silence. While the westbound lanes were still choked with fleeing cars, the eastbound lanes they were traversing were practically deserted. Gideon stared straight ahead, hands gripping the wheel, his mind still racing. Should he try calling Glinn back? The man obviously had the right connections. But he dismissed the idea quickly: Garza had made it abundantly clear that Gideon was now completely on his own.

"We know their plan now," Fordyce said. "What we need to do is contact NEST, have them secure USAMRIID, and we're done."

Gideon drove on, considering this.

"It goes without saying," said Fordyce, "that we can't do this ourselves."

Still, Gideon did not reply.

"I hope you agree. I'm calling Dart." Fordyce took out his cell phone.

"Just a moment," said Gideon. "What makes you think Dart will believe us?"

"We've got the computer. We've got the file. If this isn't proof, I don't know what is." Fordyce began to dial.

"I don't think so," Gideon said slowly.

Fordyce stopped dialing. "You don't think so."

"Dart's not going to believe us. He thinks I'm a terrorist and you're a fuckup whom he relieved of duty and who's now gone AWOL."

"The proof's on the computer."

"In a Microsoft Word file that could easily have been created or altered by us."

"...But the DES encryption!"

"Big deal. The *file* wasn't encrypted—just the computer. Stone, think: this investigation is way too invested in the jihadist plot theory. There's simply too much momentum for it to turn on a dime."

"It doesn't *have* to turn on a dime. All Dart has to do is redeploy a dozen armed soldiers to guard that smallpox vault. It's what any prudent investigator would do."

Gideon shook his head. "While Dart isn't stupid, he's a prisoner of the book. He's not the kind who thinks outside the box. You call Dart now and we'll be arrested as soon as we show up with this computer. They'll want to analyze the computer, make sure it isn't a plant of some kind. They'll debrief us at length...and meanwhile the smallpox will be stolen. Only then, when it's too late, will they believe us."

"Yes, but I know the FBI, and I'm telling you they'll cover their asses by instantly deploying at least a few troops to guard USAMRIID."

"This isn't just the FBI now, or even NEST. It's a monstrous, hydra-headed, out-of-control investigation that's no longer acting in a rational manner. They're drowning in false leads, red herrings, and conspiracy theories. We come in at the eleventh hour, babbling some out-of-left-field talk of smallpox...Think about it. Dart isn't going to respond in time, and the bad guys will get the virus. You call Dart and they win. Game over."

Fordyce slammed his fist on the dashboard. "Damn you, so what do you propose instead?"

"Simple. We go into Fort Detrick—I'm pretty sure we can talk our way in, especially with that shield of yours—and ambush the bastards when they come out with the smallpox. Catch them in the act. Then we take away the smallpox at gunpoint, hold them, and call the cavalry."

"Why not stop them *before* they get the smallpox?"

"Because we need to catch them *with* it. If we just stop them at the door, there might be a scuffle, and then we'll be arrested and they'll go free—free to execute their plot. We need proof that the crime was committed."

Fordyce laughed mirthlessly. "So, what—now you've got a hero complex? What if they show up with ten guys armed to the teeth?"

"They're not going to do that. Think about it. This plan is all about *quiet*. Draw off the security and go in and out quietly."

"I say we call Dart."

Gideon felt a surge of anger. "I *know* Dart. He was director of the lab my first year at Los Alamos. Sure, he's smart, but he's also stubborn, defensive, and rigid. He's *not* going to believe you, he will *not* put guards on the smallpox, he'll arrest us both and dick around until it's too late. Once they drive off with the smallpox, it's over. Because all they have to do is toss one of those petri dishes out the window and the United States is fucked. We're all freaked out about a loose nuke. Well, here's a news flash for you: that smallpox is *worse* than a nuke. A lot worse."

A long silence. Gideon shot a covert glance at the FBI agent. Fordyce's face was red with anger, but he said nothing. Gideon seemed to have gotten through.

"We will *not* take this to Dart," Gideon said. "We're going to do this ourselves. Otherwise, I'm out."

"Have it your way," said Fordyce, his lips tightening.

There was a long silence.

"You want to hear my plan?" Gideon asked.

After a moment, Fordyce nodded.

"We socially engineer our way in. You stake out the lobby. I go to the Level Four lab where the smallpox is kept. I'll put on a biosafety suit, unrecognizable. You call me when Blaine arrives, I ambush him in the lab after he opens the biosafe, and I hold him at gunpoint while you call in the cavalry. It'll all take place in Level Four, so even if the smallpox does escape, it'll be contained."

"What if they're armed?"

"I doubt it. That would be risky. Like I said: this whole plan is all about subterfuge and misdirection, not force. But if they are armed, I'll have the drop on them. And believe me, I'll shoot to kill if need be." Even as he said it, he wondered just what it would mean if he killed Alida's father. He pushed that unsettling thought out of his mind.

"That would work," said Fordyce slowly, after a moment. "Yes. I think that might work well."

65

Gaining entrance to Fort Detrick was a piece of cake: Gideon pretended to be Fordyce's driver and Fordyce did his thing, waving his FBI shield around and explaining they were on a routine assignment, just checking out one of many undoubtedly false leads related to the nuke alarm. He was careful to say nothing about smallpox. The lone man in the security station helpfully directed them to the USAMRIID complex, drawing their route on a photocopied map of the base, which Gideon examined then stuffed in his pocket. The man waved them through, the base's single main road winding around a golf course before heading for the main section of the compound.

At three thirty in the afternoon on a weekday, Fort Detrick was eerily deserted. Its green, extensive grounds, covering over a thousand acres, had an almost post-apocalyptic feel: parking lots were empty, buildings vacant. The only sound was that of birds, chirping in the spreading oaks.

They cruised slowly through the leafy base. It was surprisingly attractive. In addition to the golf course, it had baseball diamonds, several suburban neighborhoods of neat bungalows or trailers, a small airfield with hangars and aircraft, a fire station, and a recreational center. USAMRIID was at the far end of the base, next to the base's large motor pool—bristling with military vehicles, but apparently devoid of humanity save for a single mechanic. USAMRIID itself was a sprawling, 1970s-style building with a welcome sign on the approaching drive: The United States Army Medical Research Institute for Infectious Diseases. The large, wraparound parking lot was, like the others, mostly empty. There was an air of desuetude, even abandonment.

"Blaine called it right," said Fordyce, looking around. "Everyone's in DC. Let's hope we beat him here."

"Not cool if Blaine sees his own Jeep parked in the lot," Gideon said. He drove past the building to the lot of an unrelated complex, parking the Jeep behind a van. He shrugged into a new disguise, and they cut across the lawn, approaching the entrance.

As they'd discussed the plan, Fordyce had used the laptop's broadband card to access USAMRIID's website. In the process, they had learned quite a lot about the facility: that its name was pronounced *You-Sam-Rid*; that it had once been the hub of the country's biological warfare program; that it now served as the main center for biodefense research in the country, its primary mission to protect the United States from potential bioweapon attacks.

And it was one of two repositories of smallpox left in the world. The virus, the website helpfully mentioned, was kept in a high-security vault in USAMRIID's Biosafety Level 4 laboratory complex, located in the basement of the building.

They entered the lobby. There was a security guard at a locked entrance door at the rear, seated behind a small window of what appeared to be bulletproof glass. Fordyce was going in as himself; Gideon, on the other hand, had sorted through his arsenal of clothes, hairpieces, and accessories in order to create a new persona. He didn't have a lab coat, but he deemed that overkill anyway. Instead, he went for the tweedy, somewhat disheveled absentminded professor look. "A cliché to be sure," he'd told Fordyce, "but clichés often work when it comes to disguises. People like to have their prejudices confirmed."

Fordyce approached the guard, ID in one hand, shield in the other. "Stone Fordyce, Federal Bureau of Investigation," he said, his aggressive tone almost implying the guard himself was a suspect. "And this is Dr. John Martino of the Centers for Disease Control. He doesn't have any ID at present, but I can vouch for him."

This statement hung in the air. Fordyce did not offer an explanation for why Gideon had no ID, and after a hesitation the guard seemed disinclined to ask for one.

"Do you have an appointment?" the guard asked.

"No," said Fordyce almost before the guard had finished asking the question.

"Um, the purpose of your visit?" he asked.

"Routine law enforcement activity," said Fordyce, his tone now becoming impatient.

The man nodded, pulled out a clipboard, slid it through a slit in the glass. "Fill this out, please. Both of you. And sign."

Fordyce filled out a line, passed it to Gideon, who used a suitably quasi-illegible hand. They passed it back.

"Stand in front of the camera," the guard directed.

They each stood before the camera. A minute later, newly issued clip badges were slipped through the slot. A moment later, the steel entrance door buzzed and they were let in.

Fordyce motioned the guard over. "I'd like to ask you a few questions." Again, his tone implied suspicion.

"Yes, sir?" the guard, already intimidated, stood almost at attention.

"Has a Mr. Simon Blaine signed in?"

The guard hesitated, again decided to go with the flow, and checked his clipboard. "No, sir."

"How about a Mr. Novak?"

"No."

"Does either of them have an appointment in the building today?"

Another check. "Not on my sheet, sir."

"All right. Dr. Martino needs to gain access to the Level Four lab. How can he do that?"

"It's on keypad security, you have to get clearance and an escort."

"Who's in charge?"

A hesitation. "He should contact Dr. Glick, the director."

"His location?"

"Third floor, Room Three Forty-six. Shall I call him—?"

"*Absolutely not*," said Fordyce forcefully. He glanced at the man's

ID badge. "Mr. Bridge, here's what's going to happen. I will need your help, so please listen carefully."

He paused.

"I'm going to move into the waiting room, there, mostly out of sight, and wait for Mr. Blaine to arrive. You will not indicate my presence or acknowledge that an FBI agent is on the premises."

At this the guard swallowed and seemed to grow flustered. "Is there something wrong? I mean, maybe I should call my boss, the head of security—"

Fordyce interrupted him. "Do not call *anyone*. If you're concerned about this, and *really feel* you need to check up on me, you can speak to *my* supervisor, Special Agent in Charge Mike Bocca, of the DC field office." He took out his cell phone and looked poised to dial, his expression one of extreme annoyance.

"No, no," said the guard, "that's not necessary."

"Good. You will please continue working as if nothing out of the ordinary was going on."

"Yes, sir."

"Thank you," said Fordyce, his voice suddenly warmer, giving the man a handshake. "Good man."

The guard retreated behind his counter. Gideon watched Fordyce cross the lobby and take a seat in a small waiting area, in the corner, where he could see but not readily be seen. *He's learning*, Gideon thought to himself. Then he continued on into the guts of the building, following the helpful signs directing him toward Level 4.

66

ALMOST AS SOON as Gideon had disappeared down the hall, Stone Fordyce took out his cell phone and dialed Myron Dart's telephone number. Fordyce had to intimidate his way through several subordinates before getting Dart himself on the phone.

The man came on, sounding tense. "Fordyce? What the hell is this all about? I thought you were, ah, taking time off."

Fordyce took a deep breath. He had been going over this conversation in his mind for a while, thinking of the best way to approach it.

"I'm in Maryland..." He took a deep breath. "With Gideon Crew."

This was met with a sudden silence. "Maryland? *With* Crew?" A freezing silence. "You'd better explain yourself."

"We're here following a bombshell lead. And I mean *bombshell*. You've got to listen to what I have to tell you."

Another long silence, then a faint, muffled conversation. Fordyce wondered if Dart was initiating a triangulation on his cell signal. It's what he would do, if he were in Dart's place.

When Dart finally spoke again, his voice was like black ice. "I want to know exactly where you are and what you are doing."

Fordyce plowed ahead. "I've got a laptop computer belonging to a certain individual, and on this computer is a document dated six years ago that spells out the entire terrorist plan, from beginning to end. It explains *everything*."

Another long silence. "The name of this individual?"

"I'll get to that in a moment."

"You'll tell me right now."

Again Fordyce moved ahead. "I've got the computer with me, and if you'll give me your email address I'll send you the document."

"You are insubordinate, Fordyce. I want you to take Crew into custody and come in right now, with Crew in handcuffs and leg irons, or I'll have you arrested as an accomplice."

"Give me your email address and I'll send you this document." Fordyce kept his voice steady, neutral. This wasn't a good start. God, he hoped Gideon hadn't been right about Dart. He had to get the man to *see* the document.

After a long, ticking silence, Dart finally gave him the address. Fordyce typed it into the computer and mailed off the document.

He continued holding the line. They must have located his position by now. It was the chance he had to take—whatever Gideon thought, this was too big for the two of them to handle. Either Dart would believe him or not.

A minute ticked by. Two minutes.

"Did you get it?" he asked.

"Just a moment," Dart replied. His voice sounded thick, distracted. Another minute passed. Fordyce could hear Dart's breathing. When he came back on, his voice had changed. It was steadier, calm. "Where did you get this?"

"Off a computer owned by Simon Blaine, the novelist."

"But...in what context?"

"It's a proposal for a thriller."

"Who else knows about it?"

"Just Gideon."

"What the *hell* are you doing teamed up with Crew?"

"He's the one who found it."

"It's obviously a fake!" Dart suddenly exploded. "Gideon fabricated this—and you fell for it hook, line, and sinker!"

"No, no, no. Impossible. It was on an encrypted computer. *I* broke the encryption."

"How the devil did he get this computer?"

"It's a long story. The important thing is, today is N-Day. Which means today is the day they're going to steal the smallpox."

A beat. "You actually *believe* this?"

"Yes. I do. I'm certain of it."

"And you're at Fort Detrick now?"

"You know I am."

"My God." Another crackling silence.

"You need to get some troops out here, sir. Right now."

"How can I believe this?"

"You can't afford *not* to. A dozen troops would secure the place. Even if it turns out to be a hoax, you surely can spare the manpower—as insurance."

"Yes...yes. I see your logic. But...All our military assets have been moved out of Fort Detrick. There's nobody left on the base but low-level people, civilian doorshakers and a few scientists." A silence. "Hold the line."

Fordyce held the line. A few minutes later Dart came back on. "We've got a NEST rapid response team here on the roof. They were already on standby, suited up and ready to go. They'll be there in ten minutes by chopper. Where exactly are you?"

"In the lobby of the USAMRIID building."

"And Crew?"

"He went down to the Level Four lab, setting himself up to ambush Blaine..." Fordyce hesitated. "Look, he doesn't know I've called you. He wanted to go it alone. It wasn't worth arguing with him."

"Christ. All right. Listen to me carefully. I want you to get out of the building and meet the team when they arrive by chopper. They'll land in the parking lot in front of the entrance. Don't tell Crew—leave him alone. I don't trust him, and he's liable to do something unpredictable. The men I'm sending are seasoned professionals. They'll know exactly how to handle this situation."

"I'm not sure it's a good idea, leaving Crew in the dark."

"You yourself called me behind his back. You know the guy's un-reliable, a loose cannon. The team I send will have strict orders to safeguard him."

"Yes, sir."

"I hope to hell for your sake this is good intelligence."

"It's solid gold."

"Your job is to meet the team and identify yourself. Then you're done. They'll secure the building and the Level Four facility, they'll find Crew and escort him out. When Blaine arrives, he'll be taken into custody and this whole thing will be over. *If* this is real intelligence."

"You can't take the chance it isn't real."

"No. I can't."

Fordyce was encouraged by the relief he could hear in Dart's voice.

"We're going to secure the smallpox in a quiet, professional way," Dart went on. "That's it: no shoot-'em-up, no drama. If we do it quietly, we can roll up Blaine and his people before they even know what's happening. I've been against this trigger-happy approach from the beginning. You understand? No shooting."

"Yes, sir, I agree." Dart, for all his bluster, got it in the end. Gideon's predictions about the man had been wrong.

And then he saw two people enter the lobby. One he recognized immediately from photos he'd seen on book jackets.

"Oh, shit," he said softly into the phone. "Blaine just arrived. Along with a military officer." As he stepped back into shadow, he got a glimpse of the two bars on the man's insignia patch, Velcroed on the front of his cammos. "An army captain."

"Jesus, if this isn't confirmation…Stay out of sight. Don't stop them, don't do *anything* to tip them off. Just get out of the building when it's clear and wait near the parking lot, out of sight. Are they armed?"

"The captain is carrying a sidearm. Don't know about Blaine."

"My God," Dart muttered.

"What about Crew? I'm supposed to call him, tell him Blaine's ar-rived."

"No, no, no. Let's stick with the plan. The team's going to lift off in a moment. I'm going up there to brief them now. Let them handle it, for God's sake. We can't take any chances with the smallpox. Any more freelancing by Crew could be a disaster."

And the line abruptly went dead.

67

GIDEON WAS BOTH relieved and alarmed at how effective Blaine's plan had been at drawing off security from the lab where the smallpox was kept. With his temporary photo badge on prominent display, he had not been challenged by any of the—very few—technicians or scientists wandering about the building. The only obvious signs of security were ubiquitous cameras that peered down from the ceilings everywhere, no doubt videotaping his every movement. Were there people on the other end of the camera feeds, watching him? Under the present circumstances, Gideon doubted it. Blaine's strategy seemed to have been brilliantly effective.

After a few wrong turns, he found his way to the entrance of the Level 4 facility. Here, a stainless-steel door sported a dramatic, multicolored biohazard symbol, along with dire warnings in a dozen languages.

He peered through the door's tiny glass window and saw that it led, not directly into the facility, but into a sort of ready room. At the far end, he could make out an air lock and the decontamination shower that led into the facility itself. Light blue biosafety suits hung on racks, ordered by size. On one side of the room was a small staging area, with equipment, disused bioreactors, stacks of petri dishes, culture disks, and other supplies and equipment apparently on their way in or out of the lab.

He tried the door, found it unlocked, and entered the ready room. The far door leading into the air lock and shower sported its own biohazard symbol, and this was where the additional layers of security began: there was not only a keypad entry, but a card reader and retinal scanner as well. Once again, the ceiling was festooned with cameras. Good—everything would be recorded. He was going to need that when the time came for investigators to sort everything out.

He crossed the room and examined the scanner. This was a serious problem. Social engineering might get him past the keypad and card, but not past the retinal scanner.

Quickly, Gideon reevaluated his options. It seemed he could not surprise Blaine inside the Level 4 lab itself. That was unfortunate, and it meant undertaking a greater risk. He would have to apprehend Blaine exiting the lab with the smallpox.

He stood in the ready room, thinking. In some ways, however, this made for a better ambush situation. Blaine would go in, get the smallpox, and Gideon would surprise the man as he emerged from the decontamination shower. That was where Blaine would be most vulnerable, least suspecting an attack. And if Gideon donned a bluesuit himself, it would make an excellent disguise.

He glanced around the ready room. There were several changing rooms leading off from it, perfect places to lie in wait.

He rifled through the bluesuits, selected one his size, and brought it into a changing room, leaving the door ajar so he could keep tabs on who came in and out. He checked his disposable cell phone: one bar still. That had been his only real worry—that there would be no cell reception down here to receive Fordyce's call.

As he began donning the bluesuit, he heard the ready room door open and saw two people enter; Blaine and an officer in cammos. He quickly turned his back on them, surprised and chagrined that he hadn't heard from Fordyce. Thank God they hadn't walked in a few minutes earlier.

Surreptitiously, he observed the two; the military man was a captain, judging from the bars on his insignia patch, packing a 9mm pistol.

He appeared to be a young Hispanic, good looking, of medium height, with jet-black hair and jutting cheekbones.

Gideon quickly pulled on the hood of his bluesuit, covering his face. They had casually glanced at him through the partially open door to the dressing room, noting his presence, but without apparent concern. Now the two began suiting up in silence, working fast, wasting no time. A moment later the captain swiped a card through the reader in the far door, punched in a code, and paused to be read by the retinal scanner. A light turned green; he donned his own hood, and a moment later they had stepped into the air lock to the shower, the door sealing with a rush of air.

Gideon removed his Colt Python, checked to make sure all the chambers had rounds, and settled down to wait.

68

Simon Blaine followed Captain Gurulé into the Level 4 facility. He felt curiously calm, almost serene. It was a pure delight how beautifully everything had worked, how all the pieces fell into place, how everyone had played to perfection their assigned roles in the drama—the politicians, the press, even the public. It seemed effortless, but of course it was the result of years of meticulous planning, finding the right people and carefully enlisting them, running scenario after scenario, formulating backup plans and secondary backup plans, and playing out every possible move to the endgame and then selecting the best line of attack. All that hard work, all that time and money, was now paying off.

The only wild card had been that fellow Gideon—damn him— who not only had shocked Blaine deeply by coming around asking questions so early in the investigation, but had then seduced his impressionable daughter and dragged her into the situation in a most unfortunate way. Still, Alida, like Blaine himself, was resourceful and would survive. And once he had his hands on the smallpox and had carried out the plan, she would understand everything. She would of course see his point of view—she already did in general terms—and would be at his side as she had always been before. Always. They had an unbreakable father-daughter bond, something rare in this world.

"Sir?" The captain held out an air hose dangling from the ceiling for Blaine to attach to his suit. "It locks in with a clockwise twist." He demonstrated the movement on his own suit.

"Thank you, Captain."

As he snapped the hose in place, Blaine heard the faint hiss of air, which brought with it a scent of freshness mingled with the smell of plastic and latex.

"Who was that man back there?" he asked the captain, his voice muffled by the plastic hood.

"I didn't get a good look at him. Don't worry, he's not one of the scientists with security access to the vault."

Blaine nodded. He had put an enormous amount of trust in the captain, and it was not misplaced. Captain Gurulé was USAMRIID's most outstanding young microbiologist, vaccinologist, and biodefense researcher, one of the very few people with the clearance to access the smallpox virus. A dazzling man holding both an MD and a PhD from Penn, with uncompromising political views, competent, highly effective—the perfect ally. Courting him had been a very slow and painstaking process, but it had been absolutely critical to the plan.

The lab was virtually empty, as they knew it would be. It was true their every move was being recorded on video, but by the time anyone looked at those videos the whole world would already be aware of what they had done. The terrorist nuclear threat had done its job to perfection.

In a few minutes, they had reached the back of the facility where the *Variola* was stored in cryogenic suspension, locked in a biosafe inside a walk-in vault. The door to the vault was of stainless steel and identical to a bank safe-depository, modified by USAMRIID for its current, deep-freeze purpose. It was, Captain Gurulé had explained, used for storing the most dangerous, exotic, classified, or genetically engineered microbes.

At the vault door, Captain Gurulé pressed in another code, swiped his card, and turned a tumbler. The door swung open on electronically powered hinges, and they entered. A sudden burst of condensation from the vault's forty-below temperature clouded their visors. Blaine could start to feel the cold already creeping in. Heavy coats stood on a rack by the door, but the captain waved him past them. "We'll be out of here quickly," he said.

The door automatically shut behind them with a deep *boom* and the click of tumblers. Blaine stood still a moment, waiting for his visor to clear. Then he glanced around.

The vault was surprisingly spacious, with a large central area of stainless-steel tables. They walked past a number of biosafes and cabinets, then passed through a locked door into the inner cage of the vault. Against the far wall, bolted into a framework of angle iron, stood a small biosafe set apart from the others, painted bright yellow and covered with biohazard symbols.

"Please remain standing back, sir," said the captain.

Blaine held back, waiting.

The captain approached the biosafe, yet again entered a code, and then inserted a special key into a slot on the front. When he turned it, a yellow light began to blink in the ceiling of the vault and a low alert sounded, not loud but insistent.

"What is that?" Blaine asked, alarmed.

"Normal," said the captain. "It lasts as long as the biosafe is open. There's no one on the other end checking up on it."

Inside the safe, on racks, Blaine had a glimpse of the so-called pucks—the white, cryogenically sealed cylinders—that contained the deep frozen, crystallized *Variola*. He shuddered a moment, thinking of the lethal cocktail each puck contained: the immense amount of pain, suffering, and death enclosed in every one of those little cylinders.

The captain carefully removed one puck from its rack and examined the numbers etched into its side. Nodding to himself, he then took another, identical puck out of his biosuit pouch and placed it in the empty slot in the rack.

One puck was all that was needed. They were designed to keep the virus sealed, in a deep freeze, for at least seventy-two hours—which allowed more than enough time to accomplish their goal.

The captain shut the safe, locked it, and the beeping stopped. He brought the puck over to one of the stainless-steel tables. Blaine knew what he had to do next, and he held his breath in anticipation. It would be a delicate operation.

Laying the puck on the stage of a stereozoom microscope, the captain examined its surface for at least five minutes before making a small mark on it. Then he took a scalpel from the pouch of his biosuit and, with surgical care, cut a small tile of white plastic from the puck. Contained within that tiny piece of plastic, Blaine knew, was a tracking microchip.

The captain flicked the plastic piece to the floor and kicked it under the yellow biosafe with the side of his shoe.

Blaine shivered again. His fingers were already growing numb from the cold. The captain seemed immune.

"I'll take that, if you don't mind," Blaine said, pointing at the puck.

The captain handed it to him. "Be very, very careful, sir. If you drop it, the world as we know it ends."

A moment later they emerged from the vault, and were forced to wait once again for their visors to unfog. It took longer this time. Even so, everything was ticking along like clockwork.

They made their way back through the lab until they had reached the decontamination showers and air lock. The shower accommodated only one person at a time, and the captain entered first. The automatic door rumbled shut; Blaine could hear the hissing sound of the chemical decontaminants spraying down the captain. The sounds stopped; the outer door opened with a whoosh of the air lock. A moment later the inner door opened to admit him to the shower. He stepped inside and was momentarily engulfed in a blast of chemicals, while a metallic voice instructed him to raise his arms and turn around. Then the door opened and he stepped into the ready room—to find the barrel of a gun pressed immediately against his visor.

"Give me the smallpox," said a voice Blaine recognized as that of Gideon Crew.

69

STONE FORDYCE HEARD the chopper before he saw it: a UH-60 Black Hawk, coming in low and fast from the east. He had moved to the far end of the parking lot, near the gates to the motor pool, and he took refuge from the rotor wash behind a Humvee on blocks. The Black Hawk slowed and turned, touching down on the tarmac of the nearly empty lot. Fordyce waited for the craft to settle. As the rotors spun down, the cabin door opened and six SWAT team members hopped out, wearing full body armor and carrying M4 carbines. A moment later a civilian stepped down and Fordyce was startled, and encouraged, to see that Dart himself had come along. More proof that calling Dart had been the right choice.

He watched as they moved out of the backwash and gathered near the doors of the building.

Fordyce straightened up and came out from behind the car, showing himself. Dart saw him and gestured him over.

Fordyce jogged up to the group of soldiers, who fanned out in a semicircle as he arrived—a lieutenant, a warrant officer, and four specialists.

"Are they still inside?" Dart asked, stepping forward.

Fordyce nodded.

"And Crew? Where's he?"

"Still down in Level Four, as far as I know. As you requested, I've initiated no contact."

"Any sign of activity? Confrontation?"

"No."

"Any other security involved? Alarms or alerts?"

"Nothing as far as I can tell. It's been as quiet as a tomb here."

"Good." Dart checked his watch. "They've been inside for almost fourteen minutes, by my reckoning." He frowned. "Listen, Agent Fordyce. You've done a fine piece of work. But your job is now done and I don't want anything, and I mean *anything*, going wrong. We're going to let the professionals handle it from this point on." He extended his hand. "Your sidearm, please."

Fordyce slipped it out of its holster, held it out to Dart butt-first. But even as he did so, he was surprised at the request. "Why do you want it?"

Dart took the weapon, examined it, racked a round into the chamber, then raised his arm and pointed the gun at Fordyce's chest. "Because I'm going to shoot you with it."

A noise, shockingly loud; a burst of white; and Fordyce was punched backward, the round striking him square in the breastbone and knocking him to the asphalt. He had never in his entire life been so surprised, and as he stared wide-eyed into an impossibly blue summer sky, he was unable to process what had happened to him even as the last of his life fluttered out, blue rushing to black.

70

With the barrel of the Python on his visor, Blaine froze. Taking advantage of this, Gideon reached quickly down to the biopouch of the man's bluesuit, unsnapped the flap, and slipped his hand inside. His fingers closed over the still-cold disk, which he removed and placed in his own pocket with care. Keeping the gun on Blaine, he unsealed the hood of his own bluesuit and pulled it off, allowing him to see and breathe better.

"Gideon," was all Blaine managed to say, in a quavering whisper.

"Lie facedown on the floor next to the captain, arms extended over your head," said Gideon, more loudly than he intended.

"Gideon, I want you to please listen—" Blaine began, his voice muffled by the hood.

Gideon pulled back the hammer of the Colt. "Do as I say." He tried to control the shaking of his hands. The idea of killing Alida's father was horrifying, but he knew the situation was far too critical for him to show any weakness.

He watched as the older man lay on the floor, arms extended. They were both still in their bluesuits, their weapons holstered underneath. Disarming them was going to be awkward, and the captain in particular had the look of a dangerous opponent. Keeping the revolver aimed at him, Gideon took out his cell phone with his other hand and called Fordyce.

After a few rings it switched over to voice mail.

He put the cell phone away. Fordyce was somewhere out of range—which would explain why he'd never gotten the agent's call. He would have to deal with this himself.

"Captain," he said, "remove your hood with one hand, keeping your other hand extended above your head and in sight at all times. If you try anything, I'll shoot to kill."

The captain complied.

"Now you, Blaine."

As soon as Blaine got his hood off, he began to talk again. "Gideon, I want you to hear me out—"

"Shut up." He felt sick, tried to master the shaking of his hands. He turned back to the captain. "I want you to stand up slowly. Then, with your left hand, remove your bluesuit, keeping your right arm extended from your body and in sight at all times. If you so much as twitch, either of you, I start firing and won't stop until you're both dead."

The captain complied and—a credit to his intelligence—didn't try anything. Gideon was absolutely serious about killing them both, and they must have sensed it.

When the bluesuit was off, Gideon had the captain lie back down on the floor, then searched him, recovering a 9mm sidearm and a knife. He tied the captain's hands behind his back with some surgical tubing that was lying on the adjacent lab table.

He turned to Blaine. "Now you. Take off your suit just like the captain."

"For Alida's sake, listen—"

"One more word and I'll kill you." Gideon felt himself flush deeply. He had been trying to keep the whole awful question of Alida out of his head. And here her father was playing that card right up front—the bastard.

Blaine fell silent.

When the bluesuit was off, Gideon searched Blaine, snagging the man's firearm—a beautiful old Colt .45 Peacemaker with staghorn grips—and tucking it into the waistband at the small of his back.

"Lie back down."

Blaine complied. Gideon tied his hands with more surgical tubing.

What was he going to do now? He needed Fordyce. Having seen Blaine and the captain enter, Fordyce would surely be on his way down as backup—wouldn't he? Why wasn't he here? Had they already had a run-in with him on their way in? Impossible. They had arrived calm, fresh, unsuspecting. Had someone detained Fordyce?

It didn't matter. He needed help. It was time to call Glinn.

He took out his cell phone. Just then, he heard sounds in the hallway beyond: the heavy running of boots. He took a step back as the doors burst open, soldiers in tactical uniforms rushing in, weapons at the ready.

"Nobody move!" cried the soldier on point. *"Drop your weapon!"*

Gideon suddenly found himself completely outnumbered; six automatic weapons were pointed at him. *Jesus, is this why Fordyce isn't here?* he wondered. *They must have seen us on the monitors, sent in an interdiction squad.* He froze, unmoving, hands extended, keeping the Python and the captain's 9mm in sight.

A second later Dart stepped in. He looked around, taking in the room.

Gideon stared at him. *"Dart?* What's this?"

"It's all right," Dart said quietly to Gideon. "We'll take care of things from now on."

"Where's Fordyce?"

"Waiting by the chopper. He called me without telling you, explained everything. Said you wanted to go it alone. And I see you've managed quite well. But now we're here to take over."

Gideon stared at him.

"Don't be concerned, I know all about it—Blaine, the proposal for the novel, the plan, the smallpox. It's over now, you're in the clear."

So Fordyce *had* made the call after all. And Dart had listened—to the point of coming himself. Amazing. Gideon felt his whole body relax. The long nightmare was finally over.

Dart glanced around. "Who has the smallpox?" he asked.

"I do," said Gideon.

"May I have it, please?"

Gideon hesitated—why, he was not entirely certain.

Dart held out his hand. "May I have it, please?"

"When you secure those two and get them the hell out of here," Gideon said. "And then I think the smallpox needs to go straight back into its vault."

A long silence. Then Dart smiled. "Trust me, it's going right back where it belongs."

Still, Gideon hesitated. "I'll put it back myself."

Dart's face lost some of its friendliness. "Why the difficulty, Gideon?"

Gideon couldn't find an answer. There was something about this that didn't feel quite right; some vague feeling that Dart was being a little too friendly, that he'd come around to Gideon's viewpoint a little too easily.

"No difficulty," said Gideon. "I'd just feel better seeing it go back in the vault."

"I think we might arrange that. But if we're going in the lab, you'll have to disarm. You know—the metal detector."

Gideon took a step back. "The captain here went in with his 9mm, no problem. There wasn't any metal detector." He felt his heart suddenly pounding in his chest. Was this bullshit? Were they lying to him?

Dart turned toward the soldiers. "Disarm this man now."

The rifles came up again. Gideon stared. He made no move.

A lieutenant stepped forward, drew his sidearm, and placed it against the side of Gideon's head. "You heard him. Count of five. *One, two, three—*"

Gideon handed over the Python, the 9mm, and the Peacemaker.

"Now the smallpox."

Gideon looked from Dart to the men. The expression on their faces was more than unfriendly. They were looking at him as if he were the enemy. Could it be they still believed he was a terrorist? Impossible.

Nevertheless, something felt very wrong.

"Call the director of USAMRIID down here," Gideon said. "He must be on the premises. I'll give it to him."

"You'll give it to me," said Dart.

Gideon looked from Dart to the soldiers. He was unarmed and really had no choice. "All right. Tell the lieutenant to back off. I'm not doing this with a gun pressed to my head."

Dart made a motion and the lieutenant stepped back, keeping his pistol leveled.

Gideon slid his hand into his pocket, his fingers closing over the puck. He slipped it out.

"Easy now," said Dart.

Gideon held it out. Dart stepped forward to take it, his hands closing over the puck.

"Kill him," said Dart.

71

Bᴜᴛ Dᴀʀᴛ ʜᴀᴅ spoken too soon. Gideon clamped his fingers around the puck and turned abruptly, checking Dart hard with his shoulder, while at the same time extending his hand with the puck over his head.

"Don't shoot!" Blaine cried, from the floor. "Wait!"

Gideon stared at Blaine. There was a sudden silence. The lieutenant didn't fire. None of them did. Dart seemed paralyzed.

"Drop your weapons," Gideon said. He cocked his arm as if to throw the puck and Dart jumped back, the soldiers following his cue, alarmed.

"Don't throw it, for God's sake!" This came from Blaine, still lying on the ground. He rose awkwardly to his feet. "Dart, you *really* screwed up," he said angrily. "This isn't the way to deal with this situation."

Dart was sweating, his face white. "What are you doing?"

"Fixing this mess. Cut this off." He held out his wrists.

Dart obeyed, using a scalpel to cut off the surgical tubing.

Blaine rubbed his hands together, fixing Gideon with his deep blue eyes but speaking to the captain. "Gurulé, you can get up now, too. We don't need to keep up this pretense any longer."

Full comprehension dawned in Gideon's mind as the captain rose to his feet, his dark eyes flashing with triumph. He was staggered by the realization: Dart and Blaine were co-conspirators.

Blaine turned to the soldiers. "Lieutenant, you men, damn you, lower your weapons!"

A hesitation, and then Dart said: "Do it."

The lieutenant obeyed and his men followed.

"Give me my sidearm," rumbled Blaine, holding his hand out to Dart.

Dart handed him back the Peacemaker. Blaine hefted it, opened the gate, spun the cylinder to make sure it was still loaded, and tucked it into his belt. The 9mm was restored to the captain.

While this was going on, Gideon remained standing with the smallpox still poised threateningly over his head, his arm tense. He spoke quietly. "I'll smash this on the ground if you *all* don't lay down your weapons. On the ground. *Now.*"

"Gideon, Gideon," Blaine began, shaking his head, his voice quiet. "Will you please listen to what I've got to say?"

Gideon waited. His heart was hammering in his chest. *If he starts talking about Alida...*

"Do you know why we're doing this?"

"Blackmail," said Gideon. "I read your book proposal. You're just in it for the goddamn money."

"Ah, I see," said Blaine chuckling. "You have no idea, *no* idea, how wrong you are. That was merely a trifle, a plot point for a book. None of us is after money. We couldn't care less about that. We've got a much more important use for the smallpox. Something truly beneficial to our country. Would you like to hear it?"

Gideon remained tensed like a spring, his arm cocked. But something perverse inside him wanted to hear what Blaine had to say.

Blaine gestured at Dart. "You see, I've used Myron, here, to vet my book ideas from time to time. And it was he who told me that this idea, Operation Corpse, was too good for a book. It was something we could actually *accomplish.*"

Gideon said nothing.

"I'm telling you this because I'm pretty sure you'll want to join us. After all, you're one of the most intelligent people I've ever met. You will certainly understand. And..." He paused. "It seems you love my daughter."

Gideon flushed again. "Don't bring her into it."

"Oh, but I will...I will."

"Blaine, you're wasting time!" said Dart.

"We've lots of time," said Blaine calmly, turning back to Gideon with a smile. "What we *don't* have time for is an accident. Frankly, Gideon, I don't think you're the kind of person who'd be able to smash that on the ground. And kill millions." He raised an eyebrow inquisitorially.

"I will if it keeps it out of your hands."

"But you haven't heard yet what we plan to do with it!" This was said in a genial, protesting fashion.

Gideon said nothing. Blaine wanted to have his say—let him.

"I was in the British intelligence service known as MI6. Captain Gurulé here is CIA. Dart is not just involved in NEST but has also worked for a black agency at DIA. Because of our mutual background in intelligence, we all know something you don't, which is this: America is secretly at war. With an enemy that makes the old Soviets look like the Keystone Kops."

Gideon waited.

"The very survival of our country is in the balance." Blaine paused, took a deep breath, and began again. "Let me tell you about this enemy. They are single-minded. They are sober, extremely hardworking, and highly intelligent. They have the second largest economy in the world and it is growing at five hundred percent the rate of ours. The enemy has an immensely large and powerful military, they have advanced space weapons, and they have the fastest-growing nuclear arsenal in the world.

"This enemy saves forty percent of what they earn. They have more university graduates than America has people. In the enemy's country, more people are studying English than there are English speakers in the entire world. They know all about us and we know almost nothing about them. This enemy is ruthless. They operate the last imperial, colonialist power on earth, which occupies and brutalizes many of the formerly independent countries surrounding it.

"This enemy has brazenly and openly stolen trillions of dollars of our intellectual property. In return, they send us poisoned food and medicine. They don't play by the rules of international law. They are corrupt. They oppress freedom of speech, oppress the free exercise of religion, and murder and imprison journalists and dissidents on an almost daily basis. They have openly cornered the market in those strategic metals critical to our electronic world. This enemy, having little oil, now dominates the world's technologies and markets in solar, wind, and nuclear power. As such, they are on track to become the new Saudi Arabia. This enemy has accumulated almost two trillion of our own dollars through unfair currency and trade practices. If dumped on the world market, this sum would be enough to annihilate our currency and wreck our economy in a single day. Basically, they have us by the bollocks.

"Worst of all: this enemy despises us. They see how we conduct business in Washington, and they've concluded that our democratic system is an abject failure. And they think we Americans are weak, lazy, whiny, self-important global has-beens, inflated with a false sense of entitlement. In this, they are probably correct."

Blaine's rolling, mesmerizing speech ceased, leaving him breathing heavily, his face slick with sweat. Gideon felt sick to his stomach, as if the words had been physically bludgeoning him. Still he held the smallpox up.

"They have the population, the money, the brains, the will, and the guts to beggar us. They have specific plans to do this. *And they are in fact doing it.* While America just sits on its arse, doing nothing in return. It's a one-sided war: they're fighting, we're surrendering."

The novelist leaned forward. "Well, Gideon, not every American is ready to surrender. Those of us in this room, along with a small group of other like-minded individuals, are not going to let this happen. We're going to save our country."

Gideon desperately tried to order his thoughts. Blaine was a powerfully persuasive and charismatic speaker. "And the smallpox? Where does that come in?"

"Surely you can now guess where that comes in. We're going to release it in five of the enemy's cities. The enemy's great vulnerability is their population density and their dependence on trade. As the virus spreads like wildfire through the virgin human population, the world will impose a quarantine on the infected country—it will have no choice. We know that for a fact: response to a smallpox event is detailed in a highly classified NATO plan."

He smiled triumphantly, as if the operation had already taken place. "With a quarantine, that country's borders will be sealed. Everything will be stopped or blocked: flights, roads, railroads, ports, even trails. The country will remain quarantined as long as the disease is present. Our epidemiologist tells us it might be years before the disease can be recontained. By that time, the enemy's economy will be back where it was in the fifties. The *eighteen* fifties."

"They'll lash out with nuclear weapons," Gideon said.

"True, but right now they don't have all that many, and not of high quality. We will take down most of their missiles in flight. A few of our cities might be hit, but then we will massively retaliate. After all, it *is* war." He shrugged.

Gideon stared at him. "You're crazy. They're not our enemy. This whole plan is insane."

"Really, Gideon, you're smarter than that." Blaine held out his hand in a supplicating gesture. "Gideon. Join us, please. Give me the smallpox."

Gideon backed toward the door. "I won't be part of this. I can't."

"Don't disappoint me. You're one of the few with the brains to see the truth in my words. I'm trusting you to think about this—really *think* about what I've said. This is a country that only a generation ago murdered thirty million of their own people. They don't place the same value on human life that we do. They'd do it to us—if they could."

"It's monstrous. You're talking about murdering millions. I've heard enough."

"Think of Alida—"

"*Shut up about Alida!*" Gideon found his arm trembling, his voice cracking, the soldiers backing away in fear as he waved the puck about.

"No!" Blaine entreated him. "Wait!"

"Tell the soldiers to lay down their guns! Now it's my turn to count to five. *One—!*"

"For God's sake, no!" Blaine cried. "No here, *not near Washington.* You release that smallpox, you'll do to America what we were going to do to—"

"Look into my eyes if you don't believe it. Tell the soldiers to put down their guns! *Two...*"

"Oh my God." Blaine's hands shook. "Gideon, I beg you, don't do it."

"*Three...*"

"You won't do it. You won't."

"I said, look into my eyes, Blaine. *Four...*" He cocked his hand. He really was going to do it. And—finally—Blaine saw that.

"Lower the guns!" Blaine cried. "Lay them down!"

"*Five!*" Gideon screamed.

"Down! Down!"

The guns went down with a clatter, the soldiers clearly terrified. Even Dart and the lieutenant threw their weapons down.

"Hands up!" Gideon demanded.

All hands went up.

"You son of a bitch, don't do this!" Dart yelled.

Gideon edged around, past the laboratory table, one hand still raised, the other behind his back. He had very little time. He reached the door, pushed it open with his knee. Then he spun around, took a fresh grasp on the puck, and hurled it to the floor with all his might, simultaneously darting out and racing down the hall.

As he ran, he heard the puck shatter, the broken pieces ricocheting around the ready room—and then an absolute chaos of shouting, scrambling, running, while, rising above it all, came a great and terrible roar from Blaine, like a lion speared through the heart.

72

SIMON BLAINE stumbled backward with a cry as the puck struck the floor and split open, spewing its contents with a puff of condensation, the pieces of plastic and glass bouncing off the door frame and skittering across the floor. He could see the crystalline powder melt on contact with the floor.

With lightning clarity his mind saw the future: the sealing off of Washington and its suburbs, the quarantine, the inexorable spread of the disease, the frantic and useless vaccination efforts, the galloping pandemic, the mobilizing of the National Guard, the riots, the ports closed and borders sealed, curfews, states of emergency, bombing sorties, war along the borders with Canada and Mexico...And of course the total collapse of the US economy. He saw these things with a certainty born of knowledge. These were not speculations: this was exactly how it was going to happen, because he had *already* seen it happen to the enemy in their computer simulations, over and over again.

All this flashed through his brain in a few seconds. He knew they were all likely infected already; the disease was as catching as the common cold, and the amount of smallpox in the puck represented a staggering quantity of virus, enough to directly infect almost a hundred million people. With the shattering of the puck, it had been rendered airborne. They were already, all of them, breathing it in. He and the rest of them were dead men.

He saw all this with a horrific lucidity. And then he became aware of the shouts, the cries of the soldiers, the hollering of Dart.

"Don't move," he said in a commanding voice. "Don't stir the air. Stop yelling. *Shut up.*"

They obeyed him. Instant silence.

"We need to get the building sealed," he said, with a strange, sudden calm that surprised even himself. "*Now.* If we can keep everyone inside, we might just contain it."

"But what about us?" Dart asked, his face white.

"We're finished," said Blaine. "Now we need to save our country."

A long silence. A soldier suddenly screamed and bolted, leaping over the doorsill and tearing off down the hall. Without hesitation, Blaine drew his weapon, took careful aim, and pulled the trigger. The old Peacemaker kicked with a roar and the soldier went down, screaming and gargling.

"Fuck this, I'm putting a suit on," Dart said, his voice breaking, scrabbling at the rack, pulling down suits. "We'll be safe in the lab!" Several suits fell off the rack with a crash and now the soldiers rushed in, grabbing at suits, shoving one another, all semblance of discipline vanished.

Multiply that panic by a hundred million, Blaine thought. That's what the country was facing.

His eye fell back on the faint, damp patches where the crystallized virus and its substrate had sprayed across the floor and walls. It was unspeakable. He couldn't believe Gideon had actually done it. Blaine knew he was perfectly willing to give his life for his country—in fact he had expected to—but not like this. Not like this.

And then he noticed something.

He bent down. Looked closer. Got on his hands and knees. And then reached out and picked up the broken puck. A small serial number was stamped on the side, along with an identification label in tiny type:

INFLUENZA A/H9N2 KILLED

"My God!" he cried. "This isn't smallpox! We've been tricked. Spread out, search the building, find him! This is a different puck. *He switched pucks.* He's still got the smallpox! *He's still got the smallpox!*"

73

Gideon sprinted down the hallway. As he ran, he decided to head for the rear of the building. There might be more soldiers waiting in the lobby. Besides, the back of the building would give him the added advantage of bringing him closer to where he'd parked the Jeep, in the rear lot.

Which meant he had to find a back exit.

He raced up a stairwell to the ground floor and headed toward the back of the building, running as fast as he could while still protecting the puck. It was a huge, virtually deserted complex, and he found himself wasting time with unexpected twists and turns, dead ends and locked doors that forced him to backtrack again and again. And all the while, the clock was ticking.

He had no idea how effectively his ruse would delay their response. He had seen his opportunity and had taken it, his old skills as a magician coming in handy as he'd palmed a random puck from the lab table and substituted it for the smallpox. It had been relatively easy, given that he had worked magic tricks with many objects of precisely that size and sometimes even that shape. What that other puck contained, if anything, he had no idea, but it couldn't be all that dangerous or it wouldn't have been stacked on the outside table, unguarded. Maybe it would give them all hives.

After yet more wrong turns he arrived finally at a long corridor that ended in a glassed-in waiting area with a large exit sign and a crash door at the far end, striped white and red with an Alarm Will Sound label. He ran for the door, only to see a man appear abruptly in the lobby from another approach. It was the captain, Gurulé.

So they're on to me already. Shit.

The captain turned, saw Gideon, began to draw his weapon.

Gideon charged ahead, ramming into the captain and slamming him back against the crash door, which burst open with a piercing alarm, the pistol flying away. He scrambled for it, acutely aware of the smallpox container in his pocket, shielding it protectively with his body. The captain, sprawled across the threshold but recovering fast, pulled himself up and leapt on Gideon, trying to get a hammerlock around his neck. In doing so he left his face exposed and Gideon punched back fiercely with the palm of one hand; he felt the captain's nose break under the strike, Gurulé's grip loosening just enough for Gideon to wrench free, even as the captain landed a vicious punch to his side.

They faced off, the captain shaking his head, trying to recover his senses and fling away the blood spurting from his nose. The smallpox felt like it was burning a hole in Gideon's pocket. Whatever happened, he couldn't let that puck break.

Gurulé suddenly turned and unleashed a powerful kick to Gideon's groin; Gideon twisted to protect the smallpox and the kick slammed into his hip, just missing the puck but knocking him back against the wall. Gideon went into a defensive hunch, still shielding the puck, and the captain took advantage of his defensive hesitation to advance on him, driving a punch straight into the side of his jaw that broke a couple of teeth and sent Gideon to the floor.

"The smallpox!" Gideon gasped through the blood welling into his mouth, "Don't—!"

The captain was too enraged to hear. He punched him again in the chest, then slammed his foot into Gideon's side, almost flipping him over, the jarring movement sending the puck flying out of his pocket and skittering into a corner. For a brief, terrible moment both men stopped dead, watching as it bounced against the wall—and then rolled back a few feet, unbroken and unharmed.

Instantly the captain dove for it while Gideon, now free of restraint, let loose a savage roundhouse to the man's kidneys, laying him on his knees, and following with another kick to his jaw. But the captain, rising, pivoted with lightning speed almost like a breakdancer, lashing out with his legs, knocking Gideon back down just as he was staggering up. With an inarticulate gargle of rage, Gurulé fell on Gideon, sinking his teeth into Gideon's ear with a crunch of cartilage. Yelling in pain, Gideon slammed his fist into the man's neck, causing him to release his hold on Gideon's ear; as he turned to throw a blind punch, which missed, Gideon seized his scalp with both hands and yanked his head back and forth, like a dog shaking a rat, while simultaneously bringing his knee up into the man's face so hard it almost felt like he had caved it in. The man flipped over backward and Gideon fell on him, seizing his ears and, with them as handles, slamming the back of the captain's head into the cement floor, once, twice.

Gideon rolled off the now unconscious man. Their struggle had brought them close to Gurulé's gun, and Gideon grabbed it just as the side door to the lobby burst open and two soldiers rushed in. Gideon shot one immediately, throwing him back against the wall; the second dove for cover in a panic, firing wildly, the bullets raking the glass wall behind Gideon and shattering it.

Gideon dove through the broken glass, then staggered to his feet, bullets snicking past him and ricocheting off the asphalt of the rear parking lot. He reached the closest parked car and fell behind it as a swarm of rounds rammed through the metal. When he returned fire he could see, through the open door of the building, the white puck of smallpox lying against the wall. Even as he stared Blaine appeared, scooped up the puck, and disappeared again into the back hall, with a yell for his men to follow.

"*No!*" Gideon cried out.

He fired again but it was too late; the remaining soldiers vanished into the building with a final, desultory burst of gunfire in his direction.

They had the smallpox.

For a moment, Gideon just leaned against the car, head spinning.

He'd been badly beaten, he hurt all over, blood was pouring from his injured mouth—but the surge of adrenaline from the fight, and the loss of the smallpox, managed to sustain him.

Pushing away from the car and sprinting around the corner, he ran along the blank, windowless side wall of the building, which went on seemingly forever. He finally reached the end and tore around the next corner. The front parking lot came into view, and there on the tarmac was Dart's chopper, a UH-60 Black Hawk, its rotors spinning up. Through the open cabin door he could see Blaine and Dart already seated, with the last of the soldiers just now climbing in. Lying nearby the chopper, in a pool of blood, was a body all too clearly dead.

Fordyce.

Gideon felt a sudden nausea, a choking rage that closed down his throat. All was now clear.

He drew his pistol and sprinted across the grass toward the helicopter. As it began to rise, gunfire erupted from the cabin door. Gideon veered to another parked car and crouched behind it as rounds buried themselves in the vehicle. Half mad with anger and grief, he rose again and—bracing himself on the hood, ignoring the rounds whining past his head—aimed the captain's 9mm and squeezed off two carefully placed rounds, aiming for the turboshaft engines. One round hit home with a *thunk* and a spray of paint chips, followed a moment later by a grinding noise. More shots raked the car but Gideon remained in place, easing off a third shot. Now black smoke spurted up from the engines, half obscuring the main rotor blades; the chopper seemed to hesitate as the grinding noise turned into a strident rasp. Then the fuselage began to rotate and tilt, the bird coming back to earth hard, the tail rotor making contact with the ground and shattering, the pieces flying away with a chilling *hummm.*

Three soldiers piled out of the now burning chopper and came at him, firing their M4s on full automatic, followed a moment later by Dart and Blaine. The bullets shredded the car he'd taken cover behind, spraying him with bits of glass and metal as he crouched, only the heavy engine block stopping the high-velocity rounds.

And then the shooting stopped abruptly. He took a deep breath, rose to return fire, but realized it was a waste of ammo—they had veered away and were now out of range for a handgun. And they were no longer concerning themselves with him. Dart, Blaine, and the soldiers were piling into a Humvee, evidently the vehicle Blaine had arrived in. The doors slammed shut and the vehicle laid rubber, fishtailing out of the lot and heading for the long service road out of the base. The chopper was now leaning precariously, making a gruesome grinding sound, the rotors flapping, smoke billowing upward; a moment later it erupted in flames and, with a *thump* that made the air tremble, exploded in a ball of fire.

Gideon shielded his face from the heat with a curse. They were getting away—getting away with the smallpox. He jumped up and pursued them, running past the burning chopper to the far end of the parking lot, pulling the trigger again and again in impotent frustration until the magazine was empty.

Then he stopped and looked around, breathing hard. Blaine's Jeep was parked in the rear lot, but if he ran back to get it the game would certainly be lost: Dart and Blaine would be so far ahead by that time he'd never catch them.

The base's main motor pool stood on the opposite side of the road, gate closed. He ran across the street, flung himself onto the fence, scrambled up it and dropped down the far side. A row of Humvees and another row of Jeeps were parked to his right; he ran to the first Humvee, glanced inside. No key. No key in the second or third Humvee, either. Running wildly now, he dashed over to the Jeeps. None of them had keys in the ignition.

He turned left and right in desperation. On the other side of the motor pool were the larger military vehicles: a couple of M1 tanks, MRAPs, and several Stryker armored fighting vehicles, looking like huge, bristling tank turrets mounted on eight massive wheels. One of the Strykers had been moved into an open area and had apparently just been washed down with a hose. Gideon vaguely recalled seeing a mechanic working on the vehicle when he and Fordyce had arrived. Even as the thought occurred to him, the mechanic appeared, wrench in hand, leather holster flapping, running from a distant shed, staring at the burning helicopter. "What's the hell's going on?" he cried to Gideon.

Gideon knocked the wrench from his hand, grabbed him by the collar, pushed the empty 9mm pistol into his face, and aimed him at the nearest Stryker. "What's going on," he said, "is we're going to get into this vehicle and you're going to drive it."

74

THE MECHANIC OPENED the door. They climbed in the cave-like interior, the mechanic first, Gideon following with the gun. With the mechanic in the gunner's seat, Gideon slid into the driver's seat.

"Give me your gun," Gideon demanded.

The mechanic opened his holster, passed over his sidearm.

"Now give me the key."

The mechanic fumbled in his pocket and handed over the key. Gideon shoved it in the ignition, turned it. The Stryker immediately rumbled to life, the big diesel purring. Weapon trained on the mechanic, he quickly glanced over the instrumentation. It looked straightforward enough: before him was a steering wheel, shift, gas and brake pedals, no different from a truck. But these controls were surrounded by electronics and numerous flat-panel screens of unknown function.

"You know how to operate this thing?" Gideon asked.

"Fuck you," said the soldier. He had evidently collected his wits and Gideon could see a combination of fear, anger, and growing defiance in his expression. He was young, skinny, with a whiffle-cut; no older than twenty. His name was JACKMAN and he carried the insignia of a specialist. But the most important information was written on his face: this was a loyal soldier who was not going to cave at the muzzle of a gun if it was against his country.

With an effort Gideon forced himself to slow down, take a deep breath, push aside the fact that every minute that passed put Blaine and the smallpox farther away. He needed this man's help—and he had one shot at getting it.

"Specialist Jackman, I'm sorry about pulling a gun on you," he said. "But we're in an emergency situation. Those people who tried to take off in the chopper stole a deadly virus from USAMRIID. They're terrorists. And they're going to release it."

"They were soldiers," said Jackman, defiantly.

"*Dressed* as soldiers."

"So you say."

"Look," said Gideon, "I'm with NEST." He went to reach for his old ID but realized it was gone, lost at some point during the desperate chase. God, he had to do this fast. "Did you see that body on the tarmac over there?"

Jackman nodded.

"He was my partner. Special Agent Stone Fordyce. The bastards murdered him. They've stolen a vial of smallpox and are going to use it to start a war."

"I'm not buying your bullshit," the specialist said.

"You've *got* to believe me."

"No way. Take your best shot. I won't help you."

Gideon felt close to despair. He tried to pull himself together. He told himself that this was a social engineering situation, no different from any other he'd encountered. It was just that the risks were infinitely greater this time around. It was a question of finding a way in, discovering how to reach this man. And doing it in seconds. He looked into the frightened but absolutely determined face.

"No, *you* take *your* best shot." He handed Jackman his 9mm, butt-first. "If you think I'm one of the good guys, help me. You think I'm one of the bad guys, take me out. It's your decision now, not mine."

Jackman took the proffered weapon. His look turned to one of uncertainty, struggling with a strong sense of duty. He gave it a quick inspection, ejected the magazine. "Nice try. There's no rounds in here." He tossed the weapon aside.

Son of a bitch.

An uncertain silence fell. Gideon began to sweat. Then, in an almost impulsive movement, he passed the mechanic's own handgun back to him. "Put it to my head," he said.

Jackman made a brusque movement, seizing Gideon in a hammerlock and pressing the gun against his temple.

"Go ahead. Shoot me. Because I'm telling you right now: if they get away, I don't want to live to see the result."

Jackman's finger tightened visibly against the trigger. There was a long, ticking silence.

"Did you hear me? They're getting away. You've got to make up your mind—are you with me or against me?"

"I...I..." Jackman hesitated, flummoxed.

"Look at me, judge me, and damn it, *make your decision.*"

They stared into each other's eyes. One more hesitation—and then the face cleared, the decision made. He took the gun away, reholstered it. "All right. Shit. I'm with you."

Gideon peered out through the driver's periscope. Then he jammed the gearshift of the Stryker forward and released the clutch. The vehicle lurched back and smashed into a Humvee, knocking the heavy vehicle back several yards.

"No, no, the shift works the other way!" Jackman shouted.

Gideon yanked it back and the vehicle lurched. He floored the accelerator but the Stryker only lumbered forward, gaining speed slowly because of its great weight.

"Can't this damn thing go any faster?" he cried.

"We'll never catch them," said Jackman. "We can't do more than sixty. A Humvee will do eighty, ninety."

For a moment, Gideon took his foot off the accelerator, almost freezing up in despair. They had too big a lead—it was useless. Then he remembered something.

Pulling the map of the base out of his pocket—the one he'd been given at the front gate—he tossed it at Jackman. "Look at that. The base access road winds all over the place. We can still cut them off if we head straight for the front gate."

"But there's no road going straight to the front gate," said Jackman.

"With this thing, who the hell needs a road? Just point me toward the gate. We'll take it cross-country. And when we get there, be ready to operate the weapons."

75

Gideon accelerated the Stryker across the long parking lot, past the burning helicopter, and hit the pavement, making fifty miles an hour, the vehicle's eight wheels humming loudly on the service road.

Jackman examined the tattered map. "Take a heading of a hundred ninety degrees. Here, use this." He indicated an electronic compass on the dashboard.

Gideon turned to one hundred ninety degrees south, the Stryker leaping the curb and churning across a wide expanse of grass, heading toward a line of trees.

"What do we have for weapons?" Gideon called out.

"Fifty-cal, Mk-9 automatic grenade launcher, smoke grenades."

"Can the Stryker cut through those trees?"

"We're going to find out," said Jackman. "Shift into eight-wheel drive. That lever, there."

Gideon pulled the lever and accelerated for the trees, the diesel roaring. God, it was a powerful engine. The trees were spaced far apart, but not far enough. He steered toward an area of what looked like younger, thinner trees.

"Hold on," he said.

The vehicle struck one, then another, slamming through them with a loud *thwack* as each tree snapped off at the base, the vehicle bucking and lurching, the engine roaring, trunks flying aside, leaves whirling. A minute later they broke into a grassy clearing.

A red light glowed on a nearby flat panel and a flat, electronic voice sounded. "Warning, speed unsuitable for current terrain conditions. Adjusting tire pressure to compensate."

Gideon peered through the driver's periscope. "Shit. There are some really big oaks ahead."

"Slow down, I'll try to clear them with the grenade launcher." Jackman pressed a series of switches, and the weapons system screen flickered to life. He peered intently through the gunner's periscope. "Here goes."

There was a series of *whooshes* and, a moment later, an eruption of sound. The oaks disappeared in a wall of flame, dirt, leaves, and splinters. Even before the area had been fully cleared Gideon floored the accelerator again, the wheels spinning, and the Stryker lumbered forward, bucking over a mass of broken trunks, then plowing back in the forest, knocking down smaller trees on the far side: *whap, whap, whap.*

They broke free of the woods with a final crash. Looming ahead, across a road, was a chain-link fence surrounding a residential neighborhood: neat rows of bungalows, driveways, cars, postage-stamp lawns covered with all the accoutrements of suburban living.

"Oh shit," Gideon murmured. At least nobody much was around, the families largely evacuated. He aimed the Stryker toward the path of least resistance. They hit the chain-link fence, peeling it up like a ribbon before tearing through. He careened across a backyard, pulverizing a jungle gym and sideswiping an aboveground pool, causing an eruption of water across the yard.

"Jesus!" cried Jackman.

Gideon kept the accelerator pinned to the floor, the massive vehicle slowly continuing to accelerate. Ahead, the street took a sharp right angle. "I can't make the turn in time," Gideon shouted. "Hold on!"

A single-story bungalow lay directly before them: checked curtains hanging in the living room picture window, yellow flowers framing a beautifully kept lawn. Gideon realized he could not avoid the house entirely and aimed for the garage. They impacted with a terrific blow, the Stryker's engine screaming as they knocked aside a pickup truck, then tore out the back wall of the garage, trailing wooden beams and wallboard and clouds of dust.

"Warning," came the electronic voice. "Speed unsuitable for current terrain conditions."

Looking through the periscope, Gideon could see people running out of the houses, shouting and gesturing at him and the trail of ruin he was leaving behind.

"Sure you don't want to go back?" Jackman asked through clenched teeth. "I think you missed something."

Pushing the vehicle forward, Gideon tore through another chain-link fence on the far side of the neighborhood. Beyond an empty parking lot, a grid of Quonset huts loomed ahead, the narrowest of alleys between each of them; Gideon headed for the broadest looking of the alleys, but it wasn't quite broad enough. The Stryker chewed its way through, crumpling the walls on either side like so much tinfoil and knocking the flimsy huts off their cheap foundations.

Bounding into an open area, they blew across a set of baseball diamonds, smashed through some cheap wooden bleachers, burst through a brick wall, and—quite abruptly—emerged onto the base's golf course. As he worked the controls, Gideon remembered vaguely that a golf course was the first thing he'd seen on entering the base: they were almost at the entrance.

He rode over a tee-off area and ground his way down the fairway, the few golfers out and about dropping their clubs and scattering like partridges. He crossed a narrow water hazard, boiled through the mud on the far side, and churned over a second green, sending huge divots and gouts of turf flying—and then, as they topped a rise, Gideon could make out, a quarter mile away, a cluster of buildings and a fence that marked the front gate.

...And along the service road paralleling the golf course, speeding at right angles to them, was the Humvee carrying Blaine and Dart.

"There they are!" Gideon cried. "Bust up the road ahead of them! But for God's sake, don't hit them or you'll spread the virus!"

Jackman was frantically working the remote weapons system. "Stop the vehicle so I can aim!"

Gideon ground to a stop, gouging two huge, trench-like furrows in the fairway. Jackman peered through the commander's periscope, adjusted some gauges, peered again. The Stryker rocked slightly as the grenades were launched, then percussive flashes went off ahead of the Humvee and the road in front of it erupted into the air, chunks of asphalt spinning skyward. The Humvee skidded to a stop, backed, turned, and started driving across the grass.

"Again!" Gideon cried.

Another shuddering series of explosions. But it was useless—the golf course was too broad, the Humvee had nearly limitless paths to the base exit.

Gideon gunned the Stryker forward, peeling across the greensward. The Humvee was still outpacing the Stryker, on the verge of getting away.

Ahead, Gideon could see a few panicked soldiers milling around the gate buildings, running this way and that. "Can you call the gate?" he yelled over the roar of the engine.

"No phone."

Gideon thought quickly. "The smoke grenades! Cover them with smoke!"

They plowed through a sand trap, attained another rise, and Jackman let loose. The canisters arced through the sky, bouncing ahead of the Humvee and erupting into enormous clouds of snow-white smoke. The wind was in their favor, rolling the smoke back over the vehicle. It immediately vanished.

Gideon headed into the huge smoke bank. "Got any infrared on this baby?"

"Turn on the DV, set it to thermal," Jackman said from the gunner's seat.

Gideon stared at the banks of instrumentation. Jackman leaned over, hit one switch, then another, and one of the innumerable screens flickered into life. "That's the Driver's Video screen, set to thermal," he said.

"Nice," said Gideon as he headed deeper into the smoke bank. "And there they are!"

The Humvee was still off the road but much closer to them, moving blindly, edging from the fairway into the rough, heading for a line of trees.

Gideon peered at the ghostly image on the videoscreen. "Shit. They're going to crash."

"Let me handle it." Jackman threw himself back into the gunner's seat. A moment later the fifty-caliber machine gun erupted, firing remotely, kicking up divots of turf behind the Humvee.

"Careful, for God's sake." Gideon watched as Jackman walked the automatic fire up and across the back of the Humvee, shredding its tires. The car slewed sideways, then came to a shuddering halt.

On the DV, Gideon saw the doors fly open. The three soldiers boiled out, crouching and firing their weapons blindly through the smoke. Then two more figures emerged—Blaine and Dart—and both began running toward the gate at top speed.

"I'm going after them," Gideon said. "Give me your weapon."

Gideon threw open the hatch of the Stryker and jumped out, suddenly enveloped in smoke. He could hear the soldiers firing blindly, stupidly, somewhere. He took off in the general direction he'd seen Blaine heading, running along the fairway and quickly emerging from the smoke. The soldiers had also found their way out and turned toward him, raking him with fire. He hit the ground at the same moment the fifty-caliber machine gun sounded from within the smoke; the three soldiers literally came apart in front of him.

He jumped up again, continued running. Blaine was a hundred yards ahead, approaching the final green, but he was old and rapidly losing steam. Dart, younger and more fit, had pulled ahead and was leaving Blaine behind.

As Gideon approached, Blaine turned and, wheezing heavily, pulled out his Peacemaker and fired, the shot kicking up the grass in front of Gideon. Still he ran; Blaine got off a second shot, which also missed as Gideon launched himself at the older man, tackling him at the knees. They fell heavily and Gideon grappled the revolver away from him, flinging it aside, pinning Blaine. He pulled out Jackman's sidearm.

"You damn fool!" Blaine screamed, gasping, spittle on his lips.

Without a word, holding the gun to Blaine's throat, Gideon slipped his hand into the man's suit coat, groped about, and located the telltale puck of smallpox. He slipped it out, placed it in his pocket, and got up.

"You god*damn* fool," Blaine said, weakly, still lying on the ground.

A sudden eruption of gunfire sent Gideon to the ground. Dart, fifty yards away, had turned in his flight and was now firing at him.

There was no cover and Gideon scrambled to get low and carefully aimed, returning fire. His second shot brought the man down.

And then he heard choppers. Following the sound with his eyes, he made out a pair of Black Hawks approaching fast from the east; they slowed, then turned, coming in for a combat landing.

More backup for Blaine and Dart.

"Drop your weapon and give me the smallpox," came the voice.

Gideon turned to see Blaine, standing unsteadily, the Peacemaker back in his hand. He felt sick. And he'd been close—so close. His mind raced, trying to figure out a way to escape, to protect the smallpox. Could he hide it, bury it, run with it? Where was the Stryker? He looked around desperately, but the vehicle was still enveloped in the streaming clouds of smoke.

"I *said*, give me the smallpox. And drop your weapon." Blaine's hands were shaking.

Gideon felt paralyzed, unable to act. As they faced each other off, the choppers settled down on the fairway, their doors flew open, and soldiers poured out, weapons at the ready, fanning out in a classic pattern and advancing on them. Gideon looked at the approaching soldiers, then back to Blaine. Strangely, tears were streaming down the older man's face.

"I'll never give you the smallpox," said Gideon, raising his own weapon and pointing it at Blaine. They stood there, weapons aimed at each other, as the soldiers approached. Gideon sensed that Blaine would not shoot him—any shot had the possibility of unleashing the smallpox. Which meant all he had to do was pull the trigger on Blaine.

And yet—even as his grip tightened on the weapon—he realized he could not do it. No matter what the stakes, even at the cost of his own life, he couldn't bring himself to shoot Alida's father. Especially since it was now futile.

"*Drop your weapons!*" came the shout from the group of soldiers. "Disarm! Now! Get down on the ground!"

Gideon braced himself. It was all over.

There was a brief burst of gunfire; Gideon flinched, anticipating the impact—and yet the burst did not strike him. Quite abruptly, Blaine pitched face-forward onto the grass, where he lay unmoving, still clutching the Peacemaker.

"Drop your weapon!" came the shouted command.

Gideon held his arms out, letting the sidearm fall from his hand as the soldiers approached, warily, keeping him covered. One began to search him; he found the smallpox puck and gently removed it.

A lieutenant from the chopper crew came striding over. "Gideon Crew?"

Gideon nodded.

The officer turned to the troops. "He's all right. He's Fordyce's partner." He turned to Gideon. "Where is Agent Fordyce? In the Stryker?"

"They killed him," said Gideon, dazed. He began to realize that, in addition to notifying Dart, Fordyce—with his belt-and-suspenders FBI mentality—must have notified others as well. These weren't more conspirators—this was the cavalry, coming to the rescue a little late.

To his great shock, Gideon heard Blaine cough, then saw the old man rise to his hands and knees. Grunting and gasping, he started crawling toward them. "The...smallpox...," he breathed. Blood suddenly gushed from his mouth, stopping his speech, but still he crawled.

One of the soldiers raised his rifle.

"No," said Gideon. "For God's sake, don't."

Blaine managed to raise himself a little higher, feebly trying to raise the Peacemaker, while they stared back in horror.

"Fools," he gargled, then he pitched forward and lay still.

Sickened, Gideon turned his head.

76

THE NEUROLOGIST'S WAITING room was done up in blond wood wainscoting, neat as a pin, with a rack of the day's newspapers, a box of politically correct wooden toys, copies of *Highlights* and *Architectural Digest*, and comfortable leather sofas and chairs complementing one another at the proper angles. A row of windows, with translucent curtains, allowed in a pleasingly diffuse natural light. A large Persian rug, dominating the floor, completed the picture of a prosperous and successful practice.

Despite the overactive air-conditioning, Gideon felt a stickiness in his palms as he nervously opened and closed his hands. He walked up to the receptionist's window and gave his name.

"Do you have an appointment?" the receptionist asked.

"No," said Gideon.

The woman examined her computer screen and said, "I'm sorry, but Dr. Metcalfe doesn't have any openings today."

Gideon remained standing. "But I need to see him. Please."

For the first time the woman turned and looked at him. "What's it about?"

"I want to get the results...of an MRI I had done recently. I tried calling, but you wouldn't give them to me over the phone."

"That's right," she said. "We don't give any results over the phone—positive or negative. It doesn't necessarily mean there's a problem." She perused the computer screen. "I see you missed an appointment...We could schedule you for tomorrow morning, how's that?"

"Please help me to see the doctor now."

She leveled a not unsympathetic gaze at him. "Let me see what I can do." She rose and disappeared into an inner warren of offices. A moment later she came out. "Through the door, a right, and a left. Examination Room Two."

Gideon followed the instructions and entered the room. A nurse appeared with a clipboard and a cheerful good morning, seated him on the exam table, took his blood pressure and pulse. As she was finishing up, a large figure in a white lab coat appeared in the doorway. The nurse bustled along, handed the figure the clipboard, and vanished.

The doctor entered, a grave smile on his kindly face, his halo of curly hair highlighted from behind by the bright morning sun that streamed in the window. It made him look curiously like a large, jolly angel.

"Good morning, Gideon." He grasped his hand, giving it a warm, brief shake. "Have a seat."

Gideon, who had stood up when the doctor entered, sat down again. The doctor remained standing.

"I have here the results of the cranial MRI we performed seven days ago."

From the tone in the neurologist's voice, Gideon knew immediately what the man was going to say. He felt himself in the grip of a fight-or-flight reaction, his heart pounding, his blood racing, his muscles tensing up. He struggled to calm his body.

Dr. Metcalfe paused, then eased himself down onto a corner of the table. "The results of the test show a growth of blood vessels in the brain we call an AVM, or arteriovenous malformation—"

Gideon rose abruptly. "That's it. That's all I needed to know. Thank you." He started for the door but was arrested by the doctor, who placed a gentle hand on Gideon's arm to steady him.

"I gather, then, that I'm your second opinion and you already knew about this?"

"Yes," said Gideon. He wanted nothing more than to head for the door.

"Very well. I believe, however, you could benefit from hearing what I have to say, if you're willing to listen."

Gideon remained standing. With effort, he overcame his impulse to run. "Just say it then. Don't dress it up. And spare me the expressions of sympathy."

"Very well. Your AVM involves the great cerebral vein of Galen and it is both congenital and inoperable. This type of malformation tends to grow with time, and the indications are that yours is growing. An abnormal, direct connection between the high-pressure artery and the low-pressure vein is causing the steady dilation of the vein and enlargement of the AVM in general. In addition, part of the AVM involves a venous anomaly downstream, which appears to be constricting blood flow, leading to further dilation of the vein."

He paused. "Are my descriptions too technical?"

"No," said Gideon. In a way, the technical terminology removed some of the horror. Even so, the idea that this was going on in his brain made him sick.

"The prognosis is not good. I would estimate you have six months to two years to live—with the most probable mortality rate being somewhere around a year or slightly less. On the other hand, the annals of medical history are sprinkled with miracles. No one can say for sure what the future will bring."

"But the survival rate after, say, five years is...what?"

"Vanishingly small. But not zero." The doctor hesitated. "There is a way for us to know more."

"I'm not sure I want to know more."

"Understandable. But there's a procedure known as a cerebral angiography, which would tell us a great deal more about your situation. We insert a catheter into the femoral artery in the groin area and thread it up to the carotid artery in the neck. There we release a dye, or blocking agent. As it spreads through the brain, we take a series of radiographs. This allows us to map the AVM. It would tell us more accurately how much time you have...and, perhaps, show us how we might ameliorate it."

"Ameliorate it? How?"

"Through surgery. We can't take out the AVM, but there are other surgical options. One can work around the edges, so to speak."

"Which would do what?"

"Possibly prolong your life."

"By how much?"

"It depends on how fast the vein is dilating. A few months, perhaps a year."

This led to a long silence.

"These procedures," Gideon said at last. "Are there risks?"

"Significant risks. Particularly neurological. Operations like this have a ten to fifteen percent mortality rate, and an additional forty percent possibility of causing damage to the brain."

Gideon looked the doctor in the eye. "Would you take those risks in my position?"

"No," the doctor said without hesitation. "I wouldn't want to live if my brain were compromised. I am not a gambler, and fifty-fifty odds are not attractive to me." The neurologist returned Gideon's gaze, his large brown eyes full of compassion. Gideon realized he was in the presence of a wise man, one of the few he had met in his short and relatively unhappy life.

"I don't think the angiogram will be necessary," Gideon said.

"I understand."

"Is there anything I have to do in the meantime, any way I should alter my life?"

"Nothing. You can live a normal, active life. The end, when it comes, will probably be abrupt." The doctor paused. "This isn't really medical advice. But if I were you, I'd do the things that are really important to you. If it involves helping others, so much the better."

"Thank you."

The doctor gave his shoulder a squeeze and dropped his voice. "The only difference between you and the rest of us is that, while life is short for everyone, for you it's just a bit shorter."

77

GIDEON TURNED OFF North Guadalupe Street, driving the Suburban through the ancient Spanish gate and onto the groomed white gravel entryway of the Santa Fe National Cemetery. A dozen or so cars were parked before the Administration Building and he pulled in beside them, then exited the vehicle and glanced around. It was a warm summer morning, the Sangre de Cristo Mountains dark green against a porcelain sky. The orderly rows of small white tombstones stretched ahead of him, running from the shade into brilliant light.

He walked east, his shoes crunching on the gravel. This was the older part of the cemetery—originally built for the Union soldiers who died in the Battle of Glorieta Pass—but he could see, through the pines and cedars, the distant newer section, climbing the low flanks of the nearby ridge, where the desert had been newly covered with turf and transformed into Technicolor green. Partway up the hill, he could make out a small group of people gathering around an open grave.

He gazed over the neatly ordered files of white crosses and stars of David. *Before long, I'll be in a place like this, and people will be gathering around my grave.* This unexpected and unwanted thought was quickly followed by another, dreadful yet irresistible: *Who will come to mourn me?*

He turned up the path that led toward the group of mourners.

The details of Simon Blaine's involvement in the terrorist plot had been kept out of the papers. Gideon had expected to see a much larger crowd at his burial. He had been, after all, a well-known and well-regarded novelist. But as Gideon made his way through the severe white rows, he realized there were no more than two dozen people circled around the open grave. As he approached, he could make out the voice of the priest, intoning the older, formal Episcopal version of the Burial of the Dead:

> *Give rest, O Christ, to thy servant with thy saints,*
> *where sorrow and pain are no more,*
> *neither sighing, but life everlasting.*

He moved forward, stepping out of the shade of the trees and into brilliant sunlight. His eyes searched the crowd and found Alida. She was dressed in a simple black dress, with a veiled hat and white elbow-length gloves. He took an unobtrusive place at the back fringe of the group and surreptitiously studied her face across the grave. The veil was pinned back across the hat. As she stared down at the coffin, her eyes were dry but her face looked ravaged and utterly desolate. His own eyes remained on her face, unable to look away. Suddenly her gaze flickered up and met his for one terrible second. Then she looked back down, into the grave.

What was that look? He tried to parse it. Was there any feeling there? It had been too quick, and now she resolutely refused to raise her head again.

Into thy hands, O merciful Savior, we commend thy servant Simon...

In the week following Fort Detrick, Gideon had tried repeatedly to contact Alida. He had wanted—needed—to explain: to tell her how desperately sorry he was; to say how terrible he'd felt about deceiving her, to express his condolences about what had happened to her father. He *had* to help her understand he'd simply had no choice.

That her father had done it to himself, something she must of course realize.

Each time he'd tried calling, she had hung up. The last time he called he found she had switched to an unlisted number.

Then he'd tried waiting outside the gate to her father's house, hoping that, by seeing him, she would stop just long enough for him to explain...But she had driven past, twice, without a look or acknowledgment.

And so he had come to the burial, willing to endure any humiliation to see her, talk, explain. He didn't expect that their relationship could continue, but at least he would be able to reach out to her one last time. Because the idea of leaving it like this, raw and unresolved, full of bitterness and hatred, was something he simply couldn't imagine. He had so little time left—he knew that now.

Again and again he had replayed in his head their time together: their horseback escape; Alida's initial fury at him; the slow morphing of her feelings into something else, culminating into love—his first real love, thanks to the incredible generosity of her heart and spirit.

> In the midst of life we are in death;
> of whom may we seek for succor,
> but of thee, O Lord,
> who for our sins art justly displeased?

Gideon began to feel like an intruder, blundering in on something private and personal. He turned away and walked back down the slope of the hill, past grave after grave after grave, until he reached the older section of the cemetery. There, in the cool shade of a cypress tree, he waited on the white gravel path, where she would have to pass by on her way back to her car.

Even if you only have a year, let's make that year count. Together. You and me. We'll roll up a lifetime of love in one year. Her words. He found himself haunted by the image of her, naked in the doorway of her ranch house, beautiful as a Botticelli maiden—that day he'd driven away in her car, hell-bent on ruining her father's life.

...Why was it so important for him to speak with her? Was it because he still hoped, against all hope, that he could make her see things his way, understand the awful bind he had been in, and—ultimately, with the boundlessness of her big heart—forgive him? Or did part of him already guess that was impossible? Maybe he needed to explain simply for his own peace of mind—because, though perhaps he could never again hope Alida might love him, at least he could help her understand.

He watched the service from afar. The shifting breeze brought the priest's faint voice to his ears from time to time, a distant murmur. The coffin was lowered. And then it was over. The tightly clustered group around the grave loosened and began to disperse.

He waited in the shade as they made the long, slow, straggling procession down the hill, his eye fixed on her, her alone, as people offered her their condolences, hugged Alida, took her hand. It all took an excruciatingly long time. First came the cemetery workers; next a knot of women of a certain age, talking animatedly among themselves in low tones; next, various young people and couples; and then came the priest and a few of his assistants. He gave Gideon a professional smile and nod as he passed.

Last came Alida. He had assumed she would be accompanied by others, but she had drifted back from them and was the last to leave, all alone. She approached him, bowed by her loss but still walking proud, her head erect and staring straight ahead, moving slowly along the long, narrow pathway among the graves. She didn't seem to see him. As she drew closer, Gideon felt a strange hollowness in the pit of his stomach. Now she was almost upon him. He wasn't sure what to do—whether to speak, step in front of her, reach out—and as she drew alongside he parted his lips to speak but no sound came. He watched, struck mute, as she passed by, walking the same slow walk, her eyes straight ahead, without the faintest flicker, the faintest change of expression, to acknowledge his existence.

He followed her with his eyes as she continued down the path, her back to him now, never deviating in her deliberate, icy stride. He continued watching her dwindling black figure for several minutes more, until she had disappeared around the distant edge of the building. He waited until she was long gone, until all the cars were gone, and then waited some more. Finally, with a deep, unsteady breath, he made his own way out along the narrow pathways between the gravestones, down the graveled path, to his car.

78

GIDEON ASKED THE cabdriver to let him off at Washington Square Park. He felt like walking the last mile or so to the EES offices on Little West 12th Street—but before doing so, he wanted to hang out in the park for a bit and enjoy the summer day.

Three weeks had passed since the funeral. Immediately afterward, Gideon had fled to his cabin in the Jemez Mountains and turned off his cell phone, landline, and computers. And then he had spent three weeks fishing. On the fifth day he finally caught that wily old cutthroat trout with a barbless hook, intending to release it. What a gorgeous fish it was: fat, glossy, with the deep blood-orange coloring below the gills that gave the cutthroat its name. Certainly this was a fish noble enough to be worth releasing, as was his policy. But then, strangely, he hadn't. Instead, he'd taken it back to the cabin, cleaned it, and served himself up an exquisitely simple *truite amandine*, accompanied by a bottle of flinty Puligny-Montrachet. All without guilt. And as he enjoyed the simple meal, all by himself, an odd thing happened. He felt happy. Not only happy, but also at peace. He examined his feelings with a sense of surprise and curiosity, and he realized they had something to do with the certainty of things. The certainty of his medical condition, and the conviction that he would never see Alida again.

Oddly, that certitude seemed to liberate him. He knew now what he faced, and what he could never have. It gave him the freedom to follow the doctor's parting advice: to focus on doing things that mattered to him, and help others. Releasing the trout would have been a fine gesture; but, he had to admit, eating it had been an even rarer pleasure. Eating it had mattered to him. *In the midst of life we are in death*...It was a wise thought, true for trout and human alike.

Over those three weeks, he had done a number of other small things that mattered to him. One had been to arrange for an indefinite medical leave from Los Alamos. And when his little fishing vacation was over, when he had turned his phones back on and collected his messages at last, he found one from Glinn. The engineer had another assignment, if Gideon were inclined to take it; one of "considerable importance." Gideon was about to dismiss it out of hand, but then stopped himself. Why not? It seemed he was good at that sort of thing. If he wanted to help others, maybe that is what he should be doing.

Even his anger at Glinn for abandoning him in the field had abated. Gideon had begun to understand that Glinn's method of operation—though difficult to take in the heat of the moment—had proven remarkably effective. In this case, they had refused to help because they clearly felt that Gideon, on his own, had the best chance of success.

And so here he was, back in New York City, ready to start the next chapter in his short life. He took a deep breath and looked around. It was a beautiful weekend afternoon, and Washington Square Park was overflowing with activity. He lingered, enchanted by the bustle—the Dominican drummers whose joyful rhythms filled the air; a group of awkward in-line-skating kids in helmets and padded knees, their mothers sitting in a worried knot; a pair of men in expensive suits smoking cigars; an old hippie strumming a guitar and collecting coins; a mime trailing people, aping their way of walking to their great annoyance; a three-card-monte player shuffling his cards and keeping an eye out for the cops; a bum sound asleep on a bench. The park contained a full vertical slice of humanity, top to bottom, in all its complexity and richness and splendor. But on this day the joy, the richness seemed particularly acute. New York felt a lot different from the last time he'd been here and had his cab stolen by a loutish, half-drunk businessman.

The terrorist scare that had half emptied the city was over, and people seemed to have returned changed. They were more connected, tolerant, more in the moment, happier.

The city had changed; and he had, as well. *We all need reminding what's really important in life*, thought Gideon. These people had been reminded. Just as he had.

It was all over; the country had returned to normal. His own troubles had been resolved: the videotapes at USAMRIID, Blaine's laptop, and Dart, confessing all from his hospital bed, had filled in the gaps and told the full story. Novak had been arrested, along with other conspirators at Los Alamos and in the defense and intelligence communities. The frame job had been exposed, Chalker revealed as an innocent victim. Glinn had stepped in to make sure Gideon's own true role in the drama remained a deep secret. This was critically important to Gideon. It would ruin the rest of his short life if he became famous, hailed as a hero, his face plastered on the front pages everywhere. What a nightmare.

Then there was Alida. She was gone forever. That part of his heart he was still wrapping up and packing away. Nothing more to be done about that.

He took a turn around the fountain, and paused in front of the Dominican drummers. They were pounding away, huge smiles on their faces, bliss in their eyes, beating out the most complicated syncopations imaginable: not just two against three but five against three and what even sounded like seven against four. It was like the beating of the human heart, he thought; that first sensation we all experienced at the beginning of life, multiplied a thousandfold, and turned into something delirious, wild.

As he listened to the music, he felt peace. Real peace. It was an amazing feeling, one he was still unused to. Was this what most people experienced every day? He had never known what he'd been missing. The AVM, and the good doctor, had given him that gift, finally, after so many years of anxiety, fear, sorrow, angst, hatred, and revenge. It was a huge, even inexplicable irony. The AVM was going to kill him—but first, it had set him free.

Gideon glanced at his watch. He was going to be late, but that was all right. The drumming was what was important right now. He listened for almost an hour; and then, with a feeling of peace still in his heart, he headed west down Waverly Place to Greenwich Avenue, toward the old Meatpacking District.

EES seemed as empty as always. He was buzzed in without even an acknowledgment. No one was there to meet him or escort him through the cavernous laboratory spaces to the elevator. The elevator creaked up, and up, the doors finally opening again. He walked down the hall to the conference room. The door was closed; all was silent as a tomb.

He knocked, and he heard Glinn's voice, a terse "Come in."

Gideon opened the door and was greeted with a room full of people, and a sudden outpouring of applause and cheering. Glinn was there, in front, and he wheeled himself forward, holding out his withered arm, and kissed Gideon on both cheeks, European-style. Garza followed with a fierce handshake and a thunderous slap on the back, and then the others: what had to be close to a hundred people, young and old, male and female, of every imaginable race, some in lab coats, others in suits, others in kimonos and saris, along with a handful of what appeared to be other EES operatives with their appraising and appreciative gazes, all shaking his hand, congratulating him, an overwhelming and irresistible torrent of enthusiasm and warmth.

And then they fell silent. Gideon realized they were expecting him to speak. He stood there, flummoxed. Then he cleared his throat. "Thank you," he said. "Um, who are all you people?"

This was greeted with a laugh.

Glinn spoke up. "Gideon, these are all the people at EES you haven't met. Most of whom work behind the scenes, who keep our little operation going. You may not know them, but they all know you. And all of them wanted to be here to say to you: *thank you.*"

An eruption of applause.

"There is nothing we can say or do, and nothing we can give you, that would properly express our gratitude for what you did. So I'm not even going to try."

Gideon was moved. They wanted to hear him say more. What would he say? It suddenly occurred to him that he was so good at being phony, at spinning falsehoods, that he'd almost forgotten how to be sincere.

"I'm just glad I was able to do something good in this crazy world." He cleared his throat again. "But I couldn't have done it without my partner, Stone Fordyce. Who gave his life. He's the hero. All I gave was a few teeth."

A more restrained round of applause.

"I want to thank you all, too. I can't begin to know what you all do, or have done, but it's nice to see your faces. So many times out there, I felt like I was on my own, alone. I realize that's part of the job—part of your system, I suppose—but seeing you all here makes me realize that I wasn't really alone, after all. I guess, in a way, EES is my home now. Even my family."

Nods, murmured agreements.

A silence and Glinn asked, "How was your vacation?"

"I ate a trout."

More laughter and applause. Gideon stilled it with the raise of a hand. "Over the past few days I've realized something. This is what I should be doing. I want to continue to work for you, for EES. I think I can do some real good here. Finally…" He paused, glanced around. "I really don't have anything else in my life worth a damn. You're it. Sad, I know, but that's how it is."

This was met by another silence. After a moment, a faint smile appeared on Glinn's face. He glanced around the room. "Thank you all for your time," he said.

At this tactful but obvious dismissal, the room emptied. Glinn waited until only himself, Gideon, and Garza remained. Then he motioned Gideon to a chair at the conference table.

"Are you certain about this, Gideon?" he asked in a low voice. "After all, you've had quite an ordeal. Not just the physical manhunt, but the emotional toll as well."

Gideon had long since ceased to be amazed at Glinn's ability to learn everything about him. "I was never more sure of anything in my life," he replied.

Glinn looked at him carefully for a moment—a long, searching look. Then he nodded. "Excellent. Glad to hear you'll be with us. It's a very interesting time to be in New York. In fact, next week there's a special exhibition at the Morgan Library—an exhibition of the Book of Kells, on loan from the Irish government. You've heard of the Book of Kells, of course?"

"Of course."

"Then you'll come have a look at it with me?" Glinn asked. "I'm a great fancier of illuminated manuscripts. They'll be turning a new page every day. Very exciting."

Gideon hesitated. "Well, illuminated manuscripts are not exactly an interest of mine."

"Ah, but I was so hoping you'd accompany me to the exhibition," said Glinn. "You'll love the Book of Kells. Not only is it Ireland's greatest national treasure, but it's the finest illuminated manuscript in existence. It's only been out of Ireland once before, and it's only here for a week. A shame to miss it. We'll go Monday morning."

Gideon started to laugh. "Honestly, I couldn't care less about the damn Book of Kells."

"Ah, but you will."

Hearing the edge in Glinn's voice, Gideon stopped despite himself. "Why?"

"Because your next assignment will be to steal it."

About the Authors

The thrillers of **DOUGLAS PRESTON** and **LINCOLN CHILD** "stand head and shoulders above their rivals" (*Publisher's Weekly*). Coauthors of the famed Pendergast series, their books *Relic* and *The Cabinet of Curiosities* were chosen by readers in a National Public Radio poll as being among the 100 greatest thrillers ever written, and *Relic* was made into a number one box office hit movie. They are also the authors of *Fever Dream*, *Cold Vengeance*, and *Gideon's Sword*. Preston's acclaimed nonfiction book, *The Monster of Florence*, is being made into a movie starring George Clooney. His interests include horses, scuba diving, skiing, mountain climbing, and exploring the Maine coast in an old lobster boat. Lincoln Child is a former book editor who has published four novels of his own, including the huge bestseller *Deep Storm*. He is passionate about motorcycles, sports cars, exotic parrots, and nineteenth-century English literature. The authors welcome e-mail from their readers; you can visit their website at www.prestonchild.com.